I0692736

T.S. HOWARD

A Pyre of Men and Mountain

First published by Maelan Press 2021

This novel is entirely a work of fiction. The names, characters and incidents portrayed in it are the work of the author's imagination. Any resemblance to actual persons, living or dead, events or localities is entirely coincidental.

First edition

ISBN: 978-1-7375377-4-8

Editing by Sage Maelan
Illustration by London Montgomery
Illustration by Jake Howard

This book was professionally typeset on Reedsy.
Find out more at reedsy.com

For Sage,
who keeps me moving forward, no matter the circumstances
who believed in me when I didn't
who pulled me from a fire of my own
Ever Northward, my dear.

Contents

Prologue   vii
I: Venture   ix
II: Vengeance   xix
III: Vigil   xxv

I   A Pyre of Men and Mountain

Home   3
Tea Kettles   8
Baranor's Children   23
The Reliquary   38
Shattered Mask and Castle Walls   51
With Words Alone   58
Ocean of Temples   75
The Death of You All   89
Jaru'tal   95
Everything   109
Shattered Glass   122
Foul Concoctions   128
A Limited Capacity   133
The Source of Power   138
Olsu Varek   146
Painful Names   156
White Grave   167

Sadagon's Herald   180
Prayers or Pitch   192
Simple Lies   202
A Just God   212
Radiant Dark   218
The Third Law   227
A Steep Price   238
Something Small or Heavy   241
Bloody Arithmetic   247
What Good it Did   255
Anything but That   270
The Kindest Way   282
Faron's Good Work   298
Fighting Back   300
Freedom from a Painful Choice   306
Bloodlust   321
Forfeit Advantage   332
A Slowly Blackening Skull   343
A Weight to Save the World   350
To Become Strong Enough   363
A Pyre of Men and Mountain   372
No Matter the Cost   386
The Last Chapter   400

Epilogue   405
I: The Cruel and Corrupt   407
II: The Path through Apocalypse   415
III: The Life Spile   421
About the Author   430

I said once that these books are my soul made manifest, and I meant it; but, that is more true now than ever. A Pyre of Men and Mountain is the culmination of my work, and it holds more of myself than any book ever has and likely ever will. It is the story that has cost me the most steeply and the one that challenged what I thought I knew. It is the work I am proudest of and the work for which I am the most vulnerable.

And I lay it here before you.

T.S. Howard

Prologue

FIVE YEARS BEFORE

I: Venture

Even in the heart of a snowstorm, Sadagon never seemed to get as cold as he once did. Perhaps that was an effect of the new blood in his veins, or maybe three hundred years in Vam Aranath had strengthened his frame. Either way, the windborne snow bothered him very little.

Mounted on great white horses, Sadagon and his men blazed a steady path toward a small and insignificant village, inoffensive in its regularity. They must have seen it's like fifty times before. Even now, in the wintry dark, Sadagon knew what he would find inside without needing to see it: fields, farmhouses, a tannery, a butcher, a blacksmith if they were fortunate, and always a tavern. What he didn't know was *who* they would find.

Any light that may have shown from the mundane village was blocked by the wooden palisade that surrounded its entire circumference. It was half-buried in snow and haunted on all sides by red eyes and gnawing hunger. Inside every shadow, there was the slip of white fur, almost invisible except for the reflective eyes of the beasts who waited patiently for the snow to climb high enough for them to mantle. It wouldn't be long now.

Out of the corner of his eye, Sadagon saw Varan with the same dreadful thoughts, wordlessly gauging the snow's height and comparing it against the date. His thin lips drew into a tight line when he finished his calculations. Not good. Damn that Baranor. Not for the first time, Sadagon wished for the honest existence of gods—real gods—if only for there to be a hell for that traitor to burn in for eternity… and for a chance to see his children again.

Casting off such dour thoughts, Sadagon physically shook himself and approached the gate. It was odd to be so torn between hoping to find his family's murderer and hoping not to. He supposed it was some fight of attrition between his desire for revenge and his loathe to attempt a test he could not pass.

"Not this year," Varan said from Sadagon's side. "And not the next. Perhaps five. Ten at most."

Sadagon only nodded his understanding. This, after all, was why they were here.

"Vam Sadagon," Varan said with a modicum of hesitation. "I cannot help but feel that we are spending what little time we have left poorly. We should be preparing in Vam Aranath with your archons and leaving this search to others, no matter how… personal."

Unclenching his jaw, Sadagon responded, "I know the preparations you would take, Varan, and my mind is decided. I have to do this first."

"But why, Lord? There is too much at stake for—"

"No more," Sadagon commanded. "Now is not the time." Despite the argument brewing on his manservant's lip, he remained quiet. "We're here. Tarak and Kav, stay with the horses. Yarow, you go with Horus and clear the gate. Varan… stay with me." They obeyed with practiced alacrity. Even with the cloaks on their backs and the sheer length of time they'd been beyond the safety of a wall, they were all eager to find some separation from the monsters that stalked them, even if they need not fear them outright.

"Another palisade," Varan observed. "Even with enough resources, small villages like this won't last a year once the Veil swallows them."

"And they don't have those resources," Sadagon added. "Any excess has been taxed or sold off to Blackwood, where it will be hoarded once the Veil does come. These small places will be abandoned before the wolves can even devour them."

"This is one of the last places that will be touched. We are nearly as far south as south goes. Between that, my lord, and the disappearance of Garroh and Seris here... our chances are somewhat greater. It is possible that we have followed a false lead, but, in my opinion, Baranor is all but found."

"Good," Sadagon said without believing it.

"If I may, Vam Sadagon," Varan's voice hedged concern. "You have been... somewhat terse of late. I worry what you hope to find."

"As do I."

"I was hoping you might confide what it is you hope for."

"I haven't felt anything as strong as hope in over a decade, Varan—not even a hope for a hope. I know what your concern is, and it is not warranted. My children are dead. I know that. There is nobody to carry this burden but me." It was hard to say it.

Varan seemed to physically relax. He was more worried than he let on.

"I am sorry for it, but I am glad to hear it all the same. That said, if this is the case, my lord, why are we here? Baranor has slipped up and is all but found, and any team could have collected him for you. If not for the hope of your children, why have you come personally?"

Varan's question was met with the soft whistle of intermittent wind, unanswered until a voice came from the wall.

"The gate is clear."

Without a look or a nod toward Varan, Sadagon stepped away. "Horus?" he called. His man responded by pulling a great length of rope from a pack, the vast majority of which he let fall spooled onto the ground. An iron grapple dominated one end. Not bothering to build momentum with a spin, he tossed it straight over the twenty-foot wall, then pulled hard, setting the hooks into the old wood.

The shorter man scaled straight up until he reached the top. The tips of the snow wall had been sharp once, but that was long ago. Now they were nearly rounded with weather and age, and he slipped over them with little trouble. The rope followed him, uncoiling from its spool for several feet before the grapple gave and was ripped from the wall.

"Varan," Sadagon said, giving the High Archon his cue. Near instantly, the tall man procured a phosphorous lamp—a glass orb that shone with a violent white light. With a small twist, he held it up in a gloved hand, casting a color-draining illumination across the immediate landscape.

Long shadows leaped from the fourteen or fifteen dire wolves that followed them, lurking like vengeful ghosts. Their fur was a perfect white, except two long streaks of gray that stretched from jaw to flank. The sudden light hurt their red eyes as if it were a sun, and the would-be monsters scattered like common hounds from fire.

A few short moments later, a deep scrape sounded from beyond, and the man-door was forced open. Horus stood inside, holding the door against the piled snow. Sadagon,

Varan, Yarow, and Horus entered the village with rushed steps, then slammed the door closed. Even knowing that every man, woman, and child inside was only a few years from the belly of a wolf, Sadagon wouldn't just let them in. He wasn't that numb to the fate of the world or the worth of a life.

Not yet.

Double checking that the iron latches were secure, Varan twisted the two halves of the glass orb and severed its supply of oxygen, effectively extinguishing the light. He plunged the heatless lamp back into a satchel at his side, then stepped away from the unmanned gate and onto the rough, snow-covered street. Sadagon took the lead, and Varan quickened his pace to match. The others stayed a few steps behind.

"The map from Blackwood shows farmland this way, then a thicket of woods," Varan said. "It should serve well enough."

Nobody offered any challenge, so they clung to the shadows and forged deep into the trees. The village was small, especially when compared to the size of its snow wall. Most village's fields lay beyond their walls, untended during winter, but here, they were safely hemmed in alongside the businesses and houses—an advantage of being so far from Empyrion, Sadagon expected.

When the houses were left far behind, they cleared a circle in the snow and gathered enough deadwood for a bonfire. Its heat sustained them through the remainder of the night.

The following morning, Yarow patrolled the makeshift camp, and Horus set out to gather what information he could. Varan and Sadagon stood together, watching over a crossroad in the village. Sadagon's face was contorted into a scowl as he tried to peer past the hoods of the few men who roamed the streets.

"If it comes to it," Varan said. "There is an elder's hall where tax records are kept. We could break in and have a look at them. Perhaps Baranor will be listed—or someone bearing his description."

"He will have a false name," Sadagon replied. "And his blood is southern. More than half the men will bear his description."

"I'm afraid that's as far as my skill in reconnaissance goes. I am mostly a burden in matters of this nature."

Sadagon pondered for a moment as he studied a shorter man's face. "In my decades of service to my parents, I learned to find people who didn't want to be found, but... an inquisitor's work is a bloody and public affair. There was no guile or stealth involved—or very little. We're of equal use here, where discretion is so necessary."

"Which brings me back to the point," Varan said. "Of why you are here."

"You have asked me that question nearly every day for the better part of three months, Varan. I have answered as well as I am able."

"The heirs to the Twinborn throne are dead, and the Veil only grows. There is little time left, Sadagon." He used no honorific, indicating his levels of stress. "You know that there is no other to ascend than you?"

"I said last night that I did."

"Then you intend to take the thrones for yourself?"

Sadagon shifted uncomfortably. "After," he said. "After we've found him."

"Your children are dead, Lord Sadagon. There are no others to relieve this burden from you, and there is no room for dulcet words. If you do not take the thrones, everyone will die."

"You're asking me to become a god," Sadagon said with sharpness in his tongue. "Me, an inquisitor who hunted those who spoke out against the false gods, even when I knew they were false. Me, who brutally killed my own parents, who lost my family to—" He cut himself off.

"You're asking me to overcome my bloodlust and take up power over those you know I *hate* and rule them with fairness and benevolence. You want me to wield the greatest weapon ever created and trust myself not to use it." Sadagon's eyes searched Varan's with intensity. They were brimming and half-mad with lifetimes of grief and responsibility. "Ask me again when I find the man who murdered my wife and children and have the strength not to kill him." He looked away. "*If* I have the strength."

Finally, Varan understood. Finding Baranor was a test of self-control—finding and not killing. It was a test he had to pass. The world depended on it.

"Your hatred is not so strong as you would believe, Sadagon." His voice had adopted a tone Sadagon had not heard in over three hundred years. It was fatherly—and almost chastising. "You're a better man than you think."

"You have no choice but to believe that, Varan, and I suspect you would put the crown on my head even if you didn't."

"Then tell me this, Vam Sadagon. If you despise common humanity so greatly, why do you endure such tortures to try and save them?"

Sadagon's jaw clamped firm, and before Varan could pry it open, Horus came around a street corner and into view, hood raised and sleeves carefully covering his forearms. He carried a bundle of supplies.

"Did anybody ask who you were?" Sadagon asked as he approached. The tension had not left his voice.

"Everyone," the stalky man answered. "I told them I'm a traveler from Blackwood, wintering here by chance of the early Veil, and my supplies just ran out. They bought it well enough."

"What of Baranor?" Sadagon said. "Any word?"

"Yes," he affirmed with nervous conviction. "But... Sadagon... there's something else."

The relief that whirled through the group was not reflected in Sadagon. If they found Baranor, he would tear his heart out. He knew it with every fiber of his being, as much as he knew that he would abuse any power given to him, just like his father had.

Horus's serious expression drew concerned looks from the others. "It might be nothing, but either way, you should know." He waited again before nodding back toward the tree line. "Come on, back to camp."

They slipped back into the trees and away from the homes and shops before breaking the long silence.

"What did you find?" Varan said, speaking for Sadagon. Horus glanced between them as he deposited the foodstuffs he'd acquired.

"A name. Two names. It might be nothing."

"What names?" Sadagon asked.

Horus studied Sadagon's eyes as if contemplating how to proceed. He hesitated a long moment before speaking.

"Hadria," he finally said. "And Faron."

Sadagon's stoic expression shifted to one of melting fury, then spine-shattering pain. Varan's brow pulled into a look of careful calculation, and even the quiet Yarow looked taken aback; but, Sadagon did not see them.

He was in a tomb, carefully carved into the side of a south-facing hill. He remembered faces from centuries ago and wished he could forget. He remembered toppled walls and so many corpses; even the snow beasts could not consume a tenth of them. His hatred rekindled anew, and it followed him back to the present, where the others were staring at him with expressions of serious concern.

"How dare he!?" Sadagon tried to yell but was strangled by his apoplectic rage. Baranor would die for this.

"What does this mean?" Varan asked, searching for a method to cool Sadagon's temper.

"They are the names of—"

"I know what they are!" Varan yelled. "But what does this imply? The Twinborn, are they... alive? Are they here?"

Sadagon was too enraptured in pain to answer.

"It cannot be," Yarow said, breaking his long-lasting silence. "You killed his children."

"I was bound by the law!" Sadagon yelled in an abrupt explosion. "*Baranor* killed his children, and he took mine in their place. Vavelt and Varek are here, and they're alive; and now, Baranor is going to die."

II: Vengeance

Sadagon stood before the threshold, contemplating the impossible. A golden-haired girl of twelve years and a fair-haired boy of the same age lived inside, bearing painful names from the past. Just beyond the door stood the freedom and hope of salvation he once thought dead. Beyond the door stood those who could be gods.

They were more than just that, though. They were his children, Vavelt and Varek, even if they'd never known him. Fear stilled his hand. He had raised it to knock, but now he could not. Some paternal dread kept him from announcing himself. It took more than a moment to identify what it was.

These children were as ill-prepared to ascend to the Twinborn thrones as he was himself—less so even. They had been born to the purpose, with the intention of grooming and preparing their entire lives for rule, but that had been robbed from them. They would be half-grown now, with some idea of what life had in store for them, and he intended to rob them of that as well. Was it fair to tear them from everything they knew and place the world on their young shoulders? Was it fair of him to ask something of them that he himself was so unwilling to do?

Snow shifted to rain as Sadagon contemplated.

He could almost feel Varan's eyes on his hesitant back. *The growing Veil has no concept of fairness, and neither do hungry wolves.* That's what he would have said—or something to a similar point. He was being foolish. Why, then, couldn't he knock? Was it the scorn he would feel when his children met his eyes and didn't know his face? Was it the idea of stealing them away from some semblance of happiness?

He wasn't sure. The only thing he was sure of was that the Veil was growing, his children were alive, and Lyss was not. Sadagon had a job to do, and there was no longer a test to pass.

He knocked on the door.

Barely a moment passed before a small figure pulled it open, small drifts of snow standing erect where they had begun piling at the corners of the threshold.

It was Varek.

Sadagon instantly recognized his nose and chin, with Lyss's eyes. He was beautiful, and Sadagon could not speak. So overcome was he with emotion that he didn't hear the question prompted at him. Another, bolder voice from inside rang forward, and Sadagon's heart was pricked even further.

That was Lyss's voice—or it could have been when she was younger. It was everything he could do to not remember the mausoleum where her body was interned.

The brighter voice—Vavelt's—had asked him to come inside, so he did, automatically stepping as he processed what had been denied him the past decade. He could see them both now—his son, with Sadagon's prominent nose, and his daughter, who appeared to be the very image of her mother, save her soft blue eyes. They were both dressed in rough home-spun wool—pants and tunic. Even Vavelt was dressed as a boy, which was exceptionally rare outside of the more industrial cities.

He found himself judging the home around them as if to ensure that they had been suitably cared for in his absence. He shouldn't have cared, but he did. He would have been beyond enthused to find them only barely alive, but here they were, alive and well.

He was overcome with a burning desire to sweep them both up into an undying embrace and whisper all the things he should have been able to say years ago, but he stood rooted. They did not know him. For all they knew, they had a father.

He realized in a moment that they were staring at him, Varek with growing concern, and he searched his memory for what he'd just been asked—his name, he realized.

"We will become better acquainted," he managed to say without choking. "But for now, you may call me Sadagon." It was true enough. "As to why I'm here? Well, I'm here to speak to an old friend, and I was told that this is where he lived."

He hated the words as they left his mouth. Why not take them both and flee? They could be gone before Baranor returned, and all would be right. He banished the thought as soon as it came. Baranor murdered Lyss and stole his children to raise as his own, and now there was no longer a reason to test himself. Baranor needed to die.

"Oh, you mean Da?" Vavelt asked. Deep bitterness bit at Sadagon's heart. "He'll be home soon, but you're welcome to sit with us until then." The offer was so genuine that it made him smile—a very rare thing.

"I had hoped to find Bouren here, but I cannot state how overwhelmed I am to finally meet you two," Sadagon said. It was true in a manner of speaking. Then, caught up in his emotions and desperate to express himself in some way, he said, "You seem to be everything a man could want in his children." He nearly choked.

"Thank you." Vavelt smiled, then folded down a corner of the page in a book she was reading. Sadagon hadn't noticed it until then. She could read then. That was good. "That's a very nice thing to say. I'm guessing you have a son you'd like us to meet?"

The two children shared a knowing grin, and it told Sadagon much. Even at her age, she was sought after by the local boys. Unsurprising. Lyss had been a great beauty.

For some reason, that filled him with pride, and he smiled again. "In a manner of speaking." That, too, was technically true. His son was Varek. She just didn't know him by that name yet. He forced his mind to slow. They'd get to that. First, there was Bouren to deal with.

Suddenly, Varek spoke. "Did you say you were a friend of Father's?"

That was too great a lie to be tolerated.

"Old friend," Sadagon corrected. That still felt too far from the truth, so he added, "Long ago, in a place far from here."

His son opened his mouth to ask something else but was cut off by Vavelt's energetic inquiry. "Your accent is so smooth. Where are you from?"

It should have been yours too, Sadagon thought, feeling slighted, but he forced himself to laugh. It was easier than he expected.

"Oh, you would not know it if I told you. Suffice it to say, it is far away." He realized, suddenly, that he was dripping on the wood floor and removed his cloak. Casting about, he noticed a coat rack by the entrance and made to drape the wet article over it but stopped.

"May I?" he asked, looking Varek's way. It was best to get off on the right foot.

The boy nodded, and some of his tension seemed to slip away. Sadagon took it as a cue to continue dressing down and removed the rest of his shabby traveling clothes. As he did, he couldn't take his eyes off his daughter—his eldest, if only slightly. A burst of emotion nearly overwhelmed him, and he had to let out.

He didn't mean to speak but heard the words before he could consciously stop them. "You look so very much like your mother, young one." They both stiffened, and he wondered if he'd just said too much.

"You knew our mother!?" Vavelt cried, standing so fast her chair toppled. The purity of it could have melted any level of anxiety.

"Yes," he answered painfully. "Very well, in fact."

"How? When? Tell us about her!" Vavelt demanded, seizing her brother's wrist and tugging him near to her at the table. "Nobody here knows the first thing about her," she explained. "She died in childbirth, you see, and Father never likes to talk about her; so, I must know *everything*."

Childbirth? Is that what Baranor told them? He wanted to scream, to yell about how their 'Father' was a liar, murderer, and traitor—how their mother had died trying to protect them. He wanted to release all deceptions and tell them everything. They were family, after all, but it was not the time. Baranor had to be dealt with.

Sadagon's daughter went on, "Was she tall? Beautiful? Good at climbing trees? How did she wear her hair? What was she like?"

It hurt to remember.

"Now, that's an awful lot of questions," Sadagon said. "And I promise I'll answer them all, but let's perhaps begin one at a time, shall we?"

The anticipation that came from her nod was infectious, but it was cut off all in a moment when the door opened; and, all warmth bled from Sadagon's heart. The man who kidnapped his children and murdered his wife entered with a thinly wrapped parcel in his hands and freezing water in his eyes. He didn't seem to notice Sadagon, standing almost in the kitchen.

"Faron, could you fetch the shovel? I'd—" Baranor stopped dead in his tracks when he saw the cloak and gloves hanging on the rack, and his eyes shot upward, landing on the menacing scowl on Sadagon's face.

The aging blood drained from his face.

"Look, Daddy," Vavelt said, not knowing any better. "An old friend's come to visit you."

Save for the rain on the window, all was quiet as the two men locked eyes, Baranor's filled with dread, Sadagon's with long-awaited cruelty. The bloodlust in his heart was so powerful, he very nearly forgot the miraculous existence of his long-lost children. Baranor was his, and the time for vengeance had come.

"Hello, Baranor."

III: Vigil

Sadagon wept. Atop a throne of blackened stone, the prince of dawn and dusk, heir of Atha and Olsu, father of the Twinborn gods, sat surrounded by silent figures in robes of black. Bitter tears slipped down his cheeks to fall on the gemstones embedded into the soft marble floor. All around him, the men and women with long hoods and veils gently gripped orbs of white glass, none of them daring to speak a word.

Down the long and open length of the throne room, Sadagon's sole surviving child walked with an orb of her own, large in her hands, looking near to dropping it for her trembling. The statue-like figures all watched as she slowly walked, the long train of her inky gown trailing behind her.

The silence built, a palpable tension emanating from the tortured souls of Sadagon and his daughter as they drew nearer, one with hatred and loss, the other with stark abandonment and fear. The stillness grew to a crescendo as the girl who carried the weight of the world came to a stop before the raised dais of the thrones and lifted her orb into the air.

Light spilled from a thousand places as the hooded archons

lit their own orbs, lifting them softly until their limbs were extended. Diamonds and rubies flickered with the harsh light, glittering mournfully in their places on the walls and floor like the tears of a god.

The lamp slipped from Vavelt's fingers as she was finally overcome by the tears she'd been holding. It shattered into a thousand pieces of reflective glass and luminescent phosphorous, shimmering and scattered upon the ground.

With the silence broken, Sadagon's hushed tears became frame-wracking sobs, and his anguish filled the halls of Vam Aranath.

Alone, and with no other soul in the world left to trust, Vavelt witnessed Sadagon's pain and—willingly—ascended the dais. She knelt by his side and tenderly—fearfully—rested her hands upon his arm. She recoiled at his look of surprise but saw her brother in his features. With hope in his eyes, he extended toward her a shaking hand.

She took it, and together they wept for a lost brother and son—and for the fate of the world.

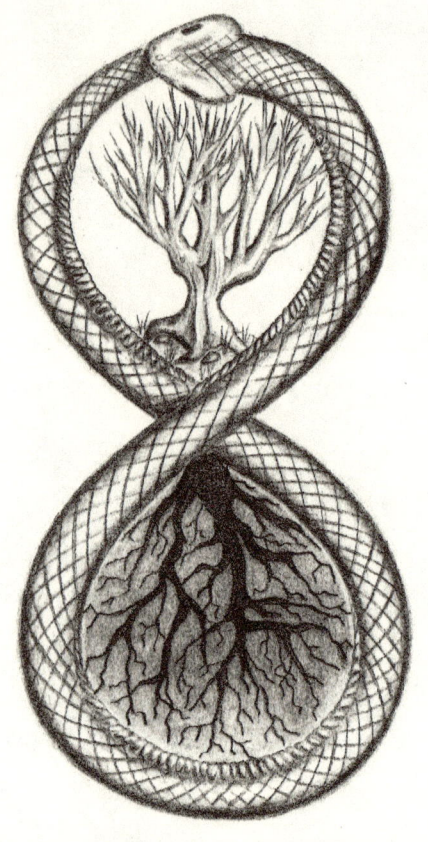

xxviii

I

A Pyre of Men and Mountain

FIVE YEARS LATER

Home

Somewhere above the Veil in the freezing white of the North, a woodfire flickered in a tower so high it pierced the roof of the sky. The top of that tower was adorned with a black iron spike, the sides of which stretched out to buttress the dome it dominated.

Just underneath that spike, a boy slept in a room built for a god. His skin was fire-scarred across his chest and shoulders, and his body was emaciated where it was not bandaged. His pale and sickly visage contrasted sharply with the decadence of the room around him.

A girl sat beside the boy, regal and belonging in the tower as it belonged to her. The way her eyes rested on the rise and fall of his chest only punctuated the sharp contrast he cast upon the temple around him, but it didn't matter. It was his.

The boy's breathing broke pattern as the drug wore off, and he shifted with a jolt.

Faron's eyes flickered open, and he found himself in a cloud. White and gold surrounded him in the softest touch he'd ever experienced, silk caressing him everywhere. It was a luxurious moment before he realized the cloud was not a cloud but thick blankets on the largest bed he'd ever seen.

The white was a reflective silk, and the gold an embroidered brocade, all of it smooth over his dry, flaking skin. Massive arches of polished blackwood connected the four posts of the great bedframe, draping a golden, diaphanous cloth in curtained sheets all about.

Everywhere he looked were the colors white and gold—the colors of Olsu.

Confusion swam with memory until the events of the previous night returned to him, and he remembered where he was. He sat up in a flash, or at least, tried to sit up, failing miserably, with horribly cramped muscles and a migraine that he felt in his teeth. He gasped and collapsed back into pillows so soft they had no right to exist in material form.

He felt eyes on him then and turned to see the form of his sister, who he had come so far to find, watching him while he slept. She didn't react, except to search his eyes in the silence. How many times had he done this? Finding her, only to wake and learn he'd been dreaming and to grasp at nothing while the sight of her slipped away.

To his great shame, Faron almost hoped that this time would be no different, that he could rouse the events of the previous night away with a few blinks of his bleary lids, that Sadagon and the truth of his parentage would disappear as mist. The white blankets would become snow, and the visage of his twin would resolve itself as the fevered nightmares of a freezing mind.

Of course, she didn't evaporate as she so often had when he woke. She was real, and so was the temple in which he slept—*his* temple. That sent a chill down his back.

Hadria's study of him became more quickened and tense as if she could sense the dour nature of his thoughts. She

4

didn't say anything, though, not wanting to be the one to break Faron's tempered quiet. What could he say, though, when he was hiding such evil thoughts?

He opened his mouth, and then, "I thought I dreamed it." Let her believe that it was a bad thing.

"It feels like a dream," she said, her lilting voice washing over him like the dulcet ring of silver. She seemed to search for more to say but stopped.

Faron examined her dress, searching for something to fill the silence. It was silver and scarlet, with long sleeves. Only one ring adorned her fingers now, and there was no diadem upon her head. Her golden hair was braided on the top and fell in delicate curls all down her back.

"You look like a queen," he said.

She smiled. "And you look terrible, like something the cat chewed up and spat out."

"I feel that way, too," he said, finding the beginnings of a smile. He could do this. She was still his sister. "I found you," he said, the emotions of the previous night returning to him in some small measure. He reached a hand toward her, almost drew it back, then trembled when she took it in both of hers. "I... I can't believe I'm not dreaming."

"Would you rather be?" The bluntness of the question shocked him. It was as if she could read his mind.

"Of course not," he said. "No. I found you."

"But not how you hoped to."

That merited a pause. He wondered for a moment how to best respond, then said, "No. No, not at all how I'd hoped. I... I wanted to... I thought you would be..."

She finished the thought for him. "You thought I'd be chained up like an animal, fattened for harvest."

"Yes," he admitted, looking away from her to hide his face. "That's what I thought—that I could find you, and that would be the end of it, that I could take you somewhere safe, away from Blackwood, away from here, and all our problems would be over." He breathed deep, eyes flicking around the grotesque room. "Now, the problems are just beginning."

"I would wish it was a dream, too," she said.

Faron imagined it then, picturing her fade away as she had so often before, and he panicked. It felt like the time he'd almost lost the wolf ring in that heated pool in Dageran's caverns. "No!" he said. "No. I won't lose you again. I cant… I can't do this with you, but… but I can't lose you again. Not again."

She must have seen the panic in his eyes because she leaned in close, long curls framing her angular face. "No," she agreed, smoothing a lock of his dark hair. "Never again. You're here now, and so am I. I'm going to take care of you, Varek."

He tried not to speak, to let her comfort be enough, but it wasn't. He could tell from her frozen body language that she had realized her mistake, but still, he had to say it. "That's not who I am," he said, and she grimaced.

"I'm sorry," she said. "I know I agreed not to use that name; it's just that I'm accustomed to it, and, well, it hurts him—Father, I mean."

"It's my *name*, Hadria. He can't take that from me, too."

She shook her head. "There's just so much you don't understand, Faron, so much hurt that you've never known, and it's so unfair—" Faron looked back to see her fighting back the threat of tears. "It's so unfair that you should come so far and through so much, and nothing is what you thought it was—not your family, your enemies, not even your name.

And now, after all of it, here I am, asking even more of you."

That broke him. "I can't do it," he whispered. "I can't do what you and Sadagon are asking of me."

"I know," she said. "But you will anyway, and I'm so sorry for it, Faron."

There was no reply to that.

"You don't have to right now, though," she continued. "We talked about this. Once, we had hoped to be a bard and a bard's guard, twins with the world at their feet and not a worry but for their dinner." She nodded. "We can be that again—for a while, a little while." She blinked away her sadness and offered him a serene smile. "You don't have to be Varek just yet. You don't have to be anyone's son or anyone's heir. You're my brother, and that's all you have to be—until you're ready."

Faron winced but tried to hide it. He didn't want to fight with her, not right now. Still, even if she could somehow look past it, Sadagon was killing and enslaving children. Faron would never be ready.

Tea Kettles

Sensing Faron's thoughts, Hadria sighed, then leaned further across the bed and wrapped her arms around him. Faron folded into that embrace, letting the heat of her melt away his anxieties.

"You never asked for this," she said. "I can't imagine what you must be going through." Faron pulled his own arms up and managed to pull himself into a sitting position. They stayed that way for a long while, regretting the long years they'd lost and the divide that had grown between them. When she finally pulled away, the white blankets slipped from around Faron's chest, exposing the mess of scars there, except where wrapped bandages held broken skin. When had he been bandaged? The last he remembered, he'd been on a one-armed couch with Synick, weeping like a pathetic child.

Hadria gasped. It was clear from the sound of it that she had seen it already but not the full extent that the fire had touched him. Why should her reaction cause him to feel shame? He resisted the urge to pull the covers higher and let her see him as he truly was: wounded, marked, and ugly.

Before he could say a thing, Hadria reached out and traced a palm over the angry webbing of his chest.

8

"Sorry," she apologized, retracting her hand. "Does that... hurt?"

"No," he reassured. "In fact, there's barely any feeling left in my chest at all, except for when—" He cut himself off.

Hadria's brows pulled into a sharp V. "Except when?"

"Nothing," he said. She didn't need to know how the fire had touched his mind just as harshly as his skin. She didn't need to know how she'd haunted him these years. She was here now.

Hadria spied the brand above his heart—an emblazoned image of a snake twisted back on itself over a dead tree with deep roots—the symbol of the gods.

"What's this?" She reached a finger out to touch it but stopped. "Faron, this is *our* symbol: the Ourodurity. How did you get it burned into you, and why is it branded directly into a fire-scar?" Her eyes shifted from the brand to the knot of damaged skin across his body, and her voice hushed. "Is this... Is this from when I saw you die?"

Faron shrugged uncomfortably. He wasn't ready to talk about that—any of it. "It's a long story."

"Brother," she said. "You don't have anywhere to be. There's nothing you have to do and nowhere you have to go. I've delegated all my affairs of state so we can be together. We have all the time in the world."

Clearing his thoughts with a shake of the head, he said, "I want to talk about *you*, walk with you. I want to *know you* again, Hadria."

She smiled. "There are ten thousand things you'll want to know, and I'm undoubtedly the *least* interesting among them; but, we have the time." Her smile was soft and warm like the red rays of morning on a leaf bitten with frost.

9

A long moment passed. "Faron?" Her smile had turned to a humorous half-grin.

"What?"

"You can stop staring now. I'm not going anywhere."

He blushed. "I'm sorry. I just… I never thought this day would come. I'm a little in shock, I think."

She stood off the bed. "Well, I'm marginally pleased to see you too, you know. It's all I can do to keep myself from squeezing you until you pop, which, by the looks of you, wouldn't be too hard." She frowned. "I plan to make the most of our time, but as for that walk you asked for, it'll have to wait. You're not going anywhere. If I knew the half of your condition when you'd arrived, I would have refused to meet with you until you'd slept a week and eaten an entire sheep. You're starved, Faron."

He frowned and looked down at his chest. It was a strange blend of corded muscle and emaciated ribs. In his prolonged journey without food, his body had almost cannibalized itself to stay alive, leaving behind only the strongest of his muscles and the most necessary. Everything else had been metabolized.

"At any rate, you're safe now, and I'll feed you that sheep myself." He noticed, for the first time, a folding table with silver bowls and cutlery. Hadria pulled the lid off a deep-bellied bowl, and steam rose from within. The scent of onions and black mushrooms was immediately evident.

"Broth?" Faron asked.

"In your condition, yes. You're somehow both starved and dehydrated. Luckily for you, though, we've both been here before." She tapped a spoon on an ornate silver bowl to drip excess broth from the bottom, then lifted it to Faron's lips.

"Drink."

He thought of protesting the command and taking the bowl himself but stopped, allowing himself to accept her help. He opened his mouth and sipped. It was salty, hot, and packed with flavor. Having eaten nothing but wolf meat the past week, if he'd eaten at all, he wasn't ready for the intensity of the soup and coughed violently. The clenching in his stomach sat him upright, and Hadria slammed his back until he stopped coughing.

"Ow!" Faron complained when he could speak.

"Who chokes on broth?" she asked. "That's like choking on water—or air!"

Faron laughed but was cut short by the compounded pressure in his head. He groaned instead. Hadria laughed for him and, before he could lay back down, stacked several pillows behind his back to prop him up.

"Let's try again," she said, preparing another spoonful. Slower this time, Faron accepted the broth into his mouth and swished it around. It was wonderful. He swallowed and was overly aware of it washing down into his stomach. Spoonful after spoonful, he reawakened his body with water and nourishment, sparking both hunger and thirst. When the first bowl was empty, Hadria let Faron hold his own, and with shaking hands, he drained it without the use of a spoon.

When the third bowl was empty, and he felt simultaneously stuffed full and starved to death, he leaned back and closed his eyes. Now that he was finally safe and out of the cold, his body was making up for the over-expenditure of energy he'd forced upon it. He was *exhausted.*

"Do you remember when you broke your arm for me?" Hadria asked eventually.

"For you?"

"Yes, for me."

"That was hardly for you," Faron replied.

"Beating the boys who harassed me into a pulp wasn't for me?"

Faron laughed. "That isn't what happened at all. I *lost* that fight."

"You gave as good as you got—better, actually. There were three of them."

"None of them had you to stick-fight with," Faron said.

"*Sword*-fight," Hadria corrected.

"They were sticks," Faron laughed. "Pretending otherwise didn't change that."

"Well, they beat and bruised well enough if I remember."

Faron chuckled, even though it hurt. "I was in bed for three days after that."

"It was supposed to be three weeks, but, well, you never were very good at following rules."

"You fed me then, too," Faron remarked. "Also broth."

"You've given me lots of practice," Hadria agreed, sitting on the massive bed. "Gods, Faron, you've always been such a troublemaker."

"Me?" Faron asked, incredulous. "*I'm* the troublemaker? The only trouble I've *ever* gotten in was keeping up with *you!*"

"Sometimes, a troublemaker is the one who gets caught."

That spurred Faron's memory. "Where's Synick?" he asked, suddenly panicked.

"He's well," Hadria assured him. "He watched us all last night and followed you here, spent the day sleeping on your floor before the door, and spent the night harassing Varan.

Unless I miss my guess, he's currently prying gemstones from the pillars outside."

Faron groaned. That sounded about right. "I'm sorry," he said. "He's... like that."

"Don't be. As far as I'm concerned, he can have all the gems on all the pillars and the floor, too. Returning you to me is a deed that cannot be adequately rewarded."

Just then, the doors burst open, and Faron glanced away from his sister, taking in the room for the first time. The bed was on a raised dais, fifteen steps above the main level, where gold and white tapestries hung from stone arches. Couches of the same color sprawled all about. Twenty-foot-tall windows stretched from the floor to the great ceiling, where several arched pillars met, creating a radial pattern that boggled the eye.

Each arch was polished nearly white, with a miniature spike at its apex like the buttress of a grand tower. To the left, two heavy wooden doors were flung open, and in strutted Synick beside the sofa Faron remembered.

"My ears are burning," he said. "So, either someone walked on my grave, or you're talking about me."

"How about both?" Hadria asked, gesturing to the empty side of the bed. "We could stab you and lie you to rest right there."

Synick stopped, staring at her. "Huh," he said thoughtfully. "That's odd. I didn't expect to like you... Damn it."

Hadria snorted a laugh. "Did you find the pillars to your liking?"

He lifted his heel off the ground to swivel his leg back and forth. Sweet clinking noises came from his pocket, and he grinned. "Sure did."

"What happened to giving up thieving?" Faron asked.

"Oh, this *hardly* counts," Synick replied. "Like stealing a rushlight or a fingernail full of lead paint."

"It's fine," Hadria said, soothing Faron. "From time to time, the earth quakes, and stones fall from their settings. They are easily replaced. This whole temple belongs to us anyway, and if you want to give something so mundane as rocks to your friend, they are yours to give."

"That's what I figured," Synick said.

Hadria's lips drew to a thin line. "How much of our conversation last night did you overhear, you eavesdrop?"

"None!" Synick promised. "After I left, anyway. Didn't hear a thing, honest." She scowled at him.

"He reads lips," Faron said. "Frighteningly well."

Synick grinned. "Still, though, technically didn't hear anything."

"I can already tell you're going to be an interesting person."

"If by interesting," Faron said, "you mean irritating and difficult."

"Actually, that *is* what I meant." Hadria brooked a smile, which Synick returned doubly.

Faron cut in. "I take it you've been awake longer than I have?"

"That's a very low bar you're setting, Faron. We're in the city of temples and light, and you *sleep*? For a full day? Your sense of adventure has always been lacking, but this? You sicken me."

"Tell me about it," Hadria agreed.

"That's not fair!" Faron defended. "I'd only just crossed the snowing mountains to get here, nearly frostbitten and fighting wolves the whole way."

14

"As I recall," Synick said. "You napped through the last fight."

"Why aren't you exhausted?" Faron retorted. "You came every one of those seventeen freezing days with me."

Hadria's brow rose at the swearing.

"Oh, I don't know," Synick said. "Maybe it's because I didn't come immediately after climbing the sacred mountains of the Kaor and racing the Veil all the way to Anveil. Maybe it's because I don't make a regular habit of starving myself nine-tenths to death and sleeping four hours a night. Might have something to do with it."

"You *what?*" Hadria asked.

"It's been a long road," Faron said.

Sighing, Hadria descended the stairs and opened the door to the hallway outside. "Bring in the pheasant," she said to a person Faron could not see. "And honey water." When she had climbed the steps again, Synick sat himself against the far wall, kicking his feet up onto the arm of a couch. "You've had enough time to allow for something more healing," she declared. It wasn't long before silver trays were brought in by gold, white, and red liveried servants bearing pheasant breast drenched in a thick, white gravy. Heavy biscuits were soaked beside them.

A stool-like tray was set over him on the bed, and his food was placed atop it. Synick was given a generous helping of the same, only he sat more properly at an ornately gilded table of polished blackwood. Despite the bowls of broth he'd only just had, Faron's stomach rumbled, and he consumed the food with gusto.

When he realized he was eating like an animal, he blushed, and Hadria snorted a laugh. "It's nice to see some things don't change."

"Don't hold it against him," Synick said through a mouthful of pheasant and bread. "He's been eating with wolves for the past week or so."

She eyed him dubiously. "He's not the only one."

"Oh, no." Synick shook his head. "I'm just slovenly."

Hadria laughed. "That's odd," she said, mirroring Synick's earlier words. "I didn't expect to like you... Damn it."

Synick almost choked on his food.

"I'm feeling a lot better," Faron said before Synick could reengage.

"You're sitting up, at least."

"Faron," Synick interrupted. "You *have* to come and see this temple of yours. The walls are covered in silver and gold, and there are gemstones *everywhere*. All the servants act like they can't see you, too, even when you talk to them, so you can just take them."

"Are you harassing my handmaidens?" Hadria asked.

"Depends on your definition," he said, waving his hand to dismiss the topic. "Faron, are you going to get up or what?"

"Please *don't* encourage him. He needs rest."

"A bath is what he needs."

Hadria wrinkled her nose. "He's right, in fact."

Faron flushed.

"Normally, we would never have sent you to bed without a bath or at least a change of clothes, but you appeared anything but normal. I've never seen a person look so tired before. Varan wanted to send servants to clean you while you slept, but I forbade him. No offense, but you looked as if you might stab someone who surprised you."

Synick grunted his agreement.

Faron nodded. "You're right. I've been weeks in the North, and I can't pretend I don't need one... Where...?" He trailed off when Hadria broke into a broad grin.

"You're going to love this," she said.

He didn't. When they arrived at Olsu's bathing chamber, Faron's jaw nearly hit the floor. The palace was so disgustingly ornate that it should have given him some indication that the utility rooms would be the same, but the sheer waste of space was astounding. The bath itself, if it could be called that, was more of an indoor cistern than a tub, recessed into the floor and stretching over thirty feet across. In the middle of the octagonal depression was a tall structure made of stone and bronze metal that he couldn't identify. All about the outsides of the unnecessarily huge room were sofas, beds, benches, and grated holes in the floor.

"It's..." He searched for the right word.

"Impressive," Synick finished for him, fingering a larger than average array of emeralds on a white pillar.

"Awful," Faron said.

"Oh, you'll be fine," Hadria quipped. "It's supposed to be *fun.* This is the personal bathing chamber of Olsu. Of course it's going to be a little over the top."

"Why are there beds in here?" he asked.

Synick coughed a quiet laugh.

Hadria rolled her eyes at him and answered, "The late Olsu was, apparently, deeply concerned with personal pleasures."

"There are more than ten in here. How many could you need?" And then it dawned on him that the beds were likely not used for sleeping, and he blushed.

"Well..." Hadria paused awkwardly, shooting Synick a quick glance, then looking away. "He was a very carnal man, according to the, uh… evidence."

Synick busted out laughing. "Atha's tits, Faron. I can't believe you needed that spelled out for you by your *sister*." He cackled madly until he noticed Hadria staring at him with one brow raised very, very high. "Uh… right." He paused. "I suppose that's an expression I'd best give up."

"Oh, no, please," she said with mock sincerity. "Continue. I only hope they live up to the legends."

"Synick!" Faron snapped with horrified eyes.

"Oh, it's fine." Hadria waved. "If you dislike that expression, wait until you learn what *you've* inherited."

Faron wasn't sure how to respond to that, so he changed the subject. "How am I supposed to take a bath in here? It would take weeks to fill it up with a line of a hundred buckets."

"Things are a bit different in Vam Aranath," she said, leading him to a back room. "There were so many wonderful things that have been lost to the world, but not here. We have a few more comforts than you might be used to." She pointed at a metal wheel attached to a great bronze tube. "Synick, would you be a dear?"

"Sure," he said with a blank expression.

When it was clear he didn't have the first idea what she wanted, Hadria rolled her eyes and said, "*Turn* it."

When he did, the sound of squealing metal followed by rushing water came over them, and Faron jumped when concentrated waves surged out of grates in the great bath. Water and steam rushed out together, and the room quickly filled with swirling eddies of mist.

"It's hot!" Synick exclaimed.

Rushing over to the bath, Faron stuck his finger in one of

the fat jets and recoiled when it stung. "Too hot," he said.

Hadria moved to another metal wheel and turned it herself. The flow increased, great laminar gushes quickly filling the large depression. "You control the temperature from here," she said. "One valve for hot and one for cold."

"How is there so much water stored in the walls?" Faron asked. "And how is it hot?"

Hadria laughed, a delighted, melodic tone. "It's not stored in the walls, silly! It's stored underground!"

That didn't make it any clearer.

"Deep below us are great lakes of lava that heat the ground and melt the snow. That water collects in cisterns and aquifers where it heats and is pumped by the power of steam through pipes to anywhere in the city."

Faron and Synick shared a dumbfounded expression. "The power... of steam?" Faron asked.

Hadria laughed again, clearly relishing the ability to confound him. "Yes! There's so much that was lost, Faron, so much to show you!"

"Wait a minute," Synick implored. "We're talking about steam? White puff of nothing? Pleasant to fill a room full of lady friends with? That steam?"

She nodded, scrutinizing gaze lingering on him a moment longer than was necessary.

"How on earth do you move water through pipes with steam?"

"Have you ever watched the lid of a tea kettle as it shakes?"

"No."

Hadria rolled her eyes. "Your lack of curiosity is worse than Faron's."

"So, you're moving all this water... with tea kettles?" Synick asked.

"Why are you friends with him?" she asked Faron. "He's pretty, but..." She hesitated. "You are... *friends*, aren't you?"

Faron cocked an eyebrow, but Synick's reaction was much more drastic. "Atha's tits, yes." He shivered. "Gods, yes. Do you think that if I were to betray my *natural inclinations*, it would be for a boy like *Faron*? No!" Faron tried to speak, but Synick shut him down. "If I were to dabble across the proverbial aisle, it'd be with someone with far broader shoulders, a square chin, muscles like a dehydrated ox, and a..." He trailed away. "Ahem. You know what? Never mind."

"You've, uh... given it some thought, I see," Hadria said with a twisted grin.

"Don't let him answer," Faron said. "It only fuels him."

"No, no," Hadria insisted. "I want to see where this goes. I'm interested."

Faron cut them both off. "So, am I going to be bathing in here alone, or are both of you going to go on gawking while I undress?"

"Well, I know one of us who might be interested," Hadria said with a pointed smirk at Synick.

"For the last time, no!" he protested. "I won't take him off your hands for you. Forget it."

"I can't believe this is happening," Faron groaned.

Hadria opened her mouth to say something but was cut short. "That's a lot of tea kettles," Synick said, staring at the nearly overflowing bath.

"Damn," Hadria breathed, rushing back to the controls. She threw her weight on one and spun it shut. Synick leaped to the other and did the same. The water slowed to a trickle and then stopped.

"Thank you," she said, catching his eye. Synick grinned at her, and when she didn't look away, that grin slipped—for only a moment. It wasn't lost on Hadria. Her gaze intensified, piercing through Synick until he broke the contact. "You hide behind that smile the way a soldier cowers behind a shield." Her voice was accusing. Synick visibly squirmed, but she nodded. "What arrows are you hiding from, Synick?"

She reached out to cup his cheek but was stopped when the long sleeve of her gown caught on the twisted metal behind the wheel. It tore, then came away covered in black grease.

"Blood and ice," she cursed. Synick had never looked more relieved in his life.

"Are you alright?" Faron asked, stepping forward, all taunts and jibes forgotten.

"I'm fine," she said, pulling her dirtied wrist away. "Just covered in this filth now. You have a point, though. You need a bath, and I need to change into something else." She pulled Faron into a tight hug, arm carefully splayed to the side. "I'll be back in an hour to see if you're finished."

Whatever she had done to Synick, he had recovered, replacing a rare blush with that slanting grin. "I could use a hug, too," he mumbled but sounded shaken. Faron shoved an elbow into his ribs anyway.

"I bet you could," Hadria said and then slipped out the door.

"What was that?" Faron asked when she was gone.

Synick didn't fall to the floor, but he looked as if he wanted to. "I have no idea. She looked at me like I'd just told her every secret I've ever had."

"You're imagining things," Faron said. "She's probably just realized that you're only half as stupid as you pretend to be."

21

"That's still pretty stupid," Synick said with a nod.

"Unfathomably."

"Right," Synick said with a shake of his head. "We taking a bath or what?"

"We?"

"Well, yeah. This thing is huge. There's plenty of space for us both."

"Not a chance in the Iron Halls," Faron declared. "Find your own tub."

"I was only joking earlier," Synick grumbled.

"There are a hundred servants outside that can take you to a bath. You can't have mine."

"Alright, alright," he said, waving his hand behind him. "I get it." With that, he was gone.

Baranor's Children

S trangely relieved to be alone, Faron breathed deep and disrobed, then stepped into the great bath. It was hot and smelled of flower oils. Grime and caked blood lifted off of him in lazy ripples, and the hot water undid months of anxious knots. It even worked in great strides to reduce the intensity of his migraine.

He had made it. He had found Hadria, and he had made it. Why, then, did he feel even worse than before?

He drifted idly for a while, letting himself feel clean for the first time in what felt like ages. This new reality was almost beyond belief. He had been able, for a little while, to force his thoughts away and enjoy his time with Hadria, but they came crashing back now. Sadagon wasn't the monster he expected, but he was a monster nonetheless. Hadria was alive and well, which was wonderful, but she was in league with the man who killed their father.

He had to catch himself as he did every time the thought came: not his father. Bouren—Baranor—was apparently not even that. Sadagon was his father now, supposedly. The idea made him shiver despite the heat, and it raised too many questions.

Faron didn't want to answer questions. He didn't want

to think about the growing Veil or the coming winter Sadagon spoke of. He didn't want to think about inheritance, bloodlines, immortality, or gods. He only wanted to be with his sister.

Hurriedly, Faron brushed the accumulated sweat, blood, dirt, mud, and filth from his body and extricated himself from the water. He pulled on the new clothes Hadria had left him—stable clothes, she had called them—and exited the room.

He was surprised to find Synick sitting in a chair just outside the door, legs propped up against the wall.

"Well, that didn't take very long," he said. "Couldn't stand to be alone with your thoughts?"

Faron shook his head.

"Thought not. You didn't, uh, bucket that out or drain it, did you?"

"Of course not."

"Right. My turn then, you prude."

"It might not be that clean," Faron suggested.

"Oh, please," Synick said, standing. "I know you're no flower, but show some humility. There's more water there than even you can pollute."

He pushed his way inside, and Faron stood in the doorway. "I was going to find Hadria," he said.

"She'll come looking for you sooner or later, and if you go wandering at random, you'll just get lost. Better to stay put."

"You waited for me." It wasn't a question. When Synick didn't reply, he added, "Why?"

"Habit, I suppose. I've gotten used to seeing you all the time these past weeks."

"You were guarding me," Faron accused.

24

"Of course not," Synick lied.

"Yes, you are," Faron pushed. "Hadria said you slept on my floor last night and have been staying within sight of my door."

"Alright, fine," Synick said. "I don't trust them. So what?"

"She's my sister, Synick—my twin. You don't need to protect me from her."

"This isn't a conversation I can have clothed," Synick said. "Are you gonna turn around or what?"

Knowing that Synick wouldn't waste any time, Faron turned and waited. He heard an enormous splash and then gasped as water landed all over his arm and head.

"Git!" Faron half yelled when Synick surfaced.

"Worth it," he giggled. "It's not every day you get to douse a god."

Faron sighed. "I'm not a god."

"That's not what *everyone* here seems to think."

"I don't want to think about it."

"We've been there before, haven't we?" he retorted.

"I don't want to talk about it, Synick."

"Definitely been there," he confirmed. "Look, Faron, only a day ago, we were starving and being hunted by hungry wolves. We were so cold most of the time that I didn't dare to check and see if my toes were turning green, and now you're in the nicest snowing palace I've ever imagined, except it's a temple, and it's yours, and everyone loves you.

"Your sister, who've you've trekked across the entire known world to find, is, in fact, not in trouble, and your mortal enemy is pretty comfortable about the idea of being your father."

"Is there a point?" Faron snapped.

"Your whole world has been turned on its head, Faron. Don't you want to talk about it?"

"No."

"Ah. I see. You do, but you don't want to admit that you do."

"I'm fine, Synick. I don't need to talk about it, and I don't need you to protect me from her."

"And what about Sadagon? Are you fine with him waltzing into your room whenever he pleases?"

"Of course not."

"So, what are you going to do?"

"I don't know."

"Are we going to stay?"

Faron gave him a questioning look.

"Do you believe them? About the growing Veil? About what you need to do?"

Faron shrugged. "Yes... I don't know." He put his hands in the air. "I can't deny it, at least."

"So, we're staying?"

"I'm not leaving my sister."

Synick nodded, letting out a pent-up breath.

Faron's brow furrowed, and he waited a moment before asking, "Are you thinking of going back?"

"No," he answered with a fervent shake of his head. "Not unless I have to. Faron, I... I actually really like it here." When Faron didn't respond, he went on, "I mean, if you end up going, I'll go with you, but if I get a vote, I'm staying here."

"What about Jesika?"

Synick stared off into the distance. "What about her?"

"Weren't you, you know, chasing after her?"

He nodded. "I was, but more like how a dog chases a horse.

The chase would stop the moment she stopped running. To be honest, we both kind of understood that it was mostly just to bug Artur. She's not… She's not what I want."

Faron nodded. "I guess that's a good thing. I don't even know if Sadagon would let me leave. He seems so sure about the Veil growing."

It was an extended moment before Synick replied. "It *does* explain a lot. Winter has been coming earlier and earlier each year, and now Anveil is swallowed months before it should be. Something is definitely wrong, but… still. Propping up a false god to unite the world hardly seems like the best option."

"You really are frightfully good at reading lips," Faron said.

"Well, I *did* hear some of it," he admitted. "It's not like you were trying to keep quiet, and besides, I had a right to know."

Faron nodded. "Well, in any case, I'm glad you're happy here, Synick."

"That doesn't mean I trust them, Faron. I believe that Sadagon means what he says, but I don't like him making it your problem."

Faron nodded again. "I'll be careful, but honestly," he said, getting back to the original point, "you don't have to protect me. I'll be fine."

"I suppose I'm just nervous. I was prepared to deal with a bloodthirsty tyrant, maybe stealing Hadria from a cell, but not this. Not…"—he waved his hands out of the water—"all this."

A knock came at the door.

"That'll be Hadria," Faron said, standing.

"Oh, yes, please, invite her in. I'm sure she'll be eager to get a better view."

"I'll just slip outside," Faron said in an exasperated tone.

"Bring me some lunch, would you?"

Faron nodded and slipped out into the hall, and there stood Sadagon.

He was huge. Compared to the easy head of height that he had over Faron and the broad, heavy shoulders, the nervous and penitent expressions he wore hardly seemed to matter.

Faron tried to speak, but his throat was filled with remembered smoke and heat. He could feel his flesh burning and melting away on his chest. That face was a sharp trigger.

"I'm sorry," Sadagon said with a step backward. "I shouldn't have come."

"Where is Hadria?" he managed to say. After only a moment, the panic subsided.

"She sent me," Sadagon answered. "And asked me to tell you that she will be preoccupied for a few hours."

Faron stiffened. "Preoccupied with what?"

"Your nameday celebration." He smiled. "And repeal of the citywide mourn."

"Can't you do those things?"

"Not if you want them to be any good," he said with a small smile. It faded away when Faron did not return it. "It's good for her to practice leadership. She will be the official ruler soon." There was a pause. "As will you."

"I'm not the ruler of anything," Faron retorted. "Is that the reason you came? To deliver a message any of your thousand slaves could have?"

Sadagon smiled patiently. "No, in fact. I offered to carry the message personally because I couldn't stay away. You're my son, and I wish to know you."

"Don't call me that."

"I'm sorry, I know it's unfair of me. Forgive me if I'm eager to use the term. It's been a point of pain for me for some years. How would you have me address you?"

Faron searched his eyes for signs of malice and was disturbed to find none. "Just call me Faron," he mumbled.

Sadagon nodded as if agreeing to a compromise. "Very well, Faron. I had intended to ask you to walk with me, but I see a panic rising in your eyes. Do you want me to take you to your sister?"

"Tell me where she is, and I'll find her myself." He was annoyed that Sadagon had been able to read him so well.

"Could you allow me to show you? You are eager to know she is safe, I know the way, and I wish to speak with you."

Faron thought for a long moment, still holding the exterior handle of the door behind him, and finally acquiesced.

"Alright," he said. "I suppose I can't hide from you forever."

"I don't know about that," Sadagon said when Faron released the door. "I know that look in your eye when you see me. I've seen it before on a night long ago and a thousand times in my dreams since—ten thousand times."

Faron knew what night he was talking about: the night of the fire.

"If the sight of me strikes fear into your heart for the next thousand years, I couldn't blame you in the slightest, and I can't blame you if you want to be rid of me."

"I do," Faron said quietly.

There was a pause, and then, "I know. It's why I've come. There is a debt between us."

A question burst from Faron, a question he had been trying not to ask for fear of legitimizing the painful truth in front of him.

29

"Why did you kill Bouren?" He clenched his jaw shut as if he could take the question back. Sadagon, though, didn't look the least bit surprised.

"Walk with me." He extended a flat, pale palm into the hallway. Reluctantly, Faron did.

"There is no way to make my actions that night sound anything other than revenge, and I won't try. I killed Baranor because I could." He acknowledged Faron's sidelong glare with a slow nod. "It was base, but please try to understand, he murdered my wife. I thought he murdered you."

"You almost did that yourself," Faron said, then immediately regretted it. Sadagon didn't start that fire. He did. Sadagon must have read the pain on his face because he didn't point that out.

"It was the greatest mistake of my life, and I have spent years hating myself for it."

Faron wasn't sure how to respond to that.

"When I set out to find Baranor, I hoped *not* to kill him. It was of… personal importance to me. When I saw you and your sister, though… I could not control myself." He turned his head and caught Faron's gaze with his electric blue eyes. Faron saw far more in them than was being said. "I thought I killed you. In my jealousy and fury, I set in motion a chain of events that resulted in me fleeing that burning home with only one of my children for fear of losing both."

He sighed deeply. "As is my apparent legacy, I have made things infinitely worse for myself—and for you." He stopped, and Faron turned back to look at him. "They say there is a brand on your chest above the fire scars I gave you—an Ourodurity. Is that true?"

Wordlessly, Faron nodded.

30

"Then that, too, is my fault. I'm sorry."

Faron had thought much the same thing over the years but couldn't bring himself to agree with the man who was laying his soul bare for him. Unable to trust himself to speak, he only shrugged.

"I hope one day you will entrust me with the stories of your past, but I will not ask for them now. I do not have the right."

It was silent for a long minute as Faron felt a hot choking in his throat. It wasn't the memory of smoke.

"Hadria mentioned something about our mother," Faron said. He was right not to trust his voice before. It wavered dangerously. "What did he do?"

"Has Vavelt not told you?"

"No, except that he stole us as infants, but... why did he do it?"

"That, too, was my fault." Faron could feel the cold remorse emanating from him like fog from frozen metal. "For centuries after the gods, we tried to isolate ourselves from the rest of the world, removing any scrap of paper that mentioned even the name of Vam Aranath and the historians who would remember it. We tried to let Alden rule itself, free of gods or god-kings, but when we learned of the growing Veil, we knew it was time to reestablish rule, if not as totalitarian and cruel as before."

Faron ignored his urge to rush Sadagon to the point and listened carefully.

"It was decided that I, being the only known descendant of either god—even the bastard child of both gods—should be the one to restore the old religion. Despite our efforts at eradicating the memory of Atha and Olsu, there were already prophecies of their eventual rebirth, leaving an obvious avenue for us to pursue. For the plan to move forward, twins would need to be born—a boy and a girl.

"The issue," Sadagon went on to explain, "was with me. I was not eager to take a wife and even less eager to bear children. It is a... sore point with me."

"How could you have known you would have twins?" Faron asked after a brief pause. "Aren't they extremely rare?"

"Less than you would think. A woman who would bear twins will often lose one or both of her children if she is not properly fed or is overworked, so it already isn't as rare as you believe. Additionally, there are ways to increase the odds—lineage, for example. The trait is one that skips generations in family lines, and I, unfortunately, have the trait from both of my parents."

Faron grimaced at the concept.

Sadagon only nodded and continued. "Further, I was required to choose a spouse who was also descended from twins, as physicians say it is the female who is more determinate in the process, and having lived almost three centuries with my followers, I knew who that was and was not willing to consummate a marriage with them."

"Hadria said that our mother was named... Lyss?"

"Yes," Sadagon said, appearing uncomfortable. "When my obstinance was made abundantly apparent to my followers, they began to search through our growing number of slaves and servants for the correct bloodlines and found several potentialities. They were removed from the other workers and groomed for my... consideration."

"That's awful," Faron said, surprising himself with his bluntness.

"Indeed," Sadagon agreed. "It was most distasteful, but my followers—and Varan—were growing anxious, and there were far more serious concerns mounting than my discomfort; so, I agreed. When they had grown near enough to adulthood, I met with them and was surprised to discover a friendship with a child from the debtor's prisons of Empyrion: Lyss."

"She was a slave?" Faron asked, surprised.

"Even before she was brought here, if not in name." Sadagon continued, "I did not love her, but... she was a person I could come to love. Given the great need, I overcame my hesitations and asked her to marry me."

"And then Bouren killed her?" Faron asked, confused.

"Not quite. As with all things, it is never so simple. This was a process of decades—you have to understand. While I grappled with my reservations, a faction grew in my supporters who wished to install the first birthed twins as gods, regardless of heritage or birthright. Baranor and his wife, Gwyn, were the first to bear male-female twins, and he led the rally to lift them up to the Twinborn throne. The lady, Gwyn, died during childbirth, and it only fueled Baranor to press the subject. This debate lasted for years until the twins themselves grew old enough to advocate for their ascension."

"What happened?" Faron asked.

"On the nameday of their eighteenth year, they staged a coup to dissolve my stewardship and take over rule of Vam Aranath. It was... unsuccessful."

"What happened to them?"

"I was forced to have them executed on a pyre," he said with clear remorse.

"Gods," Faron whispered.

"Indeed," Sadagon said. "The law required it of me, but that made it no easier a thing to do. It was the first serious crime committed by an archon since the Supernal Dusk and not an aspect of rule I had hoped to endure."

"That's horrible," Faron said, not sure if he was referring to the punishment or the fact that Sadagon had been made to carry it out—both, perhaps.

"Baranor could not be directly tied to the actions of his children, so the law did not require me to execute him as well. The decision was mine, and I allowed him to live." He sighed again. "That is another way I have failed you. It was another fifty years before I met Lyss, and she would eventually give birth to the two of you." He paused for a heavy breath. "Barely a month passed after that before Baranor murdered both her and your wet nurse, then made off with my children into the Veil."

Faron stopped, trying to comprehend the enormity of the crime Bouren had committed. It bore the hand of spite and grudgeful rage. Was the man who raised him capable of such horror?

"He really did those things?"

"Truly, and Vam Aranath has been in mourning ever since. No citywide celebrations have been held since that day, except to honor the return of your sister, and none would for another eighty years if you had not returned. This is, in part, what is keeping Vavelt so busy. Her servants and advisors are unaccustomed to celebrations on such a scale and require her attention. The city will wake from its mourn for the first time since Baranor betrayed us, and my heart is finally at rest."

"I'm sorry," Faron said with sincerity, resuming his pace.

They made their way up several huge flights of stairs. "I didn't intend to make you relive those days."

"Don't be. This story is your birthright, no matter how painful it might be for me. I only hope it helps you to understand the anger that drove me to kill Baranor. When I saw him with my children, I should have been relieved that you were alive. Instead, I was only furious at seeing what he had stolen from me."

"It took you twelve years to find him?" Faron asked. "Us, I mean."

Sadagon nodded. "The world is a big place, and Baranor carried you far, farther than I suspected. I sent men to search from Anveil to Murcosta and searched Sycele myself. You have to understand, beyond the bounds of Vam Aranath, my reach is as weak as any other man's."

"How did you find him?" Faron asked.

"Slowly. I sent men to all corners of the world to recover you and your sister if you were alive and to drag Baranor back if you were not. When I sent only two men to Blackwood, and they didn't come back, I knew that Bouren had found them first and killed them." He shook his head. "They were good men—loyal—with families of their own. I sent ten men to scour Blackwood and her surrounding villages after that and went myself when they did not return results as fast as I wanted. I was lucky enough to find you and stupid enough to get you killed."

Faron walked lockstep with Sadagon down the long halls now, both descending into silence. Faron had known what it meant when he'd set foot in Vam Aranath. It meant Ulric had been right about Bouren. He was a monster. Now, though, with the fullness of knowledge set upon him, Bouren had finally and truly died. Even the idea of him was dead. The quiet grew stifling until Faron piqued the courage to break it.

"I believe you," he said.

Sadagon stopped short. "Thank you," he said after a pause. "I know how hard that must be."

"I'm not saying I consider myself your son or that I condone what you're doing—because I don't. I want nothing to do with what you're doing here, but... I believe you."

Sadagon searched his eyes. "You are a good man," he said. It caught Faron off guard. "It is one thing for a man to be honest with those around him. It is another for him to be honest with himself."

Before Faron could respond, Sadagon stopped outside a door posted by liveried maidservants. They bowed their heads slightly as he opened the double door himself. Inside was Hadria in another scarlet gown, sifting over piles of papers, bolts of fabric, bowls of food, bouquets, and other pleasant things. She turned when she heard the door open and grinned apologetically.

"You were right," Sadagon said as he approached. "He wanted to see you."

"I'm sorry!" she said. "I've been trying to hurry, and I would have come; but, I learned the handmaiden I had trusted with planning your celebration was laying out a magenta theme. I would have come to you, but the cloths and flowers are here." A servant with loops on her shoulders brought up a bowl filled with blue flower petals. "Yes," Hadria said, shifting her attention to the woman. "Those will do. Now have them crystalized."

Suddenly, Faron felt very foolish for insisting on seeing

her.

"I'm sorry to bother you," Faron said. "I only wanted to…"

"I know, I know. Don't worry yourself," she said, putting down a charcoal pencil and rushing over. She pulled him into a hug. "You can wait here with me if you like. I still have the seating to straighten out, then flower arrangements and dresses and suits for the servants, and then I should be finished."

"It's alright," Faron said. "…Sadagon said he wanted to show me something."

"Really?" she asked, surprised.

"The reliquary," he answered. "I thought it might pique his interest—if he'll go with me."

"Not fair!" she said. "I was going to take him there." "The what?" Faron asked.

"You'll see," Hadria said. "And fine. You can take him to the reliquary, but I get to show him the observatories."

"If you ever finish," Sadagon said with a smile.

"*Magenta*," she cursed with a shake of her head. "If I'm done in a timely way, I'll look for you there." She took his hands in hers and squeezed. "I can't tell you how happy it makes me to see the two of you getting along." She offered him a smile that made everything a little easier, and then she was back to her work.

The Reliquary

Old bookshelves crafted of walnut and blackwood held texts that looked to be older than Vam Aranath itself. Between the rows of books that lined the walls were glass cases of all shapes and sizes, some with articulating doors, others sealed shut. Great circular rooms connected by hallways or massive openings in the walls were filled with ancient prizes, mementos, artifacts, and relics. It was here that Faron stared in wonder at the numberless curiosities that Sadagon had brought before him.

Over the course of the past hour, he had seen suits of armor leafed with gold from the ages before Atha and Olsu, ancient frescos that were faded and chipped, a statue with a thousand hands, skulls of ancient kings set with silver, bones from animals so large they could not be fathomed, and other items from people or places that had been lost.

Now, Sadagon held in his hands what appeared to be a book with pages made of bronze sheets. In those sheets were set a series of wheels with numbers and letters all around.

"It's a cryptograph," he explained, turning the thousand-year-old wheels. "A device used for encoding and breaking encoded messages."

"What for?"

"Wars were far more organized events than the messy affairs that take place today. A general never knew which of his messengers might be intercepted, so it was safer to speak in codes like these."

"It seems too beautiful to be a weapon of war," Faron said.

"Some weapons are more refined than others." He placed the book back on the shelf and led Faron to a smaller case, lifted off the ground by four wooden legs. "For example," he said. "This is a weapon more brutal than almost any other, a force multiplier like the world is not ready for."

Faron stepped over to see what he was talking about. It looked like a stick—a short stick—about a foot long, with a rounded pommel at the bottom and a metal tube on the top.

"What is it?" he asked.

"A flintlock," Sadagon explained. "A firearm. Olsu *hated* them. With this, a farmer could make himself as strong as a knight. A hundred men could destroy a force of any size unless they, too, had a force multiplier. Whenever the technology crept back up, Olsu would send legions to destroy the creator as well as any family they had. Sometimes, entire villages would burn."

"That's terrible," Faron said.

"It is," Sadagon agreed. "But you don't know the horror that weapons like this bring."

"It's so small," Faron argued. "How could it be so danger-ous?" The wood was polished to a deep brown.

"It launches a projectile a hundred times faster than a crossbow, and unlike an arrow or bolt, it does not cut. A man struck by an arrow will look down to see his organs cut and bleeding. A man struck by one of these will see that his organs are no longer there—vaporized if he is lucky, strewn out behind him for yards or more if he isn't."

"That… is horrifying," Faron admitted.

"It is, and if that crossbow you arrived with is any indicator, we are not far off from seeing their return."

"My crossbow?"

"Yes. It is advanced far beyond any I've seen outside of this reliquary. This is a pattern that repeats every few hundred years. Crossbows and bows become more advanced, first with springs like yours, then with wheels. Sometimes, they even had time to become powered by hermetically sealed pistons before Olsu wiped them from the earth. Following those advances comes black powder and nitrates if they are not snuffed quickly enough."

"And will you wipe them out if they come back again?"

"That depends," he said, "on you." Faron's brow furrowed, and he looked away from the flintlock. "If the world is divided like it is now and one faction rediscovers a weapon like this, then yes, I will send men to quell them for the safety of others. If, however, the world is united under your rule, men will be safe to advance under your protection if you allow it."

Faron deflated. He had been trying not to think about that.

"You can't avoid the issue forever, Varek. If you choose to remain with your sister and me, you will need to make a choice."

"Please don't call me that," he whispered.

"You would rather keep the name given to you by the man who killed your mother?"

"Please," Faron said.

"I… will try," Sadagon said. "But the issue remains. Will you accept your place as ruler of this city?"

"No." There was no hesitation. "You kill children, Sadagon. You're a murderer, and you won't make one of me."

"You know I have no love for the price we pay. Let me ask you this, then, Faron." The name seemed distasteful on his lips. "Do you believe that the Veil is growing?"

"Yes," Faron answered begrudgingly.

"Do you believe that it is a coming threat to the world?"

"It already is," he said. "When Synick and I were in Anveil, winter had already come. The Veil stretched past the city more than three weeks ago."

That seemed to catch Sadagon by surprise. "Truly?" he asked. "The mountain city is swallowed already?"

"Yes."

"Then the Veil is growing even faster than we had thought, and Anveil is in danger."

Faron nodded. "They lost most of their crops and harvest and are relying on an already dwindling supply of stores."

"I believe it. They have been subjected to increasingly long winters and ever shorter summers. They will not outlast two years, even if the snow doesn't pile high enough to let the wolves in. The threat is more immediate than even I believed."

"I should have mentioned it earlier," Faron said. "Only..."

"You didn't want to validate my words." It wasn't a question.

"Yes. I'm sorry."

"I appreciate your honesty now. This gives us an unprecedented opportunity."

"What do you mean?"

"Answer this first, Faron. Do you believe that when winter swallows all of Alden, men will kill each other for the last

41

scraps of bread?"

"I do."

"Do you believe that anyone will be left alive in ten years' time if the Veil consumes the world without crops or harvest, without walls and wood to burn? Left to their own devices, do you believe humanity will survive the coming storm?"

There was a long silence. "No."

"Do you believe that under one banner, with vows against violence backed by the threat of eternal salvation, men can be taught to survive in a frozen world as we do here?"

Another pause. "Yes."

"Then you agree, horrific as it may be, that the sacrifices we make are for the betterment of all mankind?"

"There has to be another way," Faron burst out. "There *has* to be. Why must we rule as gods? Can we not simply teach them to provide food the way you do? Can we not teach them how to be protected from the wolves? They would be safe, then, and fed."

"Faron," Sadagon said. "You *are* the other way. This is a thought that has occupied my mind for decades. It is not possible."

"Why?" Faron demanded. "We can save them from hunger, and when the snow piles higher than the walls, we can provide them with snow cloaks."

"Do you know what men will do with these gifts if we provide them with both food and protection from the wolves? Warfare. Long-term sieges that need not break apart during the winter. Without oversight, they will only use these gifts to kill each other. Freeing men from the shackles of winter is almost as deadly an idea as the return of cannons."

"What about food, at least?" Faron tried. "Could we not teach them how to sustain themselves?" It occurred to Faron that he still didn't know what they grew here in this eternal winter.

"We could," Sadagon said. "But there are still the snow-beasts. Sooner or later, they will rise above any snow wall, and a well-fed population is no different to them than a hungry one. No, Faron. The only hope is to give the world these secrets together, and the only way to do that safely is to unite them.

"Unify all men under one banner, force them to sow fields of mana and not plunder, protect them from each other, and you can save them. That is the problem we face: how to bring warring factions and jealous cities together, how to assure that they will not turn on one another. I do not doubt that you are more clever than I, so if you can suggest a way to force men to give up the sword for the plow, I will listen. If you can find a way to unite them, I will follow your example."

"Why do we have to be gods, though?" Faron asked. "Could we not unify under the banner of a king or queen?"

"Men have kings already, and kings have armies."

"So do we. If we declared ourselves kings, we could unite men under one banner without the need for the Life Spile. We wouldn't need to live forever." His cadence grew quicker. "There would be no need for..." He hesitated. "The children."

Sadagon nodded. "I know the argument well. It was my original. For the life of every child you save, a hundred men will die."

Faron was crestfallen.

"A king is a direct conflict to the authority that already exists, and if you intend to cast down the powers that be, you will have to cut through every last man at his command first. Governors and rulers will not bow to a usurper."

"How is godhood any different?" Faron asked, growing exasperated.

"It is a higher authority," Sadagon explained. "An authority which supersedes that of rule, and one men believe in. Men can only be pushed so far by loyalty to a king, but there is almost no limit to what they will do to save their eternal souls." He grimaced for a moment, then returned to the conversation. "I know it for a fact. The threat of eternity is perhaps the most powerful force of control imaginable. Even kings are ready to bend the knee for a god." His voice was smooth and sincere. "I know it is not easy, but it is the safest and most merciful way."

"There has to be another way," Faron said, though his voice carried resignation.

"If you find it, I will follow you gladly."

Faron did not respond.

"I don't say that lightly. I don't intend this as a hollow offer or to mock you. If you can find another path, I will be there by your side to implement it." He took Faron by the shoulders. "Varek. I will give up my immortality for you if you can find another way."

Surprised, Faron searched his father's eyes. There was no deception there or comfortable amusement. He meant it. That, more than anything, shook his deeply-rooted understanding of who this man was.

"I..." He tried to pull his thoughts into words. "I don't know."

"Five years ago, I made you watch as I murdered the man you believed to be your father," Sadagon said. Faron looked

44

up in surprise. "I made you watch while I kidnapped your twin and left you to die in a blaze. I set about the series of events that led to that brand on your chest, and it is I who must bear the blame for whatever horrors you were made to endure. Your pain bears my hand. Your sins are mine. The very scars on your body are my fault."

He paused for a long time. "I know what I must seem to you—a monster from a living nightmare, exsanguinating children to fuel a perverse immortality, a bloodthirsty killer, a figment of darkness and evil." His voice wavered. "Even being aware of this, I have no choice but to ask you: Can you trust me? Can you trust that this plan I have laid out for over a hundred years is not for my personal gain or ego? Can you believe that I have considered every other conceivable avenue and found them lacking? Can you accept that, despite the terrible cost, this is the best way to save as many lives as possible?"

Letting his gaze slip back to the artifacts in the glass cases, Faron swallowed hard before answering. "I trust," he said, "that you believe it." It was a far larger concession than he had been prepared to make.

Sadagon seemed to breathe a sigh of relief. "That is enough and far more than I have earned."

"There has to be another way," Faron said, finally meeting Sadagon's gaze. "I… I don't believe that you're the monster I thought you were, but… there is nothing that can justify killing children—not all the lives in the world."

"I mean it when I say I will lay down my life if you can find a way to let the exsanguinations end. The Archons of Vam Aranath will be no more. At any point, even in a hundred years, if you find a way to keep the world safe without gods,

I will keep to my word."

Faron nodded, oddly comforted. "I'll find it," he promised.

"I don't know you nearly as well as I would like, but I do not doubt it. Until then, will you accept rule of Vam Aranath? Yours and Vavelt's eighteenth nameday approaches. I plan to abdicate as steward and coronate Vavelt to her throne. With your permission, I would coronate you as well."

Faron was silent, flexing the muscles in his hands and setting his jaw.

"There will be no promises made, no expectations placed upon you. It will be symbolic, more than anything, the bulk of responsibility placed upon your sister, who is prepared for this."

"It will symbolize my approval of what you're doing," Faron said.

"It will give you the power to stop it," Sadagon argued. "If you find a better alternative, this will place you in a position to wield authority. If you *cannot* find an alternative, this will allow us to move forward with unifying the world under the names of Atha and Olsu. Will you agree?"

Faron breathed hard, confusion and desperation swirling together in his mind. What choice did he have? He couldn't deny the necessity of Sadagon's plan, but he couldn't condone the murder of children or use of slaves. It torqued his consciousness.

"I will think about it," he said.

"Very well. I am grateful for your willingness to consider."

"You speak of unifying the world," Faron began. "But you haven't mentioned how you intend to do that. How do we know that men will come together, even if I agree to be a god?"

"The third gift to the world," Sadagon said, back straight. "I spoke of an opportunity earlier, do you recall?"

"Yes. Anveil and the early winter."

"Yes. The past hundred years have not been spent idly, Faron. While I took my time finding a wife, I also amassed the means to create and support an army."

Faron stiffened. He had forgotten about that. What had the priestess, Valatha, called it? Olsu's Fist?

"We do not bring men together through the offer of religion alone. The fear that comes from starvation and dire wolves is far too powerful for that. We re-establish the old religion, then force all men to it."

Faron felt a sickness in his gut. He had suspected that answer, but it hurt to hear all the same. "And that's your third gift? Armies sent to destroy and bend all men to my will?"

"Initially, perhaps. Afterward, they will be sentinels against the snowbeasts, given by their gods to protect them, but that is not the opportunity I spoke of. An army is a force of destruction, certainly, but Anveil is already facing that threat through starvation. If we come to their gates bearing gifts of food and grain and not spears or explosives, we might just be able to install you as benevolent gods without needing to kill a soul."

Faron was taken aback. "You intend to march an army to Anveil?"

"They are the first logical target. We will be the first siege in history who comes to bring food, not to seize it."

"And if they refuse?" Faron asked.

"Then we will destroy their walls and fill their streets with wolves, and when they have had their fill, we will follow with swords and spears." He breathed hard. "It will not come to that."

"It will!" Faron cried. "Anveil believes in the strength of their walls. They will not surrender to another force, even now." He shook his head, face filled with disgust. "I won't let you do that. Anveil is a kind place with good people. If you intend to assail them, I will reject rulership of Vam Aranath and any association with you. They are good people!" he yelled. "I won't allow it!"

"It's too late for that," Sadagon said. "We march in three days' time. Believe me when I say I have no desire to harm a soul in that city, but the numbers are simple. If I have to kill ten thousand men to save a million, I will."

"Three days?" Faron asked, aghast. "You learned I was alive, and the first thing you do is mobilize your army?" Disgust played across his features.

"Faron," Sadagon said. "The mobilization has been underway for months."

"What?" Faron asked. "What do you mean?"

"I mean that the army has been preparing to march for far longer than the short span of time you have been with us. That, more than anything, is what makes your arrival so spectacular. Not only did you rise from the dead, but you did it just before Vavelt comes of age and was to ascend alone."

That made Faron's head reel. Sadagon had been planning on giving Hadria the thrones of the world alone? To rule as half the godhead?

"How would that work?" Faron asked, stumbling over his words. "How would you restore the gods without Olsu?"

"It would have been bloody," Sadagon confessed. "With only one half the godhead, many would revolt and decry us as heretics. The role of the sword and fist would have been far greater, but even that is preferable to the annihilation we faced otherwise. It is an imperfect solution but still better than the alternative."

His gaze intensified. "And that is why I am so amazed by the timing of your arrival, my son. Now, the men who would have died for crying heresy will bow to you and live. With the godhead completed, the world will be far more eager to fall into line, and the people who would have died will live—because of you."

Despite the glory of Sadagon's words, Faron couldn't help but feel a deepening pit in his stomach. With all the talk of how the world depended on him accepting Olsu's throne, he hadn't considered that Sadagon had been conducting a contingency plan in his absence. He almost felt betrayed at the thought that Hadria would continue on without him.

"And what if I don't want to be a god?" he asked. "What if I refuse and you can't change my mind?"

"I won't have to," Sadagon answered. "Because you won't leave your sister while you believe her mind can be changed, and she won't let you go while she thinks the same. The army marches within the week, Faron. Will you let her go without you?"

"You're using her against me," Faron seethed.

"No," Sadagon corrected. "I am stating fact for you. I will not force Vavelt to accompany the army for the siege of Anveil or any siege, but she will go all the same because she knows it will save the most lives. It is my belief that you will go with her rather than leave her alone."

"How will Hadria save lives among an army of murderers?" Faron asked with heavy skepticism.

"She might not—without you." His eyes were confident and full of purpose. "If an army were to arrive in the name of the gods, they would be fought off from the first. If, however, those gods came themselves in the flesh with an army behind them... no one could deny it. And if those gods came bearing gifts of food and protection, Anveil might surrender without unsheathing a blade."

"That'll never work," Faron argued. "Anveil already knows me. When the Veil fell, they pulled me from it, surrounded by snow wolves. There was a celebration where I was seen by everyone. They know me already, and they know I am no god."

Sadagon nodded. "I had forgotten about that winter tradition of theirs. Firstblood, it was called, wasn't it?" Faron didn't answer. "I don't believe that will lower you in their eyes, Faron. If anything, it may help them to revere you even more. Either way, the army marches in three days. The odds of a peaceful surrender are far higher with the Twinborn Gods at its head, so Vavelt will go. It is my hope that you will go, too. With the offer of food, protection, and induction into the old religion, the sight of you might be just the thing to spur them to our side."

Faron gave him a baleful glare. "You are a murderer. There are people in Anveil who I call friends. If you hurt them in any way, I will never forgive you."

"And I would never forgive myself," Sadagon said, surprising him again. "That is the pain we must bear. I cannot allow the Veil to destroy mankind, and I cannot suffer to harm the innocent. Something has to give."

"I will find another way," Faron spat, turning on his heel and leaving Sadagon alone in the reliquary.

Shattered Mask and Castle Walls

J ust when Synick had given up hope of Faron coming back with anything to eat, the door finally opened back up.

"Took your time, didn't you?" He drifted lazily through the still-hot water, well pruned and with no intention of getting out.

"If I'd realized you were waiting for me, I'd have come straight away." That wasn't Faron's voice. Synick snapped his eyes open to see Faron's sister standing above him, hands on her hips and a smirk across her lips.

He buckled forward, surprise getting the better of him. "Um, hello."

"Hello to you, too." Her smirk became a smile, and she sat down on a long half-sofa. "I have something for you."

"Uh, is it something you have to give me right now?"

"Oh, you don't mind, do you?" Her gaze wandered, then locked with his. Synick knew his eyes were blue, but they were nothing like the electrifying stare that Hadria possessed. That was the stare of a person who knew they were in charge. Synick understood why. She was a goddess and queen. Could he even say no to her? He swallowed, then put on his smile.

"Not at all."

She relaxed into the armrest of the sofa. "Good. I haven't forgotten what you've done for me, Synick. I'm in your debt for bringing my brother to me, and I intend to make good on that debt." Only then did Synick notice a long tube of rolled-up paper in her hand. She waved it at him. "Now, don't splash. This is the original copy."

Curious, he moved to the nearest edge and put his arms up on the tiles. Faron's sister bent down and unrolled the parchment, keeping the edges in place with four flat-edged chunks of unpolished blue sapphire. Synick smiled. This place was delightfully excessive.

Hadria looked at him expectantly, and he remembered that he was supposed to be examining the paper and not the stones. It took a moment for the shapes and scratched handwriting to take meaning.

"Is this... a map?"

"It's a deed," she clarified. "To an Aranath estate."

"A deed?" he asked. "What's it for?"

She smiled. "Well, it's for you."

Synick looked up at her in disbelief. "What?"

"It's land," she said. "And I'm giving it to you. There will be servants, of course, to manage the day-to-day affairs, and a chapel for them to worship at—you won't be expected to use it, obviously—a few dozen homes for the tithing residents, a tavern, an expansive home for yourself, and a regular income."

Synick's mouth fell wide open. "An income?" he asked. "What for?" What a foreign and bizarre idea.

"Of course. As the lord of the land, you'd receive a stipend from the tithes generated by the circulating currency.

There's also a sapphire mine tied to the deed, but it isn't technically on the same land."

"Sapphires?"

She laughed. "Well, yes. They technically belong to the godhead, but the estate will be rewarded a fee for mining and finding them, and that estate now belongs to you." When Synick did nothing but stare at the dimensions of the deed before him, she added, "If you want it, that is."

"I do!" he responded. "Gods, I do! More than anything!"

Hadria giggled. "Then, for the noble act of returning my brother to me, it is my great pleasure to deed this estate to you, Synick. This grants you the title of Vam, a Lord of Aranath." She smiled at him with a beaming toothful expression. He returned it, then further tried to grasp the size of the land given to him. It was massive. There were towers marked on the parchment, along with several smaller buildings that sprawled across what must have been several acres, mostly developed and surrounded by more of the great city.

"I... I don't know what to say," he confessed. "It's... I don't deserve this."

"I'll decide what you do and don't deserve, Synick. You brought my brother to me, and that isn't a thing easily repaid."

He swallowed hard, trying to keep the emotion from his voice. "This is more property than I ever thought I'd be allowed to set foot on."

"Well, now it's yours." She grinned. "When Varek returns, we can all go and see it if you like."

"Yes!" he said. "I'd love that. Hell's Iron Halls, I can't believe it. You'd really just give it to me?"

Her laugh was giddy and enthusiastic.

"Thank you, Hadria."

Her smile fractured slightly. "I understand Varek must have called me that for years, but I'd prefer you use my real name."

"Sorry, Vavelt," he corrected. He could remember that. "It's actually a really beautiful name."

She gave him a half-smile. "Thank you."

"Honestly, thank *you*. I've never been so excited in my life." He beamed at her. "Now, not that I'm not grateful, but is there a reason I couldn't put clothes on before you came in here?"

"Yes, actually," she answered. "It's much easier to keep you off balance like this."

He frowned. "And why would you want to do that?"

Vavelt's eyes took on that penetrating quality again, prying to see more than he offered, and Synick started to squirm.

"Because you've been lying to my brother."

Synick's defenses hardened, his earlier joy forgotten in the uncomfortable pressure of those questioning eyes. They seemed to burrow into him.

"Stop looking at me like that."

"Why?" she asked, not letting up at all. "Are you afraid of what I'll see?"

"It makes me feel naked."

"You *are* naked, Synick."

"This is worse."

"Alright, then tell me what you've been hiding."

"I'm not hiding anything," he insisted. "I haven't been lying."

"Not with your words, no."

Synick knew what she meant, but he wasn't about to admit that. "How, then?" He withered under that gaze, deep and discerning.

"I was wrong," she said. "That smile isn't a shield; it's a castle wall, and you've pulled up the drawbridge and are hiding behind the tallest ramparts you can find."

He sucked in a breath and flashed his best smile. Even his eyes were bright and brilliant. He knew because he'd practiced it countless times in the mirror.

"No idea what you're talking about."

"Mhhhm," she nodded, smiling herself now and pinning his eyes with her own. It was to be a game, then—her trying to break past his defenses and him trying to keep her out. It was a game Synick was very good at.

Unfortunately for him, so was she. A silence stretched between them, not awkward but not comfortable either—ten seconds, twenty, an absurdly long gap for a conversation—but the exchange was no longer in words. His most charming smile deflecting her will to see through it became the new medium. A full minute passed, and Synick's confidence grew. He could keep her out.

"Does my brother know that you love him?"

Synick shattered. "What?" he gasped.

"I win," she said with a small smile.

"What?"

"My brother," she said as if it were the most common question in the world. "Does he know that you love him?

"You don't know half of what you think you do," he snapped.

"Don't I?"

"No. It… It isn't like that at all."

55

"Oh, I see, *you* didn't know either."

"No!" Synick shot back.

"Then what am I missing, Synick?"

"Faron..." Synick's shoulders slumped. "Faron isn't interested in people," he said. "Not like that."

"But you are."

"Of course."

"And yet, he has no idea."

"None," he said, dropping into his arms. "Faron is my brother, and that's all he has the ability to ever be. He doesn't need... human connection. He can barely stand being touched."

"That must be very lonely," Vavelt observed.

"Good job," he said, eyes growing cold. "You figured it out. I'm more alone than I've ever been, and I'll never find a way out of it. I need something I'll never get—and have no right to ask for—from someone who will never know I need it. You broke me. I hope you're happy now."

"I'm not, actually." Long curls bobbed around her neck as she shook her head.

"Great," he snapped. "May I go now, *my lady,* or is there something else you want to take from me?"

"There is." Her voice carried an intensity as she lowered herself to her knees next to the unrolled parchment.

"What, then?"

There was an extended silence.

"Everything."

Synick looked up to catch the meaningful expression in her eyes, and she caught his chin in her hands. He froze, nearly paralyzed between surprise and longing.

Vavelt leaned in and kissed him.

The battling emotions inside his chest fell quiet as one side immediately overpowered the other, and Synick kissed back, unexpected, eager, and wanting. The rush of it overwhelmed all other senses as his sleeping mind reveled in the animal joy of being wanted.

Vavelt pulled back, and the world snapped into focus. She was grinning, and so was he. The laugh that fell from her lips was the most pure thing Synick had ever heard, and it made his heart ring to know that he was the cause of it. She smiled *because of him.* She *wanted* him.

She leaned in and kissed him again, reaching out with a pale hand to smooth the gooseflesh that ran the length of his arms and neck, and Synick was lost in it.

Somewhere in the back of his mind, a quiet regret spoke of the betrayal he was committing, but in the tide of her lips, golden hair, and soft fingertips, it was swept away.

With Words Alone

Less than an hour later, Faron had navigated the temple halls back to his opulent rooms, eyes a storm and jaw set. Hadria had not been in the offices high above where he'd seen her last, and Synick was no longer in Olsu's bathing chamber. When he burst into his rooms, he found them there together, lounging idly and laughing. Synick stood, orating something with arms high, a true grin on his face, and Hadria lay on her side on one of the white and gold half-sofas, wearing an intrigued smile.

"That's when he said," Synick declared. "'Sure, it's hot enough, but you still haven't told me where you've hid my trousers!'" They both burst into laughter before turning to see Faron glowering in the doorway.

"Brother!" Hadria said. "You're back!" Her enthusiasm diminished when she registered the anger on his face.

"Did you know?" he asked, closing the door behind him.

"Know about what?"

"Did you know about the army—about Anveil?"

She shook her head like a troubled parent. "Well, of course I knew. This is my city, Faron—*our* city."

"You knew that Sadagon intends to lay siege to Anveil, and you didn't tell me?"

Synick went quiet.

"Of course not. It was *you* who asked *me* not to make you be anything but my brother. I didn't want you to worry before you had a chance to accept your role here."

"You kept it from me," he accused, trying to keep the edge from his voice. "You knew I wouldn't approve, so you kept it from me."

"Kept it from you? Faron, you've only been awake one day, and I've only been with you for part of it. How was I meant to inform you of something you asked me not to when I've only spent a few hours with you at all?"

"He's going to kill people, Hadria. He means to lay siege to Anveil and force everyone inside to submit to our rule."

"Well, of course," she said, concern spelled across her face. "Faron, how did you think we were meant to unite the world? With words alone? Surely you had seen the soldiers patrolling the streets before you were brought here."

"I had other things on my mind," he said. "Finding you, for example."

"Alright, now hold on," Synick cut in, eyeing Hadria. "You're attacking Anveil?"

"Only if we have to," she said, exasperated. "Faron and I will lead the soldiers with gifts of grain, oil, and livestock. We will declare ourselves to them and offer gifts on condition of accepting our rule. Nothing will have to change in the city. The three governors will retain their station, only they will answer to us and take vows against violence. From there, we can leverage our foothold in Alden to bring one city at a time into our fold through diplomacy or other means if necessary."

"Really?" Synick said. "You think you can win them to

your side with bread? Just make them surrender?"

"The people of Anveil remember well the old religion," Hadria scolded. "When Atha and Olsu return from death to save them from the brink of starvation and the coming storm, they will dance in the streets, praising our return. It will be a *celebration*, brother, not a surrender."

"You're wrong," Faron said. "I know those people. They're fighters. They will not surrender to an army outside their gates, gods or no gods."

"Well, you better hope *you're* wrong," Hadria said. "Or we'll have no choice but to take the city by force."

Pale-faced, Synick interrupted, "We've been... together, all day, and you didn't mention this?"

"I'm sorry," Hadria replied. "I didn't realize that I owed explanations to you."

"There are—I can't—" Synick cut himself off. "You're really doing it? You're really going to attack Anveil?"

"We leave in three days," she confirmed. "The soldiers will be hauling thousands of pounds of grain, oil, spices, and other stores, so the journey will not be fast. I suspect twenty days from departure."

"Dead gods," Synick cursed. "Blackened, bloody corpse of Olsu."

"That is one curse I will *not* tolerate," Hadria said, but she was ignored.

"I have to go," Synick said, looking distant-eyed. "I have to warn them."

"Warn them? Synick, we have messengers for that—heralds—to begin negotiations."

"Then I'm going with them," he insisted.

"Why? You'll miss the celebration," Hadria said. "It's our

nameday and coronation of sorts. You pretend otherwise, but you're important to my brother. You should be here for him… and for me. Besides, you haven't yet been to your estate."

"I have family in Anveil," Synick said, eyeing the door. "I can't just abandon them."

"Synick," Hadria said. "You're an orphan."

"Chosen family," he replied. "Jesika and Artur and Orothorn—like you. People who showed me kindness when they didn't need to."

"I think he loves Jesika," Faron stated. Hadria coughed, and Synick blushed. "He's right, though. They were kind to us and saved me. We owe them a debt."

"You aren't thinking clearly," Hadria accused. "When the army arrives, we will send men in to open a dialogue with the governors. During that time—or before—if you're that anxious, we can send men ahead to collect your loved ones and bring them out of the city. There is absolutely no need for you to traipse off into the Veil all alone."

Synick stood there, appearing flustered and restless.

"Breathe, Synick," she insisted.

"If any harm were to come to them," he began.

"I know," she interrupted. "You couldn't bear it. There is ample opportunity to keep them from harm's way. You have to realize," she said, "that with both Varek and myself at the army's head, the chances of Anveil submitting to the old religion is far higher than a siege, especially when one of the three governors is said to be a Remembrant priest."

That quieted them for a moment, then Hadria went on, "He will be begging to swear oaths to us. With him, with us, and with the threat of our catapults and cannons, there will be no war. Even still, we will covertly send men in to extract them if it helps you feel better. I, too, couldn't bear it if I brought pain to you or your loved ones." The look she gave Synick was piercing.

"You're assuming," Faron hedged, "that I'll go with you, that I'm going to let Sadagon attack Anveil."

"No," Synick objected. "She's right. Atha's tits, she's right." He cringed as he caught himself, then turned to see her eyeing him dubiously again. He flashed a huge smile. "Sorry, my lady—*your* tits." Hadria rolled her eyes.

"Synick," Faron warned, bringing him back to task.

"If you can make Anveil surrender by pretending to be a god, then that's what you have to do. Artur spoke of the state of Anveil's military strength, and it's not good. He all but said that if Murcosta attacked again, he wouldn't be able to repel them."

"What are you saying?" Faron asked. "That I should just bend to Sadagon's will and accept godhood tomorrow? Let him use me as justification for attacking a city?"

"*Yes*," Synick said. "That's exactly what I'm saying. If he's going with or without you, then you have to go. Anveil won't stand a chance if it comes to war."

"Sadagon is mounting an invasion, and you're asking me to be a part of it?"

"Damnit, Faron, will you shut up for one snowing second?" Synick snapped. "This isn't only about you." He turned his attention to Hadria, who had been laughing with him only minutes before. "Is there any way to stop the army from marching? If Faron takes the crown, will he have the authority to stop it?"

She shook her head. "It's our army in name, but it answers

62

to Father, and Varan after him. There's quite literally nothing to be done to stop it."

Synick spun back around. "That army is going to march with or without you, Faron. This is about more than whether or not your family is morally correct; this is about Anveil."

Faron's eyes cast scorn at Synick. "I can't believe what I'm hearing," he said. "You, of all people, are asking me to condone my father's actions? I won't do it. I won't lead a snowing army to a defenseless city."

"You should listen to your friend, brother," Hadria said. "He's right."

Faron ground his teeth; but, the objections he'd been trying to smother were rekindled in a wave of anger, and they broke free from him.

"Don't talk to me about what's right," he growled, "when you refuse to denounce our father for the blood he spills." As soon as he said it, he wished he could take it back, but it was too late. The peace he'd maintained with her was tenuous, but now it was shattered.

It was obvious from the way her spine stiffened that Hadria was offended; but, her voice was tempered, and she tried not to show it.

"The world isn't a place of black and white, Faron. Your sense of right and wrong is immature. We will *save* mankind; can you not see that?"

"He's killing people, Hadria—children—and now you march an army to Anveil, where we will outnumber their fighting men ten to one."

"That is the cost, Faron. Even if every single one of those men were to fall resisting us, how many more will it save? That is a *fraction* of a *percentage* of how many lives we can save. That is a sacrifice easily made."

"It's not your right to make it!" Faron snapped. "You don't get to decide who lives and who dies."

"I am the *only* one who can make those decisions! Myself and you—we are to be *gods*, Faron."

"Not me," he said solemnly. "I want no part in this."

"A beautiful sentiment, but we're past that, Faron," Synick said. "An army is going to Anveil whether you have the stomach for it or not. The only thing to be done now is to make sure this doesn't turn into a bloodbath."

"It's too late for that!" Faron yelled back at Synick, ire rising. "A bloodbath is exactly what this is, and now, somehow, I find myself in a position where both you and my father want me to hold the spear at the head of an invading army!"

"This isn't about you, Faron!" Synick shouted back. "If Anveil doesn't surrender to your father, people are going to die!"

"What do you think he's going to do if Anveil does surrender?" Faron replied. "He's a monster who exists on the blood of children, Synick. He's going to gather whatever suitable slaves he can find and have them harvested, and it'll be *my fault*."

"You can't keep doing this, Faron!" Synick yelled. "With Dageran, you turned up your nose at the suffering we caused and used your disapproval to absolve yourself of guilt. When that farm burned, you refused to accept that you had been a part of it, but it *still burned*, Faron! You tried so hard to be separate from the guild with your moral code, but people *still died*—more of them, arguably, than if you had just dirtied your hands by choosing your own contracts and getting them over with."

Hadria lifted a long, thin brow at this revelation but said nothing.

"What are you getting at?" Faron snapped, hackles rising.

"You *hide* behind your morality!" Synick burst. "You distance yourself from the actions and consequences of evil men because you wish they didn't happen—because in a perfect world, it *shouldn't* happen. You become so obsessed with being in the right that you fail to see that *it doesn't matter,* Faron. Condemning evil men doesn't stop them. Refusing to associate with them won't stop them. You cling to your idealistic morals and comfort yourself when others suffer because at least you weren't willingly involved, but that *doesn't help*!

"For once in your life, stop worrying about if you're in the right or wrong and look at what's actually happening. You can stay on your high horse and condemn your father's army, comfortable in the fact that you won't be there when the killing begins, or you can *do something* to mitigate the damage it will cause, even if it means shaking hands with a blood-soaked tyrant."

Faron fumed, smoldering eyes locked on Synick's as he breathed deep, angry breaths.

"I can't say I agree with the method of Synick's argument, but he's right, Faron," Hadria said, in a tone intended to calm him down. "Your scope is too small. Of course, protecting the weak is the right thing to do—because life is *precious.* Is that not still true on a larger scale? I intend to stop wars—to stop rapists and bandits, cutthroats and looters. I mean to teach the men and women to feed themselves in a frozen world. We will save *everyone,* Faron. Compared to the rest of the world, what do a few lives matter in the grand scheme of things?"

"They're all that matter!" he snapped, shifting his gaze to hers. He clenched his fists to keep them from trembling. Arguing from two sides was wearing his patience to nothing.

"And what about those who will starve if we can't protect them from the Veil or from each other? What about the men and women who will die fighting over resources when the Veil turns their fields to ice? Do they not also matter?"

"Of course they do."

"Who are you to say who matters most, Faron? Who are you to choose who to let starve and who to save?"

He exhaled a puff from his nose. "What are you doing, if not that, Hadria?"

"I'm doing the only thing that's fair. I can't be the scale that weighs souls, so the only thing I can take into account is the sheer weight of numbers. If one life is equal to another, then the *only* good to be done is to save as many as is possible, regardless of the actions required."

"What good can you possibly achieve after sullying your hands, Hadria? If you have to kill one innocent to save others, then the act is pyrrhic. Any such cost is too high, regardless of the reward."

"I feel the same way," she said with a small nod. "But our feelings cannot argue with arithmetic, Varek." She ran her long fingers through her hair. "If I can save most, then *any* cost is worth it."

"You don't believe that!" he yelled, stricken. "How can you justify the slaughter of those who have already been trodden down to nothing? Children without mothers and fathers, Hadria—that is who you're leading like cattle to slaughter."

66

"You think I don't know that?" she returned, voice edged with heat. "I hate the awful cost of salvation as much as you do, but I pay it because I understand what will happen if I don't! The world depends on the unity we can give it, Faron. Do you understand what that means? How can I weigh the needs of the poor few, who salvation requires, against the weight of the *world?*"

"How can you not?" Faron shouted. "How can it be possible to say that you're helping one group while preying on another? How can you claim to protect people when you're literally *killing children?!*"

Hadria tried to answer, but he cut her off. Synick eyed him with a grave look.

"I can't believe that you believe this, Hadria, that you can be a part of this—that you think you can save people when your hands are drenched in blood!"

"Stop shouting at me!" she demanded.

"Faron..." Synick warned, and Faron realized that he *was* shouting—and pacing, too. He stopped both.

"Five years," he said through gritted teeth, forcing his voice down. "For five years, I was a soulless and a slave." He reached up and pulled the soft velvet shirt past his red, fire-scarred collarbone. "Look," he demanded, revealing Dageran's brand, deeply burned into flesh that was already melted. He felt it as keenly as the day it had been seared into him.

"You wondered where I got this? For five years, I have lived at the mercy of criminals who named me their property. I stole food from street urchins struggling to survive because they dared use my master's name in their desperation. I robbed mourning widows, burnt homes and livelihoods, all at the end of a knife."

The sharpness fell from her face. "Gods, Faron. Please, let's not fight anymore." She softened her eyes, trying to placate him, but the peace was already broken. He couldn't pretend anymore.

"Do you remember Galvin?" he asked, and she nodded. "He was competing with the Blackwood markets, so I was made to burn his farm and livestock to ash."

"Faron," Synick warned.

"He wasn't the first," he continued, guilt and passion beginning to sting the edges of his eyes. "He wasn't even the *tenth*." His hands balled into fists. "I murdered a woman. I didn't want to, but it was her life or mine, so I did it."

"Stop," she whispered. "You needn't continue."

"I was one of the lucky ones," he went on, and Synick shuffled uncomfortably. "Some were caught in the crimes they were forced to. You can guess what happened to them. Others refused outright, and their heads were chopped off where everyone could see." His gaze snapped from the floor to her eyes. "Have you ever seen a severed head, Hadria?"

"That's enough, Faron," Synick cut in, but the point had yet to be made.

"I watched a man burn to death in his own tannery," Faron pushed on. Hadria's expression grew grim. "He ran in to put out the flames that *I* started, that I *was forced* to start, and the roof fell in on him. I could have heard his screams from ten houses over."

"Faron," Synick said again louder, but he was ignored again.

"I know what it means to make people powerless. I know what it does to them. I care about them, Hadria, because I know what it means to belong to another person, to *be*

68

another man's *property*. I know, better than most, what it feels like to be both the sacrifice and the executioner. I care about the few lives because that's where I come from, Hadria. That's who I am—a slave."

His tirade finished, Faron fell into a chair and cradled his head. His migraine was returning in nauseating waves. Had he said too much? Would she run from him now, knowing the kind of monster that he was?

For all the worry he felt at the words he'd said, there was still a weight of anger driving him to say more. Something was still wrong, but he tried to tamp it down.

"That's not who you are anymore," Hadria said, sweeping by his chair. "Not any longer. You escaped them. Nobody can blame you for what you were made to do against your will. You can only be defined by the choices that *you* make."

Head snapping up, Faron realized what was still bothering him so much. The weight of the souls he carried bore down on his shoulders. They were so *heavy* now, and he was so *tired.*

"Those are no better!" he snarled, and Hadria pulled back slightly at his ferocity. "My choices nearly got Synick killed. They *did* get Ulric killed."

Hadria gasped, and Synick gave a small nod.

Hand held to her lips, she whispered, "How?"

"He helped me escape, and it earned him a knife in the back. The worst part is I didn't even consider he was sacrificing himself for me—for you, really." His eyes flicked back and forth between hers. "That's why he did it, you should know, to find and save you."

"It wasn't for nothing, then," she said, cupping his cheek with her soft hands. "You're here now."

69

Faron refused her comfort, shaking his head as he stood abruptly from the chair. The seed of anger was a storm now, building inside his chest as the anguish of his betrayal tried to rend him in two. The confession slipped from him before he could stop it.

"It *was* for nothing, Hadria, and that's what's wrong with me. In the end, *all of it* was for nothing. I tortured and killed a man to find you. He led me to a slaver who I poisoned and threw from a window. They hanged his guard for it. I impaled another man and threw him and one other thirty feet to their deaths." He bit off the words in a frenzy, voice rising with his tempo as he remembered their faces, remembered the sounds of their deaths: crossbow strings and glass, screams and crunching bones. Dead gods, the weight was *crushing* him.

"I killed men. I tarnished my *soul*, Hadria. Do you know what that means—what it really means to end lives and carry that weight with you?" His fingers formed a half cage near his heart, and his face twisted with agony as the pain he'd been trying so hard to hide consumed him. Hadria tried to quiet him with her hands, but it was too late for that. His voice rose as he paced back and forth.

"I *murdered*. I waded through an ocean of fire, of ice, of legions of teeth and living nightmare, all while bearing your screams." He pinned her with his eyes, pulling on a fistful of his dark hair. "Your screams, Hadria—gods, the screams!"

"Stop shouting!" Hadria yelled.

"Do you understand, Hadria?" Faron asked, completely unaware of everything but his own betrayal. "I escaped my own hell and sacrificed my soul for you—to *find* you!" His eyes stung as the last vestiges of control slipped away, and his voice rose high into the stone rafters. "And now, I have found you sacrificing your *own* soul to perpetuate the very hell I escaped with the man who STOLE. EVERYTHING. FROM. ME."

With the murder and betrayal in his heart laid bare, Faron expected his sister to flee from him, to hide and call him a monster, but she met heat with heat.

"So that's it!" she yelled back, not giving an inch of ground. "That's why you're so upset with me? Because I'm not what you expected to find? Because I'm not good enough for you?" She lifted her arms high to the sides. "Am I not worth the price you paid? Were you hoping for a better return on your investment?"

She went on when he didn't answer. "You hypocrite," she said. "You think that because of what you gave up, you have the right to expect me to be what you wanted? To let you *save* me?"

"No," he said, the naked truth already filling him with shame, but she didn't let him continue.

"Is this even about the children?" she asked. "How can I believe that you'll actually listen to my side of this argument when you *just* admitted that this is all really about you and what you gave up?"

"Hadria—" Faron stuttered, but she cut him off again.

"I didn't ask you to kill anyone, Faron! I didn't ask for the sacrifices you made! How dare you hold that against me when I had nothing to do with it?"

"Hadria—" he said again, but she pushed past him.

"I don't need to be saved!" Hadria shouted. "I don't need a knight in shining armor to rescue me from my high tower. I don't need to be chastised and lectured because I can control

71

my emotions and do what's necessary. Is that why you're here, Faron, to save me from my sins? Or are you only here to tell me what you sacrificed for me and how I don't measure up to the cost?"

Faron shook his head. "Hadria, I—"

"That isn't my name!" she shouted.

"I miss you!" Faron shouted back, desperate, flailing, and confused. The anger drained from them both. "I miss you so much." Faron fell back into the chair but slipped, crashing onto the floor. He trembled as the exhaustion and shame took him. "I miss the way things were. I want to *be* with you, but I don't know how. I want to forgive you for being a part of this. I want to understand it, but I can't! I don't know what to do when right and wrong don't mean anything anymore. I don't know what to do when the stakes are so high. I don't know how to do this, Hadria—how to love you without hating you, how to put this weight down."

The tears that stung his eyes slipped down his cheeks now, and he did nothing to hide them. The shame of his weakness was nothing compared to the truth of the resentment he'd been bearing, the blame for the lives he'd taken. Alone on the floor, Faron wept as his spirit fractured.

"Oh, my brother," Hadria whispered, kneeling on her dress to brush fingers through his hair. She wiped away his shame with soft hands and pulled him into a kneeling embrace. "I don't mean it. I don't mean it at all." She held him even tighter. "These aren't the words I want for you, and they aren't at all what you deserve."

Synick shuffled back and forth on his feet, his face an image of indecision.

Nearly choking Faron with her comforting arms, Hadria

went on, "I was wrong to diminish your pain. I'm sorry." When he didn't answer, she continued, "I can't imagine what terrors you've suffered to find me, and it was wrong of me to say those things. Can you forgive me?"

Looking up from the floor, she released him, and he peered into her eyes.

"Of course," he said with every ounce of fervency he could muster. "Always."

She smiled, a small thing with a tilt of her head. "Thank you," she whispered. "But more importantly, can you forgive yourself?"

Her force of presence held his eyes for a small moment, but they slipped back toward the floor before long. He didn't answer.

"Faron," she said with a chastising tone. "Look at me."

"How can I?" he said. "If the evil I've done only leads to more evil, then how is it justified?"

"It isn't," Hadria replied with misty eyes herself. "But that's the pain of a ruler—to choose the lesser of two evils and endure the awful consequences."

"Then how can I ever live with myself?"

"By helping more than you hurt," she answered. "By saving more than you sacrifice. By knowing that you do what no one else can so others can live free of your pain."

Faron shook his head. "I don't know if I can do that. I don't know how to make it right."

"Come with me," she implored. "Make it right by proving that you can look past your feelings and work together to save lives. *Help* people, Faron."

"I can't," he said weakly. "I can't let go of the ones who need to die."

"But you know that they need to," she said. It wasn't a question.

"I don't know what I know anymore," he whispered.

"Faron," Hadria said, demanding his attention. "You will make a good king—and a better god."

Surprised, he looked up at her. With an arm splayed to the side, she pulled Synick down to kneel with them, and he gently placed a hand on Faron's shoulder. His frame shook, but no more tears came.

"Admitting what you don't know is difficult. Caring about the lowest among us is beautiful, and we love you for it." She shook her head. "I'm not asking you to abandon the people you love. I'm not asking you to not care or to sacrifice them willingly. I'm not asking you to stop fighting with me about what's right and what's wrong." She studied him with those perfect blue eyes. "I'm only asking for you to come with me. I'm asking for you to not hide your true feelings from me. Argue with me *in good faith*," she said, leaning in close. "Let me in. Trust that I'm listening to you with my whole heart when you decry me and Father. Open your heart, and *listen* to me when I fight with you, too."

Faron didn't realize it, but he was nodding.

"Can you do that?" she pled. "Can you come with me to Anveil, Faron?"

Safe in the arms of the two people he loved most in the world, Faron released a shuddering breath, and he nodded.

Ocean of Temples

Synick was abuzz with excitement. He practically hopped down the snowy streets of Vam Aranath under the white and gold peaked towers, making steady progress toward something that he could call his own. He held the deed in his hands, unable to part himself from it. Beside him strode Vavelt, with a quick step and a half for each of his one. She wore a deep gray coat with long, divided skirts over white trousers. Her black boots were tall and well buckled. She smiled at him when he caught her eye, and a golden braid slipped out from underneath her hood, accented perfectly by the brilliant gold trimming of her clothes.

"Is walking really the best way to get there?" Synick complained.

"No, but it's not far, and walking is good for you. Stop complaining."

"I walked all the way across the snowing Veil; I think I've earned a horse and a little complaining, to boot."

"Synick," Vavelt said, her stride determined. "It would take longer to walk to the stables and wait on the stablemen than to simply walk there in the first place."

"Yes, but the difference is we'd get there on horses."

"What you don't realize is that you've been complaining so long, we're already nearly there."

"I'd call that a successful use of time, then."

She smiled and continued leading the way. They passed block after block, the city organized in a radial pattern with everything branching out from the great temple at the center, except to the south, which was mountainous and empty. Hills and shorter cliffs broke up the monotony of the pattern, and it was toward one of these that Vavelt was leading him.

Several minutes passed before they approached the base of a large hill. Its side was a steep slope of columnar basalt cliffs, and its base was covered in expansive buildings that seemed packed together; but, the top was blanketed in angular pines, the tips of their boughs bit with frost and bent with the weight of snow. There were several places that remained forested inside the city, but they were easily outnumbered by great feats of development. This, so far, was the largest Synick had seen.

"Almost there," Vavelt said for probably the tenth time.

Synick looked up the steps mounting the hill. "I maintain my complaint about horses."

Vavelt grinned and led him up. Synick began to feel exposed as he rose above the rooftops—well, some of the rooftops. He began huffing halfway up, and Vavelt gave him a high brow.

"Tired, Synick?

"I'm still," he said between puffs, "a little sore from walking the *entire snowing Veil.*"

"Mhhm," she intoned. "You should have used a horse."

"I..." he breathed, "hate you."

She cackled and increased the pace.

As they got higher, the wind picked up, and Synick was surprised to find he was grateful for it. Finally, they reached the top and stopped for a breath before the expansive field of pines. Vavelt turned back to appreciate her city behind them.

"Beautiful, isn't it?" It was hard to disagree. "It's odd to think that it's mostly empty."

"I can't imagine what it must have looked like during the reign of the gods."

"The previous gods, you mean."

"Yeah," Synick corrected. "Those gits."

She cocked her head. "Yes, if by *those gits,* you mean my grandparents."

"Er, yeah, that's who I mean. Still gits."

She laughed. "You aren't wrong. Ready?"

He lifted one finger into the air. "Nearly. Did you have to give me the property on the absolute farthest edge of the city?"

She laughed. "Synick, we're nowhere near the farthest edge. In fact, comparatively, we're almost in the exact center."

"Impossible," he huffed. She shook her head and pulled him along by the arm.

The path grew narrow as it wove between the trunks of the green pines, their boughs gently dipping in the breeze. Occasionally, a deposit of snow would slip off the needles, catching the early morning light and showering the ground in a shimmering display of cold crystals. Off in the distance, Synick caught a glimpse of a snow wolf lurking between the trees.

It was only a few minutes more until she turned on her heel, took him by the shoulders, and pressed him up against a trunk.

"Again?" he asked with a smirk. "Here?"

"You shush," she said, the fur on her collar tousling in the soft wind. "We're here."

Synick tried to swing his head around to get a look at it, but she brought his chin back to face her.

"Everything on this hilltop is yours. Are you ready?"

A massive grin spread across his face, and he nodded enthusiastically. "I'm ready!"

She let him loose to step out of the tree line and get his first glimpse of the place he could call home. The first thing he noticed was the estate home itself. It could have been a manor back in Blackwood, maybe two. Built all of patterned gray and white stone and constructed in an L-shape, its corners were fortified with circular towers that rose higher than anything in the city, except, of course, the central temple. It was its own mountain.

Outside the massive home was a courtyard all of stone and snow, with cold weather shrubs and plants adorning every surface that they could. Beyond them were several dozen smaller homes, some stacked together, like most in the city, and others more removed. Unlike the heart of Vam Aranath, there was space between most houses, with defined yards and even thin stone and iron fences. Black iron street lanterns were dotted between the houses all along the cobbled paths, but they were dim now.

"Do you like it?" Vavelt asked.

Synick's words caught in his throat, a thick lump forming when he tried to swallow. He opened his mouth to speak but couldn't.

"Synick?" Vavelt questioned.

"I love it," he managed to say. "It's just... It's only... I don't deserve this," he blurted out. "It's too much."

"Nonsense," Vavelt replied. "This is my city, and I decide who lives here and where."

"How can you even give this to me?" he wondered. "How could something like this not already belong to someone else? Someone important?"

"Vam Aranath stood for a thousand years," Vavelt explained. "It was expanding and growing all that time. My father has a select few archons, and they do own great swaths of the city; but, far more sections are held by the godhead, awaiting lords to rule them."

"What of the people already here?" he asked. "You mentioned earlier that there were servants who maintained the land. What of them?"

"Most of them were slaves who served out their time and weren't needed for the Spile. They're allowed to live in these homes and maintain the land at my pleasure and are encouraged to raise the children of others. No one owns this land, Synick, except for me and, now, my brother, and I'm giving it to you." She smiled at him, discerning eyes locked with his. "Take it, Synick. It's yours."

He couldn't hesitate any longer. "Well, when you put it that way... let's go explore!"

Vavelt giggled, took him by the hand, and took off running. A handful of men and women sweeping the paths or turning over the cold soil caught sight of her and stopped what they were doing to watch. Synick ran right along with her.

They started with a small block of short homes, dwarfed by the estate itself. Each home had one wall, usually the one facing the street, that radiated a surprising warmth. Some walls had small vines crawling out of plant boxes to cover them. Others were decorated with dark shrubs. Walls that weren't warm were adorned with crawling pines or even blue-throated ice lilies.

In another small square on the opposite side of the main estate house, an old man scratched a snow wolf behind the ears as if it were any dog. He eyed the two of them with reverence. Synick couldn't stop to take it all in.

Pausing to take Vavelt's hand again, he smiled, then whipped around the corner of the main house to see that the interior of the L-shape was covered in great stone rafters. The underside was swept clean of snow and was filled pleasantly with chairs of varying size and shape. The pillars supporting the heavy rafters were of an ancient rock, with wildly varied sizes of stone bricks.

Laughing like a giddy child, Synick set his fingers into the stone and began to climb.

"Stop!" Vavelt called, laughing herself, but Synick couldn't help himself. Slowly at first, then with more confidence, he found purchase for his fingers and boots and hoisted himself onto the roof. "Where are you going?" she questioned.

"Up!" was the simple answer. A lower dormer caught his attention, and he scrabbled up the side of it, launching himself onto the next level from there, then stepping carefully over the snow-covered roof to the side of a tower, where he could properly brace himself and look around.

That was when his jaw fell open. Vavelt hadn't been lying about the size of the city. Above the treetops, the entirety of Vam Aranath came into view, and it was beyond his understanding. Miles of compact temples, castles, palaces, great towers, and stacked homes crowded together and stretched into the distance as far as the eye could see, filling his vision with flying buttresses, steeples, and arches. The enormity of it boggled his mind, stretching into the north, east, and west until it blurred with the horizon.

Entire mountains must have been leveled to obtain this much quarried stone. Forests would have been wiped out simply for firewood. There were probably enough buildings here to house the entire world. How much of Alden's population had been lost since—or during—the time of Atha and Olsu? What else had been lost?

Casting his eyes around for them, Synick noticed that this hilltop was not the only space left empty. There were massive patches of cold fields breaking up the monotony of the God City, with most every hilltop left bare as well. Far away in the distance, a great flurry was falling from the clouds to dust an infinitesimal portion of the ever-expansive metropolis.

The majesty and scope of what he saw choked Synick. The reality of how lucky he and Faron had been entering the city from the south, where the buildings were so comparatively thin as to be almost inconsequential, set in on him. If they had entered much farther in either direction, he didn't doubt that they would have wandered an empty and dead city for days, weeks, or months. Synick gaped as he struggled to comprehend the size of the world before him.

A window in the tower beside him swung open, shutters swinging on well-maintained hinges. Vavelt leaned out, golden braid falling as she looked first toward the city, then back at Synick, smiling when she caught sight of him.

"Isn't it wonderful?" she asked.

It was, but that wasn't half of what was going through Synick's mind. All of this, this endless ocean of stone temples, belonged to Faron—Faron, and Vavelt. The scale of what he was getting involved in was beginning to dawn on him, and it was oppressive.

"How?" was all he could say.

"Well, it *is* mostly empty. Even with the upscaling Father has been doing over the past century or so to grow our ability to create an army, the vast, *vast* majority of Aranath is abandoned."

"How can anything be so big?" Compared to the breadth of the God City before him, Synick felt very small. Everything he'd ever seen, everything he'd ever done or ever felt, suddenly became entirely inconsequential.

"Vam Aranath grew for a thousand years," Vavelt explained, leaning her torso out the window. "With the center of life revolving around the gods, it never stopped expanding."

"I don't belong here," Synick realized.

"What?" her laugh became short and stifled.

"How did I end up here? Wrapped up in all of this?" He shook his pale head. "How did I ever convince myself that I could..." He couldn't find the words.

"What are you talking about?" Vavelt puzzled. "What has you so suddenly on edge?"

"This is the *God City*," he expounded, trying to piece his overwhelm together. "What could have possessed me to think something like this could ever have been for me?" His gaze shifted to the beautiful girl hanging out of a window in front of him. "What insanity convinced me that I could ever hope to be worthy of someone like you?"

"You're talking nonsense," she accused.

"You *own* this," he exclaimed, gesturing out toward the ocean of stone. "You. *Own*. All of this. More than that," he realized. "Soon, you'll own all of Anveil, too, then Murcosta, Istred, Sycele, Blackwood, *Empyrion*, whatever the hell else there is. You own it, Vavelt. You are a queen of queens." He struggled to find the right word, and then it hit him. "A *god*. You are a literal god, and here I am, some nobody, some recovering thief with half a brain, thinking that I can be with you, as if I'm, in any way, your equal."

He fell to a slumped sitting position on the roof, one hand on the cold stone of the tower. "I knew there was a disparity between us, but… I didn't know just how eclipsed my importance is by yours."

"Oh, Synick," Vavelt sighed, eyes softening as she took in his piteous state. "Come in, and we'll talk about it."

"How could I think that I could belong with you when literally everything in the world will one day belong *to* you?" He was growing despondent, crushed by the weight of his own insignificance.

"Synick…" she began. "Wait for me." She clambered through the window and stepped out onto the snow-covered roof. Her foot slipped, and Synick lashed out to seize her arm, but it wasn't needed. She caught herself on the sill. "I'm fine," she placated, pulling herself up to the cross-section beside him.

"I understand what you're thinking," she said, and looking into her eyes, Synick knew that she did. They were deep, sharp, and knowing. There was no smile that could keep them at bay.

He hated that.

"You think that we're too different, that we come from different worlds, and the disparity between us is too great to bridge. You think that my power will make me controlling or manipulative." She paused, looking inward. "I don't think that I am. I don't want to be."

"I don't see it that way," Synick said, finally responding. "It isn't that you're too much or too frightening. It's that I'm too little. It's that I have literally nothing to offer you."

"That is far too harsh and far too assuming. If I am, as you say, a god, then what could *anyone* possibly offer me? What connections could I ever forge, based on the metric of material need?" Synick tried to shrug her argument off, but she pressed further. "Even the matches my father imagines for me can't hold up to that standard. It can't matter to me, Synick. If I have everything, then the only thing that can ever be given to me is yourself. What about our short time together gives you the impression that I am displeased with that?"

"It isn't just that," he realized. "You're going to be... You are immortal, Vavelt. That's a line I won't cross, even if I could. One day, I'll be old and awful, and you'll be perfect. Even if you do want to be with me, which I can't understand, it doesn't matter because you're going to live forever." He shook his head, suddenly feeling very foolish. "How could this have ever worked?" What he didn't say, and what stung even deeper, was that the same was true for Faron.

"Oh, Synick," she said with softness. "When will you let go of your hatred?"

"Hatred?" he asked. "I don't hate you. Vavelt, I... Why do you say that?"

"Of course you don't, Synick. You hate yourself."

Any hope Synick had harbored of hiding his feelings was suddenly dashed away. "Doesn't everybody?" he admitted. "So what if I do? You don't know me as well as you want to think, Vavelt. If I do, it's because I deserve it." She tried to interject, but he didn't let her. "I'm a hedonist, Vavelt. I'm a whoremonger and thief. I'm a *nobody,* and you're a god. I should love you for what you've shared with me, but instead, I hate myself. I feel as if I've robbed you, and at any moment, you'll wake up to that fact and want me gone. And you know what?" he went on. "I'd understand it. I'd go because you don't deserve to be tied down to me." He looked around at the expansive lands beneath him, far too much of which was supposed to be his. He didn't deserve it. He couldn't take it.

"Synick," Vavelt asked, her voice soft like the petals of a springtime flower. "Why can't you show yourself the same love that you show others?"

Synick clenched his jaw.

"You have loved my brother for years and haven't told him because you know he can never feel the same way. You have protected him for no other reason than he needed it. You forsook the woman you were pursuing because he needed you, even if he didn't know it. You came here with longing in your heart to find family, and you're willing to walk away because you believe they need it."

She looked up at him, face white in the pale sun. "You are a *good* man, Synick. What I don't know is why you try so hard to hide it."

"Because I have to!" he cried. "Because if I let you in, you'll see that what I am isn't good; it's pathetic. If you see me... you'll leave me."

Vavelt wrapped her arms around him and said nothing. Synick bulled on. "I love someone who can't love me back, clinging like a beaten dog that still begs for scraps. Even with you, I find myself in a position where I can never be your equal, and still, I want to stay because I'm so *lonely*, Vavelt. Don't you see? I cling to anyone who won't shake me off, and everyone who comes to know me sees that. If you don't hate me, it's because you don't know me. Trust me," he spat, "when I say that you don't want me."

Barely keeping his emotions under control, Synick looked up and saw her reading him with that determined gaze again, the one that made him feel naked and unmade. This time, he made no attempt to keep her out. Let her see the demon in him. Let her run.

She studied him for a long time, nearly a minute passing under her scrutinizing eyes. It was the most uncomfortable Synick had ever been. When Vavelt spoke, it was like a wave rolling over a barrier, uncontrollable and unable to be held back for even a moment longer.

"I've been pursued by men all my life, Synick, and I've never seen in any of them what I see in you. You insist that I don't know you, but you're wrong. I know when you're lying and why. I know you wear a smile like a mask because you're frightened people will hate who you are underneath. I know that means you were betrayed when you were very young, and you've never been allowed to heal. I know that you play with words because you don't want people to know how sharp they are and how deep they cut you."

Synick flinched.

"I know that you pretend not to have a heart so others won't see how it bleeds. I know that you possess a softness that you think is a weakness. I know the emptiness that lives inside you that you've tried to fill with women and drink. I know that it hasn't worked because that isn't what you *really* want."

"Please stop."

"I know," she said pointedly, "that you aren't half the scoundrel you pretend to be. I see past your mask and don't see a cold-hearted womanizer, Synick." She paused, pulling his face down to search his eyes. "I see," she urged, "someone trying so very hard to hide just how badly he wants to belong."

Synick cried, his soul laid bare and naked before her. "Stop it," he begged. "You make my point for me. What about that could you possibly tolerate?"

"You don't understand, Synick. You don't understand at all. Everything I just said is something that you hate, but it's only half of what I see."

Synick ground his teeth, unsure how much more honesty he could take.

"I see how suffocating your fear is and how you face it anyway. I see your love for my brother—a love that, in a way, I share—and how you have sacrificed so much for him. Where you see a clinging need, I see a selflessness, a softness, and a loyalty beyond human measure. What you see as hedonism, I see as a desperate attempt to shield my brother from a need that might harm him, a need that he doesn't know. I see more in you that I don't yet understand, but I *want* to, Synick."

She stretched her torso up to place a kiss on his wet cheek. "I know what I want, Synick. I know who you are. Trust me," she said, "when I say that I want you."

Perched before the great sprawling temples of Vam Aranath, Synick forced himself to hear her words and not cast them aside. He wanted to believe. She pushed his tears away with a kiss, and, with heat rising in his chest, he returned it—once, twice, three times, an unknowable number that didn't matter and at the same time wasn't nearly enough. She melted into him and he into her, his scars healing with every touch.

The Death of You All

Faron's heart thumped a heavy, uneven rhythm in his chest, anxiety pooling in his gut. He could hear the gathered masses just beyond the tall archway. The sound of shuffling feet, lightly laughing voices, and a sense of apprehension spilled around him. Across the long upper landing, he saw Hadria, standing with three maidservants beside her. Her grin was broad and true.

With a hard swallow, he tried to return her smile. He had come so far to find her, had gone through so much pain and anguish, only for her to lead an army to dominate a city. A familiar sensation called to him, beckoning him to hide and forget himself, to drink until it didn't hurt anymore, to find a black pit and…

Faron shook himself. There was nothing good waiting for him at the end of that line of thinking. With effort, he returned her grin over a deep feeling of nausea. He had to do this—for now. Anveil depended on it.

Despite the complexity of the circumstance, her sharp grin was almost enough to banish the darkness from his mind. Eyes locked with his twin, the anxiety lost its edge, and his smile became more honest. He *had* promised to try and see things from her perspective. Whatever else he felt, he truly was beyond happy to see her—tall, beautiful, *alive*. Her hair had grown long in the time they'd been apart, falling to mid-back in long curls like a waterfall struck by the final rays of day.

Sadagon's voice rang over the small din, cutting the noise to nothing.

"My friends!" he called over them all. "Allies and loyal subjects, regicides and conspirators, I gather you today to, at long last, fulfill my oaths and abdicate my throne."

Hushed whispers ran through the crowd.

"But my service is not the reason you are here," he continued. "It was you faithful few who, through your strength of mind and soul, liberated the world from the rule of the mad gods. It was you who are due credit for the time of peace the world enjoyed. For nearly a hundred years, we prospered, our oaths fulfilled, until the world grew threatened again.

"It was you faithful few who, in your intellect, devised a way that the world might be saved again. It was you who discovered my wife and comforted me upon her death. It was you who raised the mourn at the loss of my children. It was you few who attended my son's vigil after his second death and grieved with me in my greatest hour of need. It is you few who I depend upon, and it is you few who now, at the cusp of the world's salvation, I share in my celebration!"

Faron looked up from the floor to see Sadagon, his father, lift a gleaming, naked blade high into the air. Its hilt was run with gold, embedded with rubies and sapphires. The blade itself was ornamental, far too intricate to survive a real fight.

"Returned from death—not once but twice—rises my son, Olsu Varek, sibling-heir to the throne of the world!" At the prompting of the savants behind him, Faron was ushered forward, around the corner of the great balcony and into view of the gathering.

Men and women adorned in diamonds, rubies, emeralds, gold, and silver stared in open-mouthed wonder as he stepped away from the safety of the pillars and toward Sadagon, matching Hadria across the way, stride for stride.

"Rise!" Sadagon shouted, piercing the air with the naked blade. "Rise for my son—Bringer of Light, God of Justice, God of Dusk. See his living flesh with your own eyes, and know that you few, the loyal, the silent watchers of life eternal, have today earned your reward. Today marks a new beginning for the world, a second chance to survive the coming age of ice.

"No more will the turning of the earth spell her destruction. No longer will men rape and pillage when driven by the face of extinction. This day marks the beginning of salvation for all." The congregation had grown deathly quiet, gasping as Faron stood near his father. Hadria stood on his other side.

"The gods, once dead, are born again. With you precious few, we shall spread their law once more and save the world from the coming winter. On this long-appointed day, I fulfill my oath and grant unto you the tools to work salvation!"

Staring out over the hopeful crowd that gawked at him, Faron realized, with a sinking feeling, just what they all were. These weren't just his father's supporters or political allies; they were his archons, immortal and enduring long past their allotted lifespans. Casting his eyes about the great chamber, he paled as he failed to comprehend the blood price of the men and women before him.

Every one of them had extended their lives through the blood of an untold number of children, sacrificed to

Sadagon's Life Spile—murderers, one and all.

Faron's fist trembled as he clenched manicured fingernails into his palm, shaking with the fury he had felt with every slaver before these. It was everything he could do not to scream, not to unleash his rage upon the blood-soaked archons below, not to steal the sword from Sadagon's grasp and—

Faron's spiraling train of thought was cut off as the sword flashed downward, straight toward Hadria's exposed neck. His heart skipped a beat, and time seemed to slow. In a gleam of silver light, the blade descended, and a scream caught in Faron's throat. Before he could leap for her, yell for her to move, or loose his choked cry, the sword stopped, landing delicately on her skin. He only just managed to suppress his alarm, but his jolting reaction was not lost on Hadria, who gave him an observing side-eye.

Quelling his misplaced panic, Faron was surprised to see a tear welling in Sadagon's eye as he opened his mouth to speak.

"I, steward of the world, Prince of Dusk, son of Atha and Olsu, bestow upon you, Atha Vavelt, the burden of rule for every man, woman, and child born into this age and every age to come. I abdicate my power and raise your station from heir to sovereign and goddess." The sword lifted off her shoulder, over her head, and down again upon her far shoulder. She bowed her head, a smile touching her lips. "Rule with grace and live forever." He lifted a gold diadem off a deep red pillowed stand and placed it upon her head. It was similar to others he had seen her wear but with finer and larger rubies suspended in its lattice.

Heart still pounding, Sadagon turned to Faron. "My son."

The tear that brimmed fell freely now and not alone. "Twice, I have lost you. Once, as an infant, you were ripped from me, and as a child, I saw you burn before my very eyes. Now, you are returned to me from death to restore light to the world and chase away the shadows."

His back straightened, and he made no attempts to hide the beads that slipped down his face. "I, steward of the world, Prince of Dusk, son of Atha and Olsu, bestow upon you, Olsu Varek, the burden of rule for every man, woman, and child born into this age and every age to come. I abdicate my power and raise your station from heir to sovereign and god." The sword flicked to his other shoulder. "Rule with might and live forever." From another pillowed stand, he lifted a white crown of thinly interweaved webs of gold, bearing aloft monstrous diamonds, and placed it around his head.

His hair had been shaved roughly halfway up the sides of his head, with the remainder neatly gathered together in a tie. The crown was open in the back to let it through, but where the metal touched his scalp, it was cold.

The bloodthirsty Archons of Vam Aranath applauded with exuberant claps as the crown adorned his head, and Faron resisted a shudder. He *had* to do this.

Next, Sadagon opened a small golden casket on long metal legs and retrieved two signet rings from the inside. They were large, covering the entire span between two knuckles in a twisting figure-eight of snakes consuming their own tails. Inside the circles of their twisted bodies was the familiar image of a leafless tree above deep roots—the Ourodurity, symbol of the gods—the very same as the one he bore above his heart. It hurt to look at.

One ring was made of a yellow gold, which Sadagon

slipped upon Hadria's middle finger. The other was a white gold or platinum, which went to Faron. It couldn't have fit his hand more perfectly.

When the rings were on and brandished by a proud Sadagon, the silence broke, and the crowd of no more than a hundred men and women, adorned in finery and fur, cheered in unison, applause and cries breaking forth together. It was a celebration of zealots, and it made Faron's stomach feel like lead. They cheered for the blood he would bring them, for the life he allowed them to lead.

I will find another way, he thought at them. *You cheer for me, but I'll take your immortality from you. I will be the death of you all.* The thought helped to dampen the sickness.

Hadria, smile beaming across her beautiful face, stepped forward and lifted her arms wide toward the archons, long sleeves draping toward the floor. Despite the scarlet velvet wrapped about her frame or the gold diadem in her hair, she looked the same to him as she had a lifetime ago in Ulric's tavern, singing at the top of her lungs. He heard the stomped-out rhythm, the cries of laughter as the men displayed their sons for a chance at a golden-haired grandchild.

He remembered the crystal sound of her voice and the smirk on her lips. Again, it helped to melt away the icy blades of his anxiety, and he smiled. She was the same Hadria he had always known, no matter the circumstances. With his explosive outburst from the night before exposed and unraveled, it was easier to let himself bask in the joy of her presence.

"Let the feast begin!"

Jaru'tal

Servants in a livery of white trimmed in red and gold poured from rows upon rows of doors lining the great room. *No, not servants*, Faron corrected himself. *Slaves.* For every twenty of the servers, there was only one above the age of eighteen. Upon great trays of silver and white gold, they carried heaps of steaming meat, vegetables, bread, delicacies, and a hundred varieties of drinks in tinkling glasses. Faron was surprised to see so much so quickly. There wouldn't be enough people to consume it by half.

Hadria spun to him and squealed gleefully in an excited half-curtsey. She took him by the hand and pulled them toward her side of the balcony, then down the stairs. They passed the hulking figure of a man with a long-handled axe at his hip and thick stubble on his face, but Hadria passed him without a regard and rushed down the stairs, towing Faron after her.

On the ballroom floor, Hadria whirled and snatched a crystal glass of effervescent liquid from a passing tray carried by a young boy. Lifting it high in the air, she cried, "My brother is alive!" The rigid formality of the event on the balcony seemed to have been lifted because the din of clinking glass and voices and laughter immediately took up the call, raising their drinks in the air and cheering her exuberance.

Faron simmered at the cheers and eyes upon him. If not for his bloodline, they would see him as nothing more than a blood-bag. Hadria didn't acknowledge what could only be a caustic expression on his face. Instead, she lifted their intertwined hands and basked in the adoration of Sadagon's court—*their* court.

She laughed and pulled him farther along to a raised and perpendicular table, set apart from the others. Two massive, ornate, and high-backed chairs sat side by side, great platters of food already laid before them. Hadria shoved him into one, and she occupied the other. Her back was straight, regal, and seemed to fit the chair far better than Faron ever could, even with the white crown on his head.

He inspected his clothes. The ruined fleece he'd worn under his new yet already beaten leather traveling clothes had been removed from his apartments and burned, according to one of the many servants, physicians, and savants who had come to see to his comfort that morning while Hadria and Synick were away. Now, they had him dressed in a sharp-collared, black velvet outfit, brocaded on the lapels and sleeves with leather straps across the left breast. He felt pompous, but it was the most comfortable thing he had ever worn. It felt wrong to wear it to a feast where it might be dirtied.

As Sadagon's archons found their own seats, the distinct sound of wood dragging across stone caught Faron's ear, and he looked to see Synick hauling a chair toward them. Faron found a grin as Synick heaved it up the stairs one at a time, then placed it down next to Faron's. Without a word, he plopped down into it.

Synick looked around, eyes narrowed, then said, "Snow and ice, I forgot a plate."

"That's because yours is with the other friends of the throne," Hadria said with a laugh. "Here." She reached around Faron. "Take mine."

Synick grinned as she placed it before him, and Faron basked in the warmth of the two people he loved most in the world.

Reaching forward with a long-handled fork and thin knife, Hadria sliced the breast of a large pheasant and placed it on Faron's plate, a thin smile on her face, then cut another for Synick. A bunch of white grapes followed with the largest slice of steaming mushroom he'd ever seen, which was promptly covered in brown gravy. Next came crumbly bread and his selection of at least a dozen sweating cheeses. After his prolonged fast in the White, it was almost overwhelming, but with his newfound truce with Hadria, he found he was able to let himself enjoy it.

Hardly waiting for Hadria to finish piling ever greater amounts of food on his plate, he attacked it with fork and knife, forgetting for a moment the bloodthirsty killers that surrounded him. Synick seemed to understand it as a race and wolfed down his own food in response. Hadria laughed with delight and took it upon herself to stack their supply ever higher, turning away the servants who obsessively tried to assist her.

It was the finest food Faron had ever touched, the perfection and quality of it easily outstripping the feast at the Festival of First Winter Blood a few weeks before.

Somewhere in the noisy back of his mind, Faron thought he could get used to the frequency of such feasts, even if they were held in his honor.

Hadria noticed the pause in his feasting and took it as a sign that he was finishing up.

"Had enough already?" she asked, that old glimmer in her eye. It nearly enchanted him to see. "I thought you'd go through another three birds at least, at the rate you were going."

"I've said it before, and I'll say it again," Synick said, barely discernable through stuffed cheeks. "Lightweight."

"I'm not finished yet," Faron defended. I'm only trying to figure out what this thing is." He prodded at a plump, white lump on his plate. It was warm if no longer steaming.

"Mana," Hadria told him. "It's one of our staples here, where very little else can grow."

"Mana?" Faron said, trying out the unfamiliar word.

"The bulbs of ice lilies," she explained. "They're incredibly useful. They behave much like tubers when boiled or flour when dried."

"Ice lilies?" Faron asked, surprised. "You mean to say that a staple food is a flower so rare, we found only one or two per year back home?"

"Imagine my surprise," she said, lifting a glass to her brimming lips. "When I learned that my favorite flower would be my breakfast for so many years to come."

"They're edible?" Faron asked. "Really?"

"That's a minimalistic way to phrase it, but yes!"

"But they're so rare!"

"They don't do well in the wild," she agreed. "But they are quite happy to be cultivated if you know how. Their bulbs grow fat as potatoes, and their petals are sweet as honeycomb. They grow quickly, too, despite the… inclement weather."

"If you know how?" Synick asked, still stuffing his face. "Alright, how?"

"That," Hadria replied, "is a secret."

"It can't be much of a secret if it's done by thousands of field workers," Synick speculated.

Hadria gave him a scowl. "Do you want to discuss farming, or do you want to enjoy a feast? I believe the two to be mutually exclusive."

Synick shrugged and went back to his plate.

Faron laughed. "It's almost hard to remember that it's freezing outside with all this heat and food around."

"I believe you've struck upon the point, dear brother." She popped a small handful of roasted pine nuts into her mouth.

Looking around, Faron asked, "Where does all this food come from, anyway? Cultivated ice lilies are one thing, remarkable as that is, but what of the apples, mushrooms, and… well, everything? This is the frozen snowing North."

"Well, you've got a mouth on you," Hadria laughed. Faron blushed, and she ran a hand along his arm. "We grow it, of course. You should see the grand conservatories, Faron—great structures made all of glass, heated by huge brass systems of steam. Inside them, we can mimic any climate and grow anything you can imagine. They aren't prolific enough to feed us completely, of course—we still rely heavily on mana, animal nurseries, and a host of other efforts to provide our daily bread—but it's quite possible. In fact, if you know the secret and have a green thumb, mana is so easy to grow that entire cities can subsist on it alone—in the winter, at least."

"That's remarkable," Faron said, "to think that a city can thrive above the Veil with no season of spring and no snow wall."

"Can you imagine how you would have reacted to the prospect of no snow wall five years ago?"

"I'd never have gone outside."

"You still don't," Synick quipped. "You slept so long this morning that Vavelt and I went to go see my property without you. In fact, I don't think you've left this palace since we got here."

Faron looked taken aback, realizing that Synick was right.

"It's a *large* temple," Hadria comforted. "And you need to recover. There's nothing wrong with exploring your home and taking time to rest. Gods know there's enough to see just within these walls."

Faron nodded. "I've been a bit tired," he confessed.

"You nearly killed yourself." Hadria sighed. "Take all the time you need. We'll take you back to the estate once you're feeling well."

"I bet she'll let you use a horse," Synick murmured.

Hadria laughed, and Synick smiled back at her. Faron saw something in that smile, something different. It wasn't the smile he often saw Synick wear. It was more honest. Something about that troubled him.

"How was it?" he asked. "The property, I mean."

"Wonderful!" was Synick's immediate response. "There's a forest surrounding it all, and you can see the whole world from the bedroom window."

Hadria gave a small cough.

"There are a handful of caretakers living there who used to work the fields. I'm fairly certain one of them was a

100

blacksmith, though, with muscles like his. There's a sapphire mine tied to the land as well—*sapphires*, Faron, can you believe it? There's a conservatory where I can grow anything I like, and a garden for some reason—can't really use that for much. There's an entire room with piping like we saw in Olsu's bathing chamber, with my very own heated pool set into the floor. It's incredible, Faron. I can't wait to show it to you. There's even room to build something of my own if I wanted. That's probably the most unexpected part of it, considering how closely packed everything in this city is."

Synick pasted on his old smile when he realized he'd been rambling, but beyond that, he seemed ready to keep at it, talking and talking until he was interrupted.

"That's wonderful, Synick," Faron said. "I'm glad you like it."

Synick deflated slightly. "You could be a bit more enthusiastic if you wanted. This is something I never thought would happen for me."

"I am enthusiastic," Faron said with a frown. "Really, I'm happy for you."

Synick huffed. "In Blackwood, owning property was a pipedream, even with a thief's income, thanks to Dageran's bankers. For me, this is a dream come true—and a distant dream at that."

"Who's Dageran?" Hadria asked.

That quieted Synick—and Faron, too.

"A dead man walking," Synick finally answered.

"Synick!" Hadria replied.

He shrugged. "It's true. He always thought he was a god, but now Faron really is. He'll be choking on acid soon enough or boiled alive." He grimaced. "Or stabbed in the gut, over and over."

Hadria's eyes flicked to Synick's own midriff. "Who is he?"

"The man who owns me," Faron answered. "Synick, too."

"Owned," Hadria corrected. "*Owned* you. You belong to no one, either of you."

"We did, though," he muttered. "He controlled me as firmly as a man wields a spear."

"He's where you got that brand," Hadria declared. "Both of you."

Faron nodded.

"You're right, then," she said. "He is a dead man walking. When we're finished with Anveil, I'm sending a force to 'collect' him and drag him here. You can do whatever you like with him then."

"Wouldn't mind seeing him swim in a latrine," Synick suggested. "Kinda poetic."

"Or burned," Faron said. The murder in his eyes must have been evident and unsettling because the conversation halted.

"That's enough talk wasted on an evil man," Hadria said, changing the subject. "He's as good as dead and doesn't deserve to occupy even a single moment more of your thoughts. I want to talk about *you*. You've slept like the dead and feasted like the dying, yet here you are, against all odds, alive and well. We've avoided the topic, more or less, but it's been *days* now; and, I am the very image of curiosity. I want to know *everything*."

"That is a long and dull story," Faron said. "And I don't have the first idea where to start."

"If your story is dull, Faron, it's only because you don't drink enough. I find that brightens most tales."

Hadria rolled her eyes. "Tell me how you learned about

snow cloaks. I've been dying to know."

"I... I don't want to talk about it."

Synick nodded. "Sounds right."

"Come on now," Hadria pushed, ignoring Synick. "You've been gone for years, and you've avoided answering even a single question. Please? I am *dying* to know."

He sighed. "It was a bit of an accident, actually," he said. "I had only just escaped from Aru'barrahk over their mountain when the Veil fell, racing me to Anveil."

"Yes, *that*," she said. "Do elaborate." Her tone was encouraging.

"There's not much to tell. I climbed, but I wasn't fast enough. Nobody expected the Veil to fall as fast as it did." He shrugged. "When I noticed it, I ran as fast as I could, but... it was a race I lost; and, I was fortunate enough to stumble on a lone snow wolf. I killed him, and I saw his coat. I was freezing, so I skinned him and took it. Not long after that, I came across another wolf—a group of them this time—and they left me alone. I put it together after that."

"That's not what you told me," Synick claimed. "You said you remembered Jaru'tal's cloak, and it clicked for you."

Faron winced.

"Jaru'tal?" Hadria asked. "The Dunestrider? You know him? Faron, that's amazing! He's such a kind man. How did you meet him? How is he?"

Faron shifted in his seat as a silence blossomed. He had suspected she would know him and had purposefully left him out. At the very least, Jaru'tal had confessed to knowing Sadagon quite well.

Knowing he would regret it, Faron asked, "...You know him?"

"Yes!" she said, with an enthusiasm that would haunt him. "He's a friend and of particular interest to Father, who says he's one of the few men in the world with the power and knowledge to make him a potential match for a betrothal."

Faron paled, and Synick stiffened.

"What's wrong?" she asked. "It won't happen if that's what you're worried about. He's charming but far too ambitious." She paused, reading the expression on their faces. "I understand, considering your background, that you might not be fond of him, but... what?" She cast her eyes between them. "Faron?" A pause. "... How do you know Jaru'tal?"

"I killed him," Faron whispered, gaze drawn downward.

Hadria looked as if she'd been struck by a gauntleted fist. She sank back into her chair, the blood flowing from her face.

Faron ground his teeth. "He knew how to find you!" he shouted. "He had information that I needed to *find you*. I didn't mean to kill him," he said, then stopped. That was a lie. He had meant to kill him. Faron had very deliberately chosen to murder Jaru'tal and to carry that weight upon his back.

How could he have known what that would mean?

"I had no choice!" he said, still yelling. Hadria hardly seemed to hear him. "He bought me, Hadria! He bought me like a dog and wouldn't talk to me about how to find you. I had no choice!"

Snapping out of her reverie, Hadria seemed to notice him there, suddenly standing and on the knife's edge of panic.

"It's alright," she placated but too quickly. "I... I understand. I just was... I was shocked, is all. I... I can't blame you, brother."

"I didn't have a choice!" he said, chest drawing heavy breaths.

"You're right, Faron," Synick said. "You didn't, and he'd have deserved it even if you did."

Hadria shot him a glare but let the statement stand.

Faron squeezed his eyes to banish the memory of Jaru'tal's lacerated face. It didn't work, so instead, he peered deep into his sister's eyes. They seemed to pull him in.

"No one can blame you for what you did, brother," she told him, holding his gaze, lest the panic control him. "I don't blame you."

"I'm sorry!" he said louder than he had intended. "I didn't know! I had no way to know!"

"You're right," she soothed. "It's okay. You're right. You can't be held responsible for what you did to get here. It's okay, Faron. You're here now, and that's what matters."

Faron shook as he searched her eyes, desperate to see that she meant those words—desperate to believe. Jaru'tal was a slaver, an awful and terrible person unworthy of pity, but if his death hurt Hadria? Faron wasn't sure he could live with that.

"It's alright," she said, pulling him back into his chair. "It's alright; I'm only sorry I asked. Gods, Faron, I can't imagine the horrors you've been through."

"I killed him to find you," he said, finally quiet again. Only now did he notice the dozens of archons who stared at him. It took an effort of will not to flash his teeth at them, to find a knife and throw it. "I didn't know he was your friend," Faron whimpered. "I didn't know."

"It wasn't like that," she insisted. "Jaru'tal is—was—more

of a tool than anything, and tools can be replaced. Father admired him for the positions he held and the service he rendered us, but he *wasn't* betrothed to me, brother, and he was never going to be. Gods, I wish I could take it back. I'm so sorry."

"I asked him about you—about Hadria—but he didn't know you by that name." He shook his head. "I'm a fool. I should have known."

"There was absolutely no way you could have known she would have another name," Synick said. "And besides... he was a royal git, right? And so *old.*"

Vavelt swatted at him but quickly returned her hands to Faron's arm.

"Look at me," she commanded, and Faron did. "Listen here and now. You can't blame yourself for the things you did to find me. You didn't know. You can't blame yourself for what you *didn't know.*"

Faron drew a deep breath.

"You didn't have a choice," Synick told him. "It isn't your fault the idiot tried to buy you."

Faron flinched, but it was too late to turn back the tide of words now. He'd already begun. "That isn't true," he admitted. "It took careful planning to see that Jaru'tal bought me, plans that I made."

He grimaced as he remembered the dead. "Jaru'tal's guard died because of me—and the soldiers." His heart hammered the uneven rhythm of anxiety in his chest, and he squeezed his eyes shut. "I killed him thinking it would save you—and that you needed me. I killed him because he supplied Sadagon with children, and I thought he was a monster. I thought I could kill him, and I could live with that... but now?"

He released a trembling breath. "Now, *seven* men are dead because of me—and for nothing… Maybe I'm the monster."

"No, Faron," Synick hushed, but Hadria's voice captured his attention.

"Seven?" she breathed, disbelief playing across her visage.

Faron closed his eyes, then shot them back open when he saw the faces watching him in the darkness. "If you don't count… the others." He thought of Badune'ahl and Jakab'een, who Harab had killed to strike an allegiance with Faron. "They weren't my fault—not directly." The words came out sounding like a question. He realized that that list included Ulric. It almost included Synick. Faron met Synick's eye and could tell that he was thinking the same thing, but, blessedly, he didn't say anything.

Faron forced his lids shut and looked upon the dead, broken men who waited there.

"I said I didn't want to talk about."

Synick stopped his convulsing with a strong hand on his shoulder. "That's enough," he said. "Their lives aren't worth a fraction of yours. Regardless of what Sadagon buys slaves for, they were evil men for selling them—barely even people. They tried to buy and sell you, too." His fingers clamped down hard. "They deserved what they got, and your only regret should be that I won't get the chance to kill them, too, because I would if I could; and, I wouldn't be so kind as you."

Synick's ferocity surprised Faron. He pulled away from the dead in his mind to see Synick staring daggers at him, protective and angry.

"You are not a monster," he spat.

Slowly, Faron nodded. Long breaths combined with

Synick's determination helped to ease his guilt, and a knot loosened in his chest. He nodded again, easier this time, and Synick managed to put on a smile.

"Besides, I think we're missing the really important thing here, which is that you took out a dire wolf and wore its dripping, bloody pelt on your back."

Faron paused. "Dire wolf?"

Synick jabbed a thumb toward Hadria. "Vavelt's been using the name."

"It isn't just a name," she corrected, understanding that Synick was deliberately changing the subject. "That's what they are. Any other names came about from a linguistic culling and a burning of libraries."

"Whatever you call it," Synick said, "he killed it with a box and a knife, then wore its skin on his back."

"That's... somehow both disturbing and extremely impressive," Hadria said. "But mostly disturbing."

"It was disgusting," Faron agreed, finding a small laugh. Hadria laughed with him, and for a moment, everything felt like it would be alright.

Then Sadagon stepped up behind him.

Everything

Sadagon placed his hands upon their chair backs, informal and familiar. The suddenness of it made Faron's skin crawl, though he tried not to feel it.

"It is fortunate," he said, "that you are skilled with a dagger. Any other weapon would have had no chance against Olsu's wolves."

Faron attempted to shove down the panic that rose every time he saw Sadagon. It was a reaction he could not control. He took a deep breath, promising his lungs that there would be no smoke and no heat. "What do you mean?" he asked, with a heavy exhalation. It didn't do any good to pretend Sadagon didn't exist. He had to be able to speak to him without flinching if he was going to change his or Hadria's minds.

"A sword or spear might offer distance from the wolves, but wolves don't fight at a distance. You may be able to fend off one with it; but, the rest will force their way close, and you will be defenseless. The only way to survive an encounter with more wolves than one is in their own engagement distance with a knife. If you had defended yourself with a sword, you would be dead."

"I don't like swords," Faron offered quietly. "They're

bulky—clumsy."

"Heavy," Synick offered.

"They would not have served you in this case."

"You called them Olsu's wolves?" Faron asked. "Had—Vavelt just called them dire wolves. Which one is it?"

"Well, both," Hadria answered. "Olsu bred and named them."

Sadagon nodded. "They were his method of controlling the world, and they have been quite effective."

"He created them? How is that possible?"

"Selective breeding," Hadria answered again, popping a pine nut in her mouth. "He bred those with traits he wanted, like white coats and aggression, a fear of strong light, and fed the others to them."

"I believe," Sadagon cut in, "that the fear of strong light was something of an accident—a side effect of the white coats. I don't believe that he intended to breed them with albino traits, but the results are hard to argue with."

Faron didn't know what that meant, but he wasn't about to ask Sadagon to expound.

"I disagree," Hadria said. "Olsu was nothing if not deliberate. Their weak, red eyes gave him control over them, and Olsu, it seems, was obsessed with control."

"Perhaps."

Faron grimaced. "How long would something like that have taken?"

"A hundred years, at least," Sadagon answered. "It was long before I was born."

"Well," Faron said. "That explains why this city was built without walls. There were no snowbeasts then." He shook his head. "Still, how does someone, even a mad god, just go about creating an entire race of monsters?"

"Systematically," Sadagon replied. "First, he bred them to be larger, stronger, and more aggressive. Then he gave them a taste for human flesh and released them to ravage the existing population of wolves."

Faron was almost afraid to comment. "That's horrible. How do you *breed* animals to have a taste for human flesh?"

Synick nodded at the question.

"Can we not?" Hadria cut in. "I'm trying to enjoy this feast."

"He has a right to know," Sadagon said lightly. "They, too, are a form of inheritance."

"Fine." She rolled her eyes.

"The population of archons I maintain is nothing compared to the hosts that the previous gods kept. With that came a larger demand for exsanguinations, which meant more bodies—tens of thousands of times more."

Faron put his fork down, suddenly feeling very sick.

"Told you," Hadria said.

"He fed the bodies to the wolves," Sadagon confirmed. "And when generation after generation of his pets grew accustomed to the behavior, he sent them into arenas to hunt those who displeased him for bloodsport."

Reading the expression on Faron's face, Hadria said, "I *did* tell you."

Faron swallowed hard before speaking. "The more I learn of Olsu, the more I come to hate him. I hope his end was a painful one."

Hadria paused the cutting motions of her fork and knife and looked up to study Sadagon before adding with an edge to her voice, "They were his parents, Varek. You shouldn't say such things."

Synick picked at his food, not saying anything.

It didn't reflect in his tone, but Sadagon seemed to stand a little stiffer. "It was," he said. "His screams and suffering, along with my mother's, earned me the name of Pyre."

"I hate when they call you that," Hadria cut in. "It's a disgusting thing to call a man by, no matter how vicious the gods were. Do they not pause to consider how it makes you remember?"

"It's fine, Vavelt," he consoled her. "Consideration is not a duty of our subjects and not their concern. We bear the responsibility that we must so that they may live freely."

"Well, it's crude," she replied. "Why don't they call you Vam Steward or Lord Inheritor? There are a host of names to choose from that aren't nearly so base. Naming a man after an execution is cruel."

"I'm sorry," Sadagon said. "I did not intend to speak of evil things. I had meant to ask you if you were enjoying your nameday celebration."

It all came back to him then—the Life Spile, the army. His smile slipped away.

"It's more than I'd ever imagined," Faron said honestly.

"Is more, better?" Sadagon asked.

He opened his mouth to offer a tentative reply, but Hadria cut him off. "In terms of mushrooms, it must be. You should have seen him work his way through an entire giant puffball. Gods, that was impressive."

"Disgusting is what it was," Synick muttered but fell silent again. He seemed uncommonly uncomfortable.

Sadagon lifted an eyebrow. "As steward of this world, I raised you to the position of gods not an hour gone. Does it make much sense to curse by yourself?"

Hadria smiled and laughed softly. "I suppose it does create a bit of a paradox."

Sadagon turned to Faron. "This is only a small gathering for you to be seen and known by those who will be your closest delegates and supporters. Some of them have been with me from the beginning; others were raised as archons from the children born to us and even the ranks of slaves. Still," Sadagon continued. "We lack the time to commission your portrait and distribute it among our people. The majority of your subjects will not know your face, so make a point to keep your crown and ring with you. They will know to answer to you then, should you choose to walk among them."

Faron was quiet, so Sadagon changed the subject. "There is someone I'd like you to meet, Varek, or rather, meet again." He held up his left hand, and a tall, white-haired man with a long, pointed chin stepped up to his side. Faron recognized him as the man who had shown him to a bed his first night out of the Veil. "This is Vam Varan, High Archon of Vam Aranath and the architect of your rule. He has been my right hand for over three hundred years, as well as a close confidant and friend. He is also your keeper, assistant, and most trusted protector."

The tall, slender man bent himself into a deep bow, his long hair spilling from his shoulders and nearly brushing the ground in his kneeling position.

"That sounds like my job," Synick cut in. "Only I don't need titles to do it."

When Varan spoke, his voice was even with sincere inflection. "And yet, Vam Synick, you have been titled for it."

He offered a wizened smile. "I do not infringe on your self-appointed duties. I serve in whatever capacity is needed."

Varan turned to Faron now. "It is the honor of my life to finally meet you, Vam Varek. I will be your man in whatever capacity you may require me—as a god, a friend, or a master. In life and death, I will serve you so long as I live."

"A keeper?" Faron's brow furrowed. "Are you so certain that I'll try to leave?"

"He's not here to watch you, Varek," Hadria said, using his apparent birth name. "He is your companion, to offer advice if you want it, protect you if you need it, and any other kind of support you could imagine. Really, Varan isn't here to police you. In fact"—she turned and pointed to the staircase leading to the balcony far above—"Yarow, there, that thick trunk of a man"—she waved at him fondly, and the axe-wielding man nodded in return, maintaining eye contact until she turned away—"he is my keeper, and Varan is yours. They've been spoken for us since birth."

Faron eyed the man warily. "I don't have much need of a servant," he said, trying to temper the offensive tone he knew his voice carried.

"It is not my place to judge the needs of a god," Varan said. "But I will be your sword from this day—always." Faron shrugged. He didn't seem to have much control over what happened to him in this city, regardless of his supposed title. "I will leave you to privacy with your newly reunited. If you have need of me, only lift your left arm to a square, and I will come." He showed Faron the gesture he would never use, then bowed and departed, but not before Faron caught a glimpse of the black veins crawling up his wrists.

Faron felt a distinct sickness overwhelm him. Finding this

city, its scale and magnificence beyond anything he had ever imagined, and then Hadria in it, not as a slave but a ruler, had been a shock to his senses. Now, inside the belly of the beast, he had agreed to become a figurehead for the slavers and murderers he once hunted. He wasn't sure which side of that fact disturbed him more. Either way, it weighed heavily on his chest, forcing the air from his lungs in quick, panicked bursts. Standing, he pushed himself out of his chair.

"I... I need to go."

Hadria and Synick were right in step behind him. "Brother," Hadria asked. "Where are you going? You've only stayed for the second course; the celebration will last for hours still." She looked concerned, but Synick's anxious expression was far more worried than hers.

"I have to go," he said, shaking his head. She grabbed his arm, searching his eyes.

"Olsu Varek is tired from his extended journey," Hadria announced suddenly. "I will take him to rest. Continue the feast in his name." The archons who watched them closely nodded and turned, accepting the excuse. Sadagon observed with arms folded behind his back while Hadria took Faron arm in arm and led him away through the gigantic palace. Only a step behind, Synick followed. Faron tried to control his breathing, but it came in short, ragged gasps that only brought him closer to panic.

They came upon a lonely space, filled with hundreds of delicately carved pillars the width of his arm, with a floor to ceiling space of only twenty feet. He collapsed there, back to a white column, and hugged his knees.

"What is it? What's wrong, Faron?" Hadria asked with genuine concern.

"I don't know," he answered. "Nothing. Everything."

"Are you well? Should I call for a physician?"

"It's them," Synick answered for him. "They're crowding him, cheering him on and watching him, and—I'm willing to guess—he wants to kill them."

"I'm fine," Faron answered, pulling in hard breaths. "I'm fine." The crown was heavy on his head, so he pulled it down and fiddled with it before dropping it to the floor.

"What's wrong?"

"I said I could do this," he intoned, "but I can't. I can't go through with it."

"Of course you can!" Hadria encouraged. "You only need time to understand."

"It's too much, Hadria."

She was silent for a moment, then said in a quiet voice, "Please don't call me that."

"Why?" he burst out. "Why can't I call you that? It might not be your given name, but it's the one I know you by."

"Please, just don't, especially not around Father."

Faron grunted. "That's the problem—*Father.*"

"I understand why you think of him the way you do, but he *loves* you, Faron, truly."

"Does that really matter? Does it excuse his callousness?"

"Please…" Hadria whispered. "Don't start shouting."

Faron pulled in a long breath through his clenched teeth. "I'm sorry."

Hadria breathed with him. "I thought we were past this, Faron. What's frightened you?"

Faron just shook his head.

"*Faron,*" Hadria chastised. "You said only last night that you'd listen to me and not shut me out. Now I'm trying to listen to you. What has you so frightened?"

"It's Sadagon," Synick said. "What's in your head, Faron?"

Finally, he shrugged and answered, "I don't trust him, Vavelt. I want to believe what he says—I almost do sometimes—but when I don't, I can't see anything but bloodlust in him."

"He is your father, Faron."

"Is that a reason to love someone?" Faron asked. "To trust them?"

She looked genuinely surprised. "Of course it is. What else in the world is there besides family? He is your *blood*, Faron."

Synick shuffled on his feet but was silent.

"Blood is what scares me, Vavelt, but not ours. The blood that frightens me is in the veins of Father's archons, stolen from children who are corpses now."

"Yes," she agreed solemnly. "It is frightening—a terrible necessity."

"But is it?" Faron questioned, jumping back up to his feet and beginning a furious pace. "Sadagon speaks of sacrifice and necessary evil but maintains an entire host of archons? How many lives have they consumed between them?"

"Less than will be saved," Hadria replied softly.

"That's no excuse to murder!"

"Calm, Faron." Synick's voice was firm.

He deliberately slowed his breathing but spared a moment to give Synick a short and level look. "I can see how he believes the sacrifice is necessary to prolong our lives—so the world will believe in gods—but how does that apply to his court? How is it necessary to require so much blood to extend the lives of a few supporters? How can I see that as anything but intentionally cruel?"

"The needs of the kingdom are vast, brother. Father and I rely heavily on delegation and continued loyalty."

"It could be done without the Spile," Faron argued. "Yet Father allows it because it's easier. Can you not see," he pressed on, "how he throws the lives of innocents away for the convenience of it? What does that make him if not a murderer?"

"Stop it, Faron!" Hadria interceded, patience eroded. "You don't know who you're talking about!" She opened her mouth to continue but stopped herself, taking in a deep breath to fortify her temper. Bending down, she stooped to lift Faron's fallen crown off the ground, took another breath, then finally spoke.

"I understand why you feel that way. You're scared. None of this is what you expected. You did the impossible by coming here and, no doubt, thought you'd have to find me and fight your way out, but that's not *real*, Faron." She stopped his pacing by grabbing his shoulders—his flame scarred shoulders. "You're prejudiced against him because of what happened the night he found us and what you imagined he did to me, but that's not *real*. You're judging him based on events that never happened and your own misunderstandings. Do you not see how that's unfair?"

"What I imagined he did to you is *exactly* what he's doing to others, Vavelt. How can I overlook that?"

"It isn't nearly what you seem to expect. You imagined prisons and cages where children wait to be picked off, one by one. The reality is infinitely kinder. Our wards are rescued from starvation, cold, molesters, and abuses of all kinds and brought here, where they are fed, warmed, and given purpose. They work fair hours when they are able and are free to live like they never could otherwise."

"Until you kill them."

"Yes. That is the tragedy, but it is not unfair, Faron. They understand that they have been given a lease on life. When their time comes, they come willingly, gratefully even. I know it's hard to see, but Father's work extends *everyone's* lives, not just the archons. Nobody comes to Vam Aranath unless it was the only way they could have been saved. Besides," she explained, "most never go to the Spile. That fate is reserved for a select few."

She released his shoulders to whirl on Synick. "At your estate, what commonfolk were there?"

"Old people, mostly," he confirmed. "A few with the deep skin of the Kaorn, and a few kids running around, really young—like—born here young."

She nodded. "It isn't half as bad as you make out."

Faron shook his head. "Extending a lifeline to a person does not give you the right to cut it away when the purpose suits you. I cannot see past that."

"You promised to *listen* to me, Faron. Let go of your biases and see this objectively. Father is a source for *good*. He wants to unite and save the world. There are only two ways to do that."

Snapping his head to the side, Faron asked, "What is the second way?"

"The first is by claiming ownership over the world and pressuring the major cities to accept our rule as gods, one at a time." She held his gaze for a moment. "The second is by human rule—to replace the powers that exist instead of superseding them. That way is to slaughter every man who stands in our way, make an example of their wives and children, and crush those who would oppose us until there are none left. That's how they did it, you know—Atha and Olsu. Is that what you would prefer?"

"Of course not," Faron said, breaking out of her grip. "Hadria, there *must* be another option."

"That is *not* my name," she snapped, her previous calm failing. I use 'Faron' for you because it is what you are comfortable with. Please show me the same courtesy."

Faron waved her objection away. "I only mean that there has to be another way—a method to bring people together without sacrificing children to fuel a vain immortality."

"What is it, then?" Hadria said, leaning against the fine white pillar. "Tell me what other option there is, brother. I'll wait." He paused his pacing but couldn't answer. "There is *none*," she said after a long moment. "There is no third option. We either unite men and save them from themselves, or we see what kills them first: the frost, the wolves, the hunger, or their blades."

Synick interrupted. "He isn't talking about your immortality." He looked between them. "He's talking about the archons. Aren't you?"

Hadria's eyes flitted between Synick's, and then she nodded her understanding. She softened and let out a deep breath.

"Come here," she said, holding out her arms for him. Pulling him in close, she put a hand in his recently cut hair and said, "You're right. Of course, you're right. As a direct trade of lives, Father's archons are a steep price that no one should have to bear, you least of all."

Safe in her arms, Faron felt himself become nearly overwhelmed. "I've been a slave too long to write them off as only a sacrifice, Hadria. I know what the ugly side of this looks like, and I cannot be a part of it. There has to be a way to do it without them."

"You're right, Faron," she whispered again. "The archons *are* a callous use of life. They've been of vital importance to Father's rule, but, brother"—she lifted his white crown—"we are the rulers now." She ducked her head into his lowered gaze until his eyes locked with her own. He studied her expression, wondering if she meant what he hoped she did.

"Come with me," she said. "Come with me to Anveil, and help me spare the city; and, I will do this for you. When our rule is secure, and our people are safe from the Veil, we will dissolve Father's archons."

Tears stung the corners of Faron's eyes, and the dread that harrowed him seemed to lift.

"Truly?" he asked.

"Truly," she said, holding him close, and he trembled with relief, not only for the precious lives he could save but because Hadria had listened to reason. He could still get through to her. He could still save her.

Releasing his weight as Faron stood a little taller, Hadria sighed and held him tight. "I can only imagine what you've been through—what's shaped you this way. Help me understand. Please. I know it hurts you to talk about, but I promise to listen. Tell me what's happened to you these five years. Tell me about that brand on your chest. Tell me what they did to you. Tell me who you are. Tell me *everything*."

Shattered Glass

"She looks..."

"Beautiful?" Hadria suggested.

"Like you," Faron said, a little sheepishly. "Except more how I remember you, almost—younger."

"That's because she was," Hadria confirmed. "This statue is made from a likeness of her when she was only fifteen."

"That's... young," Faron said with a furrowed brow.

Sensing his discomfort, Hadria nodded. "Yes, unfortunately. The need far outweighed propriety, but she wasn't forced into a marriage with Father. She agreed to the union."

Faron remembered another girl who had agreed to a distasteful arrangement out of necessity and wondered if she was faring any better than his mother had. Images of Clarath with torn clothing rushing away from Dageran's chambers assaulted him, arms held tight to shoulders, eyes down.

There was nothing he could do about that now.

In the gray and white mausoleum, Faron examined the statue of his mother, the lady, Lyss, and tried to think of anything but his past. Underneath the stone likeness, there was a white marble sarcophagus where her body was interred, encased forever in rock.

Shouldn't he feel something?

All his life, he had wondered who his mother was and what she was like, if not with quite the same intensity as Hadria, and now he was here, staring at her coffin like it was any other in a long line of corpses he had never known. He shuffled his weight back and forth. Somehow, his lack of emotion was more personally disturbing than the grief or mourning he had expected to overcome him. Instead, he felt nothing, examining the final resting place of a person he'd never known, who meant nearly nothing to him.

"She died not long after this portrait was commissioned," Hadria continued. "Just under a year." Her voice tinged with lament as her hand brushed the rounded surface of the sarcophagus lid. "I wish I could have known her."

"I'm sure she would have loved you," Faron said.

"Isn't it odd," Hadria said, eyes affixed to the statue. "To wish to be comforted by someone who never reached adulthood? On one hand, she was our mother, and that alone should entitle us to her care; but, on the other, she was a child. She died a child. I'm older now than she ever was, and yet, I feel as if I ought to seek her approval, win her affection." Her eyes became far away, and the motions of her fingers on the stone became more automatic. "How odd that I feel the pull to find her and let her braid my hair, to hold me awhile and tell me everything will turn out well, despite the pain of the way."

Faron wasn't sure how to respond. He felt none of what Hadria expressed, only an odd hollowness where his longing should have been.

"I suppose it is a bit strange," he managed.

"I think you're underselling it, but I appreciate your support." Her gaze broke away, then locked onto Faron's

123

with a small grin. "I think we could use some air," she said. "Let's go meet up with Synick at his estate. You still need to see it."

Nodding his agreement, Faron followed her through the great open chambers of the mausoleum. They passed under grand archways, far smaller than the ones found in the temple but still oppressively large, and long hallways full of similar statues. Every so often, a winged figure of stone could be seen, holding aloft a glowing eye surrounded by golden rays—the ancient symbol for the afterlife. Faron had seen many of its kind in cemeteries and mausoleums.

On one side, they passed a smaller room with two stone infants near a gray bowl filled with shattered glass. Faron didn't stop to ask all the oddities described to him, only pressing on, eager to be away from the surrounding evidence of mortal fragility.

Outside, the wind was white, colored with fat flakes of snow that drifted in small gusts that chilled but didn't cut. Dressed in the finest clothes of leather and short-cropped fur, Faron hardly noticed it at all.

His warmth was cut short when he turned around to take in the overwhelming temple-like structures, and a pound of snow smashed into his head. Faron spluttered, nearly knocked off his feet.

"Ah!" he half growled, but Hadria only laughed.

"You should see your face!" she howled.

Faron's initial reaction of frustration slipped away as a grin stole over his face, warm and true. Hadria correctly interpreted that grin and bounded away in pursuit of cover or, at least, distance.

Faron's first snowball hit her in the shoulder, exploding

in a soft puff on her white fur mantle. His second hit a little more squarely at the hips. He stooped down for more ammunition but not before Hadria whirled around and flung a snowball high into the air.

Faron felt a wicked smirk pull at his lips. Its arch was slow and lazy. He could catch it and send it hurtling right back at her, giving her a mouthful of her own snow. He reached up to snatch it out of the air when a second snowball smashed full in his face.

The arms that reached upward only a moment before pinwheeled for balance now, and he fell flat on his backside. The first snowball landed unceremoniously on his chest.

Through the muffling powder, Faron heard Hadria's guffaws as she rushed to his aide.

"I can't believe I got you with them both!" she said with such alacrity.

Faron groaned, wiping his face and sitting up. "I believe the sportsman-like thing to do would be surrender after a defeat like that."

"I don't take prisoners, I'm afraid," Hadria teased.

"That's alright," Faron said, leaning forward a little more. "I've never really cared for the whole concept of 'sportsman-ship.'" Flinging his arms upward, Faron threw two armfuls of snow directly into Hadria's half-smiling face.

Her spine stiffened, and she backstepped away from him. "You cheated!" she declared. "I was performing my duties as a battlefield medic!"

"All is fair in love and war," Faron quoted, "and this is both!" He assailed her with another barrage of snowballs. Hadria narrowly ducked his shots and laughed when one ball knocked the crown off her head. She gave as good as she got after that, nimbly dodging to the side and pelting Faron with fistful after fistful of dry snow until their fingers were red and painfully numb from the cold.

It wasn't until a stray shot from Hadria hit a girl barely older than herself that Faron noticed the attendants that had assembled and were now watching them, bearing towels and steaming cups of mulled wine.

"Vanessa!" she called, voice high with the thrill of their battle. Faron uncoiled his arm, disengaging from the throw he had nearly committed to as his sister rushed over to the servant. "Oh my goodness, I didn't notice you there!" she said, pulling chunks of snow from her servant's red hair. It was only when the majority of the snow had fallen away from her face that Faron could see she was smiling, still holding tight to the platter bearing the steaming wine. Nearly half of it had sloshed out onto the tray from the force of Hadria's throw, but she'd somehow held on and kept the cups aloft.

"Collateral damage is a common effect of war, my lady," she said with a knowing grin.

"You deviant," Hadria said, brushing her handmaiden's shoulders. She reached out for the tray. "You'd better take this"—she indicated toward the silver cup—"as recompense for your noble sacrifice."

"Thank you, my lady," Vanessa said with a shy bow, accepting the cup. A younger servant retreated to fetch another.

Still bearing the tray, Hadria turned around and proffered the other cup to Faron, who also took it with a grin. Hadria smiled, carrying the tray as naturally as a serving girl until her other handmaidens took it from her.

Shivering, Faron noticed the others who watched them,

dozens of servants waiting in the cold to be called upon, one young girl retrieving Hadria's fallen crown. There were archons and lesser nobles in the windows and upper walkways who gazed curiously and even affectionately down at them. Soldiers halted their patrols to witness the playfulness of their gods before continuing their mobilization toward Anveil the next morning. There were even groups of children sweeping the streets of snow, watched over by older servants who all paused to see them.

Faron ignored them all, feeling for the first time in his recent life the warmth of unfettered joy.

Foul Concoctions

Synick sat alone atop his roof—*his* roof—and idly watched the snow falling around him. It was peaceful here, his back against the warming wall, feet liable to slip and send him hurtling three stories to the stone courtyard below—just how he liked it.

Below, the servants—well, semi-retired slaves, really—milled about performing their daily tasks. Some of them stopped to stare at the eclectic manor-lord who perched on his roof, but most of them were used to him by now.How odd that he should inherit so much property and still elect to spend the majority of his time on the rooftop. Old habits, he supposed.

The towering ocean of temples that were the Vam Aranath horizon still daunted him, but it was a familiar kind of daunting, like the sapphire-speckled sky on a moonless night. The thought made him look up. The sun would be setting soon. Maybe the green curtains of light would come back tonight, and he could watch them from the vantage of his eyrie.

While he stared at the clouds like the slack-jawed idiot he was, Faron and Vavelt mounted the rise of his hillock home and spied him on his roof. Even from here, he could see them shaking their heads in unison. In so many ways, they really were so alike.

How odd that that should bring him a pang of pain.

"What are you doing up there?" Faron hollered from the narrow street.

"What are you doing out of your castle?" Synick shot back. "That's the real question. I thought you'd sworn an oath never to go outside again."

Synick couldn't hear it, but Faron grunted—well, he *guessed* Faron grunted. It was a safe guess. "It feels like it," Faron returned.

"Come down from there, you rogue," Vavelt said.

He grinned and stood, then put one hand in the open window of the tower to swing inside. The rich woods and carpets were a stark contrast from the stone shingles of his lookout.

Striding through his hallways, dining room, and parlor, Synick put on his smile then met the siblings outside. Faron was very in his element there, the wind tousling his neatly cut hair under that small circlet his sister made him wear. The clothes worked for him, too, in an 'I'm wearing a fortune and don't want to think about it' kind of way. Vavelt was no less striking, with that pleated riding dress and trousers, all trimmed in gold to accent her hair in a way that felt supernatural. Really, though, it was her pinning gaze that made him stop and swallow hard.

"Welcome to my home, git," he said, giving Faron a small bow.

He chuckled. "It's all yours?"

"Apparently. Still hasn't sunk in. Everything on this hilltop. Isn't that strange?"

Faron grunted, and Synick smiled inwardly. "It is," he said. "I wouldn't have given you half this much."

"Git."

"Oh, shush," Vavelt said, faux-slapping Faron's arm as he broke a slanting smile. "He's earned all this and more."

Faron nodded but said, "Still, it *is* a lot. It's impressive, Synick."

"It's impressive?" Synick asked. "Everything that's *not* this is *yours*."

That made Faron stop. "Hasn't sunk in," he said, echoing Synick's words from earlier. "It doesn't feel like mine. It doesn't feel like I don't belong, exactly, but it doesn't feel like mine."

"Let's make a club."

"Have you been enjoying yourself?" Vavelt asked. "You missed out on quite the snowball fight."

He shrugged. "I'll just let you stand under the west eaves and kick a few feet of snow down on you. That should make up for it."

"I don't think you understand the spirit of snowball fights."

"Spirit of winning, though."

She gave him a wry look, and his grin spread wide. "What have you been up to?" she asked.

He turned to take in the breadth of his property for perhaps the thousandth time. "Saying goodbye, I think—for a while—and hello. Really kind of a mixed greeting."

"You'll have more time to get to know it," Faron promised. "After." That was a dangerous line of thinking Faron was veering toward, so Synick changed course.

"I'm thinking I'll add a few things when I get back, or maybe I'll just tell this lot to handle it for me."

"Like what?" from Vavelt.

"Hops," he said. "Do you think they would grow along the warming wall? Let them climb an arbor like cold-weather roses, but roses you can make ale out of?"

"You want to turn this into a distillery?" Faron asked.

"Well, maybe not *turn it into* one so much as *add* one. I could grow hops along the wall if they'll take and blackberries if they don't, then put the hops in the conservatory with wheat, barley, and oats. Maybe I'll make the two of you pay to add another one where the cold garden currently is, then put in some apple trees and grapevines. Lavender might be nice, too, and a space for goats."

"Goats?" Vavelt interrupted. "What could you possibly need goats for in the process of beer-making?"

"I don't stomp into your throne room and tell you how to put down peasant uprisings," Synick grumbled. "Don't tell me how to make beer."

Faron actually chuckled, and Vavelt slapped at his arm again but with a brilliant smile and bright teeth.

"Well," she said, "I'd be interested to see what you could make up here—from a distance, of course, where the smell of the resulting vomit won't waft my way."

"There's no distance," Faron said, "where you'll be safe from Synick's concoctions. They're *unbelievably* foul."

"Nonsense!" Synick defended, hand splayed over his heart. "You're only saying that because, half the time, we drank in a tavern underground, and caves do *not* ventilate well. I seem to remember you being rather fond of cider and salt."

Vavelt was horrified, and Synick kept back a mischievous giggle.

"I said it wasn't as bad as the gravy beer; I *never* said that I

131

was fond of it."

"Uh, what?" Vavelt followed. The giggle slipped out at that. "I think," she went on, "that as my first act as Goddess, I'm going to need to create a few new laws for Aranath—this hilltop specifically."

"That's alright." Synick shrugged. "I can always move production to the sapphire mines." He paused abruptly as an idea struck. "Sapphire wine!" he exclaimed. "I'll make a white wine and dye it blue with ground sapphires!"

"Sapphires," Vavelt groaned, "are mostly corundum, and corundum," she said, "is made of dirt. It tastes like dirt. When ground, it looks like dirt. If you're going to grind sapphires fine enough to remain blue, it'll be like drinking small shards of glass, and you'll be damned if you think you'll get a finder's fee for ground gemstones and blue-glass wine."

"Worth it," he declared. "Definitely trying it now."

"The only way," Faron said, "to make sure Synick actually does something he says he's going to do is by telling him how bad an idea it is."

He nodded. "That's basically nine-tenths the reason I came with you across the Veil. You told me not to."

"And I've regretted it ever since."

"Not me," Vavelt said, pulling both of them under her arms. She sighed. "I'll try whatever poison or potion you come up with. It seems like you could use the attention."

"I could." He nodded vigorously.

"Alright, shut up now," Faron said with a small laugh. "We're going in the morning, so show us around before the sun sets and I'm forced to spend the night here."

Synick smiled, bowed, and commenced showing off the property as it was—and as it would be when they came back.

A Limited Capacity

With a white crown on his head, softened leather and white fur on his frame, and an Ourodurity ring upon his finger, Faron stood above waves of men and women in white and gold metal. Officers, with red sleeves for distinction, stood at the corners of each battalion, marking another hundred soldiers.

Teams of white horses and oxen pulled great carriages on skids, with trails of burly men between them forming long supply lines. Many were wide and uncovered, not unlike a giant sled, and were stacked high with crates, tools, planks of sawn wood, and long metal bars. Others were weighted down with massive iron and copper barrels, Sadagon's cannons and mortars. A few of the carriages were reserved for personal transportation, highly decorated and luxurious. The largest of these was stopped below Faron and Hadria, far enough below as to not impede their view of the gleaming army.

Sadagon stepped up behind them, overlooking his considerable force, and Faron tried not to smell smoke.

He's your father, Faron chastised himself.

"There are few things in this world more sobering than an army, even one under your own control," Sadagon began.

"Especially an army of slaves," Faron cut in. Hadria tensed beside him, sensing another fight, but Faron exhaled softly. It was too much effort to keep hating this man.

Sadagon seemed to sense his regret because he didn't confront the challenge. "Yes," he said instead. "A frightening thing indeed."

The vast fielding ground before them was eerily quiet, filled with as many soldiers as would fit. Not one of them moved an inch. Each plate of armor was polished to an identical brilliance as the one beside it, every soldier inside standing at attention toward the north. The silent parade would have been a beautiful display if it didn't foretell such violence.

"I thought you said you hated cannons," Faron stated, not aggressively but not kind either.

"I do," Sadagon answered. "It is my hope that they will not be needed."

"If they're so awful," Faron began, "why bring them at all? Why not leave them behind?"

"As gods, you will be expected to possess technologies and artifacts outside of modern understanding. We will need to be careful to ensure they do not fall into enemy hands, but they will be a boon to us and are worth the risk. At the very least, the cannons and catapults will put weight to our words," he replied. "If all goes well, the fear of them will help leverage our diplomacy."

"And what if everything doesn't go well?" Faron asked. It was the obvious question, but he wanted to know.

"I have taken steps to limit the damage they can cause," his father said. "Even if we are made to use them, the cannons will remain outside the city walls, where they cannot be found and studied. Of all possible outcomes, that would be the worst. If they are used, it will be in a limited capacity. My flare machine will see to that."

Faron shrugged and let the topic slide, no longer interested in projectiles or explosives. There was too much to worry about already.

"Thank you for being here," Sadagon said, speaking up again. "You, Varek, especially."

"I don't want to be," he answered. "I see this army, and my heart tells me to run."

"In a way, that is a good thing." The statement tore Faron's eyes away from the ocean of armor and weapons in the morning light. "To them, you are a god. Many of them have waited most of their lives for your return and will die for you, given the chance. There are those who would abuse that loyalty, but not you, Varek. You see them for what they are and will not throw their lives away."

Faron wasn't sure how to respond, but he was grateful when Hadria took his hand. "I know," he managed.

"There is nothing left to wait for," Sadagon declared, standing a little straighter. "Your army is ready, and so are you." He gestured down the steep staircase toward the great carriage and its four-horse team. "Go. Lead your army."

Feeling somewhat numb, Faron allowed Hadria to grip his hand and lead him down the staircase. Varan stood there, waiting to open the door for them. Faron nodded awkwardly to the tall man and followed Hadria inside. In the four corners of the interior, there were small phosphorous lamps glowing with a dim inner light that illuminated the plush red of the velvet benches and the perfectly polished blackwood underneath. Wherever there was a hard corner,

135

it was trimmed in gold.

Sitting on the far end of the bench, Synick sat with his legs propped up all the way across to the other side.

"We ready to set off, then?" he said as if he was supposed to be there.

"Synick!" Hadria chastised. "Your carriage is waiting for you only two cars behind."

"Well, yeah," he said. "But if you think I'm going to simply ride alone just so everyone can believe their gods are lonely gits, you're wrong."

Hadria alighted on the bench and settled into it. "Your driver will wonder where you are."

"He thinks I'm walking," he said.

"Walking?" she asked. "All the way out of the city?"

"Nah, of course not. All the way to Anveil."

She huffed. "Well, of course he won't believe that."

"He might, as it was, in fact, his idea. Those weren't the exact words I used—or the exact tone."

Faron groaned and sat on the opposite bench. "I'm assuming you insulted him?"

"I only asked if I could drive, how it felt to have such an easy job, and if he felt at all demeaned by knowing that he possessed no earthly talents and was so utterly replaceable." He wrinkled his nose. "Mostly. There was the bit about his legs—and his mother."

Hadria sighed. "I will smooth things over with him once we've stopped. Of course, you're welcome in my carriage, Synick. Just stay hidden when the door is open. I don't want the common people wondering who is riding with their gods."

Synick grinned. "The real question is: what guards

blundered and let me slip in here undetected? Nothing short of unprofessional."

"Mine," Faron said. "And only because I told them you were liable to try and not to arrest you when you did."

"Well, that's no guarantee that they *did* see me," Synick grumbled, prompting a laugh from Hadria.

"Yes, you're very sneaky, Synick, I'm sure."

He leaned his head back against the bench and smiled, accepting the placation as actual praise. Seconds passed, and the carriage slid into motion, the sudden movement sobering the mood inside. No one spoke as Synick's levity was swept away by the momentum of the events around them. The siege of Anveil had begun.

Faron's breathing increased in pace as his eyes cast about inside the carriage as if it were a cage and he a wolf.

"It's starting."

"It's alright," Hadria's soft voice soothed. "It's alright, Faron."

Closing his eyes, Faron braced himself against the growing weight that bore down on him. Faces stared back from the darkness, dead, hollow, and broken. They would soon be joined by more. He grit his teeth and met the accusing gaze of his victims, as was his responsibility.

"Let's go save Anveil."

The Source of Power

F aron stepped from the warmth of the carriage as the sun went low over the horizon. His back ached from long hours spent in the cramped space, but it was still far preferable to his first journey through the Veil. Chill air washed over him, and for a moment, he was tempted to step back inside; but, he resisted. The initial shock of the cold was always worse for the first few minutes. He'd be fine in a moment.

In the expansive mouth of a narrowing canyon, Faron's army sprawled out before him, pitching massive tents made of fur and leather all across an ice field. For four days, they had followed what was once a wide, twisting river, now a frozen road for the army. It wasn't as direct as a straight shot over the mountains, but the ease of it allowed for the great sleds and trains of resources that followed them, if not quite as fast. At this rate, they would arrive at the city in two or three weeks. That was a terrifying amount of time to be left to think.

Faron stared silently over the camp. It seemed to stretch out as far as he could see.

"Vam Olsu?" a man behind him spoke. "You should not risk your health in a fell wind such as this. Allow it to pass in your carriage. I will see that the snow does not pile around you while your tent is finished warming."

Varan. Faron shivered to hear his voice. How old was he? Six centuries? How many children had this man killed to live such a horrifically long time? Faron wanted to stab him in the heart. He considered doing it, too. What could they do? Varan was supposedly the architect behind his rule, but he was their god. It took his hand reflexively snatching at empty air for him to realize that he didn't have his dagger. He didn't even know where it was. The last time he'd seen it was when he'd surrendered it to the priestess, Valatha.

Faron didn't respond, instead staring bleakly over the encampment. It was a vessel of death, and it would kill in his name. *That couldn't be right*, he thought to himself. Faron was a thief—a lowly criminal—unworthy even among the ranks of Dageran's guild.

How had he come to this?

He fought the compulsion to empty his stomach. It came every time he laid eyes on it—an army of slaves for the purpose of creating more slaves and all in his name. He clenched his eyes shut.

"My lord god?"

"I'll be fine, Varan."

There was a pause, then, "It would be fascinating, were it not so bleak. The world alters its axis, and an age of ice comes for us all. The polar vortex gathers its strength and grows, and you arrive at the cusp of it all, at the absolute last moment, to gather the world into your fold. Divine indeed."

Without turning to look at the man, Faron replied, "You're one of my father's first supporters, Varan, and Atha's and Olsu's before him. You know the farce behind this better

139

than anyone. There's no need to address me like that with no one else listening."

"Indeed, I know it well enough to not call it a farce, my lord god." When Faron didn't prod him to explain, he continued, "What is a god, young ruler? Is it truly a being of power, unseen and ever-present? An intelligence, infinitely powerful, finitely caring, who favors only the strong? Or is it something much more, something far more complicated?"

"Neither," Faron said, finally turning to address his keeper. "There never was or ever will be such a being."

"To beg your pardon, God of Dusk and Light, but you are wrong—but only because you are also correct." Faron waited for him to expound, impatient and already prepared to ignore whatever was said next. A noise from behind alerted him to Hadria and Synick walking up behind them. The shrieking had muffled the sound of the carriage door. He must have roused them when he slipped out.

"In my experience," Synick butted in. "If your argument is so complicated that you have to be right and wrong at the same time, you're usually just wrong."

"Two things can be true at once," Varan said in a way that sounded like an agreement but felt like a rebuttal. "Especially when accounting for nuance."

"Oh, don't bother, Varan," Hadria said. "He's only trying to start an argument with you." She turned to Faron, the last of the sun's pale light falling gently across her shoulders. "Gods exist in the hearts and minds of the people, if nowhere else," she said. "Men are eager to attribute the good and the bad to various beings above themselves. It allows them to ignore their own faults and mistakes or circumstances of birth and assign blame to another. At the same time, it bridges gaps in their understanding, offering explanation where they can't otherwise find it."

"Isn't that just another way of saying that they don't actually exist?" Faron asked, his tone carefully meted.

"Almost," she nodded. "There might not be a god that created the world, but the idea men hold in their hearts is powerful and real. We have but to claim ownership of that idea, and godhood will exist in more than just the imagination of mankind."

Faron frowned, trying to understand. It was difficult to see through his irritation. Synick looked as if he felt the same way, inspecting his fingernails with a longsuffering expression.

"What your sister is trying to explain, Vam Varek Olsu, is that power and authority are nothing but imagined forces, yet they have a greater impact than an eternal winter. A king is only better than a beggar because they both believe it to be true. A headsman only obeys his liege because he believes he should. In reality, there is nothing separating one man from another except the limitations we force on ourselves. It is both real and unreal. Do you understand, my lord ruler? Something may be real without it truly existing. There may not be one god who created everything and watches over all, but the authority and power of such a being is indisputable. All that is required is to fill the role men have laid out for you."

Faron looked back out over the army, trying to feel anything but sick. Perhaps it would be better to feel nothing at all. That thought felt familiar—and dangerous.

"Men *wish* to be ruled, Varek," Hadria expanded. "For millennia, they have created gods where none existed because they *want* someone to rule them, which is how Atha and Olsu first came to power—after slaughtering everyone who opposed them, that is—but still, they could never have invented the image of gods by themselves. They assumed a role already created for them." Hadria took his arm in hers. "That's another reason why we must become gods and not just kings. Men desire to be ruled—*truly* ruled—not just in this life. They crave the freedom of non-accountability—to be free from their agency."

"The goddess speaks truth," Varan said, "and answers the question as well. Gods may not exist in the physical world, but they are a force more real than the sun. You are the recipient of this reality, Olsu Varek. The burden of godhood has rested on your immortal shoulders from the moment of your birth and will for all millennia. It is a very real sacrifice required of you, so I will argue that, yes, you were indeed born a god, a mantle as real as your flesh."

The crying wind occupied the space in the expanding silence.

Still staring out over the encampment of his slaves, Faron finally said, "Has it ever occurred to you, Varan, that if there actually is a god out there somewhere, we'll be damned for this?"

"Yes," he answered solemnly. "It indeed has."

"And you aren't afraid?"

Varan took a moment to consider before replying. "What is a god's greatest tool, Lord Olsu?"

Faron furrowed his brow and didn't answer. This wasn't a topic he had ever given much thought.

"Death," Varan answered for him. "Death is a god's tool—and life after death. By means of punishment on the dead, gods maintain threats on the living. But consider, even if there is a god, Varek, what power does death wield over the undying?"

Faron had never considered himself to be religious, generally seeing the Remembrants as a guild of fools, but this line of questioning was beginning to make him oddly uncomfortable.

"No god can lay claim to the souls of the immortal, young ruler, and that's you. They have no power over you. As such, that tool—the fear of death—now falls to you, to wield as you see fit."

A chill ran down Faron's spine. "This feels wrong," he said.

"Why?" Hadria asked, surprising him. "Do you really believe in a god, Varek?"

"No," he answered honestly. "But it feels wrong."

"Look at the world around us, brother: the suffering, the corruption, the coming calamity. If there *is* a god, she is either powerless to stop what is coming or cruel enough to choose not to. Either way, if we have the ability to take that power and use it for good, isn't it our responsibility to do so?"

"Whatever may await us in the heavens, whatever form of afterlife or gods there may be," Varan added, "we are beyond their reach. As immortals, you answer to no gods and fear no retribution. Whatever power and authority they held is yours now."

Faron cradled his head and massaged his throbbing temples. This was becoming far too philosophical for him to follow. "All that," he said, "to justify calling me a god in private?"

"Is that what we're arguing about?" Hadria questioned. "I

thought I was stepping into a well-meaning debate."

"I believe it would be wise to become accustomed to the practice," Varan confirmed, throwing a look toward Synick, "in the event that we are ever overheard by believers. In any case, I felt it prudent to expound upon the nature of your brother's titles."

"Oh, Varan, you know how it bothers him. At least here, let him be called by name."

"If the both of you insist, then I will, of course, relent, Lady Atha."

"You don't answer to me, Varan," she chastised. "You are sworn to my brother and should have relented when *he* insisted."

The High Archon looked genuinely abashed. He didn't answer right away, instead taking a few moments to peer inward.

"You are right, my lady, Atha. My sincerest apologies," he said to Faron. "I will strive to be more obedient in the future."

Hadria left it at that, turning back to Faron as Varan stepped away. "I'm sorry," she said. "I didn't mean to add to the lecture. I just find the entire idea so very *fascinating*."

"Terrifying is more like it," Synick said, finally speaking. "You two might not fear what comes after death, but that doesn't mean I have the same immunity."

"You?" Hadria asked. "Of all people?"

He smirked. "You don't know what's out there—what happens when we die. Maybe there is a hell."

"Vam Synick," Hadria proclaimed, "Lord of Aranath, thief and occasional assassin by trade, self-proclaimed whoremonger, and now, god-fearing Remembrant. How delightfully contradictory."

Synick smiled. "I'll never pass the chance to start a fight, no matter who I have to fight for, even a git like a god. Besides," he said. "If a god was watching just a moment ago, but not anymore, maybe I'll be due some credit in the end."

"If anyone owes credit, it'll be you, Synick," Faron joked, managing to find a smile, "for all the irritation you've caused the world. If I really were a god, you'd be damned simply for the time you mixed beer with wine."

"That wasn't half as bad as I thought it would be!" Synick defended with a long, dexterous finger extended. "And it's not like I didn't also find milk with mead. I'll be exalted, I'm telling you!"

"Not if I have anything to say about it," Hadria grimaced.

"Wait until you try carrots and gin; then you'll see."

Hadria laughed, and Faron smiled, letting some of the stress melt away. He took in the vision of her, admiring the way her hair caught the westering sun and how the jewels on her sleeve reflected the red light. He stared, letting the warmth of her smile wash over him. He stared because to look away meant looking back at his army. He stared because, without her warmth, the cold tendril of doubt would find him.

He stared because he had to.

Olsu Varek

The deep swirled in a way that elicited patterns one moment, then swallowed them the next. Separate rooms of a massive cave spun into view, only to fall into their own bottomless pits below. Throughout it all was the miserable sound of sobbing—not the crying of a baby or the innocent tears of a child but the mournful howls of the bereaved.

Everywhere Faron looked, he saw cold iron bars, rough, pockmarked, and bit with crystalline lattices of frost. Half-remembered faces scowled in between those bars alongside faces that could never be forgotten: Jakal, broken, bruised, and bleeding, with swollen purple lids; Garad, feeble, cowardly, and trembling; Haka'een, blood spilling into his mouth from a dull iron knife that split his eye, thrashing only inches away on the desert sand as his life ebbed away, his life that Faron stole.

Then there was Jakab'een, Haka's brother, who had died because of him; and Badune'ahl; a masked and veiled guard, who had failed to protect his master; Jaru'tal, whose face was a web of sliced skin and broken shards of glass, who was *Hadria's potential one-day husband.*

The rhythm of the vision grew more violent.

146

He saw two more guards, thrown from a window to crash and break, shatter and rupture upon the palace courtyard in Aru'barrahk.

They all stared at him, but the most vividly remembered weren't the ones who hurt the keenest. He saw the tanner's wife, too, a sickly, thin woman with no gray in her hair despite her apparent age. He never learned her name. He saw the woman Synick had helped him poison. He saw a group of street urchins who he'd located and sent Dageran's thugs after for using his name to survive. He saw Galvin, Clarath, Ulric, a thousand others who, to them, Faron was a byword and a cursed memory. To Faron, they were necessary sacrifices to save himself.

It was their eyes that hurt the most.

Through the bars of the cage Faron had seen countless times in his dreams, he saw his sister. Ever had she been freezing, weeping, and begging for release. Now, in a drastic juxtaposition, she was regal, dressed in the finest fur that could be imagined, draped in velvet and red diamonds with a delicate crown on her head.

He locked his gaze with hers, desperate to hide from the thousand eyes that burrowed into him. So intense was his stare, so all-consuming and terrified, that he only now noticed he was on the wrong side of the bars. The cruel cage that he had imagined for his sister for so many years swallowed *him* now, encircling his freezing frame with iron and ice.

He reached around for his lockpick and lever, but he had no pockets, no boots, or anywhere to find such a tool. Cries and whimpers assailed him from adjacent cages, dying children absorbed in the throes of their misery.

Hadria smiled at him, and he tried to push everything else out. It was alright. It had to be alright—for her. Didn't it? Hadn't he done this for her?

"You found me." Her voice was diminutive and soft.

Tears choked Faron's voice and eyes. He only nodded. The dead faces were still there, circling him from beyond the cage, and they leaned inward, inching ever closer.

"I can't do this," he cried, breath stirring the faint fog that spilled from the growing ice on the bars of his cage, spinning and twirling before disappearing entirely.

"Then come out of there," she said. "Step out of your cage, and come into the light."

"I can't," he answered, tears freezing on the cold iron below him. "I can't get out."

"You can," she insisted. "You only have to let yourself."

He looked around, taking in the wailing children in the cages beside his own.

"Can they come with me?"

She shook her head.

"What will happen to them?"

"Only what you let happen."

Faron shuddered because he knew what he needed to let happen. These were the few that the world depended upon, the few Sadagon's plan required. They were connected, somehow, to the faces that watched him, the weight that bore down on him, the lives that he carried.

"Come out of your cage, Varek," Hadria said. "Come and be with me. You don't need to do this to yourself."

"I'm... I'm Faron," he whispered.

"No."

"Please. Let me be Faron."

"Faron doesn't have the strength to save us," his sister whispered. "You need to become Varek. You need to be Olsu."

He realized then that she wasn't alone. Standing beside her, dressed in furs of his own, was *him*—or, perhaps, a version of himself. He stood with hands clasped behind his back, the way his father did, with hair trimmed perfectly underneath a tall and noble crown. He projected strength in a way that Faron could not, gazing at the children with a sad look but determined. Faron couldn't do that, but this wasn't Faron. This was Olsu Varek, the god he was born to become.

Inside the cage, Faron shrank back, away from the imposing figure. His naked back pressed into the freezing iron of his cage, and it burned. He recoiled with a sharp intake of breath, and the images of Varek and Vavelt collapsed into mist. The comfort and warmth of his sister's presence was suddenly snatched away, and he was left alone as the faces closed in on him.

Screams. They were back. The screams were *back.*

In a rush, Faron woke, head spinning and jaw clenched. Soft furs of various colors surrounded him in his tent of tightly stretched leather. A small fire flickered in an elevated hearth of iron across from padded chairs and a full-length mirror. Trunks of heavy wood held exorbitant furs and clothing for him to wear.

Faron sat up in the bed of animal blankets and down pillows, the scars on his bare chest catching the dim light. He exhaled slowly, purposefully, as the dream slipped away. It had been different this time. Ever had Hadria been the one in the cage and he trying to save her. This was worse.

A rush of bitter cold struck his damp chest as the pins of

149

the door were pulled open, and Varan stepped in. Faron let the wind and flecks of snow wash over him.

"Forgive me, Lord Most High. I had hoped to renew your fire without waking you."

"You didn't wake me," Faron answered, trying not to sound out of breath. He had grown used to the man's pandering tone these past weeks.

"Well then, in that case, I should tell you your presence is humbly requested by your father, though he won't be expecting you for at least an hour."

"Good," Faron grunted, rolling to his feet. "Where are my clothes?" he asked, casting his eyes to the chair where he had draped them the night before.

"With the washmen," Varan replied. "It is unseemly for a king to wear the same apparel more than once in a month, let alone a god such as yourself."

"I'm not a god," Faron replied automatically.

"I most respectfully disagree, my lord," Varan incanted back. It was a nearly scripted interaction between them now. He genuinely seemed incapable of calling Faron by name without at least one title, despite what he had previously agreed to. With a flourish, he opened one of the several chests and withdrew a black velvet, vested tunic with belts below leather lapels. He sighed and donned it. Sharp collars held the brim of his white fur cape in place, warming his neck. Gloves and expensive leather leggings braced him against the sharp wind and ice.

"Did Sadagon say what he wanted?" Faron asked as he finished dressing distastefully.

"Only to speak with you before the army resumes its march."

"Fine. Don't tell me. I'll find out myself." The remnants of his dream pushed his tone to bitterness.

"He is worried for you, Olsu Varek. You are his son."

"Do you have children?"

"Regretfully, it is not my place to rear a child." Faron waited for him to continue. "It is the privilege of very few to raise children among our society."

"You're Sadagon's right hand."

"Yet that blessing falls to others. If everyone were to multiply in a society of immortals, we would quickly be outpaced by the drain on our resources."

"And by resources, you mean blood."

"Even as you say, Lord Olsu."

Faron left the tent. The air outside was bitter cold and dry as well. His vantage from atop the outcrop upon which he was stationed was incredible, thousands of tents encamped on the very same lake of ice he and Synick had come across prior. He wondered if the wolves' corpses were still there.

Also overlooking the clear lake of frozen bubbles and surrounding cliffs was a tent colored gold, black, and scarlet: Sadagon's tent, which served both as his nightly reprieve and his command station. Faron was learning more and more that whenever possible, Sadagon was surprisingly practical. When Faron stepped inside, he found his father in council with five of his generals, all but one white-haired and dressed in command fatigues.

"—catapults to be used as liberally as needed, operated at a distance by the mirror and the red phosphorous, reserving the cannons as only a final resort. Once the wolves are given entrance, there will be no undoing it."

The room fell silent as Faron was noticed. The men turned

151

from their spread maps to acknowledge him.

"Lord of Dusk and Light," one balding man said, falling to a knee with fist pressed to heart, thumb tucked under the index finger. Faron remained silent, and so did they.

"Leave us," Sadagon commanded, and the room cleared. "Thank you," he said once they were alone, "for the fortunate timing. Kaarfane would revise battle plans endlessly if left uninterrupted."

"You wanted to see me."

"Yes, I have something for you—something that I promised you."

"What's that?"

"Proof—and a gift."

"I don't need either," Faron said.

Sadagon looked back at the table. "No, I suppose you don't. Still, I would like to give them to you."

"I'm already here with you, a figurehead for your army that you would use even without me, so what is it that you still want?"

Sadagon looked back up and caught his eye, wearing an expression that suggested Faron had confessed something about himself he had not intended.

"Your trust," he answered with honesty.

Faron hesitated, repressing his reflex to snap at the man. Sadagon *was* his father, even if he was reprehensible.

Slowly, he trusted himself to say, "That does not come easily." Shuffling uncomfortably, he went on, "I already know what you say about the Veil is true. I already know you're my father. What else could you say to earn my trust?"

"It's not a thing I could tell you so much as show you."

Faron thought for a moment. Already, Sadagon had shown

him his proof that the Veil had not always been so large, lecturing him on climate as they passed features that could not exist in a place that had always been frozen. What else was there to see?

"If you are to be a ruler, Varek, there are things you need to understand about human nature and about your history. I ask that you ride a few hours with me for this purpose."

Faron stifled his reaction to decry the entire idea of his rule. He was already here, and that would get him nowhere.

"Will Hadria come with us?"

"No. She is welcome to, but she has made the journey before and will not want to again. You will likely feel the same—as do I."

Faron raised an eyebrow, trying to ignore the stirrings of his emotions. He didn't trust this man, no matter how honest he claimed his intentions were. Part of Faron still wanted to kill him—to put a knife in his belly and ride off with Hadria, never to be seen again. Deeper than that, though, he felt something else, and it shamed him.

He wanted to be *wrong*. He wanted to trust Sadagon, to see his evidences and believe them. He wished he could release his hesitations and accept that whatever Sadagon did was for the greater good.

He wanted a father.

Faron ripped himself from the tent. Eddies of snow spun about him as he rushed away, fleeing the weakness of his emotions.

It isn't too late to break through to her, Faron reminded himself. Hadria was spending more and more time with Synick and had agreed to dissolve the archons, after all. That had to mean she was coming to see things from his perspective, didn't it? If anyone could sway her, it was Synick. That was what he really wanted, he assured himself, to show Hadria that she—that *Sadagon*—was wrong.

To find another way.

Otherwise, it was all for nothing. Otherwise, the weight of the souls he had chosen to carry would all be for nothing.

Faron stopped on his little hill, overlooking the army—*his* army. A hard lump formed in his throat. He didn't feel like he led an army. He felt like a prisoner tied to the back of the wagons to be used in the initial charge.

Wishing to be anywhere else, away from the confusion that assailed him, he felt eyes on his back and breathed deep. A black leather gloved hand fell on his shoulder, and he turned around.

"Three weeks," Sadagon said.

"I don't know what you want to show me, Sadagon," Faron said. "But I don't care to go with you."

Sadagon cut off his protest. "Three weeks I knew you before Baranor murdered your mother and escaped with you and your sister. It was a terrible crime and one that has hurt you more than me, I suspect. But even with that short period and the blessed time that you've been returned to me, I know you well enough to know this isn't about your sister."

Against his weakening will, Faron looked away and nodded.

"You are not like other men," Sadagon said. "You are a man of passion. Despite what you might think about yourself—about what you've been forced to do—you are a man driven by love, not hate. I see it in you—a light that guides you even in the dark."

Faron felt the skin on his arms turn to gooseflesh, water

pricking his eyes as the unexpected validation washed over him.

"You were robbed from me, robbed of the life you should have had, and I failed you in that; but, I will *not* fail you again."

Faron pulled his shoulder out of his father's grasp but didn't flee further.

"You want to trust me," Sadagon whispered, coming a step closer. "I *know* that you do. It's why you can't speak to me—can hardly look at me. It's why the thirst for murder is slipping away from your eyes every day."

"What do you want?" Faron asked. He felt exposed.

"Let me give you a chance to trust me. Let me earn your faith."

"How?" His voice was soft.

"Come with me. Give me this one chance to share this secret with you."

Jaw clenched tight, Faron turned around before Sadagon could see how desperately he wanted this. He couldn't resist his father forever. He hated himself for it, but... he didn't want to. Peering over the tops of the cookfires and tents, Faron gave one brief nod.

"I will ready your horse."

Painful Names

Synick blinked his weary eyes and trudged grudgingly along behind the soldier who had roused him. The sky was pale and dim, the sun not yet risen above the horizon. He shivered. This was always the coldest part of the night—or the morning—however he was meant to think of it. He pulled his snow cloak tighter and shuffled up the hill.

When the last vestiges of his dreams were obliterated by the chill, they came to a stop before a gold and red tent, larger than the others by more than double. He perked up.

Vavelt's tent.

The Alabaster guard—the man who had woken him and a regular soldier by all counts, save the red length of silk tied at his arm—had said something about the gods and how he was needed, but he hadn't been listening. His head was filled with sleep and thick with the previous night's alcohol.

Four men stood guard at the tent's entrance, all Alabaster Guard, and they parted to make room for him. Supposing that indicated he was meant to enter, Synick pulled back the pinned door and slipped inside.

"Took your time waking, as always." Vavelt was inside, alone, and she was giving him a wolfish grin under those bright eyes. Synick returned it. She was lounging across yet another one-armed sofa that some poor fool had to carry all the way here for the purpose.

"I might have had one too many last night," he admitted, closing up the tent flap as he stepped inside. A great bear-skin rug served to keep his boots off the carpets.

"One or twelve."

He shrugged. "I'm getting ahead of the army tomorrow. Just trying to feel ready."

"My thoughts exactly," she suggested.

Synick instantly took her meaning but asked, "What about—"

"Varek's gone," she said, answering his question before it was out of his mouth. "Gone down to Vam Bahr with Father."

Synick took the initiative and hurriedly unclasped his cloak. Vavelt laughed and closed the distance between them, pulling the fur off his shoulders and helping him shrug out of his coat.

"What's Vam Bahr?" he asked, hands binding in the jacket as he squirmed out of it with too much haste and too little finesse.

"Awful," was her answer. The accompanying grimace was telling. "Still, though, it is an opportunity, and there have been precious few of those." She extricated his arms and chest from the last protective layer on his torso, then stopped to appreciate him. The Orodurity branded below his collarbone was identical to Faron's, except for the smooth skin underneath.

"I hate that we have to sneak around," Synick said as he began working the pins on her dress. "Always slinking behind Faron's back."

"Well, we wouldn't have to sneak if you just told him."

"I will," he said, sounding dejected and suddenly tired. "What is with this lacing?" he asked, frustrated fingers trying to find shortcuts in the back of her dress. "How long have you been up that you're already dressed in all this?"

Vavelt laughed. "I have servants for that, normally, and I wasn't about to request your presence while in my slip. That would be like announcing what we're up to with a bullhorn."

He fumbled with the knots. "I've never been more eager to do servant's work in my life." She pulled her braided hair over one shoulder and ran her long fingers through it. It fell apart and unraveled without a single bend or kink.

"For all that, you do seem to be taking your time."

"Wherever Vam Bahr is, I hope it's far, and I hope Faron takes his time. This could be a minute."

Vavelt stiffened, and Synick sensed that he had killed the mood. "I'm sorry," he said, pivoting her around. "Did I say something?" He couldn't help but appreciate how smooth her naked shoulder was or the skin on her neck and nape, but now clearly wasn't the time to mention it. Her expression fell, brow furrowed with thought. She was very much like Faron in that aspect, except when Faron's brow wrinkled, it meant he was trying *not* to think.

"It's that place," she confessed, "and the thought of my father there, and that damn name."

"I'm sorry," Synick said, shivering by the door. "I didn't mean to upset you."

"Of course not." Her expression softened, and she pulled into him, warming his gooseflesh with her half-naked frame—too well dressed for Synick's preference by half.

"It's an evil place," she whispered, "and a herald of what I must do. I'm sorry, Synick, I thought I could keep my mind off it long enough to enjoy a morning with you, but I don't think I can." She pulled back far enough to eye the brand on his chest. "I'm afraid all I can think about is my brother and my father."

Disappointed but not about to make an ass of himself, Synick guided her toward the runner of her bedframe, sitting her down with gentle strength. She gathered her knees in her arms and sat still, deep in thought. Synick sat beside her for a long and quiet moment. It felt wrong to break her silence.

"I'm sorry," she said, shaking her golden head. "I shouldn't let it bother me so."

"Don't be," he insisted, his own blond hair shamed beside hers. "What's bothering you?"

"It's that place," she repeated. "The faces, the forewarning." She shook her head again. "It's an awful place, and I don't want to get into it beyond that."

"And Sadagon is taking Faron there?"

"Yes," she answered. "I wish it weren't necessary, but it is." A silence began to grow in the tent. "Synick?" she asked, dispersing it. "When he gets back, he'll need you."

Synick only nodded, attempting to suffocate the rising tension that threatened to throttle him.

"I worry about him, Synick. I worry what that place will do to him."

"Then why take him there?" he asked, voice prickling. "Why bother at all? Hasn't he already been through enough?" So much for hiding his alarm.

"Yes." Her voice was high and strained, stressed in a way he had only seen once before. Vavelt was far too collected and calculating to let emotions get the better of her. Beyond that, she was powerful, and she knew it; but, the thought of Faron in pain was enough to bend her iron will. Synick understood that.

He didn't push any further. He was being too protective again. Vavelt cared for her brother, too, and he would only hurt her by questioning that. When two trailing tears spilled down her face, Synick wished he could take the outburst back. Why couldn't he have just smiled and lied? Where was his damn mask?

"I'm sorry," he said, honest in the absence of his smile. "I just worry about him."

She shook for a moment as her jaw clenched tight, and the two tears fell alone, no further trace of her emotion forthcoming.

"It's alright," she whispered, pulling herself into him with long, bare arms.

Synick swallowed and looked away.

"I worry for him, too, of course," Vavelt said, "but it isn't for my brother that I'm crying."

That brought his gaze back, and he raised one brow in a quizzical expression.

She shrugged the silent question away. "No more of that. I haven't the room for it." She stood and stretched. "I hadn't planned on showing you quite so early, but I arranged a surprise for you. Will you walk with me?"

Picking up the change of pace, he said, "Not that I'm complaining, but maybe you should get dressed first?"

That brought her smile back, and, still shirtless himself, Synick helped work her lacing back up. A few minutes later, they were both bundled against the cold, with imposing cloaks of white fur and heavy coats. Synick half expected at least one of her guards to flash him a look of, "Already, eh?" but they didn't even crack a smile. Hopefully, that was because they believed his visit to be purely diplomatic.

This time, at least, they would be correct, sadly.

Vavelt led them away from the camp and into the frozen forest behind their elevated tents. It was eerily familiar, and Synick had to resist the urge to feel at his belt for the fire arrows he had once carried there. He wondered if he'd ever be able to outpace the fear and paranoia that had accumulated from his trip across the Veil. He was really about to go back out there?

In the maze of trees, a white figure moved, and it was fast. Synick's heart skipped a beat as he saw the form of a snow wolf, coming straight for them.

"Get back!" he shouted, reaching for his knife. It wasn't there. He cursed, realizing that he *still* hadn't recovered it from the priestess, Valatha. Casting around for a weapon, he found an ancient, dry pine bough across the ground and tried to both reach for it and step in front of Vavelt at the same time, but it was too late. The wolf was on them, and Vavelt was... on her knees?

"Francis!" she called, arms opened wide.

"Francis?" Synick asked, taken aback when the massive thing bounded over. There was no aggression in its stride, only the eager, unmeasurable enthusiasm of an idiot. With blood in its muzzle from a recent kill and red eyes to match, it came to a stop before them and rolled onto its back.

"It's your pet?" Synick exclaimed, jaw agape.

"You can't make *pets* out of dire wolves," Vavelt said, but for all that, she was bent down in the administration of tummy

161

rubs. Synick tried not to think of what the long nails on the paws might do if they clawed at her. It was small for a snow wolf, which meant half again as large as even the biggest dogs, with a jaw that looked like it could bend steel. Still, it seemed more puppy than predator.

"I've been wondering where you were," Vavelt said, scratching behind his ears and playing with fistfuls of long fur. "I haven't seen you since Vam Aranath."

Synick was at a loss for words.

"It's not that odd," she said in reply to his silence.

"Not that odd? Do you have any idea how these things hunted me on my way through the Veil? I couldn't sleep for the fear of them, couldn't get a moment's rest because when they weren't attacking us, they were stalking us, watching with those nasty red eyes."

"You had snow cloaks," she responded. "It can't have been that bad."

He eyed her pet dubiously. "I'm fairly certain it was that bad, actually. Even with the cloaks, we were getting attacked by beasts the size of horses."

"They *rarely* get that big," she said, as if that was supposed to make him feel any better. "Their hearts usually give out before then."

"I don't know about that, but their hearts *did* give out after we lit them on fire."

"That's awful!"

"Tasted awful, too, but they deserved it."

"Synick!"

He grinned.

"Were you really attacked so frequently?"

"Every day for a while, then less so until right before we

162

found the city; then a whole pack came after us."

That made her frown. "You don't actually understand how the cloaks work, do you?"

"Uh, maybe?"

She shook her head. "Synick, you can be so thick sometimes—you and my brother both." She hesitated, then asked, "How large were the wolves you cut your cloaks from?"

Synick shrugged. "About like Francis here. Maybe a bit bigger."

"Francis is a runt," she exclaimed. "He'd never have survived if he hadn't come to Aranath and been fed. You mean to tell me that you cut your cloaks from the smallest wolves you could find?"

"So what?" he asked. "They were the *first* we could find. You'd change your tune if you had any idea what we had to go through to get those pelts."

"Synick," she clarified. "Dire wolves live by an authoritarian system of strength. The weaker make way for the stronger, and the stronger lead. A snow cloak will only ward off wolves that are smaller than the wolf it was cut from."

It took him a moment, and then it dawned on him. "That's why we were only attacked by the bigger ones," he realized, "or the small ones in their packs. When we killed the big bastards, the smaller ones just turned away."

"Because the larger were the leaders, and since your pelt was smaller, they saw you as fair game."

"Damn," Synick breathed. "Ice and snow, that makes so much more sense."

"I can't believe you didn't see that earlier," she said. "Why did you think some wolves left you alone and others didn't?"

He shrugged. "I just thought some were nastier than

others."

"Well, they're animals," she said, "and that's true for all of them. The meaner ones tend to live longer and pass on the trait, and the sweeter ones, like Francis, don't often make it without a bit of help." The wolf rolled over when the scratches stopped and shoved its muzzle into her armpit. She pulled on the tufts behind his ears thoughtlessly.

"Still," she went on, "that's not what happened. The smaller wolves were turned away by the size of your pelt or because there were two of you, and the bigger ones saw you as food."

"What about your cloak?" Synick asked. "It's certainly big but not half so large as some of the monsters out there."

"Perhaps not," she agreed, "but it was *cut* from the biggest of them; and, that's what seems to matter, so long as it's large enough to cover your full back."

"That would have been incredibly convenient to know *before* we set out into the snowing North."

"Don't blame yourself," she said, standing up from her red-eyed companion. "There's no way you could have known. The fact that Varek learned of the cloaks at all is a miracle, and at least you know now."

Synick agreed, thinking of the distance he was about to travel on his own, but he said nothing.

"Come with me," Vavelt said. "It's not much farther."

They continued on through the trees, together with the snow wolf. It was unnerving to have him following beside them and more than a little surreal. On the ground, there was a set of several tracks that they followed, perhaps the first human tracks in this forest for hundreds of years. It wasn't much longer before Synick began to see a light from inside the depths of the trees.

He gave Vavelt a questioning look, and she returned a small smile, then kept trudging ahead. The light grew brighter, and they came upon a natural break in the pines. A small, almost perfectly circular clearing opened up around a single dead deciduous tree—black walnut? Its gray, lifeless branches were a stark and foreign thing in this sea of narrow pines and needles, a memorial to the life that once existed here.

On the branches of the ancient wooden carcass hung dozens of glowing phosphorous orbs, suspended in little strand nets. They were lit at a dim burn, with barely enough oxygen to ignite, and together they cast the dead tree into a shadowless, ethereal exposure. A thin fog, drifting lazily through the branches, wrapped around the trunk, catching and encasing the soft ethereal glow.

Alone, in the depths of the forest, it was the most unexpectedly beautiful thing Synick had ever seen. Vavelt watched him as he stared, caught up in the sudden beauty of such a lovely thing where it shouldn't have been.

"Do you like it?"

Synick didn't know how to answer. When it became apparent that he wasn't going to, Vavelt spoke again.

"I couldn't sleep last night and went for a walk through the trees. When I found this clearing, I…" She hesitated. "I wanted to share it with you—for it to belong not just to myself but to us."

Synick imagined her haunting the forest in the dead of night, walking alone under the trees, with the brilliance of a phosphorus lantern to stretch and cast the shadows all around her. She must have cut quite the image.

"It's wonderful," he finally said. He wasn't sure why, but something about the rarity and unexpected nature of the tree made his eyes sting. Something about how Vavelt had thought of him when she saw it made them sting more. "Thank you," he said, "for showing me."

Her eyes took on that piercing quality for a moment as she sifted through the emotion that he allowed to play across his face, then she pulled his face to hers as the tears began to escape and kissed him.

Suddenly overpowered and entirely out of control, Synick kissed her back. His hands found no struggle with the lacing of her dress this time, and hers were just as eager, just as full of compounding need and desperate finesse. Her skin flushed with gooseflesh as it was set free—but not from the cold. Her heart thrummed against his, and, with cloaks of white fur for blankets, the snow that would cover the world became their bed.

White Grave

They rode atop monstrously large white stallions, with gold and white blinders and deep black saddles. As always, the horses' flanks were covered in long, white furs. Sadagon had taken him alone, much to Varan's discomfort, and they rode mostly in silence after Sadagon's broken attempts to make conversation. Over hills and steep valleys, they traveled, ancient carcasses of long-frozen deciduous trees passing by on both sides. Around the slope of a mountain, they led the horses carefully until Sadagon brought them to a stop.

"There. Do you see it?"

It took a moment for Faron's eyes to catch what he meant. "Walls," he said in surprise. "And towers."

"A snow wall—one of the first ever erected."

"This is what you brought me to see?"

He nodded, seeming to become more tense the closer they got.

Though buried, Faron realized they had been following a path, mostly destroyed but recognizable. It led around to a crumbled gate of stone and frozen iron, their horses barely fitting under what was once a massive arch. The snow had piled high over an indeterminable period of time, and the ice under the snow was clear and blue.

"What is this place?"

"It was Vam Bahr in its prime and White Grave for nearly a hundred years after. Now it is forgotten."

"It's above the Veil."

"Now, yes. Centuries ago, it was green and full of life, though few now live who remember it. It is a place of monsters now."

"What happened?"

"Let me show you."

In the shadow of the fallen walls of Vam Bahr, Sadagon led Faron into the once-city. A now headless statue of a pike-wielding horseman stood atop a high unfallen wall, watching over them near a sloughed hill of stone bricks that had once been a majestic belfry. A broken and cracked iron bell lay on its side atop the ruinous pile, cankered with rust and forever unringing.

Further inside the gate, they were quickly met with a grisly sight. The interior of the wall was lined with massive stakes, most of which had long since snapped or been chewed away, but many stood erect, bearing ancient, skewered skeletons aloft. All of it was covered in drifts, mounds, and great heaps of snow and ice.

Sadagon rode underneath them without sparing a glance and made his way down what might have once been a bustling street. The tops of houses emerged from the ice, ancient roofs long collapsed. Faron followed, the impaled skeletons watching him from their high perches. It was little different than the faces that watched him from the dark.

"What happened here?" he whispered.

"Fear," Sadagon answered, "and hate." He guided his horse

around a particularly large mound. "After the death of the gods, I thought I had freed mankind. I freed them from their forced warfare fueled by Olsu's and Atha's bloodlust. I paid dearly for that victory."

"And this city rebelled?"

"No. I had nothing to do with what happened here. When Vam Aranath fell, I could not leave. A city newly freed does not fare well without guidance. I couldn't leave behind the Life Spile either. It was years before I could extricate myself and trust the city to Varan. In truth, I did not fully trust him then. By the time I did, it was too late."

"Why?"

"The Veil had always come to the very edge of Vam Bahr. It was the gate city to Vam Aranath, placed as high north as possible. We knew it was coming closer, but the elders of the city claimed they knew it to be a cycle. The Veil would come close for a few summers, then recede once more. When the summer Veil came right up to the snow wall, they said it would turn back. The next year, it covered half the city. They said it would turn back. The year after that, the Veil never left. By the time a consensus was formed to abandon the city, it was too late."

"Were there no messengers?" Faron asked. "Could they not have asked for aid?"

"South but not north. The rebellion struck Vam Bahr hard. Any priests, archons, or representatives of the church were strung up and executed the very first day. There were none remaining who knew our secret of travel."

"The snow cloaks."

"Yes. We kept them secret, even after the death of the gods—better to keep men away from each other's throats by

169

not allowing armies to siege one another through the winter. Despite this, messengers braved the land south, desperate to request shelter and an escorting army from Anveil. Some messengers made it. Others were torn apart by the dire wolves."

"Did Anveil send the army?"

"They did." Sadagon stopped his brilliant white horse and dismounted. "And once inside the walls, they ravaged the city."

Faron pulled his mount to a stop.

"There was no wood left to burn, no food left to eat. These people were starving and emaciated, and Anveil cut them down to the last child. When the slaughter was finished, they broke down sections of the snow wall just in case there was anyone left alive."

"No," Faron whispered. That couldn't be true.

Sadagon bent to his knees and began brushing drifts away with his hands, clearing long sweeps of glassy ice with each stroke. Faron dismounted, too, but remained standing.

"When I returned from the God City, this is what I found."

Trapped in the crystal ice lay a tangled mass of skeletons and half-decomposed corpses. The necrotic gaze of the damned peered out, as if angry, pinning Faron in place.

Screams.

Faron realized with a cough that he had been wrong. The watchful skeletons were nothing like the faces in his mind. *These* were his nightmares made manifest—the haunting dead, lingering to glare holes into his soul, entrapped where they could see out, waiting long eternities to find him.

I didn't kill you! Faron practically shrieked in his mind. *I didn't do this to you!*

Sadagon cleared one section after another in broad sweeps, revealing more and more bodies entombed in the ice. Faron gasped as he realized the mounded road was not piled nearly to the rooftops with snow but with corpses. They stood on a street of bones.

"Anveil?" Faron spat furiously, fighting his dimming vision. "They did this?"

"Their ancestors, yes."

"There are children under there."

"And women. Young and old, no one was spared."

"Why?" Faron asked in disbelief, fighting the bile that rose from his stomach.

"During the false gods' reign, Vam Bahr was an honored city, blessed with gold and jewels, food and slaves—Anveil slaves. By the will of Atha, one-fiftieth the children of Anveil were indentured to Vam Bahr to serve the will of the gods. When the armies came, they reclaimed the few of their children who had not been sapped of their blood and pillaged the city. With no gods to control them, it was a matter of only a few years to raise an army and wage war to reclaim what was theirs. When they learned Vam Bahr had no way to defend itself, they came immediately."

"These people weren't responsible for killing those children," Faron cried. "They murdered the archons who were."

"Hatred is not discerning, especially when it is earned."

Faron shook his head. "Snow cloaks. Could you not have told them how to travel the Veil?"

Sadagon shook his head sadly. "A secret then as they are now—a birthright of the gods."

"You could have told them. You could have saved them."

Sadagon said nothing.

"Why would you not tell them?" Faron pried.

"And allow the entire world to engage in long-term sieges throughout the winter as well as the other seasons? Anveil marched through the utmost edge of the Veil and still lost considerable numbers to the dire wolves, despite their force. Can you imagine the tenacity of human hatred if they were free to kill each other without fear of the wolves? The loss of this city cut me to the very core, but it would be a flake in the blizzard compared to the death that men could bring if freed from the shackles of snow."

"That isn't your right to decide."

"No," Sadagon agreed. "It is yours, and for centuries, I have made it in your stead."

"I would have saved them," Faron spat.

"I know. I'm not sure I could have restrained myself from doing the same if I'd had the choice. Don't forget that I knew nothing of this until it was long done."

Faron clenched his jaw. Why should he feel so heated for the long dead? He had not known them, yet still, he felt a fury at the injustice wrought here.

"How could anyone do this?" Faron asked into the air.

"A hundred reasons," Sadagon answered unexpectedly. "A thousand. You yourself have killed to reclaim one you love, but those are only two reasons—to protect and to avenge. There are countless others."

"But to slaughter an entire city? Men and women who only obeyed their gods?"

"Agency drives men to dark things. Vam Bahr was the first city Anveil slaughtered, but it was not the last. When the Veil continued to grow and Kearth and her villages became threatened, Anveil didn't even wait for the snow to swallow them. They sent an army to sweep them away when the first messenger was sent for aid."

"Why?" Faron asked, incredulous. "What grudge could they possibly hold against yet another city?"

"No grudge—fear. As the Veil expanded, Anveil's winters came sooner and stayed longer. Their crops dwindled, and their armies shrank. If an opposing army came to them first, they might not resist them."

"They slaughtered an entire city for what they *might* have done?"

"This is what men do when left to their own fears and devices."

"They could have offered asylum! Assimilated them into the city."

"Yes." Sadagon's voice was clipped. "And now the Veil has grown so far as to threaten Anveil with the ruin it brought to cities now forgotten. Once, their summers were long and their reach far, but that is long past. Anveil lacks the strength it once had. Now winter is consuming them, and it is their turn to be slaughtered by their neighbors who fear for their own lives and diminishing crops."

"No," Faron replied. "That can't happen."

"It must never happen again." Sadagon's voice was suddenly honed with a metal edge. "This is your purpose, Varek. Stop the wars of survival and fear. Teach them to endure the coming winter, and all without giving them the means to destroy themselves."

Faron was silent for a long moment. "I don't want to be a god," he whispered.

"I know." Sadagon stood behind him and placed comforting hands on his shoulder. He allowed it, eyes locked with the desecrated dead. "It is a terrible burden to bear and not one anyone should have to endure, but that is your legacy. You are the grandson of both Atha and Olsu. This is why you were born."

"What if they don't accept me?"

"They will, one city after another, until the entire world is safe under your protection."

"And what if they don't?"

"Then Anveil will be lost, a sacrifice required to spare the world from the fate of this city."

Faron grimaced, looking away from the dead faces. "I've seen enough."

"No, you haven't." Sadagon released his shoulder and gestured for Faron to follow. Hesitantly, he looked away from the woman's half-decomposed face that held his eyes so firmly and followed. Would she haunt his nightmares, too?

Off the road rose a small hill, the south side of which was steep and barely touched by the snow. At its base was a set of half-swallowed stairs leading up to a stone doorway, a winged woman and climbing roses carved masterfully across the breadth of it. Pillars held up a triangular headstone, marking the hill as a place of internment, and beside the pillars was a chain of steel that shone nearly as bright as silver.

"Where are we?" Faron asked nervously. Sadagon had fallen into a tense quiet. He didn't answer, instead reaching up and pulling on the chain with a heavy hand. After an initial jolt, it pulled easily, and the door opened with creeping slowness. A stale wind rushed from the opening and drowned Faron in the scent of dust and damp. It faded

174

after only a moment.

When the door opened completely, Faron could see carved steps leading down, quickly disappearing in darkness. Sadagon held aloft a small orb lamp that sparked and fizzed with the same cold light as Synick's fire arrows except brighter. It seemed to burn the very air, casting sharp shadows but lighting the staircase well. They didn't have far to go.

Following Sadagon, Faron descended the twelve steps and found himself facing an eyeless statue at the far side of a low-ceilinged room. It was a man's form, thin and hooded with stone eagle-feather wings. It held, by a chain, a radiant eye that seemed to emit bright streaks of light in all directions like the ones in the Vam Aranath mausoleum.

Adjacent to the statue on both sides of the room lay two stone sarcophagi, delicately gilded and beautifully carved.

"When I returned, I found them slaughtered with the others. I wasn't here to protect them." Tears brimmed in his eyes.

"Who?" Faron dared ask.

"My wife," he answered with solemnity. "My son, who I abandoned to the Veil."

"This was your home?" Faron asked in shock.

Sadagon breathed deep. "When I wasn't off for years at a time assassinating dissidents for my parent-gods, I was here, living in secret with a family that was forbidden me. I had this place built for them, to honor their memory and remember my failure."

He placed his palms on the sarcophagus on the left, a long-dead array of flowers perfectly preserved at its base, yellow and withered.

"They raped her before they killed her. I wasn't here to stop them. They had no reason not to—no humanity to persuade them, no afterlife to compel them."

"I... I'm sorry."

Tears flowed freely down Sadagon's stony face. "I know. You are many things, Varek, but not needlessly cruel or uncaring." Choked gasps escaped him, and his shoulders shook.

Slowly, awkwardly, Faron placed a gloved hand atop his father's shoulder. Sadagon seized it immediately and kissed it before pulling it against his cheek.

"What was her name?"

"Her name was one of several things Baranor stole from me—to wound me in his spite. It is there."

Faron leaned forward and read the name in shock.

"Hadria?"

"She was my wife, and I miss her still."

Faron sat in dumbfounded silence as a missing piece of his understanding clicked into place. "Her..." He swallowed. "Is that why...?"

"Why your sister is offended when you call her that? Yes. She is protective of me."

Faron processed this in silence. "Does that mean that my name... Faron?"

"Is the name of my son, your half-brother, and he has been dead for three hundred years—a name given to you to cause me lasting anguish."

Faron staggered back to the adjacent coffin, and sure enough, carved deep into the ancient stone was his own name, covered in dust and cobwebs. Seeing it gave him a strange feeling of disassociated dread.

Another feeling, unfamiliar and rare, pulled at him. The fatherly image Faron held of Bouren began to fade. Faron knew without doubt that Bouren—Baranor—was not his father, but the reality of what he'd done was finally sinking in. Faron felt the skin tighten around his eye as a corner of his vision went dark, but something changed. The black spot evaporated and faded away. The charred skull that haunted him wasn't there, as if its power over him had been diminished by the two names carved into a tomb in the side of a south-facing hill.

Bouren was dead, and with that death, something else was born—something new. As the images of his old father slipped away, Faron began to accept that Sadagon was his father, in love as much as blood.

And he forgave him.

"I show you this not to persuade you to give up the name," Sadagon spoke through his pain. "I understand that it is part of who you are now. I show you so you might understand the history that brought you here and believe my conviction to do what is right, no matter the cost. I brought you here to see that you are my son. I know you have doubted this fiercely, wished against it even, so I offer this proof that you may know my sincerity." He opened his hopeful arms to receive him in an embrace. "And I love you terribly."

His own tears welling, Faron fell into his father. For just a moment, a fractional pause in time, Faron didn't pull away, and he let himself forget the pain. The weight of a literal world slipped off his shoulders, and he forgot about the fates of the millions that depended on him, the men who were very likely about to die, the uncounted slaves with no savior. For a brief moment, he let it all slip away and allowed himself to simply feel the comfort of a family.

His shoulders shook as he was wracked with choking tears, not of sadness but relief, the way a man cries in a desert when he stumbles upon an oasis. For only a moment, he set aside his hatred and let himself be comforted by a father.

"Do you see, Varek," Sadagon said, "the harsh truth of the world? There is evil in the hearts of men. They hurt and slaughter each other instead of working together, inflaming issues when they could solve them. Do you see the truth I aim to prevent? This is what drives me, Varek: to save others from my fate—my family's fate. Can you see why I must go through with this, regardless of the price? Can you see what we must do?"

Faron choked on his tears. "I understand now."

Sadagon seemed almost taken aback. "I am not alone, my son. I am not the first man to lose his family to hatred or fear. If I do nothing, there will be death and destruction sown again. Anveil, Murcosta, Empyrion, Fayevew, Sycele—everything will come to an end eventually. First, Anveil, as they flee the Veil, then others will follow. Men and women, children and infants—all will come to the sword or the tooth in the end, or the frost. Widows will be made without need; orphans will starve. Cities will crumble before the growing winter—needlessly, Varek. I can end this cycle. I can save countless lives. There are untold millions who need salvation, born and yet unborn. I can save them, Varek. *You* can *save them*."

Tears still fell from Sadagon's eyes, stronger now than before, but it did not distort his face. "I know you have survived the cruelest evils. I understand what was done to you and how it has forged you. I know how you must see

178

me—a swallower of souls—but I have to ask you, my son—to *beg* you—will you help me to protect the children of my family's murderers? Will you help me to protect the world from the coming snow? To protect the good from the evil and the evil from themselves? I beg you, my son, will you do what is right, no matter the wrong, to *save* this world? I *vow* to honor the sacrifices that will be made, but I cannot do it alone. I beg you, Varek, will you help me?"

Faron—Varek—wiped his own eyes as the only certainty remaining to him was stolen away.

"Yes."

Tenderly, Sadagon pulled him into a second embrace. "My son, you have died twice and come back from death, but today is the day you are truly restored to me." He buried his face in his son's hair, and Varek allowed it.

Sadagon's Herald

"Are you sure you want to do this?" The question was posed innocently enough, but Synick could sense the apprehension that Vavelt hid. Snow cloak or no snow cloak, she was worried. Faron was, too, but in his own quiet way.

When he returned from Vam Bahr, Faron hadn't been the wretch Vavelt had prepared him for, but neither was he whole. He fidgeted nervously, and Synick would bet his soul that he hadn't slept last night. Synick set his jaw. Faron was safe here, even if he'd finally resolved to let himself be called Varek, and he'd be fine without Synick. Jesika, though? She could die without him.

"I'm sure I don't want to let one of your men do it for me," Synick answered, "and that I owe this much at least to Jesika and Artur, too, if he'll come." He spoke while tightening the straps on the saddle. The huge white horse below it rolled one big red eye at him, but Synick ignored him. It might look like a snowbeast, but unlike the wolves and other white things out there, this creature didn't eat meat.

The one convenient aspect of traveling the Veil was that he didn't need to bother with massive waterskins and could instead carry greater supplies of food with him, including a large bag of white ice lily bulbs for the horse. That was good because if he could keep it fed, he could ignore the nagging feeling that maybe *this* horse *did* eat meat. Among Synick's few less-charming qualities was the fact that he was made of meat.

He packed another bag of feed.

"I'm not asking for you to let my men do it on your behalf. I'm only asking you to let them go with you."

"They'll only slow me down," Synick objected.

Faron spoke up. "That isn't true. If anything, you'll slow them down. You're really not much of a rider."

"You're one to talk!" Synick replied.

"Maybe I'm worse," Faron admitted, "but the point is, they have more experience riding through the Veil. They won't slow you down. Synick, it's stupid to go alone."

"Didn't stop you," he grumbled.

"No, you did, and now I'm stopping you. They're going with you, Synick, so stop complaining."

Synick had no intention to stop complaining, but before he could make that known, another person came up from behind. Synick turned to see whose heel was crunching the snow underfoot and saw Sadagon standing there with a large tan bundle in his arms. He swallowed. Synick had hoped to slink out without confronting this man.

"I assume," Sadagon said, shifting the wrappings to reveal an armful of gleaming weaponry, "you would like to have these back?"

Synick perked up, hiding away the nervousness he felt at his involvement with the man's daughter. His expression became truer when he recognized his throwing knives in that bundle.

With his treacherous emotions tucked safely away behind a smile, he said, "I've been wondering where these ended up! You would be right."

Sadagon placed the bundle on the edge of a huge, flat sled. Soon it would be piled high with tents, tables, chairs, and chests, but for now, it was empty. From within the resulting pile, he lifted the belt of knives.

"The priestess, Valatha, said you managed to slip these past her guards. I don't know if that's a testament to your resourcefulness or the ineptitude of my men." He handed them over. "Either way, I thank you for not using them."

Synick returned a sheepish grin. "No reason it can't be both." He fingered through the blade handles to be sure each knife was where he'd left it.

Sadagon chuckled. "I suppose not." Next, he hefted Faron's metal-frame crossbow and pushed it into Synick's arms.

"Wait a moment," Synick objected. "This isn't mine."

Faron shook his head. "Take it. You'll need it more than me out there."

"Fate willing," Vavelt said, "you'll never have a use for it again."

Faron shrugged, and Sadagon nodded his agreement with one terse bob of the head.

"I also," Sadagon resumed, "took the liberty of fetching some quarrels for you." He lifted a quiver full of crossbow bolts. Thick, broad blades adorned the heads, with wicked curves for the severing of tendon and nerve. The sight of them made Synick's brows rise. "Wolf heads," Sadagon said, "should you run across anything not afraid of that cloak. Heads like these are ordinarily reserved for proper bows, but that spring-fired metal crossbow has an extraordinarily heavy draw."

Vavelt rolled her eyes. "You and your weapons. You're like a boy with wooden swords."

"So were you once," Faron cut in. His grin split his face now. "I didn't go a single day without collecting a few bruises."

"You probably deserved it," Synick said. Vavelt nodded her agreement. Synick turned to Sadagon. "Thank you," he said. "I hope I don't have to use them, but... well, I kind of hope I'll use them at the same time."

Sadagon's face brimmed with the biggest smile Synick had ever seen from him. "I know exactly how you feel." When he finished admiring the razor barbs, he handed them over.

Synick reached out to accept them. The movement shifted the crossbow to the side, and it fell. With a small shriek, Vavelt reached out and caught it by the bow.

Faron grinned, though he tried to hide it, and Sadagon laughed. "Let me lend you a hand." Turning from the pile on the sled, he unaffixed the clasps at Synick's neck and removed the snow cloak from his back.

Faron spun his head around, the blood draining from his face.

"He's fine!" Vavelt protested. "There are no wolves in the middle of camp, and we all have cloaks."

"Still," Sadagon reaffirmed. "Best to hurry." He let Faron hold the cloak, then took the metal lever bow and slung it across the saddle's pommel. "There," he said. "Now get those on properly."

Synick didn't need to be told twice. He threw the knife belt over one shoulder and the quiver over the other, then lowered it until it was at waist height on his back. Sadagon nodded approvingly when he tightened the cross straps to secure it in place. Taking the cloak back from Faron, he pinned it into place at Synick's back, and Faron finally took in a breath.

Vavelt gave him a small frown and took up his arm in hers. "Father," she said. "Don't you have something that *isn't* a weapon to give him?"

"I do," her father replied. The grinning hobbyist disappeared, and the stoic ruler resumed his place. From the pile, he withdrew a glass orb like the ones hanging from the corpse of the dead tree in the middle of the sleeping forest. Synick stifled a cough in his throat and looked to Vavelt. It was plain to see that she was also thinking of that moment they had shared together under the glowing branches of that ancient tree. Synick caught his momentary lapse in concentration and plastered the smile back across his face.

"A gift for you," Sadagon said.

Synick cleared his throat. "I still can't believe that you use flash stone for something so common as lanterns."

Sadagon smiled. "It's phosphorous, but yes. I'm surprised you know what it is at all, by any name."

"I worked under a glass smith for a short while, and he kept some of it around. Faron—er—" He cast his eyes to look at Faron, who was beginning to shuffle uncomfortably. "Varek and I used some with lamp oil to fight off packs of wolves on the way here. It's fantastic stuff. Are these lamps ever-burning?" he asked.

Sadagon's smile cooled to a disturbed frown. "Already, phosphorous weapons are returning and spring-fired crossbows, too? Warfare has accelerated faster than I had hoped. If we're already here, then flintlocks won't be far off either... and cannons."

Vavelt left Synick's side and was by her father in a moment. "It's not so bad as that," she said. "They aren't yet common-place. Synick rediscovered the phosphorous arrows himself." She turned to face Synick. "Isn't that right, brother?" She paused.

Faron nodded. "A stroke of genius, really." He and Synick shared a look, and Synick knew that he was thinking of Orothorn and his glass forge. He had helped perfect the fire ampoules before they left and had promised to make more with the intention of selling them. Neither of them said anything.

"I doubt that others have found them yet," Vavelt said, filling the silence. "Warfare isn't so advanced as that."

Sadagon nodded. "I hope that is the case, else our catapults and cannons won't be the overwhelming advantage we need them to be."

Synick arched a high brow. "What exactly is a cannon?" he asked.

That brought the heavy silence back, and once again, Vavelt rushed to fill it.

"Great projectile weapons made all of metal." She dropped Faron's arm to put a comforting palm on her father's chest. "He's worried because they have the capacity to knock down snow walls or anything else that might stand before them. They've been lost to the world since the rise of the Twinborn millennia ago, but if they were to return..."

It was Sadagon who picked up as her voice trailed away. "It would be nothing short of a world-ending event, a cataclysm more dangerous than even the growing Veil."

Faron had grown pale. Synick eyed him with low brows. He was often quiet, but the silence he exuded now was nothing short of traumatic. He was remembering something unpleasant, and Synick expected it had something to do with the trip he'd taken with Sadagon the day before. He dropped the subject.

"That lamp," he said, bringing the topic back to the point where it had been derailed. "Is it ever-burning?"

"No," Sadagon answered. "But it is telling that you ask. What gave you such an idea?"

"Because I tried to make one," he replied. "At the glass forge, I tried to seal it away and make an ever-burning lamp but couldn't get the damn things to light up once the glass was sealed."

Lifting his hand to display the orb, Faron's father twisted it, revealing two seamless halves, and it burst into brilliant, harsh light.

"The trick," he said, "isn't to seal the phosphorous away but to leave a small gap to let oxygen in to burn. The more oxygen, combined with more phosphorous, the brighter it becomes." He twisted the orb again, and the light flickered before going out entirely. "Then cut it off when you have no more need of it or if it begins to burn hot."

"That's... *really* bright," Synick said in awe. "Much brighter than the stuff I had."

Vavelt giggled at something, but her mirth was lost on Synick.

"It's more pure," Sadagon replied. "Refined from wolf jaws. I assume the phosphorous you're accustomed to is processed from aged urine?"

"I, uh—" Synick's face screwed up. "Oh gods, I hope that's not true."

Vavelt choked on a laugh, her bright eyes extracting every

ounce of his discomfort. Synick's face was one of disgust, but even it fell when he noticed that Faron wasn't joining in to capitalize on his discomfort. His eyes were far away, and he looked like he might be sick.

Sadagon saw it, too, following Synick's gaze, and the levity evaporated.

"In any case," he went on. "It isn't an 'ever-burning lamp,' as you put it. The phosphorous reacts with the air and burns at the contact. It will run out eventually, and you'll be left with nothing but a smoke-stained orb; so, try not to use it unless you have to." With that, he handed the orb over.

Synick frowned. "Sounds like a pretty useless lamp then, if you can't use it much."

"It's not for lighting your way," Sadagon explained. "You have oil for that. It is to keep the wolves at bay. The white light hurts their red albino eyes, and they fear it like fire."

Synick nodded, comforted by this new possibility. "Thank you," he said. "Truly. It's a wonderful gift."

"It's the absolute least I can do. You're doing me a service, even as you serve your own interest."

Synick didn't respond, too busy staring into the fine cuts along the sides of the glass sphere. He looked up when Sadagon pointed out a small, bulbous pouch attached to the saddle. "It may be safely stored here," he said, indicating that Synick should put it away. With only a slight reluctance, he did. "There is enough in this lamp to burn low for a week. Leave it on when you sleep, and know that the wolves will not seek you out."

That was a great comfort, and Synick breathed easier.

Sadagon paid his son another long look as Vavelt turned away from him and whispered softly into Faron's ear, holding him as if he might fall at any moment.

"There is one thing I need from you, Vam Synick."

Synick arched a brow, looking between Vavelt, who returned to her father's arm, and Sadagon. "What's that?"

"These lanterns are a powerful tool of deception. I give you one to aid in your journey but also to grant you legitimacy." He glanced at Faron again. "We must do everything in our power to ensure that Anveil will be safe. For that, I want you to deliver a message for me."

That caught Faron's attention. He looked up finally and seemed to notice that Vavelt was whispering to him.

"Me?" Synick asked. "Why not one of your men?"

"I believe you are more suited for the task."

"Hear him, Synick," Vavelt urged.

"What message?"

"Take the lantern to the governors' keep, and warn them that we're coming. Tell them of my army and weaponry. Give them time to ruminate in fear and fight amongst themselves. When we arrive, they will be ready to surrender."

Synick cast a glance to Faron, and he gave one brief nod.

"Alright," he agreed. "I'll do it, and then I'm going to get my friends out."

"Very well. If your message has the desired effect, you will save everyone in Anveil, not only your friends, but take care that my cloaks are not discovered by any but who you bring with you to my camp."

"I'll do it," he said with a resigned nod.

"Thank you, Vam Synick. Go in my name, as my herald. Tell them the Twinborn Gods are born again, and they come with fire, cannons, and ten thousand men for their thrones."

"Thank you, Synick," Vavelt said.

Faron finally seemed to regain a little strength, and he used it to step forward and pull Synick into a weak hug.

"Be careful," was all he said.

Synick gave him a fortifying grin. "I've got your crossbow for that." He looked at Vavelt, who was looking at him, too. He felt the tugging inside himself, the urge to pull her into a deep embrace and run his fingers through her hair, but... this wasn't the time—not where they could be seen. Swallowing his want, he gave her a brief nod.

"I need to go," he said.

Vavelt stepped closer, and it made his heart skip a beat. "First," she said, "I have something for you, too." She reached into a pocket sewn into her snow cloak and withdrew a small black velvet pouch. Synick frowned as he extended a palm to take it. She set it down with a small 'clink' that made his brows rise.

She puffed out a laugh through her nose and smiled with her lips pressed together. Tugging on the drawstrings, Synick looked inside to see several large sapphires, cut and reflective beyond the quality of any he'd ever seen. He sucked in a sharp breath.

"From your estate," she explained with a grin. "That you might remember what waits for you back home."

That hit like a hammer in his gut. *Home.* Synick clenched his teeth to suppress his emotions and wondered where on earth his smiling mask had gone. His fingers turned white as he gripped the pouch tight.

"You and your rocks," she said with a delighted smile and earnest cadence.

Synick tore his eyes away from Vavelt. "Thank you," he muttered, beginning to feel exposed and observed.

"Go now," Sadagon said. "Carry my message, and warn those you love."

With no rebuttal or parting quip, Synick climbed into the saddle and tugged on the reigns. The large horse began to turn, but suddenly, Sadagon caught the reigns.

"Wait," he said, then moved back to the sled. "This belongs to you."

Synick glanced down to see his dagger in the polished black sheath. "My knife!" he exclaimed. He drew it out to see the wide serrations on the lower back that served as blade-catchers, should the need ever arise. The deep prongs were all still intact, testifying to how little they'd actually been used. The wolf blood had been cleaned from it, and it gleamed with a new polish.

"Thank you!" he said, genuine delight overcoming the hard lump in his throat. "I can't believe I almost left without asking after it."

"The lapse in judgement can be forgiven, considering the manner of your departure."

Synick buckled the stiletto dagger and sheath onto his belt, happy to be reunited.

"Now go with my blessing," Sadagon Pyre commanded as he stepped back. "And my thanks. The lives you save may forever go uncounted, but know that you will have our undying gratitude."

Clutching the sapphires to his chest and speaking volumes with quiet eye contact between Faron and Vavelt, Synick swallowed hard and turned the horse around, then spurred it forward and didn't look back. He ignored the soldiers that were to be his guard as they fell in line behind him and tried not to think about just how literally Sadagon meant those last two words.

Prayers or Pitch

Three days in the Veil brought Synick and his company back to the shadow of Anveil's snow wall, a black and imposing structure that stood a hundred feet into the air. It rimmed all the base of the lonely mountain like a picket fence around a tall cottage. High above the wall, the peaks of the mountain city towered, packed to the brim with bustling people and neatly organized stone houses. The fields surrounding the city were long blankets of uninterrupted white, bare until the snow retreated and the wolves with them.

Synick took a deep breath as he let it all impress him. The return trip had been far more comfortable than the previous one, but he was still eager to be out of the Veil. At a steady trot, relaxed and easy, he left the tree line behind, and his guards followed.

"Get the flag ready," he said. Wordlessly, they did, and Synick was pleased to notice a slight headwind picking up. The long white, gold, and red-trimmed banner would ripple nicely for their approach. After only a moment, he could hear it whipping. Synick thought the occasion merited a word or a quip but didn't bother. These men proved to speak very little, even to each other, and his wit would be lost on them.

He suspected it had something to do with lifelong slavery, forced induction into a military, and indoctrination.

Under the noon sun, Synick could see men atop the wall scrambling in confusion at the party beyond the safety of their walls, vulnerable to the Veil at their backs and seemingly unaware of the danger they were exposed to. He smiled to himself and approached the gate.

For a long moment, nothing happened, and the thought crossed Synick's mind that they wouldn't let him in. Faron had said that they'd practically blown the doors open to rush out and seize him from the Veil, fighting back the tide of hungry wolves that followed. That certainly wasn't the case now.

Finally, the doors opened inward, large drifts outlining their closed position. The opening immediately filled with ten black-clad wardens, six with pikes and four with crossbows, but they weren't meant for Synick.

"Get inside!" a familiar voice cried. "Hurry!" But there was no rush. From the bag on his saddle, Synick retrieved Sadagon's lantern and lit it. Its light was harsh. If there had been any wolves near enough to pounce, their red eyes would have been turned aside. The light had a similar effect on the men, who shielded their faces with forearms as Synick and his guards rode past.

Seconds later, the doors slammed shut, and Synick cut off the lantern. The torches in the tunnel seemed every bit as bright as empty space for a few quiet moments, and then their eyes adjusted.

"What are you?" that voice asked again. Synick looked up to see faces filled with fear and disquiet, except for the blocky features of the one man he recognized.

"Hello, Artur."

"Dead gods," Artur breathed, coming close. "Synick?"

"Yeah," he said, "and funny you should mention them. That's actually why I'm here."

"You are alive?" It was the kind of question that needed answering only with jibes.

"Depends on your definition. Now, I hate to be in a hurry, but I have a message for the governors. Will you escort me and be sure they grant me an audience?"

"How?" he asked, open-mouthed and bewildered.

"Typically, by coming with me, maybe telling the guards to stand down and listen to me. How am I supposed to know?"

"How are you *alive*?" he clarified.

"It's a long story," Synick sighed. "Come with me to the keep. You'll hear it there."

"Black corpse of Olsu, what is going on, Synick?"

"Well, exactly that, to be crass, and you're probably going to want to give up that curse sooner than later. Come on, to the keep. You'll hear it all there, and we'll talk more after."

"What was that light?" he asked, clearly shaken. "What are you?"

"Can we go, Artur, or do you want me to just go on my own? I can get in the keep by myself if I have to."

"No." He shook his head. "No, I will take you, but I will demand explanations before this is over."

"You'll get more than that before this is over, Artur, and you'll wish it was all you had." With the tunnel cast in silence, they departed and climbed the spiraling road that would take them to the keep.

Before long, Artur escorted him across the great courtyard at the base of the governors' keep. It was a wide field, just below the very peak of the mountain. Dead clovers littered the ground between the stone paths where the snow and ice had been sufficiently cleared to see them.

It occurred to Synick that Anveil was an austere place, nearly devoid of any form of decoration. There were no fountains, statues, benches, or trees—just a minimal field, pushed up against the keep with a small balcony for the governors to dictate from high above.

The militaristic simplicity of the tiered city seemed to send a message, but Synick couldn't be bothered to unravel it. He had his own message to give.

Once Artur pushed the keep doors open and let them inside, Synick saw how the interior matched the rest of the mountain: plain and unbecoming a leading class, but that wasn't what was bothering him. This was the seat of the city's power. Shouldn't there be more to *steal*? There was barely a luxury to be seen, and it made him scowl in disapproval.

You're past that, idiot, Synick reminded himself. *You're a property owner.* He was done with thieving.

Probably.

Down a long hallway, Synick and his guards came to a pair of heavy doors, behind which the three governors sat at a triangular wooden table—two elderly men and a woman at the far end. No platform raised them, and there were no jewels anywhere on their person—to be seen, anyway. Synick recognized the woman from the Festival of Winter Blood.

"You are the ones seen from the wall?" the younger of the two men asked. His voice was pitched as if he'd spent most of his life singing.

Synick cocked a brow. Apparently, a messenger had made

it here before him—a messenger to declare a messenger.

"I know your face," the woman realized. "You were an honorary member at the feast of Firstblood, the one who later disappeared with the Wolfheart. How did you come to walk the White unharmed? Why are you here?"

"What is your name?" the older man asked.

"The important question," the first man said, "is how have you survived outside the safety of our walls? Have the snowbeasts all gone south? Are you a spy from Murcosta? An assassin?"

Synick sighed. There was no sarcastic response strong enough to get him out of delivering his message, so he might as well get on with it.

"Those things would be simpler," he began, "but no. I'm no spy. I'm a messenger. My name is Synick, and I come with a warning."

"Keep your warning until you've explained how you traveled through the snow. That, above all else, is paramount. I don't want to hear another word until I know how you've done this." The woman scowled at him as if it would force him to divulge his secrets. Instead, he resolved to lie.

Synick thought for a moment and then spoke. If a small lie could lend him legitimacy, then it would only help. "I was granted protection from the wolves by those who own them, the ones who gave me this message." That, at least, had a glimmer of truth to it.

"Protection? What is that supposed to mean?" the woman asked. "Given how?"

"Own the wolves?" the old man said.

A question was forming on the first man's lips, too, so Synick reached into his pouch to silence it before it began.

From it, he withdrew Sadagon's perfect orb, then twisted.

Color vanished from the room as garish light exploded over them, bright as the sun in the palm of his hand. The glass remained cool to the touch. Synick held the orb aloft, razor shadows cutting lines across the room.

"My message is this," he declared. "Above the Veil, there is a city, an entire empire where this is a mere trinket, a city of white and gold towers, with technologies you've never imagined."

The oldest among them gasped. "The Lost City?" he breathed.

"Yes," Synick confirmed but was cut off.

"Impossible," the woman snapped. "The Lost City is a legend, a myth, a story for the weak-minded."

"Oh, it's definitely all those things," Synick replied. "But it's also real—a city without walls, where these are nothing but pillar decorations." He threw a second pouch onto the table, and it clinked admirably on the hard surface.

Artur made to open the pouch himself but was stopped by a raised hand. The younger governor took it instead. Vavelt's sapphires clattered onto the hard wood surface, joined by the pocketful of other gems he'd pilfered, all glittering fantastically in the white light. They were larger than most stones found on necklaces or rings and were worth their own fortune.

All except Artur gasped at the unexpected riches.

"You stole these?" the woman asked.

"No," he shook his head. "They were a gift, a small thing given without much thought, easily parted with compared to the treasures stored up there. In the God City, these are quite literally paperweights."

"The God City," the old man whispered to himself. "City of Temples, City of Light. Then it is real."

"Keep your religious rambling to yourself, Artima. Your extremism will see you expelled from this council."

"The old man is right," Synick said, steering the conversation back toward his message. "Religion is exactly why I'm here. The God City is real. I've been there. It was the birthplace of Atha and Olsu—and their grave." He lifted the orb a little higher and set his teeth. Now came the most difficult lie. If Dageran were here, he'd smell it on him in an instant, but Synick could sell it to these people.

"This is what I found above the Veil and what I've been sent to tell you: Atha and Olsu are reborn. They live again, and they're coming for their thrones."

The woman and younger man stared with disbelieving eyes, doubt battling confusion across their faces. Synick could see that they didn't want to believe, but there was little choice. The unearthly phosphorous, bag of gems, and even his presence cut through any doubt that could be had. There were forces at work that they didn't understand, and they knew it.

Only the old man, Artima, seemed sure in his reaction, and it was the most surprising.

"Truly?" he asked in his weathered voice. "The gods have returned?"

"They have," Synick confirmed, his gut twisting. "And they come for your oaths of fealty."

"Fealty?" the woman asked. "To a dead god?" She huffed. "I think not. Anveil is an independent state, and we will not swear fealty to anyone, no matter who they claim to be. Even the strings of Empyrion have been cut for over a decade."

"No!" Artima cut in. "We are but stewards. Long have the Remembrants foretold of the Twinborn's rebirth."

"Superstitious drivel," she shot back. "The gods have been dead for centuries, and Remembrants hold no authority here. I see no reason why we shouldn't just throw this Fayorian back into the White."

"Well," Synick quipped. "Because I just came out of it, for one, and it's not exactly the death sentence for me that it is for you." She wasn't listening, though.

"Don't you see?" Artima cried. "They come to save us from the long winter! The gods have heard our prayers, and they live again."

"*Yes,*" Synick said, surprised to have found such an immediate ally. "That's *exactly* why they've come. In exchange for your oaths, they bring enough seed and grain to overflow your stores and will teach you to survive the growing Veil."

"The Veil *isn't growing!*" the younger man snapped. "There are no grounds for that alarmist claim. The Veil will recede as it did twelve years ago, and our summers will return."

"Perhaps." Synick shrugged. "And then it will come back again, twice as far, to swallow you whole."

"That isn't the point, Radast," the woman said. "If there really is a relief on the way, I suppose it won't be delivered without terms?"

"No," Synick answered. "No, it won't. The gods are bringing a mountain of supplies to save you, but they aren't asking for your fealty. They're demanding. With this supply train is an army of ten thousand men and women, with weapons and abilities beyond your understanding." He let that sink in for a moment. "They come to save the people of Anveil, but make no mistake"—he pointed at the woman—"they see you as usurpers, and they will tear this city down to get it back if they have to."

"Ten thousand men," Radast breathed, "from beyond the Veil? Impossible."

"The wolves belong to the gods," Synick replied. "As do the souls of us all." He felt sick to say it. "Ten thousand is only the beginning."

"Can we stand against such a force?" the woman asked, looking at Artur.

"No," he answered in a brief, clipped voice. "Perhaps, if our stores were not so thoroughly depleted and if this army of the gods did not walk in the White. As it is... no, with a certainty."

"Ice," she cursed.

"Young lord," Artima asked. "Where is the divine army? When will they be here?"

"Don't tell me you're already planning on capitulating to invaders who aren't even here?" the woman spat. "Who might not even be coming?"

"We are but stewards, Galena," Artima responded in his soft voice. "Not heretics."

"Heretics?" she shrieked. "Of a dead religion? Have you lost your mind, Artima? Have your years as a Remembrant priest so thoroughly addled you that you believe the first hint of a rebirth?"

"He came out of the White!" Artima cried. "First, that young Wolfheart, and now him. He carries an ethereal light and has seen the God City. Times are changing. How can you *not* believe, Galena? How can you see this boy alive and safe from the wolves and not heed his message? The gods have returned to save us, and you seek to anger them? Your rashness would doom us all."

"Enough," Synick snapped, hand slashing through their argument. "There are ten thousand soldiers marching through the Veil as we speak. They will be here within three days, maybe four. Either way, you'll soon see them for yourselves." He reached out to collect his gems. "I've delivered my message. Now prepare your prayers or pitch. Whatever you do, the blood of Anveil be on your heads."

Simple Lies

A shattering bowl punctuated Synick's entrance back into the Foxglove Inn, slipping from the fingers of a pale-faced innkeeper.

"Synick?" Jesika gasped. "How? What are you..." She stared at him. "You were dead."

"Only on the inside, I'm afraid." Synick gave her his best grin, but she wasn't sold.

"How are you back? They found a rope leading down the wall. They said you killed yourself, along with the Wolfheart boy."

He only shrugged. "It's a long story."

That earned him an empty wooden tankard thrown at his head. He deftly plucked it out of the air and learned that it was, in fact, only half-empty, right up until a hops-heavy beer splashed out onto his face.

Squinting hard, he puffed the draft from between his lips and nostrils. "Well, the service is better than I remember," he said.

In a flash, Jesika stepped forward with a rag in hand. "Oh, you blue-eyed bastard," she said, then was on him. Synick was blinded for a moment as the beer was swabbed from his face, then again as Jesika removed it and forced her face into his, kissing him suddenly.

Synick barely had time to register what was happening before the two warring sides of him began fighting. One portion of his heart craved the validation and victory that came from a kiss given so willingly and from so beautiful a woman. The other felt panic and betrayal. Before either side could manifest, Jesika pulled away.

"You've got some nerve, bastard," she said. "Coming in here every day and making me love you, then disappearing without a trace, then coming back when I'd given you up for dead."

Synick was tongue-tied, thinking only of Vavelt and how she would react if she'd seen what Jesika just did.

"I," he started, then coughed. "Jesika, I—"

"There's no need to pretend, Synick. I don't care about the game anymore. I thought I'd lost you, and I didn't know what that meant to me until I did. What happened to you? Where have you been? How did you survive beyond the wall?"

Synick was losing the point. "I met someone," he stammered, trying to regain control of the conversation. "I met someone I love, Jesika."

She froze, eyeing him for a long moment.

"You mean to tell me," she said, after a quiet pause, "that you slipped out of the city in the dead of night, walked among the snow wolves and didn't die, and have come back after all these weeks just to tell me that you don't want to be with me?"

"Well, no—"

She cast around for something else to throw, then settled for the wet rag. It missed as Synick tossed his head to the side.

"Listen," he placated. "It's not like that. I actually like you very much. It's just that—" He was cut off.

"You met someone?" she finished for him. "Who, Synick, a wolf? Is that what you've been doing out there? You really expect that you can just waltz into my tavern after vanishing like that and return just to turn me away?" She seemed to decide on a different approach, her throwing hands occupying themselves with his hair now. "I don't think so," she said. "I might not care to, but I can play the game just as well as you—better, even. I'm a woman who owns property, Synick. I get what I want."

She pulled him in for another kiss, but Synick managed to pull away this time. "Really, Jesika," he said. "That isn't why I'm here. I'm not playing games."

She grinned, then nodded. "Sure, blue eyes."

"I mean it!" he said, an edge of desperation creeping into his voice as he attempted to disentangle himself. "I'm here for an entirely different, platonic reason."

"Platonic?" she asked. "Isn't that how you described your relationship with a whorehouse in Blackwood?"

"Well, yes." He blushed. "But I'm not allowed there anymore after a misunderstanding with a poetry book and one too many men with no appreciation for multitasking. That's beside the point," he added, finally escaping her arms. Synick briefly realized that before he'd left, he'd spent so much energy pursuing this woman that he had no idea what it was like to be pursued by her—or anyone for that matter. 'Hunted' was the word that came to mind. For a fraction of a second, he lamented not being able to experience that, but that was only his self-loathing speaking. He shrugged it off.

"Listen," he said. "You're right that I chased after you, but that isn't why I'm here. This is a matter of life and death."

That stopped her. "My life?"

He nodded. "Among others, but yours is one of the few I care about. You asked where I've been? How I survived? You're right, Jesika. I did leave Anveil, and I did walk the Veil." He stopped to breathe. "You won't believe what we found out there."

"You're serious," she realized.

He fixed his ruffled hair. "Serious. We found a city, Jesika—the God City. It's been waiting in secret for centuries, but not anymore." He drew another long breath. Now came the lying. "The dead gods are born again, Jesika. That's what we found out there. They're reborn, and they've sent an army to reclaim the world."

"An army?" she asked. "You can't be serious." Her brow furrowed into sharp lines, and she said, "Where's your friend? The Wolfheart, Faron."

More lying, if only barely. "Dead," he said. It was true enough. Faron was Varek now, in name and purpose. The boy Jesika had known was gone.

"Atha's tits," she cursed. "I'm sorry, Synick. After everything you did to find him... I'm sorry."

"He's in a better place now," he replied. That, at least, was technically true. He was a god, after all.

The silence endured a little longer until Jesika, probably trying to change the subject, said, "Synick, you really mean there's an army coming this way? From a mythical city? In the dead of winter?"

"Unfortunately, yes. An army of the gods, with weapons and technology beyond our understanding. They're coming, Jesika, and if the governors don't surrender right out, all of

205

Anveil will burn."

She shook her head and gave him a discerning eye. "That can't be true. It isn't possible. You're raving, Synick."

"Maybe." He shrugged. "But it isn't impossible, and it is true. I've already told the governors, and Artur can confirm my words when he gets back. He's strategizing with the other wall captains now."

"Dead gods," she cursed. "Artur is taking you seriously? And the governors? Synick, if I find out that you're lying to me, I'll—"

He cut her off by brandishing the orb Sadagon had given him. With a twist, it burst alight and robbed the walls and floor of all color. She gasped, and the room filled with choked cursing. Cutting off the light, Synick realized that the tavern wasn't empty, and the half-drunk inhabitants were all watching him closely.

Jesika seemed to notice too because, blinking, she took his arm and led him to a corner near one of the four fires where they could talk in more relative privacy.

"That's flash stone," she said, a little surprised. "In an ever-burning lamp, like the one you were trying to make with Orothorn. He called you an idiot for trying. How did you make it?"

"I didn't. This is a common lantern in the God City. It was given to me, Jesika."

"It's… bright," she said. "Like the sun, but cruel and white."

"Brighter than anything Orothorn has ever made. Wouldn't you agree?"

She nodded.

"I'm not lying, Jesika. The God City is real, and their army is coming."

"Through the snow, though?" she pressed. "How? Even an army would be hunted down by the wolves."

Synick's thoughts reeled for a moment. There were so many things he wanted to tell her and so many things that he had to keep secret. The snow cloaks were a key aspect of Faron's and Vavelt's power, and it was imperative that they stayed that way. Still... he *was* hoping to take her out of the city, wasn't he?

"You can't tell anybody," he hissed. "Especially not Artur."

"Tell him what?"

"It's the cloaks," he said, "cloaks cut from the pelts of snow wolves."

"He had one, too," she realized. "Faron. He was wearing a bloody pelt when Artur found him."

Synick nodded. "He discovered it then, the idiot, racing against the snow with nothing but his knife. It was apparently more of an accident than anything. After that, we made a pair in secret and went north."

"But aren't they plagued?" she asked, brows drawn together. "Aren't they said to infect anyone who touches them?"

"Evidently not," he returned. "If I had to guess, I'd say that's a lie spread to keep people from ever finding out about them."

"Dead gods," she breathed.

"Not dead anymore," he reminded her. "That's kind of the whole problem."

"You have to be lying," she claimed, the desperation of an unwilling believer tingeing her tone.

"It would be simpler," he agreed, "and better for everyone, but I'm not. It's really there, Jesika—a city bigger than you can imagine nestled away in the far North, white stone and gold towers as far as the eye can see, oceans of temples under a green fire that burns in the night sky."

She caught the longing in his eyes and saw that he was telling the truth.

"They call it Vam Aranath," he said. "Where Atha and Olsu rule together."

"You sound like you want to be there," she observed with a nervous expression.

He moved on from the point. "They're coming, Jesika. They're coming to reclaim their thrones, and they're starting with Anveil."

"Why are you telling me all this, Synick?"

"Leave with me," he said, eyes shooting up from the floor to meet hers. "Leave with me to Vam Aranath."

"What?"

"I've been over it a thousand times in my head," Synick said, standing from the chair she'd put him in. "Anveil is doomed, Jesika. Unless the city surrenders, the coming army is going to knock its walls down."

"What!?" she said again, louder this time.

"I heard it from Atha myself," he went on. "If Anveil doesn't surrender, they're going to burn it down and fill the streets with snowbeasts. Even as we speak, Artur is coordinating a defense with the other wall captains. Tell me, Jesika, do you think he will give up without a fight? That he won't try to rally that rabble of wardens to repel the invaders, whoever they are?"

She was silent.

"Of course he won't," Synick answered himself. "I did everything I could to try and persuade the governors, but there isn't a chance in Hell's Iron Halls that everyone will simply accept an invading army. Anveil is *doomed*, Jesika."

"How can you know that?" she asked. "How can you know what abilities and weapons they possess? How do you know all this, Synick?"

"On accident, mostly," he equivocated. "I somehow managed to stumble into favor with both Atha and Olsu in my time above the Veil. It was them who sent me, Jesika, to warn the governors. I came on their behalf."

"So you're aligned with them?" she asked, mouth agape. "You are their ally?"

"It's difficult to say," he began. "There's so much you don't know, Jesika, but in their own way, they're here to save Anveil."

"By threatening to kill us all?" Her voice was reaching a shriek.

"In their minds, it would intimidate the other cities into surrendering all the quicker. From what I understand, they're trying to take over the entire world, and they're willing to make an example of Anveil if they have to."

"Blackened corpse of Olsu," she spat. "This can't be happening."

Synick pushed the point. "I'm welcomed there, Jesika. Atha herself gifted me land with a home, mine as long as I live. You should see the towers, Jesika, and the fire that hangs in the night." He waited a moment, then said, "We'll be safe there, Jesika. Come with me. Don't be here when the army arrives. Come with me to Vam Aranath."

When she replied, her eyes were filled with pain. "Damn you, Synick." She shook her head. "Damn you. You want me to flee with you to some fantasy city? Leave my brother and inn behind and just run away with you?"

"Yes," he breathed, closing his eyes. "Please."

"Damn you," she cursed.

"You could have an inn there," Synick urged. "A tavern like a chapel. There's easily enough space just on the land Atha gave me."

"I can't just leave my brother," she shot back.

"Your brother is *why* you have to leave. He's going to *fight them*, Jesika."

"And what if he doesn't? What if he surrenders?"

Synick shrugged. "Then I suspect he'll wish he did fight."

"What does *that* mean?"

"Come with me," he pressed. "Please."

"I *can't*," she insisted. "I can't just leave, Synick. This is my tavern—my home."

"None of that will mean anything when you're dead," he snapped. "None of that will mean anything when your home is nothing but a ruin—a dead place haunted by wolves, murdered to intimidate the other cities."

"You don't know that will happen," she said, quiet and without conviction. "You don't know it."

"I know it."

"But what if they don't? What if they come and Anveil surrenders? What if I left for nothing?"

"Then we could come back!" Synick said. The other patrons glanced at him, nervously trying not to overhear. "But that doesn't matter because it's foolish to believe. Please, Jesika, consider it. I've thought it over a thousand times. The only place that will be safe from Vam Aranath *is* Vam Aranath, and it just so happens that I'm currently in favor with *both* members of the godhead. *Please*," he pushed.

She shook her head. "Why are you even asking me?" she

pried. "You said yourself not an hour ago that you don't want to be with me, that you found somebody else in this veiled city. Why have you even bothered to come back?"

"Because I have no family to speak of, Jesika, and that leaves me free to choose my own. You are my family—you and Artur if you can convince him to come with us. Yes, I love someone else, but... I love you, too, in another way. You gave me a home when you didn't have to. You were kind to me and Faron, and I'll be damned before I let you die in this city. Come with me, Jesika, and live."

She shuddered, breathing in and out for a long considering minute.

"If the army comes," she finally said. "If the army comes, then I'll go with you. If the army comes and the governors don't surrender."

Synick's eyes lit up. He had been prepared to debate her long into the night.

"After," Jesika amended. "I'll not leave unless I have to. If it comes to a war, then I'll go with you, but not before."

Synick studied her eyes, reading the meaning that lay behind them.

"Alright," he agreed. "After." He gave her a reassuring smile and pulled her into an embrace. Behind her back, his smile slipped away.

A Just God

A contingent of honor guard atop white horses surrounded the gods' white and gold carriage. The runners at its base left long furrows in the snow wherever it passed. Surrounding soldiers wore a distinguishing length of thin, flowing red silk on their right arms, tied at the bicep. Five rows of more ordinary men garbed in white and gold armor marched ahead of the procession, with five more behind, all of them with snow cloaks that fell just past their midbacks. Behind them all were long sleighs with flat beds packed high with bread, roots, meat, and spices.

Together they cut a wide gash through the mostly undisturbed snow toward the gates of Anveil. Wolves followed the caravan at either side, wild and untamed. They eyed the group with hungry eyes but kept their distance.

From inside the opulent vessel, Varek peered through the glass at the frozen world beyond and the looming black wall of Anveil. From atop a down-cushioned bench, he tapped his leg with anxiety.

"I'm nervous, too," Vavelt said from across the carriage. Her bench was adorned with stacks of red velvet pillows. "You can let me do most of the talking if you want."

"It's not that." Varek shook his head.

"Then what?"

He turned to see Vavelt measuring him with her eyes. How he had longed to see them so often before. How many times had he imagined their reunion? A hundred? A thousand? And nearly as many different scenarios it might happen in, but never had he pictured this.

Finally, he answered, "No matter what happens today, I will be betraying someone."

She shook her head. "There is no treachery because there is no choice, and you made no promise. There is no other path, brother."

Looking back out the window, he confided, "I feel as if I'm choosing between cutting off my right hand or my left."

"The choice is your left arm or a finger from it. That is hardly a choice."

"I know."

"Then why do you act so wounded?" she asked, then cut herself off. "No. I don't mean it like that, but Varek, you behave as if you are being asked to put the knife to your own throat."

"That's what it feels like."

"Why? You seem to think that you're switching sides, but that's not at all the case. We're on the *same* side, Varek. We're protecting the sanctity of life."

"I know," he nodded. "And I understand better now, but I can't help how I *feel* about it."

"That makes sense." She nodded. "I'm proud of you, though."

Varek nodded in return. She had said it multiple times already.

"I know why it needs to be done, but that doesn't make it easy. Life hardly feels sacred when it's sacrificed on such a scale."

"You were willing to sacrifice yourself to find me."

"That was my choice, Had—Vavelt." He caught himself before saying the name. He understood now. "And when I learned you might still be alive… well, I barely had a life to give. It hardly felt like a choice when the other option was to do nothing."

She moved across the carriage to sit beside him and lay a hand on his knee. "Is that so different from what we do now? Stopping war and famine, uniting the world when the only alternative is to do nothing? To let the world be swallowed by frost and ice, colored only by the blood of the few who remain to fight over the last scraps of bread?"

"I suppose not."

"Then why do you mourn?"

"I don't mourn," he answered. "Not exactly. I'm with you. I understand that it's necessary. It just doesn't feel right, choosing who lives and who dies."

She was silent, her eyes a soft mirror of understanding. She reached out and pulled his head into her chest. "I know. It is a terrible responsibility." For several minutes, she gently supported his head with her frame, and he relished in it. Varek couldn't remember a single instance in his life where he felt so comforted.

Eventually, Vavelt spoke again. "I know it's an awful thing to say, but for the sake of all life, if anyone must have power over life and death… I'm glad it's you. The very fact you don't want it means you will respect the sacrifices made. You might even say the greater sacrifice is within *you*—to carry this weight that no one should have to. You will be a *just* god, Varek."

There was an extended pause as Varek considered the weight he already carried, the souls who he had elected to kill in finding his sister—Haka'een with a blunt knife through the eye; Jakal, broken and defiant; Garad, unyielding in his apathy. Those had been the easiest of them.

Then there was Jaru'tal, who had been so easy to carry, despite the gruesomeness of his death, only for him to now weigh so powerfully on his shoulders. He had been a friend of Vavelt's. Snow and ice, he was her potential fiancé, and now he was dead and his guard with him. Worse were the soldiers who had done nothing more than get in Varek's way—and even Ulric.

Could he carry any more?

"Tell me more about our mother," Varek whispered, pushing his mind to something else—*anything* else.

Vavelt craned her neck away to eye him but seemed to understand. "Varan says she was warm and generous, not at all what you'd expect from a former slave. She was kind to everyone but didn't allow anyone to talk down to her, regardless of station. It's probably why Father chose her, to be honest."

"What does Sadagon say about her?" Varek asked.

"You mean, what does *Father* say about her."

He looked down but nodded. "Right."

"He doesn't, mostly. Losing her was hard on him, like losing his first family all over again."

"I understand."

"Damn that Baranor, the frostbitten bastard."

Varek remembered the frozen faces in the ice at White

215

Grave, and he agreed. It took a particular breed of cruelty to wield the names of a dead family like a weapon. It was made worse that Varek had loved him.

"Father vowed to never love again after that. I've been working with him, though, and he's coming around. He needs love and compassion if he's to ever heal—not solitude."

Varek didn't know how to respond to that.

"It's hard," Vavelt continued, "finding a suitable woman to court him. Most are either too afraid of his station or too ambitious to be a real match, and that's if he doesn't dismiss them the moment I present them."

"You're trying to find a match for Father?" Varek asked, surprised. "He dismisses them?"

"Yes. He won't allow himself any comforts in the world at all. He seems to believe that it's his duty to suffer for his failings."

Varek swallowed hard. That sounded uncomfortably familiar.

"Are you sure he appreciates you meddling in his affairs?"

"Affair is exactly the right word. I even brought the priestess, Valatha, to try and bed him, but apparently there's a history there I'm unaware of."

Varek blushed at the thought and at Vavelt's openness. "I'm not surprised," he managed. "She seems… forward."

"Well, anyway, what he doesn't appreciate now, he'll come to appreciate eventually. He's so determined to hold himself back from any kind of joy—like he's punishing himself—but it isn't good for a man to be lonely." She shoved him off her shoulder and gave him a pointed look. "Speaking of which…"

"What?"

216

Her look became flat.

"What?" Varek repeated.

"You know what. Is there no one in your life? No person you fancy?"

He shrugged. "There's never been time for it."

"Time for whoring, though, no doubt." Her tone would have been condescending if not for her wicked smile.

His mind flicked to Clarath, the girl he'd helped bring to Dageran. "No," he said with more acid than he'd intended. "They're no better off than slaves, most of them. I have no right to inflict myself on anyone, paid or not."

Her expression grew surprised at his outburst but immediately softened, and she pulled him into her embrace again.

"I'm sorry," she said. "You really are so like Father. I shouldn't tease."

He breathed deep. "I don't have room for love, Hadria—not when there are real problems to solve."

There was an awkward pause, and Varek cringed, knowing what she would say.

"Please don't call me that," she said. "I know it's hard, but please. My name is Vavelt."

"I know." He nodded. "I'm sorry." He meant it.

She released a sigh of relief, then resumed the conversation. "We'll take care of that. You're here now, and that's what matters. We're family, Varek, and I'll take care of you—help you to heal."

The comfort of her words and touch fought with the reluctance of what he was about to do. Both mixed inside, battling for dominance, when the carriage slid to a stop.

Radiant Dark

"Why are we stopping?" Varek asked. "Father said they accepted our invitation to open a dialogue." Before Vavelt could answer, a blazing light exploded all around them, bright as the sun but harsher and colorless. It seemed to come from everywhere. Despite the difficulty, Varek peered out the window, filtering the light through his hands. The glass was dappled, but he could still see the forms of his soldiers outside, several of whom held tall standards bearing large orbs at the top. They looked like white spears of starlight.

Varek barely had time to wonder why the display was necessary before he remembered the hundreds of wolves following them. They had come in packs and coalitions of packs, watching the advent of Sadagon's army and hoping for prey. Even in the noon sun, overcast as it was, the phosphorous lanterns were strong enough to burn retinas, and they pushed back the snow wolves.

The wild hunters that stalked them fled now, red eyes fearful and damaged from the soldiers' high lanterns.

Black-garbed men atop the enormous walls must have seen the impossible display themselves because once the snow-beasts dispersed, the great doors began to swing inward.

They began moving again, continuing on under the wall, and Varek breathed a long sigh of open relief. Vavelt didn't seem nearly as concerned, simply pulling her window shades down and returning to her previous posture.

"Well, they aren't pouring pitch on us," she said. "So that's something." She smiled as if that weren't an actual possibility.

"They'll want to negotiate before they begin an open war," Varek guessed. "But still, I'm surprised they didn't demand we leave our honor guard outside the walls. There must be a hundred men with us."

"It's nearly half that amount," Vavelt corrected. "And it must mean they know they are in no position to bargain."

Varek nodded. "Good."

"If anything," Vavelt mused. "This is a sign that Synick provided them ample time to consider. Who knows how we might have been received without him."

Varek hoped that was true. He had been unable to release the image of Synick dead somewhere, frozen under a growing pile of snow. This, at least, was some indication that he had made it to Anveil safely.

Imperceptible daylight streamed back into the window as they emerged on the far side of the wall, but the phosphorous lanterns were not extinguished. The blinding light that pushed back the snowbeasts served a similar purpose on the citizens of Anveil, who crowded together in a fearful perimeter. All around the square, they shielded their eyes, awed and hesitant. Varek didn't blame them.

The carriage slowed to a stop as the runners came up on stone, cleared of all snow within the gate. For a long moment, the world was still. Varek could see through his mottled glass window the thralls outside and could just barely make out the soft noises of frightened whispers.

"Ready?" he asked.

"Not yet." She stopped any movements he might make with a hand, then pointed up. On the roof of their carriage, there was a whirring of gears, quiet and efficient. Even knowing it would happen, Varek wasn't ready for how the world seemed to shift outside. The white lights of the Alabaster Guard winked out, the unnatural brightness quickly fading away. The world felt dim in the comparative dark, but it didn't last long.

A wash of heavy redness pulsed from the carriage. Four massive orbs atop the roof had opened, and inside them, another of Sadagon's secrets was igniting: a *red* phosphorous.

Beginning as a small radial of gentle illumination, the light intensified and deepened, pulsating as it grew, and like moths to a flame, all eyes answered its sanguine call. Row upon row, as the crowds fell under the oppressive light like a brilliant blackness, the people of Anveil were quieted, exuding the hush of the grave.

Varek swallowed. Was it possible that his drumming heart was the loudest thing in all the city? Outside the carriage, in a world utterly without sound, Varek saw a tall shape dismount from a gigantic horse. In the eerie light, it was red as exposed flesh.

"Almost," Vavelt whispered, handing him a small orb of his own. He didn't reply, except to take it.

"Rejoice!" the dismounted man called, shattering the silence and seizing the attention of a city. Varek instantly recognized Varan's voice—his keeper and Sadagon's most trusted archon.

"Rejoice!" he yelled again. His shouts seemed somehow

amplified by the terrified crowds and cold light. "Rejoice, Anveil, for your sins are forgiven. Rejoice, Anveil, for your souls will be the first in the new world to be promised rest."

Not a single sound came from the florid crowds.

"Take heart!" Varan cried. "For in this eleventh hour, the masters of this world and the world beyond have returned to save you from your sins and from your hunger. In this final moment, the Twinborn have come again to reclaim what is theirs and save you from the growing Veil."

Hushed gasps ran through the crowd as what must have been a rumor was suddenly confirmed. Varek's heart raced even faster. They *were* expected. That must mean Synick had made it, but he couldn't think about that now.

"I am Vam Varan, priest of Atha, priest of Olsu, High Archon of Vam Aranath, and herald of the Twinborn." The crowd was even more silent now if that were possible, and there was no denying the fervor behind Varan's words. He spoke with the earnestness of a true believer.

"I saw, three hundred years ago," he shouted, "when the gods departed. I was there, three hundred years ago, when they were slain." Ripples of whisper washed through the crowd but not with the doubt Varek had expected. Underneath the heavy, stifling light of the carriage's lanterns, perhaps Varan's words didn't seem so incredible.

He went on, voice growing even louder, "I have watched, for three hundred years, as sin flourished and went unpunished, all of you left to atone for the fate of Atha and Olsu. I have watched, for three hundred years, as the Veil grew and threatened to swallow you. I was there, three hundred years later, when the prophecies were fulfilled and the Twinborn were born again! I was there, three hundred years later, when the lords of humanity returned and named me their herald once more!"

The whispers stopped as Varan's ranting shouts came to a climax. "And I am here now to declare to you that death will have the victory no more! Today, the dark regains its fetters. Evil shall be shackled, for the gods have come again for their thrones. Today, wickedness dies, for the gods have come to claim your souls."

The speech was punctuated by the distinctive sound of a massive sword drawing from a sheath, followed by hundreds of rustling feet and shifting weight.

"Who will stop them?" Varan cried. Through the glass, Varek could see Varan's naked blade sweeping in slow arcs toward the onlookers. The light reflecting off its gleaming surface was hungry and deep. "Who will speak to deny the throne of Anveil to their gods? Who will forfeit their soul to the Iron Halls to obstruct the work of gods?"

He was met with silence.

"Who will stand in the way of heaven!?" Varan practically screamed. "Who will oppose the godhead?"

Eerie silence swallowed the city once more.

"Then kneel!" Varan commanded. "Kneel before divinity! Kneel that you may beg to give your supplication! Kneel that you may be saved! Kneel that your hungry may be fed and your naked clothed. Kneel that your souls may be saved and your enemies burned by the power of heaven. Kneel to beg for your forgiveness. Kneel that you may be untouched by their light! Kneel that you may be graced with the glory of Vam Atha, ferryer of souls, wielder of mercy, Goddess of Dawn. Kneel that you may be graced by the glory of Vam Olsu, thrice defeater of death, meter of justice and retribution, God of Dusk. Kneel for the arbiters of your soul. Kneel!" he screamed. "For your gods!"

That was their cue. Varek reached for the crown on the seat beside him and placed it on his head, then smoothed his shirt and stood. He had to stoop inside the carriage but only barely.

"Your lamp," Vavelt said. Varek glanced at her but then remembered, twisting the two halves of the perfect sphere until its blinding radiance filled the interior of the carriage, clean and white as snow. It was a low burn, but Vavelt glowed with it.

The door opened. As the world entered Varek's view, he was surprised to find that many of the citizens of Anveil *were* bowing—most of them, even. He swallowed hard and exited the carriage, hand in hand with his twin. The white lights in their grips pushed back the dark radiance of the red phosphorous but not far. Together, the two of them seemed to radiate the only color and true light in the world, encased in a halo of white.

The sun was nothing compared to their brilliance, a weak and shameful yellow to be scoffed at and dismissed. Here, under the overcast sky, Varek and Vavelt were gods.

The thralls shielded their eyes from their gods, whose skin burned with a glory that seemed to force back even the oppressive red light and was far too dangerous to look upon. If Sadagon's illusion could be pierced, they would have seen Varek's black and red clothes, gold brocade over silk and lace, and leather epaulets that lent him an inhuman physique, but the light was too strong. To any that had eyes to see, Varek and Vavelt appeared as burning silhouettes or pillars of heaven.

There were none left who remained standing. Every single person, to the last man, had fallen to their knees. Many were openly weeping. Whether from fear or salvation, Varek didn't know.

Showered in blinding light and looking for all the world as its source, Varek and Vavelt stood over an ocean of bowed backs. Varek wondered briefly if Artur was among them. Every soldier in their escort was on a bent knee, one fist to the ground and one to the heart with thumb tucked under the index. Even Sadagon and his archons bowed low, if only with one fist and not so deep as the lowly soldiers.

In the threatening silence, Varek and Vavelt descended a set of golden steps slowly and one at a time. A veiled palanquin of white steel waited for them at the bottom, wrapped with vines of gold and speckled with giant rubies. It gleamed when their halo swallowed it. Without a word to the gathered crowds, they stepped inside, and the diaphanous drapes were pulled shut.

Unlike the carriage, the cushions here were white and neatly trimmed in gold—the colors of Olsu. Once seated, Sadagon and his archons rose, followed by the soldiers. A black-garbed warden made to stand as well but was pinned by a sudden, paralyzing glare from Varan, whose intricate steel armor was deathly red in the wake of the carriage.

No one else moved.

Two soldiers with lengths of flowing silk on their arms pinned the drapes of the palanquin, providing a false privacy. The white veil that surrounded them was sheer, and their figures could be determined through it but not as well as the crowds could be seen from within.

Eight men took their places at the long arms of the vehicle, lifting it off the ground and into the air. The sudden movement shuffled the thin veil around them, and the light dappled as if through water to play out on the cold ground below. White battled red where they passed. The bearers took position in the center of the procession and began the long trek to the governors' keep at the top of the city mountain.

Vavelt turned to give Varek a small, excited smile, and he returned it. Even from inside the small vehicle, the way their orbs made the shadows and light flicker and play together through the veil almost convinced Varek that his sister truly was a god. Witnessing the display from beyond the confines of the palanquin and inside the cage of that red phosphorous could leave no doubt whatsoever.

As the palanquin and the gods inside slipped away, the oppressive redness began to recede. The lights atop the carriage dimmed, and color and noise together ebbed their way back into the world. Somewhere a child was crying, and Varek heard Varan's voice rise again from behind.

"Rise!" he called. "Rise now, and accept the bounty of Atha and Olsu. Receive the banquet they have given you."

Safe from the bloody illumination, a murmur rose among the crowd, who seemed to wake from a half-sleep and find that they could breathe again. The sounds of excitement and joy took hold as everyone came forward to accept the foodstuffs Varan had brought them.

Well under the ambient excitement of the crowd, Vavelt whispered, "*That* went well!"

Varek allowed himself a small breath of relief. It was working. It was actually *working*. The men and women in that crowd were every bit alive as he and Vavelt, and now he was more confident than ever that they would stay that way. Perhaps the soldiers and cannons would have no place in this.

"Let it stay that way."

The Third Law

Varan rode up beside the palanquin, once again mounted on the back of his great white horse, Nobility. A majority of the envoy stayed behind with the great sleds, doling out foodstuffs and resources to the suddenly eager and vivacious crowds of Anveil.

"Amazing," he said to them near an undertone, matching his speed to theirs. "You were utterly breathtaking, my lords."

"Thank you," Vavelt replied with a slight nod and a smile. "You were quite impressive yourself, if a little intimidating."

"Forgive me, Lady Atha," he replied. "I only betray the confidence I have in you with my words and the exuberance I feel at uniting the world once again under the most competent and deserving rulers I have ever known."

"High praise," she whispered back, "from a six-hundred-year-old man."

"And not given lightly. I have waited a long time for this day, and I could not be more pleased."

Vavelt looked around. "Where is Yarow?"

"Leading the convoy with Vam Sadagon." Vavelt didn't seem to catch the sight of him but relaxed. "The three governors will be next," Varan said. "Remember that they are beneath you—so far beneath you as to not even merit a word unless it is entirely necessary. If you must speak at all, remember that they are not your equals and are as children to you, holding a thing that does not belong to them."

"That should be simple enough," she replied. "I'm nothing if not arrogant." Varan smiled in appreciation of her levity, but Varek did not share it. His heart thumped with the weight of all the souls who depended on him, both those who had to die and those he had to save. It was hardly a moment for light-heartedness.

At the very top of the mountain city, at the great, un-adorned doors of the governors' keep, they were halted by a group of black-clad armsmen who "requested" the bulk of the contingent stay outside in the large field beyond the keep's balcony. With a flick of the wrist, Sadagon dismissed the majority of the men, who took up position blocking the roadway. The palanquin was set down, a white carpet rolled across the stones for their gods' feet, and they were led inside. Only those soldiers bearing red sashes across the bicep—the Alabaster Guard—followed, their silk marks drifting behind them as they moved, nearly as light as the wind.

Once inside, the pale winter sun was immediately cut away, but it made no difference. The sun was a weak thing compared to the brilliance he and Vavelt held in their hands. It was so bright and white that it nearly drowned out color, except the gems that twinkled like dying stars in Vavelt's hair and dress.

They passed several doors on either side of the windowless hallway, stopping before four men gripping spears in front of what could only have been the council chambers. Like most of the building, or the city even, it was free of unnecessary embellishment, but the doors before it were massive and full of self-importance.

Before they even arrived, the men pulled on two great handles set into the wood and heaved, gliding the doors upon oiled hinges. Inside sat two men, one in his late fifties and another that must have been nearly twice that, and one woman, whose age Varek would have placed somewhere between the two men. She, at least, he recognized from the Festival of Firstblood.

Varan approached the rulers of Anveil, Yarow beside him, his face hard as stone. "Kneel," he commanded, as he had to the commoners. "Kneel before your ancient gods in supplication and prayer. Beg for the right to surrender the rule which you have stolen from them."

The younger of the men cleared his throat with what seemed to be disbelief. "We have allowed you into our walls to discuss why a foreign army is brought to bear on our gates and discuss terms, not to surrender like cowardly dogs. You cannot expect to storm into my city and seize it with mere words." He gestured to the men at his back, two behind each member. "You are in my keep, and we will answer to no authority here but our own."

Varan's eyes darkened, and Varek realized why he was Sadagon's right hand. That gaze could have burrowed through cold stone. Vavelt's keeper, Yarow, stood beside him in menacing stillness.

"The Twinborn live again, for whom you are merely unlawful stewards. I present them to you now to accept your immediate surrender of their humble city. You may be permitted to rule in their stead, but I will instruct you one final time: Kneel, and recognize the authority of your gods." His hand rested upon the pommel of his wide-bladed sword.

"Lower your heads, or you will lose them."

"Your men outside are surrounded, as are you in here. You waste as much of your time as mine with this idle posturing," the middle man said. "And these gods you claim are hardly more than children. Can they not speak for themselves? I would hear how they—"

He was silenced before he could utter another word. Silvery steel rammed into the chair just beside his head, and he flinched, nearly losing an ear to Yarow's axe.

He screamed, flinching away. Yarow had moved like a flash of lightning, still one moment, uncoiled the next. The nervous guards leaped to arms, drawing swords and jumping into action, but stopped behind the knobby hand of the old man.

"Stop!" he said quietly, though it sounded as if he had intended to yell. "By the gods, stop."

The nearly dead governor yanked on the axe handle, but it barely trembled at all.

"Stop?" he asked. "They tried to kill me! Arrest them!" He released the handle to point. "Arrest them at once!"

The guards didn't move, though, stilled behind the gnarled fingers of the old man.

"Be still," Yarow commanded in a low growl, then yanked the axe out of the chair. They were the first words Varek had ever heard him speak.

"Peace," the old man wheezed. "For gods' sake, peace."

Having apparently learned his lesson, the first man pushed back into his chair with dark eyes but was silent.

"Radast may not remember the stories, but they were more than that in my youth." The old man breathed deep as if simply speaking was exhausting. "I am not fool enough to disbelieve the legends of the Twinborn, and neither am I confident in the strength of our walls. We have invited your forces into our gates and even our fortress without contest." He bowed his aged head slowly. "Lady Atha, Lord Olsu." He spoke the names like they belonged to heroes from epic fantasies. "You are welcome in these halls."

The six guards stepped back as well, looking more relieved than angered, though terrified to the last.

"Welcome," the woman amended, "but not rulers. We have invited you in faith, opened our gates when we could have poured pitch and loosed arrows, and you have already violated that faith." She glanced with distaste at Yarow. "Violence is not an acceptable tool of diplomacy."

Sadagon stepped forward then, and both Yarow and Varan moved to the side in deference. "Violence," he said, "is the most likely outcome of any conflict."

"And who, exactly, are you?" the woman asked.

"To be more specific," he continued. "Violence is the most likely outcome of *this* conflict."

"You threaten us?" she asked. "After we've opened our gates to you?"

"Your gates?" Sadagon asked. "You sit on a throne that does not belong to you, and you have the gall to feign offense?"

The first governor, Radast, looked as if he wanted to speak, but the hole in his chair and woodchips in his lap kept him silent.

"Who *are* you?" the woman asked, more fervently this time.

"I am Sadagon Pyre, World Steward and Father to the Twinborn, and *you*," he said, "are Lady Galena, second governess of Anveil, daughter of Domithrane, mother of none." He smiled as if to let her know he was in control. "A usurper."

Radast became even more uncomfortable, but Galena didn't seem phased by Sadagon's knowledge.

"Usurper?" she spat. "I was democratically elected!"

Varan huffed.

"That does not give you the right to rule in the gods' stead without their consent or permission," Sadagon condemned. "Those people you govern belong to the Twinborn."

"And what of your gods?" Galena asked. "Do you speak for them?"

Varan stepped forward again, powerful shoulders encased in gleaming steel that extended in fine plates to the very tips of his fingers. "*I* do," he declared. "The words of Atha and Olsu are not for the likes of you. You will address your lords only in answering unless an invitation is extended to loose your unholy tongue. A second transgression will not be forgiven."

The old man interjected again, careful to address Varan. "Elder Galena means no offense, High Archon. That is your title, is it not? Please, forgive her. She only wishes to convey a sense of concern for our home and the well-being of our citizens. I beg you to see her concern as a love for your people."

"Their people?" Radast gasped. He silenced when Yarow snapped his head toward him.

"I'm afraid I must agree with Radast," Galena said. "You speak as if Anveil is already under your control, but I am still a governor." She shot the old man a baleful glare. "Extend your terms, that we may consider."

Sadagon leaned forward, and Varan stepped back. "You

don't comprehend the gravity of your circumstances. The High Archon speaks for the gods, but I speak for their armies. Even now, our forces assemble catapults to rain fire down upon you. Through the grace of our gods, we possess weapons with the capacity to reduce your walls to rubble, to tear them down in a matter of minutes." Sadagon placed both palms on the table as Galena's face paled. It was abundantly clear to Varek that he had done this kind of intimidation before.

"It is not our soldiers that need frighten you. It is the fire of heaven I can fill your streets with. It is the dire wolves I can set upon you, who are no threat to me or my men. It is the possession of your souls and the eternal promise of the Iron Halls that awaits you."

With a sneer Varek had not seen from him before, Sadagon leaned in close. "You think your pitch will save you? You think your arrows can keep me at bay? I can take your walls from you. I can reduce your *wardens* to meat for wolves." He spat the name. "I can burn this city to ash, and I can do it all without losing a single soldier."

"Please!" the old man wheezed. "I implore you, lords, allow us to—" He was cut off.

"It would be a worthwhile sacrifice," Sadagon expanded. "The souls of those lost would be put to rest, exalted for the example they left behind to the rest of the world who would capitulate without question before the naked power of the gods."

Varek and Vavelt stood behind their father as he threatened the governors, as still as they were silent, radiant orbs giving off that intensely steady light. The oldest man looked directly at them.

"Please, my lords." He seemed to think better of his actions and looked to Varan. "May I address the Twinborn directly?"

It was a long moment before he responded. "With reverence and the condemnation of your soul, should you fail to please them."

He nodded, then returned his gaze to them. "Vam Atha, lady most gracious, have mercy upon us, I beg of you. I am a Remembrant priest, a follower of your order. Even in your death, I have followed your ways."

Galena rolled her eyes.

He looked to Varek then and continued speaking. "Vam Olsu, lord most powerful." He was silent for a long moment and appeared to be nearly overcome. "Wolfheart."

Varek almost flinched at the name. They recognized him then.

"I knew you were no ordinary man when I first laid eyes on you. It was why I petitioned to have you named Wolfheart in the stead of our wardens. When they pulled you from the Veil, unharmed by the snow wolves, I knew it was a sign, but I did not know what you were. I plead your forgiveness for my ignorance."

Varek said nothing, only waiting for him to continue.

"Anveil is a religious city, my gods. Show mercy, I beg of you. Allow us to hear and accept your terms."

Radast finally regained his nerve enough to speak. "Yes, extend your terms that we may review them and come to a formal conclusion within three nights. The lords and lady will be given board, but the bulk of your forces will be asked to retreat beyond our walls as a courtesy while we consider."

"There is nothing left to consider, Radast." The old man's voice was wispy and full of air.

"We will not simply hand the city over to this new threat, Artima," Galena snapped.

"Anveil's rulers were always stewards ruling in the gods' name and by their forbearance. We cannot negotiate with gods," the old man argued.

"What did I say, Radast?" she said, turning to the skinny man. "Did I not warn you that his archaic ways would sow disunity? That he was unfit?"

The old man sighed. "I'm afraid I must apologize for my companions' shortcomings again, ancient ones." He bowed as he spoke. "You must forgive them, I beg of you. They only follow the first of three wartime laws of our people, laid down after the Supernal Dusk."

Sweat slipped from the temple of a guard.

Galena furrowed a brow and turned to inspect the elderly man.

"The law states, in more or fewer words, that under no circumstances, unless faced with certain and utter destruction, is the council permitted to cede to a force of any size, at any stage of occupation, the control of Anveil."

"Artima, you old fool," she said, wardingly but quiet.

"The second describes the requirements, if such a situation were to arise, for the council to administer a surrender. The vote must be unanimous."

"What are you on about, you gangly wretch?" Radast spat. "I will make no such vote with you, and neither will Galena."

"And why not?" Artima whispered. "There could be mutual benefit to such an arrangement. The gods, after all, already have their thrones in the Lost City. Surely they will spread further than Anveil and will need stewards to watch over their flock while they are away." He shifted his old frame in the uncomfortable chair. "And who better to be relied on than those who waited an entire lifetime for their return? Who better to aid their gospel than those who welcomed them with open arms, who proved beyond all doubt their loyalty to the old ways?"

Galena gripped the arms of her chair with bone-white fingers. "Traitor," she whispered.

"What?" Radast gasped, looking back and forth between them. "What are you saying, Artima?"

The old man looked over a shoulder to a guard whose gaze was already locked with his, and he nodded. For a long moment, nothing happened, and Artima nodded again, a kindly gesture from a withering man; and, the guard flashed an arm upward and then down, stabbing governor Galena between the shoulder and neck. Another guard seized her from the other side and forced a gloved hand over her mouth, silencing her as she tried to scream. The knife fell again in the chest and in the back as she slumped forward.

Pale-faced and slick with sweat, Radast leaped away from the hands of the other guards who sought to betray him, dashing out of his chair and across the room. He came to an abrupt stop in Yarow's gauntleted hand, his fingers curled up around a fistful of the governor's tunic.

"No!" Radast cried, trying unsuccessfully to scramble away. "You will have my vote! I will support your claim!"

Yarow looked to Sadagon, who gave a very brief nod.

With the effort of a man brushing off an insect, Radast was thrown back into his seat. "No!" he cried, just before Yarow's axe split his skull.

"Be still," Yarow grumbled once again.

Varek recoiled at the sudden bloodshed and almost

shouted at Yarow before remembering his place. He looked to Vavelt, who hid her reaction far better. She didn't look frightened at all. If anything, she seemed curious. Sadagon, too, didn't seem the least bit surprised. Instead, he wore a look of unimpressed frustration, one brow lifted slightly above the other.

Settling back into his seat, Artima appeared as if nothing out of the ordinary had happened. The guards, though, who had only just betrayed their governors, dropped their bloody knives and fell to their knees.

"The third law," Artima continued beside the two fresh corpses, "a contingency for war-time, states that if any members of the council are to fall in battle or illness or age, their power is vested in the members who survive them."

His ancient eyes addressed Varek, peering deeply. "Vam Olsu, Lord of Dusk and Light, Meter of Justice and Keeper of Souls, Wolfheart and Champion of Firstblood, I knew there was more to you from the moment I saw your face. I beg your forgiveness for not seeing the truth then as I do now. Welcome home, Lord of Lords and Lady of Ladys. Anveil is yours."

A Steep Price

At the top of the mountain, on the highest balcony of the governors' keep, Varek stood with Vavelt, looking over the city. Blinding luminosity shone from the gates at the bottom of the mountain where great phosphorous lamps burned to keep the wolves at bay. That light reflected off the perfectly polished armor of thousands of Sadagon's soldiers as they streamed into the city streets, filing up the organized paths to make room for more and more occupiers. In the fading light, it was possible to see the white and gold reflection of their troops, even from their distant balcony.

"Two lives," Vavelt spoke beside him. "Two lives, brother, to purchase all this."

Varek couldn't trust himself to speak.

"A steep price," she went on, "but far less than what it could have been—far less than what it *would* have been, had you not been here."

"I know," he managed to say.

"Look, brother." Vavelt pointed far down below. "Do you see the supply train coming in?"

Faron saw it only as a larger than average disturbance of the white phosphorous.

"It isn't just troops we're bringing but food, seeds, and supplies. Try to think of all the mouths you can feed now. The people you saved will be hungry."

"We can set up distribution centers in the morning," he said, but it wasn't where his mind was at. He thought only of the added weight that he carried. Jakal, Garad, Haka'een, and even Jaru'tal had all been evil men, despite his relationship with Vavelt, but that didn't change how they stared at him from the darkness. The others were worse—a man in Jaru'tal's employ who had done nothing but fail to protect his master, two guards who were selected to be his escorts, a tanner, and a woman he didn't know. Now that weight was added to by the souls of Radast and Galena, both of whom had shown him kindness in his first appearance to Anveil. That had been such a wonderful time.

Now they were dead.

The combined weight of their lives was a lead blanket on his mind, stifling his will to think clearly. Could he carry their weight, too?

Vavelt turned to examine him as the silence stretched on.

"Varek?" He looked away from the scene below and let her gaze catch his eyes. Her face was fringed with concern. "You promised not to shut me out," she reminded him. "What are you hiding behind those furrowed brows?"

He took a fortifying breath. For her—he could carry this weight, not for the world but for Hadria. He cringed slightly and corrected the mental mistake. Vavelt. He could bear the weight of these souls, for *Vavelt*.

"I'll be alright," he promised. "I have to let this happen."

She wrapped her slender arms around him, the exact support he needed. A long moment passed that way, with

239

both of them staring at the parades below, no sound except the whistling wind.

"I'm proud of you," she finally said.

Varek melted into her embrace, allowing himself to accept the praise and trying for all he was worth to not think about what came next.

Something Small or Heavy

S ynick looked through the clear glass window at the soldiers who stomped through the streets, decorated like peacocks in their white and gold armor. Jesika stood beside him, apprehension spelled out across her face.

"We should have left," Synick said, for what must have been the hundredth time.

"You keep saying that," Jesika responded, "but nothing has happened. The governors surrendered the city, just like you said they wouldn't, and things have been peaceful so far."

"There's a key expression in that sentence that I think is lost on you."

"Oh shush, blue eyes."

"I get the feeling you'll be the death of me," Synick said with only a little sarcasm.

"Why's that? Because the snark I keep you from spouting will build up inside you until it explodes? Or because I might stab you?"

"Been stabbed." Synick absently ran a finger on the scar tissue along his lower stomach. "Not a fan."

"I wasn't exactly going to consult you on it."

Synick didn't have the presence of mind to retort.

Jesika looked away from the window to eye him up and

241

down. "I know you're worried," she sighed. "I am, too."

"Then we should leave." She opened her mouth to respond, but Synick beat her to it. *"This is my inn,"* he mimicked, *"and I'll burn before it does."*

She snapped her mouth shut. "Bastard."

"Beautiful bastard," he corrected. "I like that better."

Jesika snorted.

"I thought you were above flirting with me now, seeing as you've thrown your lot in with a particularly handsome snow wolf."

"Simple statement of fact."

With a rush of chill wind, the front door slammed open, and Artur strode inside, the very image of a thunderhead breaking upon an unsuspecting shoreline.

"Artur!" Jesika chastised. "You'll break the glass, you oaf."

"The governors are dead," he declared with all the subtlety of a boar. The few men and women committed enough to their liquor to frequent a tavern in the middle of an invasion snapped their heads up at the news. "Betrayed by that superstitious fool, Artima, who turned the city over to the invaders."

Jesika forgot all about the glass in her door. "Dead?" she asked. "Betrayed?"

"And now," her brother continued, bulling over her questions, "battalions of the foreigners are led by Artima's own men, issuing warrants to surrender our weapons and armor." He scoffed. "As if there's anything left to confiscate. They seized our stockpiles already. With Artima's men, they knew exactly where to look."

Jesika gave Synick a nervous look, but he wasn't about to intervene.

"Entire garrisons now without bows or spears. What are we to do when the snow climbs the walls? How are we to repel the wolves?"

"Haven't you seen Olsu's lights?" Jesika asked. "Or his men, even? Let them handle it."

"Them?" he roared. "Handle *my* wall?"

"Oh, shush," Jesika returned. "You're the captain of a wall garrison. That *hardly* makes it your wall."

"Mine more than theirs," he stated. "And there is a difference between a *captain* and a *wall* captain."

"And what are you going to do?" Jesika folded her arms indignantly. "Keep your halberd hidden in your trousers? Fight off the whole army yourself?"

"I will *do* whatever I can. Artima's treachery does not mean I must bow down and accept these invaders as my masters, and my men feel the same."

"You're being foolish," Synick finally interjected. "There's nothing to be done, Artur."

"I will not hear of foolishness from you, a man so impotent he cannot even kill himself properly."

Jesika's jabs meant well, but this from Artur got under his skin.

"You're right," Synick snapped. "Go ahead then. Jump back out into the streets, and take on Olsu's Fist. See how long you last against ten thousand men. I'm sure it won't be much different than stabbing wolves who can't fight back from the comfort of your stone wall." Artur pounded his fist to get a word in edgewise, but Synick didn't let him. "Go on. Go and fight them. If you're the kind of man who's stupid enough to throw his life away like that, risking everyone else's in the process, then nothing of value will be lost."

Artur punched him across the face.

Synick rolled with the blow but still fell onto his back from the force of it. He got up far enough to sit before realizing that his hand was on his knife. He deliberately let it go.

"Artur!" Jesika cried, jumping between them and beating her brother helplessly with small hands. "You stupid, fat bastard," she yelled as she pummeled him pointlessly. "Can't you see he's right? You can't antagonize them. They're willing to kill us all just to prove a point."

"Alright, alright, leave off." He brushed her hands away and stepped around her.

Still on the ground, Synick looked up at the bigger man. "Get the brutishness out of your skull yet?"

"Don't think I didn't see you grasp at that dagger, Synick of Faye."

"Don't think I couldn't have used it, ice brain."

"You two," Jesika cut in, "can both get the brutishness out of your skulls by hauling Artur's snowing arsenal to be confiscated." She flashed a look at Synick. "And don't think I don't know about the dagger at your belt or the entire belt of knives you wear under your coat, blue eyes."

Synick grinned, but only because she'd missed the throwing knife in his boot. "You know," he began. "You're really not in a position to be ordering me about, seeing as we're not tied down or anything."

"No?" Artur asked. "Then how do you know about the knives hidden on his person, little sister?" His eyes were equal parts suspicious and accusing. She silenced him with a flat stare, which he returned tenfold to Synick.

Synick grinned. Half of the start of his relationship with Jesika had been an effort to torment Artur, and it appeared

Jesika was still invested in that particular sport.

Synick smiled and, picking up the game, said, "You're welcome to guess, Artur."

His flat stare became a glare. "If I guess right, I might kill you."

"Shush, the both of you," Jesika commanded. "Artur, you are being a hapless child. You're wrong whether you know it or not; so, stop your whining, and do what I tell you."

"Don't ask me to surrender to them, sister. I won't do it."

"Yes, you lumbering idiot, you will do it." She looked between the two of them. "*Both* of you will. And if you aren't thick as thieves by the time you get back, I'll find whatever weapons you wool heads have hidden away and kill you with them."

"Better leave something small then," Synick half-whispered to Artur.

"Or heavy."

Jesika shoved at Artur. "*Help* him up, oaf."

"You expend too much effort for this fool who does not return your sincerity, Jesika." Artur's voice was broad and meaningful as if he'd only just expressed what he'd actually been thinking.

Jesika, in response, only shoved at him harder.

With a sigh, Artur extended a hand to Synick. "Forgive me for striking you, Fayorian." Synick accepted his help and got to his feet.

"Now go and get your weapons out of your rooms, bastards."

Looking somewhat abashed, Artur turned and headed for the stairs. Before he'd gone half a step, Synick tripped him with a foot, sending the big man crashing onto the floor with a solid exhalation of breath and clattering of steel.

"Your apology, Artur, is accepted."

Bloody Arithmetic

S till atop the governors' keep, Varek stood with Vavelt in the thin air. The light was gone, and the city gates were shut. The greater half of the army had slowly snaked their way up the mountain, and now they were entrenched on every tier.

Behind them lay a massive glass orb, bigger even than the four mounted on the carriage that bore them into the city. It contained a massive white stone safely encased in a vacuum. At its sides were two concave mirrors, held in place by the iron mounts that lifted it all off the ground.

Far below, at the bottom of the mountain and over the wall, set just behind the tree line, was its opposite—a cannon loaded with red phosphorous. Together they were an instrument of death for every man, woman, and child who dared oppose Varek, and he hated it.

"Perhaps we should go inside?" Vavelt suggested, touching his arm. "You've gone pale."

"I'm fine," he insisted.

"There's nothing you can do for them right now, Varek. Stop worrying."

"Worrying is the only thing I can do," he replied. "One child from every seventh house is going to die, and I'm allowing it. I have to allow it."

"Oh, my brother," Vavelt keened. "It isn't so bad as that. That is the number to be taken, but not all of them will go to the Spile. Most will become soldiers or be committed to the fields to support those soldiers. Very few will have to die."

Varek nodded, trying to feel reassured, and his sister pushed up against his frame, leaning on him in a supportive kind of way as if the added weight gave him the will to stand taller.

"Do you remember what we talked about after our coronation?"

"We fought," he remembered.

"Yes." She smiled. "After that, though."

"The archons." He said it with a touch of bitterness. For every archon whose life was to be horrifically extended, the life of one child would be required roughly every ten years.

Vavelt interrupted his thoughts. "I meant what I promised you, brother. When the archons are no longer needed, and we can return to Vam Aranath with the world safe under our rule, we will cut them off from the Spile."

Varek checked over his shoulder to be sure they weren't overheard. "That is a distant promise," he said. "And little comfort to the people here."

"It will be a comfort to most of them," Vavelt insisted, "because we won't need one in seven, Varek. We won't need one in twelve. The archons don't know it, but without them, we'll barely need to maintain our populations at all."

"How many?" Faron asked.

"One in *twenty*," she said with a small smile.

That was a weight off his soul—one weight among many.

"And we can make them do that?"

"We can," she affirmed, "if we both agree to it. If it's just me, Father or Varan could outnumber us, but if you agree..." The implication was clear. If he agreed, he would have blood on his hands, but more lives would be saved.

"Yes," he breathed. "I can agree." More weight on his soul to carry.

"It's the right thing," she said.

"I know." Tiny specks of snow blew up over the ramparts, slicing across his face like cold knives. "I know. I have to let this happen."

Several minutes passed in the chill wind before Vavelt shuffled and pulled her arm from Varek's.

"I think you've dedicated enough of your energy to this, Varek. You've seen everything there is to see from this tower. It's time you stop putting off what you want to be doing and get it done."

Confusion played across his face. "What do you mean?"

"I know that it's bothering you, Varek, and the majority of the army's movements are complete. Synick is down there somewhere. Send for him."

"There's no need for that," he suggested. "I'll find him myself."

"You're going to search the city at random?" Vavelt asked. "He could be anywhere. Besides, Father will be returning with the reports any moment now, snowing fool. He has the good sense to ask us to stay here but won't hesitate to galivant about the city himself while an occupation is underway."

"It isn't random. I know where he'll be."

"And what if a resistance mounts and some peasant runs you through with a pitchfork?"

He offered a small smile. "I've faced far worse than

249

peasants and pitchforks."

Hadria huffed. "You know where he'll be?"

"Yes."

"And it isn't far?"

"Yes," he promised.

"Good," she snapped. "Then send some guards to find him and bring him here." She cut him off. "You are a *god*, Varek, and none of this can be done without you. If you are killed or hurt, the entire world will pay for it."

"I can't…" He paused, finding no legitimate rebuttal. "I suppose I can do that."

"Suppose nothing. It is the obvious course. Heimar!" She raised a single hand, and a clean-shaven man with graying temples rushed forward.

"Yes, Lady Atha?"

"Gather ten men and send them in search of a young man by the name of Synick of Faye. You will recognize him by his fair hair and a scar above his left eyebrow. He is handsome and will undoubtedly give you lip. Find him and bring him here with all speed."

"Yes, Vam Atha." He gave the double-fisted bow and turned away.

Varek stepped forward. "You'll find him at the Foxglove Inn or the glass smith's forge across the street," he instructed.

"As you say, Lord Olsu."

The guard left by the balcony's only door.

"Thank you," Vavelt said, "for not fighting me. You really are too important to be doing such things."

Varek knew better than to disagree.

"Look!" she called, stepping up to the balcony's edge. Varek peered over to see a man in black armor riding at a canter through the sharp snow. Even in the city walls, there was a white cape on his back like all the soldiers, but Varek could tell it wasn't an ordinary horseman.

"Father's returned! Come on," she said. "Let's meet him inside."

A few minutes later, they were warming in the council chamber, Sadagon's black plate dripping where the patches of ice had begun to melt. His delegates and generals stood against the far edge of the room. Varan and Yarow were gathered around the central table where the two governors had been killed only hours before.

"I trust all is well?" Varan asked.

Sadagon nodded. "Indeed. The demilitarization went better than expected. We've set up forty-seven check-ins for compulsory but willingly surrendered armaments so far, and all of them have reported hundreds of weapons registered and confiscated. There have been very few pieces of armor handed over, but that is to be expected for a population of this kind. Most sets were confiscated at the barracks by Artima's men. General Kaarfane estimates we've taken roughly eighty percent of the weapons of any meaningful size."

"I doubt," Varan added, "that you will take many more without searching every street, house to house, the risk of which would far outweigh simply moving forward immediately. Let those who resist feel a false sense of security in hiding their arms from us, and mark the names of those who cooperated as trustworthy or, at least, low risk. They could be helpful once conscription begins."

"I agree," Sadagon said. "Kaarfane, see that it happens." A balding archon at the side of the room nodded his head in response.

Sadagon paused to dry his hands on a towel, then handed it to a servant. "I have also placed permanent regiment fortifications on every level, with rotating patrols between them—as many as twelve on the bottom level and three on the top. Between that and the flare machine, we will be able to respond to any form of violence within moments, if not instantaneously." He nodded slowly, and the room fell eerily silent as if no one wanted to follow where his logic was leading.

"The city is secure," Varan ventured when it became evident that no one would say it for him. His voice was strangely hesitant. "There will never be a better time than now."

The statement was met with nods and curt coughs, but the silence crept back into the stone room.

Eventually, he pressed on, "It would be best to move before the commonfolk become more familiar with our presence. We would not want to lose the suppressive element of fear." All eyes turned to Varek, though Sadagon was the real power in the room, and they all knew it. If there were going to be a holdup in the order that was to be issued, it would be with him.

He set his jaw. This was the part he wanted nothing to do with, above all else. This was the betrayal he had to commit—the weight he had to carry.

"Do we have to?" Varek caught a glance from one of his guards, but he didn't care. "Do we really have to?"

Vavelt, still holding his arm in hers, flicked a concerned glance up at him.

"What do you believe?" It was Sadagon who spoke, and the question was a dangerous one. Even with the recent truths brought to light, Varek was liable to lash out—or run. He felt the need to go on the attack welling inside his chest but, somehow, tamped it down. The look from his sister's eyes showed concern more than anything.

"I think the peace we've won is fragile. It won't survive if we start taking their children."

"You are likely right," Sadagon nodded. "But you must consider the longevity of your reign. If you are to take more cities than this, you will need an ever-growing army, fields to feed that army, and hands to work them. We will, of course, conscript where we can, but a rabble of mercenaries is no tool for a god. You will require indoctrination as well as service—a loyalty deeper than reason or expediency."

Varek was familiar with the argument. "But one in seven?" he asked. "That hardly seems a merciful forbearance." Vavelt's face suddenly relaxed, and she gripped him tighter.

"Mercy can only come from a strong hand when justice is forestalled. You cannot offer mercy if you cannot choose to give justice instead, and you cannot wield justice if your position is weak. This strength," he continued, "will empower you with mercy."

"We understand that," Vavelt said, speaking up for Varek. She squeezed his hand. "Olsu and I have discussed this at length, and we've come to a compromise. We believe that it is possible to both show mercy and grow our strength by limiting the number of those drafted from one in seven to one in twenty." She gave him a shared smile. "The difference may be made by combining our distribution centers into volunteer centers. When our people come to receive our gifts of sustenance, they may also be encouraged to volunteer themselves for labor or their children into our priesthood."

Varek hid his wince. They hadn't talked about that, but that was probably because she had just thought of it. It was a good idea, no matter how distasteful. Still, he gave his sister a grateful nod. One in twenty was less than one in seven, and that was a difference in human life.

A difference in weight upon his soul.

Sadagon had to think only for a moment. "Very well. Who am I to argue with the gods?" He smiled, if a bit nervously. "It will be one in twenty, with the gods' blessing."

What Good it Did

"What kind of idiot owns four halberds, six swords, five spears, twelve daggers, and an axe?" Synick asked, walking down the dark street with Artur.

"Enough of your complaining. The wheelbarrows did most the lifting."

"Yes," Synick replied. "But *some* lifting is, by its very definition, too much lifting."

"And that," Artur said, "is why you are a gangly thing. And don't act as if you didn't also have several weapons, though small."

"Still do, too," Synick smirked.

"I noticed that as well."

From a hidden pocket in his coat, Synick pulled out his dagger. "I'll be dead before they get this from me, and not even then if I can help it."

"It is special to you?"

Screams came from the road just above them. Synick and Artur shared a brief glance, then bolted that direction. Up a flight of long steps and doubling back around the corner, they caught sight of the commotion.

White and gold soldiers stood outside an old stone building, pulling on the arms of a group of poorly dressed children. There were patches at their elbows and knees, rough lines where an unsteady hand had mended tears, and an undeniably underfed look to all of them. Synick knew what the building was even before he saw the wretched old woman who ran the place—an orphan hall—and it was being raided by Faron's soldiers. There was only one possible explanation for that.

"What's going on here?" Artur hollered at the men before him. One or two of them turned to see him, barely older than Synick himself, but most kept on pulling the children away from their caretaker.

"They're taking my wards!" the old woman cried. "Help us!" She pulled at the fingers of one man, trying to pry them off a girl of perhaps fourteen years. They smashed her into the ground with a gauntleted backhand.

Synick thought she was finished after that, but she bounced back up with the alacrity—and bones—of a person half her age. "Please!" she kept on, as if nothing happened. "We've done nothing wrong!"

"Stay back!" the man closest to them yelled, his finger pointing. "By the wisdom and mercy of Atha, these have been recruited into the service of the war effort."

"But they're children!" the old woman cried, back at the hands of the men hauling her wards away.

"It is children that are required," the same man said.

Artur chose that moment to open his big mouth. Synick was every bit as disgusted as Artur at the display, but he had the good sense to keep quiet about it.

"Release them at once!" the big man demanded.

"Artur," Synick hissed, but he wasn't listening.

"You claim to be exercising mercy? Then let these go!"

The man who was obviously in charge rebutted, "We don't answer to your authority, citizen, and neither are you meant to understand the gods' ways. Return to your homes before you break curfew."

Artur didn't back down, blowing up his chest as if he could intimidate a group of seven men in scale and plate armor with his brawn and bones alone. To Synick, he looked like a small dog barking at wolves.

"I am Artur of the Winter Wardens, wall captain of the east face. I have been tasked with the protection of these people from the evil beyond the Veil, and from where I stand, that includes you. I demand you let these innocents go at once." He pushed up to get directly in the face of the man addressing him but didn't get far. The soldier to the side planted a metal-clad fist in Artur's face before he could say anything else, nearly sending him to his knees. When he regained his balance, the man wasn't using fists anymore. He held a stout sword in his hands, the tip pointed straight at Artur.

"Ah!" he grunted, backing off a few steps and holding a hand to his nose. Synick grabbed him by the crook of his arm and was almost certain that he'd charge if let go. Artur glared at Synick but didn't bolt ahead.

From the corner of his eye, Synick saw shapes emerging from the darkness. They weren't the only ones who had noticed the fighting, it seemed. Dark-haired men and women rounded the corner, angry sparks in their eyes. Synick's stomach dropped when he saw them.

"Come on, Artur. We have to go."

Artur wasn't listening. He had noticed the forming mob as well, but he was grinning.

"Return to your homes!" the leader called. "You are interfering with divine will."

The mob crept closer. "They're children of Anveil. Let them go!" one woman yelled. She held an old kitchen knife in her hands.

"By word of the gods, return to your homes!"

"Piss on your gods!" she cried, meeting with unanimous cries of the others, including Artur.

"Weapons!" the soldier ordered. The men under his command unsheathed swords and brandished spears, releasing the children they'd been hauling toward an empty cart. The frightened orphans fled back to the old woman, who held her arms above them like a mother hen.

"I will not warn you again," the man yelled. "Leave, or there will be bloodshed."

"Then there will be blood!" Artur shouted, rushing the line of armed men. The rest of the mob went with him, wielding whatever weapons they could find. One had a pitchfork, classically unreliable. Another had a mace, in open defiance of the weapon ban. Alternatively, another man had nothing but a large glass bottle, but it would bludgeon just fine.

"Stop!" Synick shouted, tearing on Artur's burly arm.

"Let go of me!" he growled, but only because he didn't see what Synick did.

All the way down the long road—this tier of the mountain city—groups of soldiers were arriving at homes in seemingly random intervals, pounding in the doors and storming inside. Some of them were headed their way.

More caged carts pulled onto the roadway, drawn by the huge white horses of Vam Aranath. One group of men, not far from their own cart, backed out of a home with a door on shattered hinges, taking a teenage boy with them. He fought against their efforts to prize him away from his mother, but there was nothing for it. She couldn't maintain her grip with a baby in her arms.

Synick watched in the distance as the weeping woman fell to the cold stones, protecting the baby from the fall with her own body, and pulled even harder on Artur's burly arms.

"No!" he yelled. "Get back, you great idiot."

Artur whirled on Synick with fire in his eyes. "Let go of my arm, Syn—" He cut off when he saw what Synick was staring at. Soldiers were stealing into the homes of Anveil and leaving them one child less than they'd had before.

Men and boys from homes not targeted by soldiers poured out to defend their neighbors' families, brandishing whatever weapons they could find. More people flooded the street from the level below, where the soldiers hadn't yet gathered, ready to dive into the fray. For all their numbers, they were no match for an army.

The knife-wielding woman ran up on a spear, gutting herself with a gasp. The man behind crushed a white and gold helmet with his mace, but a sword bit into his neck. The bottle wielder managed to deflect a sword strike and knock out two opponents, but the others weren't so lucky.

One man lost his throat to a common axe, another to a sword. Vam Aranath steel split skulls, ruptured organs, and eviscerated the weak resistance. For every soldier that fell, at least ten commoners followed them.

All down the long road, it was the same, soldiers and civilians screaming as they killed one another. What had begun as a single, isolated skirmish had devolved into a full battle—no, not battle, Synick corrected himself. This was going to be a massacre.

"We have to get out of here!" Synick yelled at Artur.

"No! We have to fight!"

Fighting wasn't the word Synick would have used to describe what was happening. He watched in the distance as a man's head fell to the ground, cut clean off by an over-sharpened halberd.

"There's nothing you can do here, Artur, except help start a war. We have to go!"

"Then go," Artur shot back. "And if you are such a coward, give me your knife."

"This isn't a fight you can win!"

Artur yanked his hands out of Synick's grasp and picked up the fallen pitchfork. With no response other than a filthy glare, he turned and charged the line of soldiers.

"Shit," Synick swore. A hand seized his ankle, and he swore again.

"Help!" a weak voice cried. He looked down to see a man with an arm cut off and side gashed open—the bottle wielder. Synick shook him off with a sickness in his gut. There was nothing he could do to help him, except to perhaps cut his throat, but that wasn't Synick's job. He'd be dead within the minute anyway.

Synick fought his rising bile and watched as Artur sparred with a man spinning a fine-tipped spear. It didn't last long. The soldier cracked Artur across the skull with a surprise strike from the haft, followed up by ramming the blade deep into a woman's chest.

Artur fell to the stones.

Gritting his teeth, Synick dropped to his knees, yanked his last balanced knife from his boot, and threw it spinning toward the soldier. It struck home in his neck, just above the white breastplate. The knife was small enough that he might survive if he got help fast enough.

Maybe.

That couldn't be Synick's problem.

Ducking around two occupied combatants, Synick seized Artur's hand and yanked. The ground was slicked in blood, almost already frozen, but his boots were hobnailed at the toe. He quickly slid Artur away from the fighting. Around them, the white and gold militants were fortunately too occupied to pay any attention to someone who wasn't actively fighting—fortunately for Synick, anyway.

The spreading pool of blood stopped at the edge of the fighting, and dragging the big man became much harder. Breathing heavy, Synick tugged Artur around a corner and shoved him up against the wall. Blood trickled from under his neat mess of short black hair, but he was still breathing. He was napping, more than anything.

Synick slapped him, but he didn't wake up. He slapped him again. Still nothing.

"Freezing idiot. Freezing, snowing idiot." Synick cuffed the big man again, this time not caring if it roused him or not.

With few other options left to him, Synick watched as the citizens of Anveil killed themselves while he hid. The man he'd stabbed in the neck didn't get up.

"Damn you," he spat at Artur. This wasn't his job. Synick's role was to rob the swords from soldiers' sheaths and purses from peasants, not this bloody, god-awful fighting. The snow wolves above the Veil had been bad enough, but *people*?

Minutes later—though it felt like hours—the tide of the

battle became more obvious, and the commonfolk ran. Blood spilled from throats, arms, and severed arteries onto the cold ground, freezing but not losing its coppery scent. Only then, in the comparable quiet, did Synick vomit.

Amid the distant screams of the upper and lower tiers, the soldiers sheathed their weapons and resumed their work, reclaiming the children they'd come for and taking others in their stead if they'd run. Sadagon's men pulled the corpses to the side—there must have been a hundred of them—just far enough for the caged carts and horses to pass through, and left the dead in the resulting silence.

Synick threw up again. With the soldiers gone, there was finally room for the real fear he knew would come. Blades and open wounds were terrifying enough, viscera and marrow trickling into the hungry night, but they were nothing compared to the lines of fire Synick expected to see falling from the sky.

With the white and gold men gone from this part of the mountain, there was nothing to stop Sadagon from using his catapults to firebomb the city, as he'd promised to do in several proclamations, should there be any form of resistance.

Well, the people had resisted, thanks to Artur, killing themselves and several soldiers in the process. Synick waited, surrounded by gore on the ground but watching the sky for the true threat that it bore.

It never came. Hours later, shivering and half frozen without his snow cloak, Synick watched as Artur finally roused. He held up a giant paw to his head and groaned.

"Shut up," Synick immediately snapped at him. "Don't even think about complaining."

"What happened?"

"You did, you brute."

"The children!" he remembered. "The soldiers!"

"Both gone."

"And you did nothing to stop them?"

"Oh, there was plenty done to stop them. Go see what good it did, Artur." He jabbed his thumb around the corner of the stone building that was their shelter. Wobbling dangerously, Artur rose to his feet, bracing his back against the wall. Even then, he almost fell. He was certainly concussed.

"Dead gods," he whispered at the carnage. "Melisa, Grayham," he said, recognizing the corpses.

"You called for blood," Synick spat, still sitting against the wall. "Well, there it is."

"How dare you?" Artur said, spinning on his heel. "How dare you make light of these deaths?"

"You think I'm trying to be funny?" Synick said. His mask of a smile was gone, the bare grimace on full display underneath. "These people are only the beginning, and you had a direct hand in it; or, was that someone else who cried for blood?"

"They were taking our young!" Artur yelled. "And you stopped me from fighting them."

"They *took* your young," Synick corrected, "whether you died in the process or not, but that didn't stop you, did it? You saw the reinforcements coming and the same thing happening halfway across the mountain, but that didn't stop you at all. *This* is the hill you chose to die on and lead these people to their deaths on."

"They died fighting to protect the children of Anveil!" Artur shouted back, hackles raised. "What were *you* doing,

Synick?"

"They died for nothing!" Synick shot back. "They died escalating a war they can't possibly hope to survive! I tried to stop you, Artur, to stop them all, but you didn't listen; and now, these are nothing but food for wolves, and you know what? That isn't even the worst—" Artur cut him off.

"Better to die for Anveil than live a coward!"

"You can't help them!" Synick screamed back. "There's *nothing* you could have done to protect them, and that's assuming they're even in any danger."

"Are you so great a fool, Fayorian, to think there could be any intention for these children that is not hostile?"

"I know *exactly* what lays in wait for the children they took, and trust me when I say it's far worse than what you're thinking; but, if you want to help them, this sure as Hell's Iron Halls wasn't the way to do it."

Artur was growing increasingly agitated. "And what would you have done, foreigner? What method would you employ to stop the abduction of thousands if not resist?"

"Go to the source of the problem," Synick declared. "Cut the head off the snake. This abduction was doubtless orchestrated by Sadagon, but they ultimately belong now to Atha and Olsu."

"Your idea," Artur said, "is to murder the so-called gods?"

"No!" Synick snapped. "Gods, Artur, what's wrong with you? Are you trying to get everyone in this city killed? My plan was to *talk* to them—to make sure the children are safe or even have them returned."

"Then you are a fool," Artur condemned, "as well as a coward. You talk when you should fight."

"You don't know what you're talking about, you ice-

264

brained boar. I'm doing everything I can to keep you from starting a war because I see the bigger picture!"

"And what picture is that?"

"The one where Anveil burns. The picture where Sadagon decides you're more trouble than you're worth, and it's easier to simply break the other cities' spirits by catapulting fire over our walls and reduce Anveil to ash." He coughed and spat bile. "I'm talking about the image I have ingrained in my head where Sadagon fires his weapons on your walls and smashes them to bits, as if they were never there, filling the streets with starving snow wolves. That's the picture I'm talking about, Artur—the one with corpses everywhere, the one you're welcoming when you start fighting in the snowing streets."

Artur seemed momentarily perturbed. "You don't know they have weapons like that," he replied. "For all you are aware, you perpetuate a lie to frighten us into passivity."

Synick suppressed the growling coming from his throat. "You don't know what you don't know, Artur! You literally grasp so little of this concept that you can't understand just how much you don't know." Synick knew his true sneer was showing, but he didn't care. Let Artur see his teeth. "You have no idea the death you'll bring down on us, of the lengths Sadagon will go to subdue *everything*. You're going to get us all killed."

"Don't hide behind the threat of weapons that might not exist so you don't have to admit that you don't have the stomach to fight," Artur accused. "You are afraid because you've never done anything for anybody but yourself! You are a selfish, spineless child who's never known the sting of sacrifice. You are a coward, Synick, and I will never see what my sister or anyone else sees in you, if there even is anyone else. I suspect you're lying about that as well, luring my sister to you with the lies of your game."

Springing off the ground with a wild snarl, Synick kicked one foot off the wall, seizing a fistful of Artur's hair and wrapping around him until he was behind the bigger man, yanking his head back.

His voice was a wash of icy chill. "Have you ever even killed a man, Artur? Do you know what it does to you to split someone's organs and watch the life leak out of them?" Artur was deathly still, barely breathing; and, Synick realized that he held his knife, and it was pressed to Artur's throat. "I have. I do." The scar along his abdomen seemed to flair with pain. "Don't speak to me about sacrifice when you don't know the first thing about me."

Artur swallowed hard.

"You don't have the faintest idea what I've given up and what I stand to lose. You don't understand what *you don't understand,* Artur. You're escalating a helpless situation that you can't control, and Jesika refuses to leave this doomed city; so, when you start a war, you're making it my problem." He bit his tongue. "You want to help Anveil? You want to keep the children they took safe? Then *listen* to me." He shoved Artur away and fell back onto the ground, feeling nearly defeated. The dagger dropped beside him.

Whirling around, Artur looked ready to pounce or run but hesitated when he saw Synick leaned up against the wall. He eyed him up and down as if seeing him for the first time. When the silence stretched on unbroken, he spoke.

"What are you trying to tell me?" the big man asked.

Synick took a long, cooling breath, trying to release the

anger. The air smelled sickly sweet.

"Sadagon controls the gods' armies," he said. "But whatever happens to the children... they belong now to the gods themselves, and I'd be surprised if they knew about this attack. If we can get word to them, they can keep the children safe."

"Why would they listen?" Artur asked. Synick could tell he was trying to keep the edge out of his voice. "What makes you think they are not the very ones who orchestrated this injustice?"

"Because," Synick said. "The god, Olsu... is Faron. And Atha is his sister."

"Liar," Artur accused but was silent after. There was no rebuttal available to him. He squirmed for a moment, then said, "You really want me to believe that the Wolfheart is Olsu reborn? That pale boy who I risked my men to pull from the snow is a literal god of legend? Is that what you're telling me?"

"Keep your snowing voice down," Synick reprimanded but without enthusiasm. The dead did not listen. "Yes, that's what I'm telling you. How else do you expect I earned the favor of the godhead? Olsu is Faron, and if we can get word to him, he can release the children or at least keep that warlord, Sadagon, from razing the city with his catapults."

"Favor?" Artur asked. "What on earth do you mean?"

Synick hesitated. "Jesika... didn't tell you?"

"She's told me nothing besides the way you've turned her aside for another."

Synick exhaled slowly, understanding dawning on him. "She has no intention of leaving," he realized. "She's been letting me believe this whole time that if things went bad,

267

she'd leave, but… she hasn't even told you?"

"Leave where? Tell me what?"

Synick sighed. "It doesn't matter. I can't even convince Jesika, and she thinks she loves me."

Artur huffed, then the cadence of their voices chilled as they remembered they were standing in the carrion of a slaughter.

"You really mean it, don't you?" It sounded like a question, but it wasn't. "Faron is alive and behind this invasion?"

"It's more complicated than that, but yes."

"I thought he was dead," Artur eventually said. "Killed like all the fools who venture into the White—like how you should have been."

"Not dead," Synick replied, "and being a god now, he probably never will be." It didn't hurt to reinforce the lie, Synick thought. Anything to keep Artur from further escalating the violence.

"I see," was all he said.

"The catapults are real, Artur," Synick told him. "The firebombs are real. The *gods* are real. This is the only way."

"And you believe that he will listen to you? That he was not the one behind this attack?"

Synick nodded.

It was quiet for a moment while Artur considered. "Then we need to get word to him," he finally said. Synick was surprised at his change of heart, but he suspected his knife had something to do with it.

"No." He shook his head. "*I* need to get word to him. We might find more soldiers on the way and more people resisting. I can't trust you to not try and help them."

"There is a curfew setting," Artur said. "If you are caught, you might need my help."

"That's exactly what I mean. I can't have you breaking into fights with half the army on the way up the mountain. Trust me," he said, cutting off an argument. "I'll be much, *much* faster alone, and I'm just as likely to get caught as you are to not. Besides," he went on. "You need to tend to that concussion. I'm taking you back to the Foxglove, where you're going to stay, and then I'm going up the mountain."

"If you will not take me," Artur said, "then I will stay and tend to the dead. They will need pyres."

"No!" Synick snapped. "We're taking you home, and with any luck, no one will know you had anything to do with this. Others will honor the dead, but if you're found here now, you might join them."

Artur cleared his throat, looking into the night toward the bloody streets. "Alright then. You're right."

Forcing himself to his feet, Synick left their alley and stepped among the piled bodies. "Stay close to me. I'd rather not be seen until we're a few streets away."

"Synick?" Artur asked. He looked as if he might vomit at any moment. "I apologize for what I said to you. I was wrong. You are… I am…" He looked away from the freezing dead. "Sorry."

"Good."

Anything but That

"You should sleep, Varek. You're pushing yourself too far."

Varek stood at the edge of the keep's courtyard, tired eyes drifting over row after row of dark-haired boys and girls. Their diminutive frames shivered in the cold, and their faces were wet with tears. Mixed among them were several adults who had volunteered themselves into service, as to not be parted from their children. Others weren't nearly so fortunate, their small, bereaved faces haunted with the final memories of their parents who had fallen on swords trying to protect them, ultimately, for nothing.

More weight to carry.

"He is right to push himself," Sadagon said. "The least we can do is witness such an awful sacrifice."

Wind tore at his hair, bitter at the top of the mountain, but he hardly felt it. He couldn't possibly be made to feel more cold inside.

"This is my place," he muttered. "To let this happen."

"Varek, you're pale," Vavelt said. "Please, let me finish this task."

Sadagon turned away from the children to face them. "You shouldn't dissuade him, Vavelt. Your heart is in the right place, but Varek has committed himself. Let him see this through." With quick snaps of his wrist, Sadagon unclasped his snow cloak and draped it over his son's shoulders.

She wrung her gloved hands. "I know, but I wish it weren't so heavy a burden. I can see your heart breaking, Varek."

He couldn't deny it.

"They're freezing," he said, pushing the subject away from his own discomfort. "We can't keep them here much longer."

"They're hungry and tired as well." Sadagon stood with his hands behind his back, eyes affixed to the unfortunate few corralled by the Alabaster Guard before him. "The accounting is nearly finished, and these will be brought into the keep for the night, where they will be fed and given rest. It is a small comfort," he said. "But know that these before you will never know hunger again. Many of them were pulled from the orphan halls or found living in thieving dens in the sewers. They will never again feel the bite of isolation or neglect."

Varek grit his teeth. He hadn't agreed to that. He had bloodied his hands and given his approval for one in twenty, not for orphanages to be emptied entirely. Still, it made sense. Soldiers had died during the excursion, and for each one lost, two would be needed to replace them. The numbers had to be made up somehow.

Numbers. That was how he needed to think of them—a balance of arithmetic. Perhaps that wouldn't hurt quite so keenly. With the pale faces below him, it was a hard illusion to maintain.

Sadagon continued, "I know it hurts, Varek, but you shouldn't let that pain keep you from your victory. For every *one* here, there are *ten* that would be corpses if not for you—hundreds, even. Anveil surrendered to their gods with hardly a hint of rebellion. Rarely has progress been made with so small a loss of life."

"Except these." He didn't need to gesture.

"Each of them has siblings, parents, and friends that will live because of their sacrifice. Beyond that, Anveil's walls remain undamaged, the city un-torched and unmolested. Men will sleep tonight that would otherwise be dead by the sword. The unfortunate few women will mourn for a single child, opposed to all of them dead by the fangs of white wolves—because of you, Varek. You saved these people—you and your sister. Where an entire city would be destroyed, only some of these few will now die."

He brought Varek's gaze to his own with two strong hands on his shoulders, not aggressive but passionate. "I know that's hard to see with children corralled before you, but look at them, Varek." He let the silence punctuate his words. "The Veil is growing. They were already dead. You have given those deaths purpose by saving the lives of every other soul inside these walls."

The sentiment resonated with him, but he wasn't quite sure why. Something about it seemed familiar.

He let his eyes sweep over them, just behind the encircling soldiers. It was a pathetic sight.

A girl not yet in her teens held a boy younger still, pulling her hands through his hair and singing softly. Another girl, older, sobbed furiously by herself, wrapped tightly in her arms. Two boys a few years younger than himself bit and kicked at each other, screaming profanities and throwing punches. The Alabaster Guard did nothing to pull them apart. A small boy sat quietly under a too-large coat, shock clearly spelled across his face. A mother held her daughter, bravely keeping back her tears to lend her child strength. They would soon take oaths and be separated.

Varek's eyes flicked from person to person, all similarly beleaguered, until he caught someone's gaze. A boy nearly his age glowered from the crowd, staring murderous intent directly at him. *You did this*, those cold eyes said.

I did this, he agreed, back bent with the weight of it.

Vavelt noticed the silent exchange and understood the unspoken accusation. She lifted her arm to a square. A few moments later, Yarow, her stout keeper, appeared, severing the link between the boy and his killer. She pointed a long finger at him.

"Set that one apart from the rest," she commanded. Wordlessly, Yarow obeyed.

Varek furrowed his brow. "What are you doing?"

"These are yet to be dedicated to the Fist or field. This one is dressed in rags, and his nose has been broken more than once. He's a fighter. I'm setting him apart to become an officer, where his aggression may be of some use."

Varek gave her a questioning look.

"He'll be kept from the Spile," she clarified. "Permanently." She pointed at the keep behind Varek's back. "You've saved this one. Now go. Synick is more than likely here by now, and you should see to him. The counting is complete anyway."

Varek looked to his father, who kept a hand on his shoulder still. Finally, he nodded. "Go. See to your friend, and deliver to him my thanks."

With an imperceptible nod and one last look over the crowd of children, Varek turned his back and refused to turn around. Five men trailing by his side, he made his way back to the keep's foyer.

When the doors were flung open, Varek saw him there on a deep blue sofa pinned with wood buttons. His head was kept aloft by only his hands, and he looked more tired than Varek had ever seen him before. Deep bags lined his eyes, and his hair was matted with sweat. His knee bounced unconsciously, which was odd for him, but it stopped when he looked up and caught sight of Varek.

A true grin displaced the worry on his face, not the slanted smile that meant he was hiding what he was thinking. He looked for all the world as if he'd been just now pulled from the Veil and not nearly a week before.

"Well, you look awful," Synick said with a smirk.

Varek laughed, his frown melting away as Synick stood and accepted his embrace.

"I was so relieved when Artima told us that you'd made it. I looked for you around every corner all the way here."

Synick snorted. "Oh, please, getting back was hardly even a challenge. I had an advantage I didn't last time."

"An escort?"

"Well, that, and I didn't have you with me. Was just a simple matter of walking to the closest tavern really."

Varek grinned. "And the wolves?"

"Left me alone, more or less, same as you." Synick looked down at Varek's regal clothes. "You're dressed like a git."

Varek couldn't agree more. He glanced down to see the gaudy brocade and gold-buckled belts and caught sight of Synick's clothes as well. His cuffs, pantleg, and boots were covered in a dried blood.

"What happened?"

The smile fell, replaced by a stoic emptiness that betrayed an inner sickness.

"I killed someone today."

"Gods…"

Synick flashed a false grin that disappeared as quickly as it came. "I'm alright, but… we need to talk, Faron."

Varek nodded. "What happened? Is… are Jesika and Artur alright?"

Synick stiffened further. "For now. I'm worried that they won't be, though."

"Tell me."

Synick sat back down on the blue sofa. "I tried to convince her to leave with me. I wanted to flee the army and take her to Vam Aranath, but she won't go." He shrugged. "She won't even tell Artur that I asked. It's their home."

Varek paused, brows furrowing. "That's… actually a really good idea. I'm sorry I didn't think of it."

He shrugged again. "There's nothing for it. She won't leave until she has to, but it'll be too late by then."

There was an extended quiet.

"You said you killed someone," Varek whispered. "Who?"

Synick turned his palms up. "I don't know. One of your soldiers."

Varek felt sick. "Synick, that's… Oh, gods." What was he meant to do here? How did he help? Killing one of Olsu's Fist was punishable by death, but this was *Synick*. At the same time, whoever he had killed was also Varek's responsibility—another life on his back.

"What happened?"

"I surrendered my weapons—well, some of them—with Artur, and then there were soldiers. They were…" Synick looked as if he would be sick. "They were rounding up children, Faron, putting them in cages. I can only assume why."

Varek was silent.

"At first, I thought you didn't know, but then I saw the group in the courtyard… Why, Faron? Why are you doing this? I thought you were trying to prevent this. I thought you and Vavelt agreed to cut off the archons. I thought the whole idea of you coming here was to convince people not to fight."

"I know."

Synick grappled with his next words for a long time, looking on the edge of breaking out in shouts. "I'm worried, Faron."

"So am I, Synick, but… I have to see this through, don't I?"

"How far, though, Faron? When will this stop? What happens when Anveil starts fighting back so hard that you start taking real losses? Will you burn down the city because you have Blackwood to intimidate?"

"No!" Varek said. "Those are my father's words, not mine. I won't let that happen. Nothing is worth that price."

"Well, that's where things are headed," Synick said. "Anveil isn't just going to lie down and accept you stealing their children. They're angry. The people don't even believe that Sadagon has cannons. They don't understand what they are. They're taking to the streets with snowing kitchen knives." He shook his head. "You've started a war, and Jesika won't leave; and, I'm… I'm *terrified* that Sadagon is going to finish it."

"It *won't* come to that," Varek said. "It. Won't."

Synick dropped his head into his hands. He looked *so tired.*

"I want to believe that."

"I promise it," Varek insisted. "It won't happen—not on my life."

"No!" Synick snarled. "Not that. Don't you swear by your life. Anything but that."

Varek was taken aback for a moment, startled out of the argument.

"Take it back."

"I... Synick, I don't mean to let him use the cannons."

"Take. It. Back."

"You know what I mean, Synick. I will not let it come to that."

"And what if *he* does?" Synick lowered his voice. "Snows, Faron, what if *she* does?"

That chilled Varek to his core because it was possible, but also because it was what he'd been afraid to utter. Both Sadagon and Vavelt were so determined to save lives that they would do almost anything to achieve it. Faron wasn't half so strong as that.

He shook his head. He couldn't think like that. Faron was weak, but he was Varek now.

What was Varek capable of?

"I don't know, Synick."

"That's what I'm afraid of, Faron. You swore to me that you would stop Sadagon from taking any more children for the Spile, but now you're helping him do it. How far will you go to do what he says is right?"

"I don't have a choice! I have to let this happen." He sounded hollow. "The Veil is growing, Synick. It will swallow everything before long, and if I don't have the means to protect the world, everyone will die. If I can't sow the fields to feed them, provide the men to protect them, and keep them from starting wars over resources, they're *all* going to die."

"You're starting wars *here*, Faron. Sadagon's solution is causing the very thing he's trying to prevent."

"I need the men, Synick. I need an army. I need the food—so *much more* food." He shook his head, tears brimming. "I can't let them starve. I can't let the wolves have them. I have to protect *everyone*. How can I do that without the children?"

"You really think you can let this happen? Not just to raid the homes of the upper classes, but to empty the *orphanages*, Faron? Your soldiers are packing them into cages like sheep to the slaughterhouse."

"They're not all for the Spile," Varek defended. "Many will be soldiers. Others will work fields of mana, and... I don't intend to let them be consumed by the archons. I got through to her, Synick. Don't you see? We'll cut the archons off and save the children they would have consumed."

"No?" Synick asked. "So the few that will be needed," he said, "are for you?"

"No!" Varek cried. "I won't trade their lives for mine... I don't want to."

"And what if you have to?" Synick pressed. "What if it will 'save more lives?' "

"I am doing everything I can to make sure that doesn't happen."

For a long time, Synick let the silence stand. "That's what I mean, Faron. How long until you decide you have to let that happen, too? How many things are you unwilling to do that you'll have to 'let happen?' You've said that you'll stop

Sadagon because what he's doing is wrong, only to let them happen because there's no other way. Where does that end? How much wrong can you do in the name of what's right?"

"I don't know!" he cried. "Why are you asking me this? Over and over again, I don't know, Synick! I don't know what I have to do! I don't know what I'm capable of anymore. I don't know what's right and wrong or even who I am anymore." Varek's eyes were red, and his pulse raced under the weight that was his to carry. "I am trying to save *everyone*, Synick. *Everyone.* Everybody in the *world*! What am I supposed to do about the few who fight me for it?"

"Let them," he whispered, finally coming to his point. "Let them fight, Faron."

"That's your solution? To let people rebel against my army?" Faron stopped, stunned by the words he'd uttered. "How has this fallen to me?" he asked the open air.

"Let the ones who will fight you fight," Synick said, almost in a daze. "And let the ones who will follow you come. You could let them choose."

"And what if they choose to kill each other?"

"They can't," Synick breathed, "if you take them away. You could take them to Vam Aranath, Faron. You could save the ones who want to be saved. Offer them a new life like your sister did with me."

Varek was stunned for a moment but then asked, "And what about everyone else? What about the ones who stay behind? The growing Veil will *kill* them, Synick. If I have the power to save them and don't use it... isn't that the same as killing them?"

Synick shrugged, and Varek suspected he'd revealed more with that motion than he had intended. "Let them freeze. It isn't your responsibility, Faron, no matter what your father says."

"No?" Vavelt's voice rang out from behind them, sharp but not cutting. "Then whose is it? Who else will protect them if not us?"

Synick's head snapped up, and for a moment, he looked frozen in time. "Vavelt," he coughed, strangely reverent. She stepped into the foyer, then swept across it. She brushed Varek's arm as she approached but surprised him by passing by and pulling Synick into a full-body embrace.

"I'm glad you're safe," she said. "We worried about you all the way here, and even now, there are skirmishes throughout the city." She released him. "Still, you shouldn't talk about things you don't understand. It only makes this harder."

"There has to be another way," Synick pushed, resisting her. "Vavelt, you must see that there is some middle ground between destroying a city and extinction."

"It's good to see you, too," she said with a small, distracting laugh, then went on, "You're right, but not in the way you think you are. Abandoning those who aren't so fortunate to understand the threat facing them is *not* an acceptable solution, but... Father has found another path—a third option."

Varek perked up at that, but Synick only raised a thin brow.

"Synick," Vavelt said. "Is that blood? What's happened to you?"

"It's not mine."

She paused, actinic blue eyes flitting between his own, then stopped her questions. "I see."

"What is it?" Varek asked, fully aware of the desperation in his voice. "What way has Sadagon found?"

"Come on," she said, reaching her arms out to lift Varek to his feet. "Let him tell you. He's on the balcony still."

Varek nodded, hope in his heart like a small flame against a fierce and shrieking gale. Maybe there was a way to save them all.

The Kindest Way

The wind outside was intermittent and whipping, like falling down a frozen waterfall with a hangover. It was difficult work for Synick to not wrap his arms around Vavelt, but now was *not* the time. They stepped into the late-night air to find Sadagon there, broad shoulders cutting an impressive image as he brooded over the fate of a nation.

Synick paused his breathing, paralyzed by more than one kind of fear. The man was intimidating, to be sure, a three-hundred-year-old god slayer and genocidal commander of armies with an unshakeable moral foundation, but even more terrifying than that, he was the father of the woman Synick was sleeping with and the person he loved more than anyone in the world. It was unfortunate that they were two separate people.

He stood with his gloved hands clasped behind his back, long white hair neatly gathered in a tie. A too-thin leather coat protected him from the steep wind, but he didn't appear chilled in the slightest. His nose was white, and Synick knew that if he could see the skin on his arms, it would be smooth and unperturbed, except for the black veins underneath. Beside him was a giant glass sphere, elevated off the ground by four iron legs and surrounded by two collapsible mirrors on a track along its circumference.

Synick swallowed hard, and Sadagon spoke. "They fight," he said. "Always, they fight. I had hoped that our light and power would control them, but of course, they fight."

"Only because we made them," Faron said, but there was no accusation in his voice.

"Yes, because we made them. They fight for their children, and they cannot be blamed; but, neither can they be commended. Those children will save the other cities when their time comes, and that cannot be compromised."

Finally, he turned around. "Hello, Vam Synick, confidant of the Twinborn."

Synick scratched at his neck. "Um, hello."

"You found a way?" Faron asked, eager and hopeful. "You can stop the fighting?"

"I believe I can."

"How?"

"By making them understand," he sighed. "I've received word from my generals that, at last count, the skirmishes in the city have already taken the lives of one hundred and eighty-nine individuals. That is, in my opinion, an entirely conservative estimate. I suspect they will find by morning that the death toll has reached well into the high hundreds on the very first night of the occupation."

Faron made a choking noise.

Sadagon shook his head. "Anveil's walls hold only an estimated seventy thousand. These losses *cannot* be sustained."

"Vavelt said you found another way?" Synick asked. "What is it?" A suspicion grew in his hidden heart.

"To rectify something I had not considered. There is, it

seems, a disadvantage to holding power beyond common belief—the common people do not believe it." The wind punctuated his words with a particularly powerful gust. "They fight, dying in droves and killing my troops, because they do not believe that we can do what we've threatened to do. They feel safe in their ignorance."

Synick's gut twisted. He knew it. Of course Sadagon's idea was just to start killing people.

"So, what?" Synick began. "You're going to fire your cannons and bring the wall down? That's brilliant. They'll definitely understand how powerful you are when they're being torn to shreds by the wolves."

"No!" Varek yelled, surprising them both. "No, you can't! I won't allow it. You said you found a third path!"

"He won't, Varek," Vavelt interjected. "That isn't what he intends. Please, listen to him."

Sadagon took a deep breath. "I understand your hesitance, Varek. I feel the same thing, but please, can you trust me?"

"No, Faron," Synick whispered, and Sadagon visibly cringed at the name.

"I... I can. I trust you." The words were weak and feeble.

"Do you remember, weeks ago, when you swore to me that you would find another way—a third option?"

"I do."

"And do you remember how I swore to follow you, should you find it, even to my death?"

Faron nodded.

"Can you trust now that I have considered all, and this is the middle path that we must take? Can you follow me, with the same promise that I once gave you, except to live and not to die?"

Faron drew a shaky breath, and Vavelt stood with him, bracing him with the strength of her arm and soul. "What is it?"

"They do not believe the power of our weapons," Sadagon said, "and your friend is right that it would be folly to use our cannons. There is no coming back from that level of destruction, but…" He exhaled a long breath, mist puffing from his lungs. "I propose a demonstration."

"What does that mean?"

"The catapults," Synick realized. "He means to fire on the city with the catapults."

Faron's mouth fell, and Synick could see that he was crushed. He grit his teeth and wished he could take back the words, but they were true. Faron had allowed himself to hope, opening up to trust his father, and now he was paying for it.

Damn him.

"Yes," Sadagon said. "Yes, that is what I intend."

"No!" Faron yelled. "You can't! You said you found another way! How is this different? How is killing them one way any better than another? I can't do it! I can't let you kill them."

"Peace, my son. It isn't what you think." He gestured with a large palm. "See my flair machine. Do you know what this is?"

"I do," Faron replied, "and I'll be damned before I let you use it."

"Please, Varek. You said you would trust me. Can I not show you?"

Faron breathed long and hard, then nodded. "Show me."

He gestured to the two levers on the sphere's opposing legs, firmly attached by a system of gears.

"It is a beacon," he explained. "A signal for my catapults."

"Tell me how this is different. Tell me how this saves Anveil."

Sadagon nodded as if at a sage question. "These mirrors," he said, sliding the collapsing mirrors on the surrounding track, "are limiters. With them, I can stifle and control the light." He reached out and slid the plates along a greased track, slowly and inch by inch. There was a scraping noise as the individual mirrored sections crossed and slid across one another, expanding and collapsing to telescope out and shift in size. Vavelt held the opposite side, preventing it from following across the track. Sadagon brought the edges nearly together, almost entirely surrounding the evil thing. A metal pin slid down to latch the mirrors in place.

"The mirrors will rebound the light, creating an upward beacon to signal the catapults to fire." He indicated toward the small gap between the mirrors. "And from here, a sliver of light will fall upon the mountain and over the wall. That light," he went on, "and the city inside that light will be a target for my catapults and nothing else. One sliver, to be fired upon in demonstration of our ability and our resolve. One sliver and no more."

Faron looked like he was going to be sick. "How is that any better?" he asked, almost choking on the words.

"Because if I light this beacon with this degree of shades, my catapults will take the lives of perhaps three hundred individuals in a matter of minutes, and then they will be stopped. Anveil will know the power that we wield and that we are willing to wield it. They will know to fear us and not fight back. If others are to follow, Anveil. Must. Fall." He punctuated each word with heavy importance. "One way or another. With this, though," he said, "we can end the bloodshed, once and for all."

"That's your third option?" Faron asked, torn apart by the very same hope that held him together only moments before. "How? How can you expect me to go along with this?" He waited, then said, "How can I let this happen?" as if to himself.

"Can you not?" Vavelt asked. "Can you let the fighting continue another day or two or three, only to decide then that the catapults are needed? Could you live with yourself, Varek, knowing you could have stopped the fighting and saved them by this one show of force?"

He didn't answer, his breaths growing heavy and short.

"It is the most merciful route," Sadagon said. "Imagine the resistance we will find in Murcosta or Empyrion if they learn Anveil repelled us. How many lives will be lost in those battles if they are to come to pass?" The wind stood in for Faron's response. "With this one display, Varek, we might save this city and all others after it, but if Anveil does not surrender—and soon—it will only spell further bloodshed."

"Stop!" Faron cried. "Please stop! I can't bear it."

His quick gasps threatened to tear Synick's heart in half. He knew what Sadagon and Vavelt didn't. He knew what Faron was capable of. It made his mind for him.

"Don't then," he cut in. "Don't bear it, Faron. Please. Don't take this path. You know you can't."

"I don't know what I know!" he responded with the high tones of anxiety. "I don't know what I have to do or what I should do."

"This," Vavelt said. "This, Varek. It is the kindest way."

"Really," Synick asked, shocked by her callousness. "This is the kindest method you can think of? Nearly doubling the dead in a matter of minutes? You can't be serious, Vavelt."

"I am," she said, silencing him. "Because kindness isn't the only scale to be measured but life as well. I might be a god to them, Synick, but that does not give me the right to weigh the worth of lives. If I favor the worth of souls in Anveil above that of the world, it will be costly. The only fair metric is that of numbers. The only way to do what's right is to save as many as possible, regardless of my personal feelings."

"And what are your personal feelings?" he demanded. "What do you think this will do to you, Vavelt? And what about him?" Synick screamed, pointing at Faron. He was sickly and pale, nearly green in shade and tone. "What will this do to him? Do you have any idea how it will affect him, Vavelt? How it will follow him for the rest of his life?"

Faron looked shaken. "Stop it, Synick," he said.

"No!" he cried. "No, I can't stop, Faron. I can't, and I won't. You know I'm right. You know what this will do to you. Do you really think you can follow through with this?" Adopting a phrase Faron had begun to use, Synick said, "Can you carry that weight?"

Faron broke.

"NO!" he screamed, the sound tearing from his throat. "No, I can't! I can't bear it, Synick, but how does that matter against what I have to do? How does that matter against the weight of an entire world?"

"You can't be responsible for that, Faron! The fate of Alden cannot fall to one person alone." Synick shot a look of sharpened steel at Sadagon. "Regardless of the power you've been given."

"Someone must save them," Sadagon cut in, meeting

Synick's eyes with a look to melt iron and ore. "Or they will *all* die."

"Yes," Synick spat back. "*Someone.* How very convenient that it so happens to not be you."

"I…" Sadagon hesitated, words catching in his throat. "I am not right for that kind of power."

"And he is!?" Synick cried. "She is? You couldn't stand the burden of what you intended, so instead, you pass it on to your children?"

"Stop it, Synick," Vavelt commanded. "You don't know what you're talking about."

He didn't stop, though. "You," he accused, "are a coward, Sadagon Pyre."

Sadagon didn't immediately respond. Synick expected him to return his heat or at least have him taken away, but he only stood there, searching Synick's eyes with that same look of intensity Vavelt had inherited.

After a long moment passed, he said, "Perhaps you are right, but that does not mean I am wrong. The world expects a Twinborn godhead, so that is what I have given them; and, that is the part we must play. Words do not change that now."

"You're right, Synick," Vavelt said, her tone pleading. "I *don't* want to do this. I don't know what it will do to me or if I'm strong enough, but I know that I can't favor one life above another. What is that if not evil?"

"Favor no one, then," Synick said. "But let them *choose.* Tell them of the growing Veil and of the wars that will follow, and let them *choose* to come with you to Vam Aranath. Protect those that ask for it, and save your army for keeping peace. You *don't* have to do this, Vavelt." He turned to see Faron. "Or you."

Sadagon shook his head. "Vam Aranath will not hold them. You are wise, Vam Synick, to suggest such a thing, but we lack the means to provide for such a population. Our food stores were nearly exhausted simply by the relief we brought to Anveil. We cannot save them there." He turned back to the city. "Even if we could, you would simply abandon those who do not believe our words? You would abandon those who do not heed our warning? There is no arithmetic to balance how many would come and how many would refuse." He shook his head again. "I'm sorry, but no. This remains the only way. The mercy of numbers is the only scale allowed to us."

"Spoken," Synick said, "like a god. Remind me," he asked, "who it was who is not suited for this kind of power? Remind me who it was who abdicated his stewardship to his children because he could not bear the weight of what must be done?"

That hit Sadagon like a brick to the chest. He opened his mouth to reply but found no words. He shifted his grip on his forearms, folded behind his back, and tried again.

"Thank you, Vam Synick, for showing me my place. You are right. Let the gods decide." His tone was easy, but his gloved fingers upon the stone parapet betrayed a deeply rooted stress in his claw-like grip. He turned to face his children. "What," he asked, "will you do, Atha and Olsu?"

Faron looked as if he hadn't heard, eyes firmly planted on the cold stone of the balcony.

"Choose quickly," Sadagon advised. "Every moment is counted in the lives of those who fight still."

"I don't know!" Faron shot back at him. "I don't know what to do or how this has fallen to me."

Vavelt paid Synick a pinning look. "You aren't helping,

Synick." He waited for her to explain, but she didn't, only returning her attention to Faron.

"My brother," she whispered to him, sorting his hair with her white-gloved hands. "You are so much stronger than you know."

Faron shook his head, his shoulders trembling.

"I know," she said. "I know. It's an awful thing, a terrible thing, but somehow, it falls to us to decide." He still didn't respond. "No one should have to bear this burden, least of all someone as pure and good as you, but for what it's worth, brother, if anyone must choose, I'm glad it's you."

He shook a little harder. "I can't," he said. "I can't choose who lives and who dies, Hadria. I can't choose."

Vavelt threw a look over her shoulder at her father, but he remained unchanged. If he heard his son use the painful name, he didn't show it. Vavelt let it pass.

"Neither can I," she admitted. "I don't have the right. The only thing we can do is what's fair—to save as many as is possible, no matter who, no matter the cost."

Faron's frame trembled through sharp inhalations and shaky breaths, white mists marking each exhalation. Synick tensed, ready to leap. He looked as if he might fall at any moment, but before Synick had to intervene, Faron braced himself against Sadagon's flare machine, palms heavy against the glass orb. Vavelt reached down to trace a finger along his cheek, and he finally looked up to see her.

"What's *fair*, Varek. What's best for everyone. You know what that is."

Slowly, he nodded.

"I hate it," she said, her own voice on the edge of breaking. "Three hundred lives—gods, I can't bear it—but if nothing is done, the dead will outweigh that in two or three days anyway, with no end in sight. We must show our hand, Varek." She nodded, fighting back a welling in her own eyes. "If the violence is to stop, we must show them what we can do."

Sadagon stood with his back to the great slope of the mountain, watching as his children defended him.

"And what if it doesn't work?" Synick interrupted. "What if the threat of your catapults spurs them to even greater violence? What if you lose your grip on the city and they don't fall to you the way you hope? What will you do then, Faron? Will you raze the city? Will you use the cannons and tear down the walls to show the rest of Alden that you're willing to make good on your threats? How many will you save, Faron, if you have to tear down the wall of every city that opposes you?

"Have you considered that?" Synick ranted on. "That if you destroy Anveil, it won't intimidate the other cities but spur them against you? Turn the tide of their favor when they could have been persuaded?"

Sadagon only watched them fight.

"Stop it!" Vavelt called at him. "Stop it, Synick! You don't know how hard this is for him already."

"I do!" Synick retorted, his mask missing somewhere. "I do know him, Vavelt, better than you do, to be sure! You say how awful it is that he has to be the one to bear this weight, but you don't know what it will do to him." He choked, remembering the long sight of a wide bridge suspended high above a meaningless depth of deep and dark forgetfulness. He coughed on the words, "You don't know what it will drive him to."

Faron couldn't respond. Synick could see that he tried, but he lacked the strength. Already, this was too much for him to bear.

"Answer me!" Synick yelled, desperate. "Answer me, Faron. Do you think you can do it? Do you think you can live with who you will become at the end of this road?" When Faron didn't answer, he shouted, "Don't tell me you can let this happen!"

"I don't know!" Faron screamed, looking as if he'd been roused from a terrible dream. His eyes were wide, fearful, and bloodshot, and Synick would have sworn that he was hiding an incising headache. His face was covered in sweat, despite the cold. The smile he'd worn only an hour before looked forever lost as if he had never smiled before and never would again.

Faron turned to Sadagon. "I can't carry them!" he screamed. "The children, the slaves, the ones who will die. I can't carry any more! I can't let you kill them." He looked back at Synick, eyes a storm of terror and fatigue. "And I can't let them kill each other! There's nothing I can do to save them all, and I can't just let them die."

Synick rushed forward and seized Faron, pulling him away from the orb to face him. "And I can't let you kill yourself!" he cried, releasing what he'd been trying so hard to hide. "I can't let you do this, Faron!"

Faron shoved him away harder than Synick expected, and his grip broke. Faron staggered backward, off-balance and reeling. Synick tried to leap forward and catch him but was too late. A few quick, stumbling steps brought him to the wall of the keep, where he cracked his head against the stone—hard.

"Varek!" Vavelt gasped as he slid down to a slump.

Sadagon leaped forward like a charging bear, but Faron's eyes were still open, if unfocused. "What do I do?" he asked through trailing tears. "I can't do it, and I can't stop it. I can't... I can't kill them. I can't carry them all." He clenched his jaw, but his lip trembled still. "I cannot carry this weight."

Gently, Sadagon slipped a hand behind Faron's head, and it came away bloody. "Be it on my head," he begged. "Let these be on *my* head."

"And mine," Vavelt spoke, her chin jutted out in defiance. "You have carried enough, brother."

Faron shook his head in fatigued defiance but said nothing. Synick was profoundly proud of him for that, even if he couldn't quite finger why.

Standing in the open sky of the tower balcony, Synick faced the depth of Faron's inability to act and understood what he had to do. Sadagon, in his unshakeable morality, would go to any length to save his world, even if it meant sacrificing his son in the process. Synick couldn't let that happen. If there were to be a sacrifice, it wouldn't be Faron for the world.

It would be the world for Faron.

There was no price Synick would not pay to keep him safe. Everyone else could freeze.

The path before him clicked into place, and he knew what he had to do—the one way to protect his chosen family. He prepared himself to lie without his mask.

Faron's lids slid shut, and his breathing began to steady.

"This is our burden to bear," Sadagon said, still kneeling and cradling Faron's head. Safe from his son's fledgling eyes, Sadagon's tears loosed. "Our terrible responsibility:

to protect as many as we can from the growing Veil, no matter the cost, no matter the blood, no matter the damage to ourselves. I am sorry, Vam Synick."

"It isn't me you'll apologize to, Steward," Synick said.

"I know you're trying to help, Synick," Vavelt came in. "But please, stop. We know what we have to do."

"Then do it," he said. "But give me time. I have to get them out."

"Jesika?" she asked, her lips curving slightly downward. The expression was not lost on Sadagon, who looked to burrow into him with those augur-like eyes. Without his smiling mask, Synick knew the man could see everything hidden there, but he no longer cared.

"Yes," he said, worried, even now, that she would hate him for it.

Vavelt sighed. "Bring her then, and let me protect her. Let me see the woman who can hold your attention against a god."

Sadagon didn't seem the least bit surprised, but he did look angry.

Despite everything—Faron, the Veil, the dangerous knowledge of what he had to do—Synick felt a lump in his throat.

"It's not... It isn't what you think," he said. "It's... It's hard to." He sighed. "I don't love her," he swore. "I don't. I just... I mean, I thought I did, but—" He pulled a fistful of hair in frustration.

"I understand," Vavelt said, her tone laced with resignation. "You love so strongly, Synick, more than anyone I've ever known. You hide it—bury it deep inside—but it's true." She shook her head, golden curls falling delicately around her neck in the dance of her forgiveness. "How can I hate you for holding so tightly to the one thing you've always needed and never asked for?"

Sadagon's prying eyes formed the shape of a question, but Synick ignored him. It was Vavelt who held his attention—Vavelt, and Faron, who seemed almost peaceful in his unfeeling and unconscious state.

"Bring them," she said. "Jesika, Artur, whoever you call your family for whatever reason. We will wait for you. Bring them to me, and I will keep them safe."

Almost choking on the tears that he suppressed, Synick nodded. "I'll try," he lied. He knew they would not come, but there was work still to do this night; and, he needed the time—desperately.

Vavelt reached out and felt his hair in plain view of her father. She pulled on his chin to guide his eyes away from Faron and toward herself. After only a moment, he let her, breathing hard and jaw set tight. The intensity of that gaze would have burned anyone but her, the one person who knew his secret.

"I love you, Synick."

"I love y—"

She cut him off. "Don't. Don't say it until you mean it. I know who you love."

He tried and failed to hide his trembling.

"Let me protect your family, Synick. Let me protect your heart. Bring them here, and let me shelter them from the work we must do."

Synick stood in the silence that was his conviction. Vavelt could protect the people he cared about from the flames, but about his heart, she was as wrong as wrong could be.

He watched as Sadagon lifted Faron into his arms. For all

296

his gentle care, the choices Sadagon drove him to would be Faron's death.

Synick had to save him from those choices.

No matter the cost.

No matter the blood.

Faron's Good Work

F aron dreamed he could not breathe—not a long dream, where he evaded pursuers or hunted the men who held his sister captive, but a constant, never-ending dream, where he held his breath as the life ebbed away from him.

He didn't remember it, but it was more memory than fabrication. The dark and gleaming figure of Jakal hovered above him, a constant pressure that prevented his lungs from drawing breath. Beyond Jakal, a heavy, sooty smoke filled the air, clawing, cloying, and tearing at his lungs.

The pressure of Jakal's form shifted to that of a cage, with him inside and his sister out, but it didn't last long. Before he could even reach for the ice-bitten bars, everything was replaced by the eternal memory of a man lying hard on the sand, spilling rivulets into the earth from a stolen knife that split his eye. His body shook, clinging to life despite a sundered brain, and Faron was made to watch.

It was, after all, his good work.

He still couldn't breathe. Hands held him down, pinning him in place to make him see the death he'd caused, and then those hands burst into flame, melting the skin on his chest and shoulders, burning, burning, *burning*. He shoved the flaming pillar away with desperate hands and hidden strength, but it wasn't enough. His hands burned now, too, the skin boiling and evaporating and melting away in a way he would never recover from.

A blackened skull watched it all.

Fighting Back

With the exhausted determination of a man about to lose everything, Synick slipped back into the Foxglove Inn, long hours before the sun would tinge the sky with the first gray hint of day. He had expected Jesika to be asleep upstairs in her room, but she was kneeling over something by one of the four fireplaces, all of which were lit. They were burning high, unusual for this time of night, and she jumped when she saw him.

"Synick!" Jesika said, face flushed. "You're finally back!" She looked every bit like a guilty child, and Synick's half-sliver of hope died when he saw why.

Gathered around the fireplaces and at the polished wooden tables were dozens of children and nearly half that many adults, all bruised, battered, and bandaged. They were too busy staring with hollow eyes through chilling bowls of soup or crackling fires to take notice of Synick. This wasn't the despondency of orphans or the hopeless. These people had walked Hell's Iron Halls.

"Jesika…" he started, but she didn't let him finish.

"I won't hear it, Synick. I know what you're thinking, but he didn't have a choice. Nara knew where his son was being held, and when the troops moved, there was an opportunity."

She gestured around the room, then filled the silence when Synick didn't respond. "They needed somewhere to stay."

Nara… Synick recognized that name and, after a recollective moment, put a face to it. It was one of the men under Artur's command who had pulled Faron from the White back before all of this began.

"Artur?" he asked. "He attacked a garrison?"

It was suddenly clear where the children had come from. The question he had come to pose hung half-formed on his lips, wanting to be asked but knowing better than to bother. There was no point anymore. Jesika was rooted here as firmly as if each of these children were an anchor around her neck. Even without them, she'd never intended to leave.

That only cemented the reality of what he had to do.

With a long breath and a resigned air about him, he asked, "Where is he?"

"In his rooms upstairs." Her answer came with a relieved exhalation. Synick guessed that she'd expected a long fight. He wanted to give it to her, but there was no point in it. Instead, he abandoned his instinct to banter and cut straight to the point.

"I need him."

Searching his eyes for any clue of what he was thinking, Jesika began to nod, then turned and went up the steps. Synick wasn't sure if he was meant to follow, but he did.

On the upper level, she knocked on the nearest door. There was no answer. She knocked again, then, thinking better of it, tried the handle. It wasn't locked.

Artur sat on the edge of his narrow bed, staring at open hands. There was a bandage around his head and more on his bare chest and arms.

301

"Artur?" Jesika called, voice uncharacteristically soft as if she were trying to speak to an unaware deer without it bounding off. "Synick is here."

Artur didn't answer, and Synick knew why. He'd seen Faron in this state hundreds of times before. His hands were shaking, and his breathing was quick. Synick was watching a man who was grappling with his sins. To Synick, it was as plain as day that Artur had just taken a life and wasn't prepared for it.

"Let me talk to him," he asked Jesika, and thankfully, she slipped out and let the door close behind her. With little hesitation, Synick approached the bigger man and sat beside him. He reached out to turn Artur's palms down, then asked, "How many?"

He didn't jump or turn to see who was speaking. "Four—two for Nara, one for Harfor, one for me."

"It's not easy, is it?"

"They were alive," he said. "Thinking, walking—and then… and then we…"

"You killed them," Synick finished for him.

"We broke them," Artur coughed with a hollow ring. "We broke their bodies with metal, pulled their insides out of them. They were only boys. One of them tried to… tried to put himself back together."

"I know," Synick interrupted, thinking of his own victims, recent and distant both.

"I split his stomach open," Artur choked. "I ruined his body and, and… it wasn't quick, Synick. It wasn't fast or painless. There was no glory or victory in it. He… he saw what I'd done to him and looked at me like he couldn't believe. Then his mind was gone. Just… gone. But… he's *still* looking at

302

me, Synick."

"I know."

"Do you think it's real?" Artur finally looked at him, his eyes pleading. "The gods? Souls? A heaven and hell? Did I destroy that boy? Did I send him to another world, or is he gone now, his flame forever extinguished?"

Synick knew better than to answer that. "I don't know," was his compromise. "It's a good question but not one you should ask, Artur. There's no comfort in it, not either way."

He took a shuddering breath. "You were right," he said. "What it does to a man."

Synick suspected that, in this moment, any other man would lose his tears, but Artur held his own captive.

"How can you bear it, Synick? How can you forget?"

"You never forget," Synick said, offering a small flash of a false smile. "All you can do is be damn sure that you believe what you're killing for." Faron's bereaved face struck him then. "Anything else is to kill yourself in the process."

Synick set his jaw.

Artur breathed in and out for a long time, deep lungfuls that seemed to lend him fortitude. "For Anveil," he said. "For her children and her walls."

"For Anveil," Synick agreed. "For Jesika. For you and your family. For Faron."

That pulled Artur out of his reverie. "Faron?" he asked. "Did you find him? Can he help?"

"He can't."

Artur almost looked relieved, then his face pulled into a questioning look of puzzlement. "Why, then, are you here?"

"Because," Synick said. "I'm going to do something very stupid, and I need your help."

Artur's puzzled expression didn't lift.

"Come on, get dressed."

There was a quiet moment, long enough for the space of several heartbeats, and then Artur's mourning gave way to inquisitive determination. He stood, dressed quickly, and followed Synick through the downstair's door of Jesika's tavern. Jesika, thankfully, did not come with them.

"What are you doing?" Artur asked in the wintry mountain air, windborne snow swirling around them.

"Faron can't help us, but we can help him."

"Help him how? Where are you taking me?"

"Only across the street for now, and then you're going to collect Harfor and Nara, or whoever will come with you, and you'll take me to the bodies of those soldiers."

Artur looked around as Synick pulled him into Orothorn's glass smithy. The open design allowed cold air into the forge, but there was no heat to cool now.

"What?" He seemed taken aback, but Synick didn't stop to explain. There was very little time left. "What could you need with them?"

They stopped before a large metal safe built into the wall. It wasn't there the last time Synick was here, and he was certain he knew why.

"What are you doing, Synick?" Artur repeated the question with more fervency, then raised a brow as he pulled two lengths of metal from a pocket and had his way with the lock.

"What I told you not to," he replied. "We're fighting back."

"But why are we here?"

"Because," Synick said as the doors to the massive safe drifted open. The dim light reflected off of five rows of perfect glass arrows, all with a bulbous container toward the end and a lump of something hard and white in the head. "If you're going to do something stupid, at least be smart about it."

Freedom from a Painful Choice

I n the whispering wind beyond the wall of Anveil, Synick lay prone behind a sinuous snowdrift, wresting the lever of Faron's metal crossbow into place. The string hummed as it snapped into its catch, and with a soft clinking, Synick lowered the fire ampoule into the slot.

It was a beautiful thing, made all of glass, with a white speck of phosphorous in the pointed head and a reservoir of oil in the hollow section at the haft. It was of a far finer craftsmanship than the ones Synick had created, but then, Orothorn was a master. Regardless of the unnecessary quality, Synick felt a sense of ownership over these beautiful fire arrows. He, after all, had invented them—or, perhaps, *reinvented*.

Artur shuffled uncomfortably beside him, the very image of a man whose skin was crawling.

"Stop wiggling," Synick snapped.

"I can't see at my back like this," he complained.

"Nor we," Nara said, thumbing at Harfor. They were Artur's men, under his command on the wall, but now they were hiding in its shadow. This was Synick's territory.

"Shut up about your backs. You don't need to see the wolves to know they're there. They probably smelled you coming down the wall and have been watching ever since."

Nara checked over his shoulder, an action that required him to move completely onto his side.

"You're wasting your time," Synick said, peering through the tree line before them. "Even if the snow wolves do attack, seeing it coming a few seconds early won't save you. Either the cloaks are working, or you're already dead."

Harfor swallowed. "He doesn't exactly inspire confidence, does he?"

Artur gave him a silencing look. "If Synick of Faye says that the cloaks will work, then I believe him. That's all there is to it."

"There's blood on mine," Nara said.

"That's typically what happens when you rob the dead," Synick responded, still sighting down the shaft of the lever bow.

"Will it... attract them?"

"You're full of blood, Nara. Have they come to gnaw your head off yet?" That quieted him. "I can't find any others," he concluded. "Only the fifteen," Synick said. "One row, all spread out."

"And the cannons?" Artur asked.

"I can't find them."

There was an uncomfortable silence. Only the wind spoke to punctuate the terrible danger that represented. Small lights flickered through the trees before them, cookfires of Sadagon's army. There was a slight susurration from that direction but not enough to be understood.

Artur spoke then, "Before we were removed from our walls, a portion of the army broke away and entrenched on the opposite side of the city. Could this western camp have them?"

Synick thought about it. There was a certain cruel efficiency to that. Flood the city with fire from one side and wolves from the other—a terrible maelstrom of teeth and flame.

"It's possible."

"Dead gods," Harfor cursed. "How are we to reach them before morning?"

Synick shook his head. "We don't. I doubt there's anything we could do to harm the cannons anyway. They're solid metal. A little fire won't bother them." He lowered his voice. "Besides... Sadagon won't use those cannons. They'll be the death of every living thing on the mountain, and he's occupied with minimizing casualties." He nodded. "The catapults are the real threat. He won't use the cannons." Again, he nodded to himself. "They won't let him."

"So..." Harfor posed. "You're calling his bluff?"

Synick didn't answer.

Nara filled the silence. "What if there are more catapults on the western side with the cannons?"

Synick cursed. "Then that side is dead. What do you want me to do about it?" He bit off the rest of his raw retort and said instead, "No, no, I don't think there are more. The snow wolves fear fire. If Sadagon tears the wall down and fills it with fire, it will keep the wolves out, same as stone. No, this is all of them." A lengthening quiet sought to undermine his words, so he added, "I'm sure of it."

"There is a sense to that," Artur offered. "Either way, if we do nothing, both faces will burn. If we destroy these and the other side retaliates, we will destroy them next and the cannons with them."

Synick shrugged. That was wishful thinking, but whatever brought them along worked for him.

"But you're only guessing," Nara protested. "You don't know that!"

Synick glanced at Artur. "Who did you tell them I was?"

"Nobody." He gave a little grin.

"Accurate enough." Synick looked back to Nara. "Maybe you're right, but it's what I would do in his position."

"So, it's a guess?"

"Yes, Nora, it's a guess."

"It's Nara," he corrected.

"I don't care. Artur," Synick said, catching the other man's attention. "We don't have much time left. Are you ready?"

The big man looked up at the sky as it began to glow with the first hint of gray. "As ready as one can be."

"Remember," Synick said. "You have to break the glass. If the vial just lands in snow, it won't do anything. You have to shatter it."

"Damn that Artima for taking our crossbows," Artur said.

"We'll be alright," Nara spoke. "There's not much I can't hit with a sling."

"I'll be alright, too." Harfor nodded, but it wasn't incredibly convincing.

Synick let the moment settle. "You all know what to do then?"

They nodded.

"Remember," Synick whispered. "They'll have searchlights. If you get caught in one, try to hide behind your cloak and get down. If you're lucky, they'll mistake you for a wolf. Hide, if you can, until you can get back to the rope."

"We know, Synick of Faye," Artur said, but he was wrong.

309

They didn't know. They'd each and every one of them sworn that they were prepared to die for Anveil, but that's what they were expected to say. The truth was, this was a suicide mission. Synick ran a finger along the etched filigree of his—or rather, Faron's—crossbow haft, then corrected himself. This was a suicide mission *for them*.

He bit the inside of a cheek. Could he let Artur go along with this? The odds of them all coming back were slim, to be generous, and Artur was, despite what he would say, Synick's chosen family. He bit down harder on his cheek and tried to stem the flow of thoughts. Artur had his own reasons for coming. He had every right to be here—Nara and Harfor, too.

They had volunteered, after all. The moment Artur told them about the fire arrows, they'd scrabbled to help, no matter how poorly equipped. Part of him wanted to turn back, to tell them it was a fool's gambit, but he didn't. Destroying these catapults would free Faron from the choice of using them—a choice that would kill him, no matter the decision.

There were no other options left. Synick would trade their lives for Faron's if he had to—even Artur's. He ground his jaws together to cut out the sharp whistles of the wind for a moment. If Artur died out here, Jesika would never forgive him... but she'd be alive, wouldn't she? Alive to hate him all she wanted.

There was no other way.

"Move," Synick commanded, banishing the thought. He didn't know how this would end. Maybe they'd get through it? "Nara to the rightmost, Artur five in, Harfor to the far left. Wait for my signal, then count to thirty, then *move*."

Prowling like the wolves they feared, they split apart and approached the exposed line of catapults just before the tree line. In the near-perfect dark, Synick lost sight of them almost immediately, except for a few half-glimpsed disturbances in the shadows. The catapults, at least, were clear to him, caught without camouflage in the light of the stars.

Synick repositioned on his snowbank, guessing at how long it might take them to get within slingshot range of Sadagon's weapons. While he waited, he sighted down Faron's crossbow, estimating where to best place his signal. There were several bright spots below the long end of his bolt, where cookfires burned low and might now be providing warmth for groups of white and gold soldiers. Beyond that, there was little to observe except the seemingly endless expanse of tents that could have been trees in the dark.

With every passing minute, the sky threatened to further its gradient from black to gray. Synick waited a few breaths longer, blood pumping drumbeats through his ears, then set his jaw. That was long enough. Lying prone, he set the stock of his crossbow against his shoulder, then leaned his head down to get a clear look at the encampment through the iron sights.

He didn't have many spares, but if he achieved the proper angle, he suspected he could launch the phosphorous bolts about five hundred yards out. The catapults—and edge of the camp—were roughly one hundred and fifty yards away. That meant that, if he was lucky, he could place the first bolt three-hundred-odd yards deep into Sadagon's army. That ought to draw their attention long enough... hopefully.

Letting out a slow breath, Synick placed his finger on the

small trigger, then squeezed.

Something moved behind him.

Synick yelped as he flung the crossbow aside, turning to see a white wolf just at his back, red eyes pinning him down. His knife was out of its sheath and in his hands in an instant, but just before he had it in the thing's neck, he stopped.

"Francis?" he asked incredulously. Sure enough, Vavelt's pet monster had found him. It was smaller than most snow wolves—larger than a sheepdog and smaller than he was long—but its eyes and teeth were still considerable threats.

"What are you doing here, you dumb dog? You scared me half lifeless!" The wolf's only response was to keel over in supplication for tummy rubs. Synick glared at him, then glanced at the graying sky and down at the catapults. "I really don't have time for you," he said but found a moment to provide a few small scratches. "I'm actually more of a cat person, to be honest. Now get away. I've got work to do."

The wolf made no move to obey, instead making it perfectly clear how entirely insufficient his administrations had been. Synick, after all, had two hands and had only used the one.

Pulling his white cloak tighter against the wind, Synick looked out into the night but, this time, saw something that hadn't been there before. Red eyes, barely visible in the dark, stared back at him, hungry but patient. He swallowed hard. Synick couldn't afford to waste any of his firebolts here.

"On second thought," he muttered. "Maybe you can stay. Watch my back, Francis." Synick shook his head, then, trusting his cloak and the added threat of Vavelt's pet, gently picked the metal crossbow back up and lay prone again. He'd wasted too much time. They'd be in position now, waiting for him, wondering if something was wrong.

Without a moment to spare, Synick pulled the stock against his shoulder, tipped the point up approximately thirty degrees, and fired. The glass bolt shrieked as it flew, giving a long, clear note in indication of its direction and speed, but was otherwise invisible. Synick held his breath for a few seconds, but nothing happened.

With a bitter curse, he yanked the circular lever and forced the string back into place. He loaded it with another glass bolt from his pouch, sighted down the bow, and fired again. There was a clean whistle, a silence, and then a flash of brilliant whiteness. Synick grinned as a fire bloomed across what he only hoped was a series of tents. It was too far and too dark to be sure.

Despite that distance, a cacophonous presence of alarm filled the encampment, and in a stroke of pure luck, Synick's first phosphorous bolt went off, exploding in a fireball ten times the size of the first one. His eyes went wide, showing their whites as he swallowed, wondering what on earth he'd hit.

Francis became alert, muzzle pointing like a hunting dog toward the flame, a growl in his canine throat. The army buzzed to life before them, partially visible down the slight incline. They watched as the shadows of men flocked to the distraction, just as Synick had hoped. Ignoring his own orders, he quickly loaded another bolt and brought his aim much closer—around one hundred fifty yards, Synick guessed.

He took a steadying breath. That was a difficult shot—for Synick, anyway—maybe impossible for something small like a deer or a man, but the catapults were anything but small.

It would be like hitting the broadside of a barn. True, Synick had been told he *couldn't* hit the broadside of a barn, but that was only because he'd been aiming at the squirrels to the side of it at the time.

He grinned, his adrenaline bringing him back to task, and shoved the memory away. This wasn't the time. Letting out the long breath, he braced against the snowbank and let the catapult center in his round iron sights. His slight shaking came to a stop, and he released the bolt. Another whistle, then a blossom of yellow light as the oil bloomed across the catapult's wooden surface.

Perfectly on cue, two more catapults went up in flame, then a third. The nearness of the fire illuminated the line of death machines, and Synick grinned again. Artur and his men were right about those slings. They got the job done.

Yanking the rounded lever across the length of the shaft, Synick reloaded. Three more catapults went up in flames before Synick was finished, and he added a fourth with only a few seconds to aim. That one exploded as well—like the fireball in the camp—a huge white ball of smoke and light that belched into the sky, throwing another nearby catapult onto its side, smashing into a thousand slivers of timber and iron when it came down.

Francis yelped, turned, and ran off with his tail between his legs. Whatever accelerant Sadagon used for his catapults, it didn't burn like kitchen oil.

So bright was the fire that Synick caught a glimpse of Nara, and he realized that the adjacent catapult wasn't the only thing that the explosion had thrown. Even from here, he could see plainly that Nara was burning and not moving. Synick swallowed hard.

His life for Faron's. For Jesika's.

Synick wondered if Nara had had time to feel betrayed. Hadn't he just rescued his son? Synick held down his bile and quickened his pace. There were more catapults to destroy, more vehicles of death to be removed from Faron's arsenal of life-ending decisions.

Soldiers filtered out through the trees, buzzing insects around a burning hive. Synick added one more for them to panic over, then one of Artur's near where Nara had fallen, then the leftmost catapult on Harfor's side.

As the new fires blazed alongside the old, it became clear from Synick's distant vantage that the soldiers had spotted Artur and Harfor. Whether they had heard their slings or caught sight of them in the yellow light, Synick wasn't sure. All that mattered was that they were advancing in a tight row in columns between the three remaining catapults. They would be on Artur and Harfor in seconds.

Synick showed his teeth as he slammed the lever down, tendons popping in his shoulder from the over-rushed action. There were still three to go. How could he take them all down *and* provide cover fire for his friends to escape *and* escape himself?

He couldn't. That was the only answer. He could only hope they had the sense to run. Straining his thief's eyes to their utmost, Synick sought out something small beside the weapon nearest Artur. It was nearly impossible to see, and perhaps he was only imagining it; but, there was a dark shape that could have been a series of barrels stacked together—an ammunition supply, perhaps? Centering his iron sights, then pulling upward just a hair, he pulled the wonderfully small trigger and waited.

A fluting whistle. A light. Screams, but no fireball. Synick cursed and reloaded. He'd struck a passing soldier in the leg, the resulting splash lighting him and at least three others on fire, but they would be extinguished soon by a combination of snow and common sense.

Synick ground his teeth and reloaded. He ignored his panic and tried the shot again, hoping against hope that Artur would see what he was trying and run.

In the exact moment that the bolt flew, Synick's target lit up, wreathed in a splash of fire. For a moment, he thought that his first bolt had spread and miraculously caught, but no. Artur hadn't run. He hadn't seen what Synick was aiming for. He'd stood his ground against the advancing armies and continued his work on the catapults.

A heartbeat passed, and an explosion rent the night, a billowing, belching, bulbous ball of flame that swelled to swallow and throw the catapult—and the men—within its reach. If there were screams, they were drowned out by the fire, but Synick doubted there were screams. They were too near for that, too immediately broken by his explosion. He thought he saw limbs and viscera in the human shrapnel that followed, and despite his adrenaline or the weight of his need, Synick vomited.

There was not a shadow of a chance that Artur had not been caught by the fireball. Synick wretched at the death he had wrought, of the soldiers and for his family. Artur hadn't run, and Synick killed him.

His life for Faron's.

Two catapults remained, separated in the line by the brilliant torches that were the remnants of war machines. Numb, sick, and filled with shock, Synick mechanically began to reload. The remaining catapults stayed dark. Either Harfor had run, or he was already dead. It was left to Synick then.

As he lined up another shot, not daring to hope that he could take out more soldiers with another explosion, a resounding *boom* filled the night, reverberating deep in his chest, loud and percussive enough to stop a heart, but that wasn't what stopped Synick's breathing.

A sickly red pillar of light flew into the sky, arcing slightly above the sprouting trail of red smoke in its wake. The world was filled with bloody illumination, like that from the carriage upon Faron's and Vavelt's arrival to Anveil. It seemed to float in the air far longer than it should have, or perhaps it was simply still ascending, launched higher into the night than Synick's perception of depth could comprehend.

Synick didn't know what the pillar of light meant, but he did know that it lit him like a pale mirror. The soldiers below turned their faces his way, and they began to charge. An arrow screamed past him, going wide by several feet, but that was still too close. Synick spat a curse and, taking only a moment, fired another shot. The closest catapult burst alight, and he ducked behind his snowdrift to reload. A muffled *thwap* told him that the far side of his cover had been hit, augered by an arrow or bolt. Another three arrows followed it.

Synick swore and threw himself atop the mound that was his cover, desperately loosing a hasty shot. It went high, igniting against several tall lodgepole pines in the tree line behind. He ducked back down but not before he noticed the dangerously reduced gap between himself and the advancing

317

men. They had broken their orderly ranks and were charging at a sprint now, each man with the fullness of his speed.

Synick reached a trembling hand into his pouch and withdrew one final fire ampoule. It was his last. Coughing a half-formulated curse, Synick loaded it in and got ready to fire. Time was precious, but he took a breath to steady himself all the same. He had to make this shot count, even if it killed him.

Just before he could leap the mound and take aim, the red light died away, billowing trails of rouge smoke blending in with the other colorless and numberless clouds above.

The world around Synick fell into a blissful darkness, and he seized the moment, sighting down to line up a perfect shot. It was then that he saw, illuminated by the fires of the war machines, that lines of men had surrounded the final catapult, shielding it with their bodies. Others had rolled the stacked barrels away, understanding what Synick had done with them. Synick corrected his aim, a hair higher than he would have liked, and took the shot.

Just above the heads of the human shield wall, the final catapult caught fire as oil and phosphorous splashed across its upper surface. Synick gasped in relief, then cast about for an avenue of escape. Indistinct figures still rushed at him, having closed more than half the distance. One figure, though, caught him by surprise, running wildly from the side and panting like an animal.

"Synick!" he breathed, causing Synick to jump like a whirling cat. It was Harfor. He'd run ahead of the soldiers, if only barely.

"Get down, you idiot!" he rasped, but before the man could respond one way or the other, an arrow took him in the neck.

Synick spat as he caught the spray of blood in his mouth. He pushed down the resulting dry-heave and threw the crossbow aside. There wasn't time to strap it to his back, and he needed to be quick. He spared half a thought to hope it wouldn't be found, then got up and ran.

One or two arrows whistled past, but before any could burrow into his back, a light like a dying star exploded from the mountain, white, cold, and brighter than a thousand suns. The soldiers froze in place, dropping their weapons and throwing up arms to save their retinas.

In the time that it took Synick to take three steps, he realized what it was. Sadagon's flare machine poured radiance from the tallest peak of the mountain, white and brilliant and deadly, but it wasn't a sliver. It wasn't the razor of light that Sadagon had promised—a measured response to demonstrate his resolve. It was a nearly full radial of unshuttered phosphorous that showered every inch of the city and the world beyond in a death sentence, except one dark expanse where the keep itself blocked the light from the western face. Like a star come to earth, it pulsed a colorless light across the entirety of Anveil and Sadagon's weapons beyond, marking all of it for the fire. Synick realized then what the red flare had been, and this was its answer.

Sadagon had called for the destruction of Anveil.

Faron had let him do it.

Synick had been right, then, to destroy these catapults. That, at least, meant something.

Safe behind the hard, dark line that was the shadow of Anveil's wall—the only shade in the world—Synick fled for the rope at its base. Behind him, men cowered from the light and didn't dare look his way.

Out of breath but not caring, Synick seized the rope and set his foot to the wall.

And then the world stopped turning.

Behind him, in the open light of Sadagon's flare, ten huge balls of fire flew—impossibly—into the sky.

Synick's heart missed a beat, then two, as the trailing orbs arched high overhead, their smoke trails caught in Sadagon's blinding light. They soared over the wall, then crashed into the city. He looked around in desperate confusion until he saw where the firebombs had come from.

A second row of catapults concealed deep within the trees.

The night rained fire on Anveil.

Bloodlust

Varek woke to the sound of cannons and earthquakes. Phantoms of Dageran and the dead fled his waking mind as he threw the blankets to the side and leaped from the bed. The world shook with the reverberations that pulsed through the mountain.

He stumbled blearily, then remembered where he was. Varan was there, just inside the door, holding a coat and a pair of trousers.

"What's happening?" he asked, though he already knew.

"The eastern encampment fired a distress flare," Varan explained while Varek stumbled into his clothes. "Our spyglasses confirm the catapults are under attack, my lord."

Another volley of blasts shook the keep. Shirt half on, Varek burst through his door, across the hall, and out onto the balcony.

"Stop!" he yelled as he exploded outside into the cold light. Sadagon was standing there, hands braced against the parapets of the tower, silhouetted by the unbelievable radiance of his flare machine. His shadow loomed over the city for miles, unbroken and perfectly cut. Vavelt was there as well, pulling on her father's arms in an attempt to seize his attention and creating a behemoth shadow of her own.

In those shadows, Anveil burned.

"Stop it!" Varek yelled again. "Father, stop this! What are you doing?"

Vavelt's words were the same. Varek rushed to her side to try and catch Sadagon's eye, then noticed the work beneath them. Far below, pinpoints of light traced across the blackness of the sky, arching before great columns of smoke until they smashed into the illuminated city, exploding in great percussive blasts that shook the very mountain. Buildings crumbled under the force of it, and alongside it all rang the patterned detonations of what Varek could only assume were Sadagon's cannons, pulverizing the western wall. It was a scene from Varek's nightmares.

"Vavelt!" he cried, pulling on her own arm. She spun to see him, only just realizing he was there. Her own eyes were wide and brimming, and Varek realized that she, too, had only just been seized from sleep. She was dressed in only a sleeping gown, unfit against the cold. "The light!" He pointed at the giant claw-footed orb. "We have to put it out!"

Abandoning their father, they rushed to the flare machine and, together, managed to pull the shades across it. As the curtain of light swept closed, Sadagon noticed them, as if for the first time, and spun around.

"No!" he shouted. "Stop!"

"This is my city!" Vavelt shouted back at him. "How dare you?" Her voice was ragged and aghast, breathless as if she could not believe her own words. "How dare you, Father?"

"Look!" he said, forcing their hands away from the shutters, and the world was white again. Even through closed lids, the light burned.

"No!" Varek cried, stumbling over his words as Sadagon

dragged him away from the orb. Vavelt threw herself back at the shades, trying with a single-minded determination to cut off the beacon, but with no one else to hold it down, it only slid around its oiled track.

"Father, stop!"

"Look in the sky!" Sadagon commanded again. His finger traced a long and sinuous low-hanging cloud. It was unnatural, heavy, and red. "The distress flare has been signaled. The catapults are under attack."

Varek failed to rip his arm free. "Synick is down there!" he screamed.

Vavelt cast tall curtains of light around the mountain with her chaotic attempts at shuttering the orb until she threw her body across the glass and managed to reach both ends of the shade. She plunged the world into darkness as she pulled them together, and the final mirror slid into place. A singular, radiant pillar remained, spilling light into the night sky like a beam of pouring iron.

"Shut it!" she screamed as Varek reached her. Her arms trembled against the strength of the springs. "Shut it off! Father, shut it off!"

Varek seized at the lever and heaved with all his strength, but it wouldn't activate on its own. "Help!" he cried.

The desperation in their voices cut through Sadagon's panic, and he heard. Turning, he reached for the other lever, hesitated only a moment, then lifted it back into place. Two halves of the orb twisted against each other, pulled by a blackened worm drive at its core, and sealed the device shut. The levers returned to their upright positions, their passage marked by several distinct clicks. Instantly, the light began to lessen, the oxygen inside burning away until the white pillar thinned, dimmed, and extinguished entirely.

The last of the firebombs fell as the echoes of the cannons died away, along with countless human lives.

Vavelt released the shade, and it sprang away from her to collapse on the far side of the orb. Whatever device Sadagon had used previously to fasten it down was missing. Trembling, both she and Varek fell against the machine. It was hot, but Varek's fire-scarred hands could barely feel it.

"You said you would listen," he said, voice barely above a whisper as the world fell still. It was quiet, the way a dying flower is quiet when cut from its roots. "You said you would let us choose." His voice was hard for a moment but only long enough for the distinction to be lost as it quivered and fell into desperate, choking sobs.

"YOU SAID YOU WOULD LISTEN," Varek screamed, throat tearing from the force of it. "You said it would be my choice—our choice—to choose what happened to Anveil!"

"They attacked my catapults!" Sadagon said, fear in his tone. "Do you understand what that means?"

Vavelt shook against her father's beacon.

"If they came close enough to my weapons to sabotage them, they could know *anything*. Not only might they know enough of my catapults and cannons to see their return, but if they've slipped past the walls, then they have our cloaks as well. Don't you see, Varek, what has happened? If they've gone beyond the wall," he continued, the whites of his eyes showing. "Then they know *everything*. They know enough to level the field of power. They know about the catapults. They know about the cloaks. They might even know that we are mortal."

"We don't have time for this," Vavelt said. "We have to find

324

him." She pushed herself off the massive orb.

"They destroyed the entire front line of catapults," Sadagon said over her, looking back over the city. "There aren't one or two men responsible, Vavelt. If they got so far as that, there is an entire resistance waging war against my machines. Do you understand? An army, empowered by my cannons, unshackled from winter and her wolves by my cloaks. This is the worst possible outcome." He visibly shook. "There is no coming back from this. There is no saving this people from what they know. The only option left is to start over."

"No!" Varek shouted. "You said it would be my choice! You said I could choose to let cannons return and flintlocks and black powder!" He shook his head, his grimace bare for his father. "You liar."

"There was no choice!" Sadagon returned, more firm now. "There was no alternative, and there still is not. Go and find your friend—fate willing, he will live still—and when you return, the bombardment will continue."

"No!" Faron seethed. "You have killed enough already."

"And if we do not continue, more still will die—ten times more, a hundred times. What do you think will happen when human bloodlust is unleashed upon the other cities with the combined power of cannons and snow cloaks? Do you think wars will reserve themselves to the laws they are currently bound? Do you think that if Anveil is allowed to keep her walls, she won't tear down the walls around every. other. living. thing?"

Varek could see from his distant eyes that Sadagon was no longer looking upon Anveil but into the depths of a distant tomb, empty, except for two stone sarcophagi.

"There," Sadagon went on, in a whisper broken by gasps,

"is evil in the hearts of men, Varek. There is no choice."

"You said it would be *my* choice!" Varek accused. "You said it was my right to let technology progress."

"I did," he conceded. "I did not say, though, that it was your choice to slingshot technology by anachronistic centuries by bestowing *my* weapons upon them."

"Come, Varek," Vavelt urged. "We need to go."

Varek stood as high as he could, teeth bared against his father's will. "You will *not* fire those cannons again."

The tension between them was gristly and hot.

"Go and find your friend." Sadagon cast a look toward Vavelt. "If a friend he remains."

Varek looked toward his sister, but she turned away. "We need to *go*, Varek." Her voice was growing urgent. Following her lead, they turned and rushed past Varan to flee the balcony. Varek was surprised to see that he looked sick and pale.

"Guard them," Sadagon commanded. "Even now, the resistance could be building. Follow five at a time, with no less than fifty men. Keep them safe."

Varek had no intention of waiting for an escort. He strode toward the stables to appropriate a horse, then spared a glance for Vavelt, who was lock-step beside him.

"I'm not waiting," he warned her.

"Good." She met his eye then, shrugging into a coat someone had handed her, and it was almost like it had been so many years before when their glances told stories and passed plans.

They understood one another. With a strength lent from desperation, Varek smashed his way into the stables, unhooked a large saddle, and strapped it on Noble, Varan's great beast of a snow horse. He knew that Varan would be watching but didn't care. Tightening the straps in quick sequence, he readied the saddle, climbed in first himself, then offered a hand for his sister, who took it and rode pillion behind him.

"Don't spare the horse," she whispered, lifting a radiant orb above their heads to light the way. "Go!"

Trusting her to hold on, Varek flicked the animal into action, and it tore down the mountainside. The catapults only reached so high, but when they left the tallest several city levels behind, their ashen touch was everywhere. Burning homes and crumbled stone marked the path all the way through Anveil, the wailing and screaming of the injured punctuating the newly added weight that was Varek's to carry. The catapults had been limited to the eastern face of the mountain, but their reach was long.

Screams. Such awful, present, *real* screams. And the smoke.

Varek grit his teeth as the hooves pounded on the pavement, urging the horse to greater and greater speeds in the hopes of drowning out the cries of the dying with wind. Each low whimper and mournful howl would haunt him for eternity, and he knew it. Still, he rode, eyes streaming and carefully avoiding the darkest shadows, tearing down the city streets until they came to the Foxglove Inn.

Vavelt's gasp when they found it was worse than all the screams in all the world, except, perhaps, her own, that had shadowed him nearly to the grave. The inn was a ruin—a smoldering crash of iron and stone, small flames still licking at the wooden interior wherever it could be found. Crushed stones and splinters scattered into the street.

"No," Varek breathed, unable to accept what he was seeing.

"No." The flesh on his arms and neck spiked into harsh points, rough and cold, underscores for the quick gasps of breath that escaped his chest.

"It can't be," Vavelt whispered beside him. "Let it not be."

With no words to damp his festering shock, Varek dismounted and stepped delicately through the rubble. Soft and steady wind tugged eddies in the air as the ash and snow settled in indeterminable similarity. Vavelt dismounted and followed behind.

By the hard light of her orb, Varek came to see patches through the rubble—an arm here, a leg, the long ends of a head thick with hair. Small bodies with limbs at odd angles harrowed him from their newly fallen tombs, crushed by the stone bricks of the walls and roof, crushed by the catapults he had brought, crushed, as if, by his own hand.

Screams.

A familiar blindness threatened to protect him from what he saw.

"They are… they were children," Faron choked. "There were children here."

"He must be here," Vavelt tried. "He must. Look with me, Varek." She lifted a loose timber and pitched it aside.

"They were so small."

"Synick!" Vavelt called. "Synick!" The poisonously hopeful cry was echoed far throughout the city as other survivors searched for fallen family. Sharp shadows sawed back and forth as Vavelt moved the light to peer through holes in fallen walls or under precarious sections of roof or stone. She shifted a table to reveal the glassy eyes of a small girl, innocent and lifeless.

They hit Faron's soul like a weight of lead and iron.

More weight to carry. More faces to haunt him from the dark.

Faron cowered from that gaze, turning instead to find the hints of a small arm. He hid from it, swiveling toward a crumbled wall that barely concealed a mother clutching a son. An upturned table revealed a spattering of blood, and he fled from it, too.

No matter where Faron turned, he couldn't escape the death around him. They were so young. There were so many.

Hadn't he once sworn to protect them?

When had he fallen to his knees?

Vavelt was there then, looking down at him with wide and worried eyes. She was shouting. Faron hid his face from her. He couldn't stand her shouting.

He couldn't stand at all.

The world spun, and all he could see was his twin's illuminated face against a slowly lightening sky.

"Get up, Varek!" she yelled, and he was surprised to find that he could hear. She was shaking him by the shoulders as best as she could with only one hand. "You have to get up! He could still be here!" Her attention directed away from him for a moment. "Get back!" she shouted. "Get away from him!" The concern in her voice roused Faron from his sleeping shock, and he sat upright, apparently having fallen to the rubble. His hand reached for a knife that wasn't there.

He looked around to see lines of close soldiers surrounding them, with more approaching. "I need you," she said to him in high and hurting tones. "Please, Varek. He could be here." Her head snapped up. "All of you," she commanded. "Clear this rubble. Look for survivors." She turned back to him.

"This isn't your fault, Varek. You didn't do this. Now please, help me."

The ends of his fingertips buzzed with a numbness. "I couldn't save them," he rasped, "and now I have to carry them." He shook. "All of them."

"You didn't do this!" she cried. "Please, Varek, don't do this now! Synick could be here. He could need our help!"

That, for now, brought his mind around to the task. He could carry this weight—for now.

For Vavelt. For Synick.

With heavy breaths, he returned to his feet and searched through the corpses that were his to carry, hunting for a familiar face. His breath caught when he found one, but it wasn't Synick. Varek came face to face with a sight so forlornly similar to what he'd seen at White Grave but so vastly more terrible.

It was Jesika, lying amidst the wreckage of her inn. Her face was almost clean, despite the char surrounding her, hair brushed smoothly to the sides, with long streaks down her face where tears had passed fallen soot, then dried. The tears were not her own.

Several heartbeats passed before Varek realized what it meant.

"He's alive!" Varek cried. "Vavelt, he's alive!"

Abandoning her search and climbing the rubble pile to his side, Vavelt hurried to see what he did, but before she could, Varek whirled on her.

"We have to go!" he declared, suddenly rushing back to the horse.

"What's wrong?" Vavelt asked. "Where is he?"

"Jesika is dead," Varek managed. "She's dead, and Synick

knows. We have to go."

"Where?" she asked, chasing after him, then stopped short, and Varek saw that she understood.

Forfeit Advantage

"I worry, my lord, that you push him too far, that he is overtaxed."

"My concern is the same," Sadagon replied to Varan. "He cannot separate himself from the individuals. I worry that it will cause him lasting pain, but I do not know how to spare him."

"You worry," Synick said under his breath, quiet and secret. "But you kill him still." The wind swept across Synick's ears from his crouched position atop the keep tower, and he missed what was said next.

"His anguish is plain, my lord," Varan said when Synick could hear again. "And I would be lying if I said I did not understand it as well. It is… harder than I anticipated to kill without feeling, no matter how necessary. The urge to offer mercy is powerful, even knowing the consequences."

"It is a heavy burden," Sadagon agreed.

"Heavy enough," Varan said, "to make one wonder."

Sadagon's look was hard—hard like the edge of a knife brandished in fear.

"Wonder what?"

"If he might, in his own methods, find a better way."

"His method would condemn hundreds of thousands to

slow and terrible deaths for no crime worse than lacking an understanding of the threat that comes for them. It is no solution, Varan."

"I am aware of its flaws, my lord, but now…" He paused.

"Now that you've had a taste of the work, you want to spit it out?" Sadagon demanded. "Like a child presented with an unsavory meal, you would pass this burden? At the price of lives?"

Varan didn't immediately answer. "You told me once that you could not trust yourself with this level of power. You told me that you feared Olsu lived on in your heart. Do you remember, Vam Sadagon?"

"I do, Varan, and I fear it still; but, now is not the time to be weak—not now when so much hangs in the balance."

"You told me then that if this power was not taken from you—"

"I would abuse it, I remember," Sadagon cut him off. "But that is not what this is, Varan. There is no other way! Look at me. Do I look like a man consumed with vengeance and rage?"

"Worse," Varan crowed. "You look consumed with fear. There is no evil ever committed that can rival that done in the name of fear." That silenced him like a bag in his mouth. "You told me," Varan went on, "that you could not wield this power without using it. You said I would not care and place the crown on your head regardless, so I listened to you, Vam Sadagon. I found a way that others might carry this burden, free of your hatred and fear. I found Lyss to bear you twins who might ascend.

"I found a way that you might pass your power to those who never knew your pain because I believed you, Sadagon."

His voice became fatherly and familiar. "But what I did not expect was for you to pass your strength to your children, to give them your parents' thrones, then hold that power anyway—to refuse to let it go and believe in the will of another."

"That is enough," Sadagon spat. "You go too far. I do only what is required, Varan. My justice is meted and necessary."

Varan did nothing to show that he agreed. "You once said," he whispered, with no honorific and so low that Synick could not hear but read on his lips. "That if this power were not taken from you, you would use it to kill. You were angry in those days, and rightfully so. So angry at the world who had taken so much from you, and now that anger is gone; but, the fear is not. The fear has only grown—like a tumor—and I believe you now, Sadagon. I believe you now that if this power is not taken from you, you will use it only to kill, not because you want to, but because you are so afraid that you think you have to."

Synick hated the ancient man a little less.

Sadagon was so shaken by the words that he physically took a step back as if he'd been run through like a boar.

"Do you mean to tell me," Sadagon said, and again, Synick had to read his lips to understand. "That all this time, you believed that I am a coward?"

"No, Vam Sadagon," Varan hissed. "Never that, Inquisitor, Insurrectionist, and Lord. I only mean that there could yet be a way to persuade the world to its salvation, by the means your son's companion described and not with force."

He went on, with a jaw tightened against the horror of his own words, "That your back is bowed enough, and if there is a way to step aside and let others decide, it is now, like you said you should." Varan winced as if the words were knives and his throat an eviscerated mess.

Sadagon was a long time in answering. "You will not speak to me of this again." It was equal parts command and threat. "Ever, Varan. Do you understand?"

Varan stopped, hesitated as if he might say more, then was silenced by the heat of his master's glare. "Yes, my lord."

Synick gripped his dagger tighter. For a fraction of a moment, he had almost felt a sliver of hope.

His mistake.

"Might I offer a suggestion, my lord, for this current path?"

"Speak, but know that I'm quickly becoming disillusioned with you, High Archon."

"Blueclutch, Vam Sadagon. Your children are innocent and pure. I worry, more than I had expected, what this night might do to them. Drug them, my lord, and let them sleep while the work is done. Let us carry the sins of this night in their stead."

From his shadowed vantage, Synick could see the perturbations of Sadagon's disagreement. "No," he said. "I cannot, Varan. He will never forgive me."

"He might not," Varan agreed. "But isn't that better than letting him see the bloody banner we must raise for the world?" He let the words sink in. "Let him not see it. Let him not hear it. Let it not plague him as he promises it will. We can give him that, at least."

"What is this strange, new empathy from the High Archon?" Sadagon questioned. "What is this new distaste for the distasteful? Ever have you been the one to carve the headstones of the doomed that others might live, ever the man to weigh the sacrificed against the saved and say it is salvation." Sadagon's eyes were burning with bloodshot and red. "What now," he asked, "is this weakness that drives you?"

"Weakness?" Varan asked, peering over the edge of the tower balcony toward the mountain that burned below. "Is that what this is? Is discovering how far one should venture into wrongness to find right weakness? Because I believe I have found it." He nodded. "Perhaps I am weak, then. I am… sorry. I will…" He breathed hard. "I will forfeit my title of High Archon and my rights and privileges as Vam and will endeavor to bring you a more worthy archon when we return to Vam Aranath." He was trembling as he spoke. "I am sorry for my weakness, my lord."

Sadagon seemed to find the words disturbing. "No, Varan. No. Do not think of it. You are not a dissenting voice but a voice of reason. I would be remiss to cast aside your thoughts after so many centuries spent beside my father." He shook his head. "You're wrong that I am becoming him, but I am wrong to call you weak."

Varan recovered from the precipice of tears. Synick frowned. Part of him had wanted to see a six-hundred-year-old aristocrat cry by the sight of his evil work. Old grudges boiled up in him, and he let them—old memories of a childhood long past where he was a worm surround by sharks. He shifted his grip on the dagger and flicked his tongue over his lips.

"Is there a way, then," Varan asked, pushing forward, "that we might spare your son from this night?"

"No," Sadagon argued. "If I am unsuited, as you say, then I must start trusting him eventually."

"He is a boy, Sadagon." Something in his tone must have struck a nerve because Sadagon whirled around, tearing his eyes from the long slope of the mountain.

"He is my son!" he shouted.

Synick slinked back, away from the edge of his perch. He hadn't expected Sadagon to turn so quickly. A brief look upward was all that would be needed to give him away. Fortunately, he didn't look up. No one ever did.

"He is my son, Varan. He is born to this purpose, by your own design." He hesitated to draw a shaking breath. "By my own unwillingness."

"That is my very point, Vam Sadagon. He is your son. If we must choose this path, can we not at least spare him from it? Yes, he was born to the purpose, but he was robbed of the preparation and fortitude we hoped to give him. His return to us is a gift that cannot be overstated—a miracle, even—but he is not ready. Let him sleep, Lord Pyre. Let him sleep, and let us beg his forgiveness when the work is done."

A pause, and then, "Very well. Varek shall sleep, but not Vavelt. She has the fortitude to see this through. One of my children needs to grow and to lead, even if from a tower where no one can see."

"She is ready," Varan agreed. "I suspect she inherited the greater measure of your strength, my lord."

Synick ground his teeth.

"Perhaps." It wasn't a concession. "Prepare wine for their return, and drug Varek's." Synick watched as he seemed to think for a moment. "And put something in Vavelt's to calm her, in case she returns without that Fayorian dock rat."

Synick exhaled half a chuckle. He'd been called worse.

"We'll see who's the rat." His voice was inaudible, even to him.

It struck Synick then why Faron and Vavelt were not here.

They were out looking for *him.* He grit his teeth. All the better. The image of Jesika's dead face stung his eyes, and he blinked hot tears away. He had loved her, if not in the same way that he loved Vavelt... or Faron. It was closer to the love for a sister, or at least, he imagined it was. Still, it felt like a hole in his chest to find her there, dead and buried under an inn that became her coffin.

He clenched his teeth even tighter. After all that, after all Sadagon had done to him, here he was, preparing for another act of genocide as if it were an unpleasant bit of medicine that simply had to be swallowed. It was almost like he didn't know Faron at all, as if he had no idea what it would do to him, sleeping or awake. Sadagon was so obsessed with saving the world that he had no care for who he destroyed to do it.

Synick wasn't nearly so deluded. He had no care for the world or for cannons, for sacrifice or salvation. He had sacrificed enough. With Jesika murdered and Artur gone, Synick wanted one thing, and it was something he could have—to protect Faron. He clenched his teeth to dull the ache of his failure. He couldn't think about Jesika right now or Artur. He could do this.

"Do you think they will find him?"

"I hope not," Sadagon admitted, then added in response to Varan's arched brow, "They are involved, the boy and my daughter. I cannot blame her for seeking comfort, but still... he is problematic."

"You have no idea," Synick whispered, anger flaring. "Frost-bitten bastard."

"And what if he does come back?" Varan asked. "What will you do?"

"He will be dealt with," Sadagon sighed. "Somehow."

"She will know," Varan said, "if you have him killed. She has every resource you do and perhaps more. She will know if you kill him."

"I didn't intend to kill him."

"Or drive him off."

"Perhaps," Sadagon said again. "Let us hope it doesn't come to that. Let her grieve here and then move on."

"If that is the case," Varan began. "She will never forgive you either."

"Go, Varan. Prepare wine for their return."

"Go," Synick agreed, whispering under his breath. "Piss off."

"Yes, my lord."

Synick watched as the tall archon stooped in a slight bow, then disappeared. He stood still as a gargoyle as the man passed through the door and entered the high-ceilinged room directly underneath him.

For the briefest moment, Synick almost reconsidered. Could he reason with the ancient man? No, of course not, and even if he could, Synick didn't want to. He blinked away the image of Jesika's dead face, teeth clamped together hard enough to make his ears ring.

No, there would be no reasoning with Sadagon Pyre. Even if he could be made to see what his actions were doing to Faron, Synick knew better than to forfeit an advantage. That, at least, was one lesson he was grateful to Dageran for.

Five accelerated heartbeats passed in the mournful shriek of intermittent wind, then seven, then twelve. Synick drew and held a breath, waiting for a pause in the air's breath. It slowed, then shifted direction.

He jumped.

With a moment of wind at his back, Synick flew, nothing more than a blur in the air, and then he landed hard. With all the force of a fifteen-foot fall, Synick drove his knee into Sadagon's back and his dagger into his shoulder. It was like smashing into a brick wall. Shockingly, Sadagon almost withstood the momentum, but Synick managed, barely, to crush him against the parapet.

He cried out like all men do when they meet their end, but Synick didn't let the exclamation gain strength. Ripping the blade out of Sadagon's collarbone, Synick shoved his hand over the man's mouth. Sadagon bit at his hand, but Synick had expected that, which was exactly why it was coated in a dust of blueclutch. Sadagon wasn't the only one willing to exploit the drug.

A weakness stole over the ancient man, and Synick, with the utilitarian brutality Dageran had taught him, plunged the knife into Pyre's chest.

Through muscle and skin, Synick punctured a lung, then yanked the knife out with a curve and a twist, just in case. As Sadagon tried to scream, Synick flipped his grip to a proper forward carry and sank the knife again into Sadagon's back, the other lung this time.

With limp muscles, torn lungs, and a slowed heartbeat, Sadagon had no air to expel. His screams were audible only to Synick, who read them on his lips. Somehow, with strength Synick would not have guessed, Sadagon stumbled to his feet and whirled around to face him. Synick let him. It was, after all, the perfect opportunity to disembowel him.

Flesh came away on the blade catchers at the back of the blade as it was ripped through Sadagon's stomach, blood draining from him like wine through a sieve. The ancient man looked down at his destroyed organs and up at Synick with eyes that reflected nothing but a question.

Synick spat in his face. "Who's the rat now, madman?" He shifted his grip on the blade.

The lack of fear in Sadagon's eyes was the most unnerving thing Synick had ever experienced. He didn't scramble away, backpedal, or make an attempt at deathbed vengeance. He only stood there, letting his hand fall away from the hole in his gut as his sap spilled out to bloom and freeze on the stone.

Synick felt a spike of fear as Sadagon masterfully slowed his breaths and took a step toward him. He fell to his knees, but that didn't free Synick from his gaze.

"Why?" he asked without air and without sound.

Synick didn't answer, breathing hard.

Sadagon brought a hand to his throat as if to ask why Synick hadn't simply slit it and been done with it.

Synick just shook his head with a cruelty and a menace.

"What," Sadagon found the air to utter from his growing pool of stolen, sanguine liquid, "a waste of blood."

Flaring with sudden rage, Synick snapped forward and kicked him off the tower.

"For Jesika," he said, surprised at how pitched his voice had become. Perhaps that was because he realized that what he did would earn the eternal hatred of the only two people left in the world that he loved. But let them be alive to hate him.

Over the parapet, the tyrant fell, twisting once to crash onto the courtyard below, his body broken, eyes locked with the sky.

"For Faron."

A Slowly Blackening Skull

Sadagon's body slammed into the courtyard.

Vavelt saw it first, and when she did, she screamed a scream that pierced Varek to his core, down through the very marrow of his bones. The horses reared and bucked, and Varek fell, hackles raised. He landed hard on his back, heaving as the air rushed from him. Dizzy and breathless, he rolled away from the exhausted horses that nearly crushed him with their hooves and hacked a heavy vomitous mouthful of air until his lungs expanded to breathe in again.

It didn't feel like air. It was smoke, hot and cloying and full of remembering. He retched, trying to push out the smoke, but there was nothing in his lungs to expel it with. Strong arms hauled him to his feet, and for a moment, he almost believed it was his father. A breath came then, and he gulped it down to cool his blistered throat.

He saw then that it wasn't Sadagon. It was two soldiers who had managed to keep up with his mad dash up the mountain. Sadagon was a mangled mess barely a dozen feet away. Vavelt was there, already dismounted and at his side. The air felt hot again.

"Father?" Varek heard her say, surprise touching the edges

of her tone. "Varek, he's alive! We need a physician!" Four separate soldiers broke off from the bulk of them and dashed inside the keep.

Varek tore from the arms of his men and dashed to Vavelt's side. Sadagon's eyes were open, unfocused, and blinking. The rise of his chest was a weak and small thing.

"What happened?" Varek cried, but he knew. He shouted again for a physician.

"Father?" Vavelt said, her voice a panicked maelstrom. She was no longer screaming, but her face was filled with the same fear and shock Faron had seen in her that night of the fire. "Father, stay with me!" Her usually dulcet and musical voice caught the attention of the dying man, who locked his eyes with hers.

"Hadria," he whispered, a name so soft it was almost inaudible over the wind.

She recoiled, looking more disturbed by the word than the deep wounds in his body. Varek watched as a spark reached her eye, and the panic returned tenfold.

"No," she whispered. "Please no. We can fix you."

"Where is the physician?" Varek shouted again.

It was slight, but Sadagon shook his head once, then coughed a mouthful of blood. Vavelt was there in an instant, one hand holding up his retching head, the other pressed to the deep slash in his gut. It poured blood around her fingers at an alarming rate, even for the sight of him.

"I'm sorry!" she breathed. "I was too late. I should never have left you. I'm sorry, I'm sorry, I'm sorry."

Only then, clouded by smoke, did Varek think to look up. What he saw choked him even further.

"No. Oh no, Synick?" he cried, voice deep with dread.

"Synick!"

Synick's head disappeared behind the parapet.

That, for a moment, brought Vavelt's eyes off her father, and they were filled with denial. She locked her gaze with Varek and then back to their dying father.

"You'll be okay," Varek insisted. "Hold on, don't go. Hold on." A breath caught in his throat, and he became nauseous. "Where is the physician?"

Did he really have to do this? Did he really have to watch his father die—*again?*

He heard a scream and looked to Vavelt, but it wasn't coming from her, even though the voice was hers.

He swallowed hard.

The already ajar keep door slammed open, and an aged man with thinning gray hair appeared. Several others followed him with bags and metal devices. He spied Sadagon and came to an abrupt stop.

"Help him!" Varek shouted, but the physician didn't move. "Help him!"

"No," Sadagon panted with no air for anything else. "I am... too far." It took more than two shuddering breaths to form the words.

"No!" Varek shouted, more ferociously than he would have expected. "No, don't go. You can't! I can't do this again!" Vavelt's eyes caught him. They were sharp and full of knowing, greater now than the weight of fear that was also there. Varek silenced himself.

"I see her," Sadagon insisted with the grim certainty of a man who saw eternity. He shook as he fought for air, eyes focused on nothing. "My family," he crooned. "My wife... calls me."

"And Lyss," Vavelt whispered with a brave nod. Her lilting tone was returned. "She will be there."

Crowds gathered beyond the courtyard.

Sadagon nodded, a softer movement than a declination. "Lyss." More blood. "And Hadria. And... and *my son*."

With strength Faron had never known, Vavelt pulled her eyes and lips into a smile, a soft and selfless expression to comfort even the dying and the damned.

"They're waiting for you," she promised. "Just beyond."

"Finish... the work," he begged. "You are... strong."

More blood.

More smoke.

She gave a mournful nod but kept her tears secret. "I will," she vowed, then, "Go to them. Rest. Be with your family. I will finish your work, I swear it."

Growing paler by the moment, his anxiety seemed to bleed away, and he managed to find a single nod. "The Veil," he coughed with one final sanguine expulsion, eyes widening toward the sky. "...lifts."

And then he was gone.

Everything stopped. The wind gasped its silence as it ceased to blow. The snow stopped falling. Varek stopped breathing. Sadagon's heart stopped beating.

Sadagon—Vam Pyre—was dead.

The lie fell from her eyes, the smile falling to an open-mouthed gape as her breath caught between sharp inhalations and uncontrollable, low gasps. Tears fell on their father's body, and a moment passed in suffocating silence.

A howl, inhuman and harrow, tore from Vavelt's throat, splitting the air and returning the wind to violent lashes as her lamentation rang across years.

Screams.

Banished screams ripped Faron apart, returning in a flood of present and past, overwhelming any sense of self he still possessed. He was gone, in that flash of a moment, appearing in a glowing hell all his own.

Fire climbed the walls beside him, crawling up the stairs and across the landing toward where he was pinned by a smoldering and smoking beam. He couldn't breathe for the pressure and for the black skull that grinned at him.

Paralyzed, immobile, petrified, and unbreathing, Faron tried to look away from that skull. Cracking skin and boiling blood pulled whatever was left of his then-father into a smile, burning eyes drilling straight through him.

He tried to yell, tried to scream and get away, but there was no air—only smoke that burned and blistered inside his tortured lungs. His hands and shoulders *burned*, the flesh on his chest melting away. He was there. He was there. Dead gods, he was *there*, burning alive and pinned where he couldn't look away.

The skull was Bouren, the kidnapper who claimed to be his father. It was Sadagon, his true father, a man who would burn half the world to save it. It was himself, charring in the furnace of weight that was his to carry.

It was too much.

Screams.

Skin melting from the heat of the past, Faron's vision began to go dark. It welled up from the bottom right corner of his perception, growing until it covered the gruesome corpse that haunted him. For a moment, he could almost breathe until the faces came to fill the dark. The sound of them filled his ears, a wail to drown out even Hadria's wretched scream.

347

For an indefinite eternity, Faron burned in a flame of hurt and harrow.

He didn't know how long he was there, withering in the blackness of his mind. He didn't know how long he tried to hide from the eyes that pinned him. He didn't know how long he could carry them.

Could he carry any more?

Several lifetimes later, he was there again, kneeling and completely unmoving. Vavelt was before him, holding his face in two bloody hands. She was crying, appearing as destroyed as Faron felt, and speaking as well, though he couldn't hear it.

Finally, his eyes shifted and brought her into focus, and she gasped as if she'd almost lost him, too.

"Varek!" she said, her throat hoarse. "Varek, come back to me!"

He swallowed to find that his own throat was raw. Sadagon's body had been moved, and they were surrounded by Alabaster Guards who, in turn, were surrounded by gaunt and ghoulish survivors of the flames. In the chaos that was Anveil's death rattle, thousands of desperate people fled through the streets to cower on the west side of the mountain where the catapults could not reach them.

In that mad exodus, hundreds of individuals had been forced upward, where they crowded around the keep and around the body of a god. From that crowd, Faron could hear the whispers, emboldened and fearful both, about the dead father of the gods and what that implied for his children. If not for the ranks of tall shields and long spearpoints, they might have rushed the keep there and then.

Vavelt spared a glance for them, and Faron swore that he

saw pity in her eyes, then pulled him upright to sit. "Oh, Varek," she said, falling on his neck. "Where were you?" When he didn't answer, she went on, "Don't you leave me, too. I need you, brother. I need you. I can't do this alone."

"I'm here," he said, his voice small. Vavelt crushed his chest with her arms, but it was good.

It helped to expel the smoke.

A Weight to Save the World

Numb, weak, and barely able to keep his feet, Varek let his sister take him by the hand and lead him through the keep. A blur of stone walls and hallways passed through his mind without touching his memory, and suddenly they were on the tower balcony.

Synick was still there, slumped against the outer wall in a pool of freezing blood, his dagger forgotten beside him. Ten men surrounded him, barely able to fit with their weapons drawn and raised. When Vavelt pushed through her soldiers to face him, he slowly looked up, then turned his face away.

"I'm sorry," he whispered, almost entirely inaudible.

"Get. out," Vavelt seethed through her teeth.

Synick began to tremble.

"Get out!" she shouted. "All of you, out!" The soldiers shuffled as they realized she was addressing them. "Go! I will have the head of any man on this tower in the next ten seconds."

With the exact obedience they'd been born for, the soldiers sheathed their swords and quickly filed through the doorway, none of them wanting to be the last left with their goddess's rage. One man's poleaxe struck the doorframe and clattered to the ground in his haste, but when he reached for it, Vavelt's glare stopped him short; and, he fled, leaving it on the stone.

Only two remained—one stout and thick like a sun-bleached willow root, the other unnaturally tall with silver hair—the gods' keepers.

Alone at the peak of the world, the three of them shook in the quiet wind. Varek spoke first, afraid for Synick for his sister's wrath.

"Synick," Varek breathed, voice rough and hoarse. "Why..." He couldn't finish the question. He knew why.

In the single most shocking event of Varek's life, Vavelt knelt in her father's blood and pulled Synick's face close to her own, extending to him the same mercy she showed Varek. There were no words between them, no words to hide behind, and no words to explain. No words to question, and no words to threaten. For a moment that seemed to stretch unnaturally long, Vavelt peered deep into Synick's eyes, flitting back and forth like frightened starlings or hunting hawks.

There was weight in the silence, and Varek didn't dare break it.

"Oh, Synick," she eventually said. "What do I do with you?"

Silence was his answer.

"Why didn't you run? Why did you let them catch you?"

Pain outweighed despondency in his eyes, and Varek ached to see it. "Because if you want me dead... I don't want to live."

"What do I do with you, Synick?" she asked with less sureness than before. "What do I do when I want you dead but can't live without you?" Fresh tears slipped down her chin. "Why did you have to do it, Synick?"

That caught Varek off guard.

"You don't know him like I do," Synick breathed. "You don't know what he'll do."

"He did only what was needed! What is *still* needed!" she shouted, then stopped when she saw that Synick wasn't talking about Sadagon. Her eyes turned to Varek, who looked to the ground in turn. It couldn't hide his shame.

"You don't know what it will do to him," Synick said, finally releasing small tears. "You weren't there."

A breath of quiet inquiry dispelled from her before she asked, "What is he talking about, Varek? What have you not told me?"

To answer was to live that moment over again—to be on the bridge again. He stayed quiet.

"I wanted to take it from you," Synick gasped. "You don't know what he'll do if you fire those catapults, Vavelt. I wanted to *take it from you.*"

Varek clenched his jaw as he began to hyperventilate. Sadagon *had* used the catapults, and now there were new faces in the dark. There were *so many*. He seemed to see them coming from the shadows, but there was one shadow he could remember, deeper than the rest, that was empty—a weightless void where he could fall forever.

"It was you," Vavelt said with a tone of sudden understanding. "It was you who attacked the catapults."

He didn't answer, but he didn't deny it.

"Synick!" she cried, standing and backing away from him. "You did this!" she accused. "You murdered my father for something you made him do!"

"I didn't!" Synick replied. "Sadagon fired those catapults, not me!"

"You forced his hand!" she said, taking another step back.

352

"Synick, how could you? You sought to undermine me? My rule? What have you done?"

"I had to, Vavelt! For him." He pointed a long finger toward Varek, who was growing numb. "For you. He was going to kill them all. Anveil. *Everyone.*"

"He was going to save the world!" she shot back. "The whole of it! What is one mountain city at the edge of the map compared to the millions in Empyrion? What have you done, Synick?"

In half of a heartbeat, Synick was on his feet and upon her, hands on her face. To Varek's great surprise, she didn't pull away. Yarow took one leaping step forward but paused just as quickly when he saw her reaction.

"I don't care about Empyrion!" he said, the fervency in his voice hot enough to melt the tears that froze upon the stone. "I don't care about Sycele or Blackwood. Let Istrid *freeze*, Vavelt. Let it wither and die."

"Stop it," she commanded, but he didn't.

"Let it all die, Vavelt. I don't care. If Faron is the sacrifice that the world requires, then it can freeze. If the cost of salvation is letting you lose your soul by massacring a defenseless people, then to hell with salvation!"

Varek eyed them, a hair's breadth apart, torn and silent in the tension. Vavelt was just as quiet for a long time, lip trembling in the exchange.

Eyes filled with hatred, pain, and pity, Vavelt seized a fistful of Synick's hair and pulled him down into a kiss, her face wet with tears, both his and her own. So strong was her grip that Synick couldn't have fought it, but he didn't.

Unbelieving that he could still be surprised, Faron watched in shock as the only two people he loved excluded him from

353

a love he could never share, and something inside him broke.

Finally, Vavelt pulled away and pushed Synick off of her. There was a hunger in his eyes that Faron had never seen before and didn't understand. He shirked away from it. It was the hunger that comes from eating too little and waking a greater need.

"Arrest him," Vavelt commanded.

"What?"

Yarow didn't hesitate, moving like a crocodile in a swamp. Rousing from what felt like a slumber, Varek seized Synick's fallen dagger from the ground and stepped in his path. "Get back!" he barked. Yarow stopped, then gave Varek a long look. It felt like an eternity but only lasted a fraction of a second. Yarow turned to step around Varek, but he pivoted to keep in his way. "Get back!" he said again louder.

"I am not sworn to you," Yarow said in a rare display of language. He tried to step around again, but Varek stopped him.

"You don't *touch* him!" He moved again. "Not one finger."

Something burned in Varek's chest. Seeing Synick with his sister had woken a protective beast he didn't know he possessed, and he was angry.

"Don't, Faron," Synick said, his voice now diminutive and diminished. "I'll go."

"No!" he shouted over his shoulder. "No, you snowing won't, damn you!"

"If she doesn't want me," Synick returned, "then I don't want to live."

"What about what I want?" The screamed statement brought a silence with it, a slow, stuttering sharpness that was as unfamiliar as anything could be. Synick was caught in the net of quiet, still as a snake poised to evade a killing blow. Vavelt even paused to dissect his mental landscape with that cold stare she sometimes wore.

Varek couldn't meet their eyes. Yarow tried to push past him again, and the quiet snapped.

"Not. one. finger," Varek growled at his sister's keeper through teeth clenched tight and grinding. His fingers wrapped and unraveled and rewrapped around Synick's dagger. "Or I will kill you." The words weren't spoken as a threat but a simple statement of indisputable fact.

"Brother!" Vavelt interceded. "You don't have the authority."

"I have a knife."

"Don't, Yarow," Vavelt said. "Stand down. I don't know what to do, and it doesn't matter."

"It matters to me."

"He killed our father!"

"He killed Jesika!" Synick started, but Varek cut him off.

"If it had been Synick in that tavern, I would have done it myself!" The words came off hard and grimy, stealing the vitality from him as they escaped. He realized as he said it that it was true. He hadn't meant to speak them, but there they were, ugly and naked.

A long moment passed, filled with the tension of betrayal and stinging loneliness. Finally, Vavelt said, "Yarow, Varan... leave us, please."

Neither one of them moved.

"Yarow!" she snapped, and finally, he shifted. Varan looked to his god and sworn master for guidance. Varek delivered him a flick of the wrist, and he followed, leaving the three of them alone at the peak of the world.

"How?" she asked when they were gone. Her hurt was clear across her expression. "How can you say that?"

"It's the truth."

"Faron—" Synick said but was cut off.

"It's the truth!" He was yelling again. "There is no one on this earth that I wouldn't trade for him." He breathed hard as the words betrayed him.

Synick froze.

"So much," Vavelt said, horrified and quieted, "for your morality."

"I have no morality anymore!" Faron screamed, cutting to the crux. "You've taken it from me! You live by your blood calculus, but I can't, Vavelt! I don't know what I am or what I'm willing to do. I don't know what's right or wrong or how to trade one life for another. I can't trust myself anymore, Hadria, but no matter what else, I can't lose him." He trembled as he withered under Synick's stare. "Some weights are heavier than others."

"Trust *me*," Vavelt told him, offering her compassion when he needed it most. "Trust in our father." A small, sharpened inhalation cut off the final word, and Synick looked away. "Trust what he would have done."

"I don't…" Faron began and then changed tack. "I'm not strong enough."

"Neither am I," she confessed. "I've tried to be. I've… I've tried so hard to grow, but I'm not strong enough to do this alone." She peered deep into his eyes. "But we're not alone."

"Strong enough for what?" Synick dared, but Vavelt's angry glance shut him down.

"I know how it hurts you," she whispered. "I know how you see things that aren't there. I see how you hide from the shadows. I see the way you aren't really here sometimes." She held his rough face in her soft hands. "I see how your fear haunts you from the past, but… I see things, too, Varek."

She gasped a heavy breath. "I see… a hungry ribbon of white, swallowing all the world like a wildfire of snow. I see the huddled masses hiding under their too small walls until the day a thousand red eyes peer down to find them." She stopped to take a calming breath.

"Don't say it," Faron begged her. "Please."

"I see them," she said. "Starving, cowering from the wolves mantling their buried walls. I see pyres of men—*mountains,* Varek—mountains of bodies from the wars that the Veil will bring. I see human offerings to the wolves, the weak and the small given up to appease their hunger."

"You don't know that will happen!" Synick burst, but she only shook her head piteously.

"It already has, Synick, and if you hadn't murdered my father, he could have told you."

That hit him like a mace, and he flinched away, retreating into a wounded silence.

"So long as the strong can force the weak to their will, all the Veil will bring is apocalypse. It will happen," she said, "because it has happened, and nothing since has changed." She turned back to her brother. "That's the truth, Varek, the hideous truth that I've come to understand. If there is a god in this world, it is the Veil, and she has come to claim us."

The lethal cacophony of metal on metal and metal on bone rose up from the west, and all eyes turned to see it; but, it was blocked by the body of the keep. The din of dying men and women seemed to underscore her words.

"Anveil resists us," Vavelt said, her frightened tone evapo-

357

rating as she seemed to rouse from her reverie. "You know what that means."

"What?" Synick forced out. "What are you talking about?" He was near to panic, which told Varek that he already knew.

Varek shook his head. "I'm not strong enough," he whimpered. "I can't."

"You mean to destroy Anveil," Synick said, voicing his dangerous suspicion. "Still? Vavelt, you can't!"

"I have to, Synick, because I *can.*"

"I… I don't want to," Varek found the strength to say.

"Then don't," Synick urged, suddenly very near. "Don't do it, Faron." In a burst of movement, Varek found his hand inside both of Synick's, nearly cradled for the soft firmness of his grip. "This isn't you. This isn't what you'd choose." Synick nodded a harsh, hawkish movement. "This was his," he said. "Your father's."

Varek could see the fear in him.

"You don't have to do this, Faron!" he yelled. "You don't have to make this choice! I took it from you! I… I tried to… " He gripped Varek's hand harder still. He paused, and his voice turned soft. "Please, don't do this."

The look Varek returned him was one of fearful confusion, repulsion, and longing, all in equal thirds. "I don't want to, Synick, but… what will happen if I don't?"

"You have a choice," Vavelt intervened, "that no one else can make. Anveil or the world, Varek? That is the choice before you, and there is no easy way."

"What of my path?" Synick interjected. "What about Vam Aranath? Bring them there! Why can we not take my way?"

The sounds of dying men and war cries subverted his question.

358

"Even if that were still a choice," Vavelt answered. "You would bring those who will follow you and doom those who do not. They will kill each other, they will starve, and they will be feasted upon by the wolves—millions of them, Varek, each and every one of them a person, living, feeling, who you could have saved and chose not to because of the hardness of the way."

"Why?!" Synick demanded as he dropped Varek's hand. "Why can you not show them mercy?"

"Because of you!" Vavelt snapped with unexpected sharpness. "Because you have forced my hand, Synick!"

"How?" Synick bellowed. "Fine, conquer the world to save it, but what has changed? You've had your show of strength. Now let them surrender if they will."

"Listen, Synick! Does Anveil surrender?"

Varek, surprising himself, was the one to speak. "They won't," he said. "Not now. Not when they know we can be killed." The sound of villagers slaughtering themselves against an army fell on his ears from the decreasingly distant west, and Varek couldn't deny it. "Anveil will never surrender now."

"You've given Anveil the power to destroy us, Synick—the power to destroy the world."

"I haven't!" he screamed. "I haven't, I swear!"

"You took fighting men beyond the walls, gave them snow cloaks, showed them my catapults, and all to take a painful tool away from me," Vavelt cursed.

"They're *dead*, Vavelt," he coughed. "I told no one else. They're... they're *all* dead." He choked on his words. "All of them."

"How can I believe you, Synick?" she cried. "After all you've done? Even if I could, this is too far gone."

"How?" he yelled at her.

"You killed Sadagon," Varek answered for her. "Synick..."

"You showed them exactly how mortal I really am," Vavelt cut back in. "Everything my father worked so hard to build, the illusions he put in place to deify me, *ruined* because you had to have your petty revenge."

"He murdered her!" Synick shouted.

She pointed to her chest. "My father can be killed, Synick. *I* can be killed. What manner of god would I be if I can be felled like a common foot soldier?"

"No," Synick breathed, light hair shaking. "It won't work, Vavelt. You can't contain this. *Someone* will survive. Someone will live to flee and tell the world what happened to Sadagon."

"Then they will also tell," she said with a metal edge, "that this mountain was his pyre."

"You can't honestly believe this is right!"

She whirled on him then. "Genocide by omission, Synick. Is that what you would have us commit? If you think the fate of Anveil will weigh heavy on our souls, how heavier still is the rest of the world?" She turned away, and Varek tried to control his breathing but couldn't. She came close then and held her brother's neck in both hands.

"You don't want to do this," she said, "because you are merciful." A small nod. "I love you for that, but you cannot give mercy without strength, and this is how we gain ours." She hesitated, and then, "And I am not strong enough on my own. Please, Varek... help me to be strong." She extended a long arm, tears falling as she nodded. "Please."

Breathing hard, Varek looked up at her and took his sister's hand.

She lifted him to his feet, not by the strength of her arm but with her gaze and the strength of her need.

She *needed* him.

Eyes locked together, Varek stood despite the growing weight that bore down on his shoulders.

Hadria needed him.

Synick was saying something, furiously trying to pull on Varek's attention, but he had none to give. All his consciousness was tied up in the ever-shifting balance of lives and what was necessary to save the greatest number of them. The wind at the peak of the world was fierce now, growing with the dawn.

Varek half watched, half moved as Vavelt placed his hands on their father's flare machine. Never letting her gaze fall away from his, she skirted the sphere and found the lever on the opposite side.

"There is no morality in favoring one life above another," she reminded him as fighting raged around the mountain. Her trembling tone betrayed the fact that she was reminding herself as well. She *needed* him. "There is no choice between Anveil and the world."

He nodded.

"There is no scale for the worth of a life. Weak, strong, young, old—there is no measurement for the price of a soul." Her voice became higher and tighter as she forced the words out.

Varek's breathing quickened, his eyes stinging again.

"The only thing we can do," she said as her throat constricted, "is save as many as we can—no matter who, no matter where… no matter how."

361

Varek braced himself.

"Do you understand?" she asked through her own flowing tears. "Do you see, little brother?" She nodded as she spoke. "Anveil for the world. Our weight to carry." Her own breathing became quick, faster even than Varek's, as her voice strained in a torturous crescendo. "Now!"

Vavelt heaved on her lever, the cold glass groaning as the worm gear inside began to twist. Fighting the weight that bore him down, Varek began to pull. A gear clicked as the lever moved. He pulled harder, panting quickly but out of breath.

Another click.

A soft glow began to radiate from the white stone.

Click.

Almost there. Almost there, and it would all be over. Almost over, and he could forget. Hovering at the knife's edge of hysteria, Varek pulled.

And then Hadria looked away.

To Become Strong Enough

creams. Screams among fire as the dead sought him out. Screams among a growing expanse of darkness that tendrilled upward to cover his vision and protect his sanity. Screams in his mind and in his ear from the dead and the dying. Screams from the past and the present. Screams from a girl he thought he'd lost, and from himself who he was losing.

Faron choked as the air became smoke and his skin melted away. He coughed on the sickly scent of the man who was his father burning on the lower level. He became blinded by a writhing darkness as the blackening skull charred before his very eyes, popping and melting in a way he wished he could not remember. The darkness blinded him, that he might forget.

Other dead rushed to fill that blindness, ghosts filled with a vengeance for their murderer. Every time before, Faron had seen them all, but this was different. This time he *couldn't* see them all.

There were so many dead now that he didn't even know of, their amorphous faces shifting in the dark to become the myriad he had lost in Anveil. Behind them were masses innumerable. Behind them was an ocean of desperate faces, seventy thousand of them but what felt like millions, all begging to know why he'd let them die.

In the darkness of his mind, Faron fled from the violence he'd committed and the violence that was set before him, but there was nowhere left to turn. There was nowhere to escape the actions that had brought him here. There was nowhere in the darkness to escape the faces.

He remembered then a different kind of darkness—a quiet deepness where there were no faces, no screams, no accusations, and no guilt. No broken children or shattered bodies—a deep blackness where there was nothing but a weightless void where he could fall forever and forget.

Why couldn't he find that darkness? He remembered it from some distant past, deep and endless, longed for from the safe constraints of a subterranean bridge.

Where was its promise of forgetfulness now?

Faron convulsed on the high tower keep, vision stolen away by the hordes of the dead that he carried on his soul. Tense, tearing movements jerked his muscles in discordant direction as he fell into a seizure on the ground. He felt, as he fell, that he was tearing at the silver ring he still wore. It didn't help.

He couldn't do it.

A low sense of self returned to him, and he became aware of his muscles twitching and jarring of their own accord. He took control of his body and found he could open his eyes.

They were both there when a soft light returned him to the world and banished the dead—the only two people he could ever love, the only two people who could ever love him. They were screaming.

Sound rushed back to meet him, and he almost wished it

hadn't, carrying with it the windborne cries of the broken and bereaved from far below. Faron tasted metal and smelled smoke.

Screams.

Faron only shook his head.

"It's alright," Synick said, failing to project a calmness. "It's alright. You're safe. Breathe."

Seeing his eyes focus, Vavelt swallowed her panic, hiding it away to a secret place. Still, her sorrow remained, visible and heavy. "I'm sorry, little brother," she said, wiping away the lines where water streamed down his face. "I'm sorry for the weight you carry." The slip of silver tears spilled onto his chest, but she pulled the beautiful lines of her face away from a grimace so he wouldn't have to see it.

"I'm sorry," Faron finally said. "I'm not... I'm not strong enough, Vavelt. I can't do it. Right or wrong, I can't carry them."

"That's alright," she said, echoing Synick's words. "I... I can do it," she stuttered. "I can do this for you." A soft lying nod. "Let it be me, and not you, who carries this burden. Be it on my head and my soul."

Her sharp blue eyes pitied him for a moment more, then she stood and moved to her lever once again. She spared a moment to look at Synick, who was crouched low with both hands propping Faron's head off the hard stone. He was pale.

"Synick?" she asked, vulnerable and shaking. "... Will you help me?" One exposed tear squeezed from her shameful eye.

Synick looked to her, to the orb, and to Faron, then shook his head only once.

Vavelt set her jaw with a bitter tear, and all signs of her weakness disappeared, the flow of tears suddenly shut off by the sting of it.

She pulled the lever.

Click.

Faron's heart skipped a beat, and panic consumed him. He knew then what he had always known but never had the words for. No matter what she said or what Dageran had insisted back in his guild, nobody could carry Faron's sins for him. The death of Anveil was his weight to carry, no matter who pulled the lever.

And he couldn't carry any more.

He wouldn't, no matter what that meant. Even if it was wrong.

Back bent by the weight of a mountain, Faron climbed to his feet, shaking and nearly falling, except for Synick's arm.

"No!" he yelled. "Stop, Vavelt! Please! Don't!"

"I have to," she cried, pulling down ever harder. She was rewarded with a small clicking noise.

The glass groaned.

"No!" Faron yelled. "Vavelt, please, no. Let me take them to Vam Aranath! Let me save those who will follow. No more, Vavelt, please!" He hadn't realized it, but he was on her, fighting to pry her hands off the lever.

"That isn't enough!" she shouted. "I can't let so many die, Varek." Her breath was short and her words tight and pitched. The lever clicked again, his attempts to prize it from her only contributing to the overall force.

"Stop!" he cried. "Vavelt, please!"

"It's alright," she said through clenched teeth, fighting him with a strength he didn't know she possessed. "I... was born for this."

He wrapped his arms around her waist and tried to lift her away. "Please!" he said when the lever clicked again. "Please, stop. I can't carry them! Let me choose a different way."

"I," she said, "can carry these, brother." She didn't sound so certain. "It's what Father would have done, no matter the cost... no matter the blood... no matter the pain."

Faron's panic grew as he recognized the familiar words, and he knew she wouldn't stop.

"For the world," she whispered through her exertions. "For Father. Put me down... I can do this."

Click.

Synick was there then, adding his hands to the lever. For a moment, Faron was terrified that Synick was helping her pull, but no, he was prizing her fingers off the machine one at a time as she panted and heaved heavy breaths.

"I'm sorry," Synick said, head shaking, quick and terrible. "I'm sorry. Please, forgive me." And then her grip was lost, and the lever snapped upward, scraping a long gash into her arm and crashing into Synick's wrist with a sharp crack. He gasped a harsh inhalation but managed to extricate his arm from between the iron lever and the glass. It dangled limply.

Faron froze, petrified between their pain, and was relieved when the glass rotated slightly and was still.

Vavelt cried out but not for her own pain. Ignoring her long, bloody scrape, she cradled Synick's wrist and immediately prodded it in three places. He winced.

"Damn you," she cursed them both. "Damn you, why can't you trust me!" She released Synick's hand and brought her own marred arm up for inspection, and then Faron saw it.

The gray fabric of her sleeve had been severed and torn

away, leaving her arm naked and visible underneath. A red line marked where the lever had passed, a scraped-off section of skin, and below that line was a dendritic webbing of blackened veins.

Faron's heart missed a beat, then two. The color flushed from his face as he became a pale shade, and his strength fled him. His legs buckled, and he fell to the side of the flare machine, barely keeping on his knees.

"… Haddie?"

The feeble weakness of his tone stole a glance from her, and she saw what he was staring at. She covered her arm quickly, snatching it away from him, but it was too late. He had seen it. The marks were there, lighter than on Bouren or Sadagon, but they were *there*.

Hadria had used the Life Spile.

"Hadria, what have you done?!" Faron exclaimed, horrified and unbelieving.

"What I had to!" she howled in return, hurt by the accusation in his tone. "Because it was me who had to carry this world alone!"

Mouth agape, Faron shielded his eyes from her and saw Synick staring hard at the floor.

"You knew?" Faron recoiled. "Synick, you *knew*?"

"Of course he knew!" Vavelt shot back with tears in her eyes. "He knew because he's been with me for *weeks*, Varek. We've been together ever since you arrived in my palace, and *still*"—she shifted her eyes toward Synick—"you choose my brother over me. After everything I've given you, seen in you—even after I've *loved* you and forgiven you for loving another—you still choose him over me." Darkened wrist exposed to the morning light, she rounded on Faron. "Even you, Varek, when it matters most, chose your own path over mine, even when I carry it for you."

Faron was hardly there.

"But I'm nobody's first choice, am I?" Vavelt went on, voice tense and eyes welling. "When you found me, and I wasn't good enough for you, I forgave you. When you begged me to change and let you save me, I *forgave* you, even though I wasn't good enough for the price you paid to find me. Now you call me Hadria, who I was over who I am. Even Father, back in that awful fire, tried to take *you* first. He only got me because I took your place, thinking I was *saving* you." Her lip trembled. "And still, you can't trust me. Even *my* sacrifice, my decision isn't good enough because I'm nobody's first choice." Her eyes shot accusation at Synick. "Even a cast-out thief with no other options."

Synick looked away, incapable of finding the right words.

"Vavelt," Faron whispered. "How could you? How could you do it?" His eyes had never left the scars on her wrist.

"YOU STILL AREN'T LISTENING TO ME," she screamed back at him, storming away to the far side of the keep where she spied the fallen poleaxe. Deep breaths meant to temper her calm only shook her frame and stoked the fire of her anger. "That's all I've asked of you from the beginning, and you still. aren't. listening!" Visibly shaking, she knelt down and picked up the weapon, a crushing hammer head on one side, a tall axe on the other.

"Why did you do it?" Faron yelled as if she hadn't just picked up the wicked weapon.

"Because I am not strong enough for this!" she confessed, dragging the poleaxe across the stones. "Because you were dead, and *I* had to be resolved to save this world on my own!

Because I'm so afraid, Varek! How can I be the scale that balances all life if I can't even let *one* die? I did it, Varek"—her shudder shut her eyes for a long moment—"so terrible a sin, to numb myself to the pain I must cause."

"You didn't have to!" Faron screamed. "You didn't have to do it!"

"I didn't want to," she vowed, coming closer, an image of panic and regret. "It haunts me!" Her voice was tight and tense, high with a manifest fear. "But unlike you, brother," she trembled. "I lack the freedom to not outgrow my weakness."

"What are you doing?" Synick asked her, shattered wrist held in the crook of his arm. "Vavelt, put that down. We can still fix this." The sound of his protestations mixed and died with the noise of Anveil's resistance, nearly now to the keep itself.

She heaved the poleaxe into the air, torn sleeve falling to expose her blackened veins. "I," she said, "*am* fixing this, no matter the pain."

Faron looked up, a semblance of lucidity returning him from shock long enough to see her standing above him with the long weapon.

"Don't, Vavelt!" Synick cried out, reaching with his good hand, but it was too late.

Faron's eyes widened as she brought the hammer side down in a whipping arc, straight on top of him.

"No!" Synick screamed, throwing his body over Faron's in a desperate and twisting movement, but the blow never came.

Directly above them, a high tonal cracking scraped across their ears, combined with the ring of hard metal. They looked up to see the poleaxe rebounding off the flare machine, a series of cracks clouding the orb.

"I had to be strong enough," she whimpered, "for Father, for this." Breathing too quickly, fingers shaking to almost drop the handle, she lifted the axe again and brought it down hard, crashing through the lightning-arc mark of cracks in the glass.

The orb shattered, splinters of glass caving inward, caught in the sudden wind that was the vacuum filling and the phosphorous igniting.

The world became white.

A Pyre of Men and Mountain

Light exploded from the peak of the mountain to the absolute base, over the wall, and onto the armies camped beyond. Every home, shop, and street corner was painted with it, and like ants on a hive, the people of Anveil hid from the light, crowding and fleeing to the dark western face of the mountain if they could and cowering if they couldn't. For a breathless moment, there was nothing. The wailing and clamor of the skirmishes came to a stop, the desperation from the peak fell silent, and even the wind shirked away from the power of the light.

Soundlessly, flaming projectiles arced high into the air, still far below them, long tails of smoke caught in the illumination. They rose and rose, higher and higher until they stopped, seeming to hover in the lethal quiet, and then they descended. For a few unthinking heartbeats, Faron hoped against hope that they wouldn't land on anyone living. Cannons fired before the fireballs could fall, and Faron felt the reverberating tremor as they slammed into Anveil's wall.

The firebombs impacted, and Varek was broken. He had made his choice—right or wrong—and it had been taken from him. More bombs joined the first, and the cannons kept firing. Faron found himself leaning halfway off the edge of the parapet, joining his screams to the slaughter below him.

Anveil burned.

Protestations and desperation died in his throat, sharp gasps consuming his voice.

His sister spoke, and her tone was barely more controlled than the huge fires that sprung up all over the city. "Anveil for the world," she choked, her tone high and near to cracking. "I… I can bear this… Can't I?" She dropped her poleaxe, and it fell the long distance to the courtyard below.

Faron couldn't bring himself to look at her.

"Look at me, brother," she said. "This was my choice. I did this."

Faron could barely hear her words for her pain.

"Your choice!?" he cried. "Yours? What about my choice!?" Synick was beside him. "What about theirs?" He pointed out over the mountain. "What about their choices, Vavelt? I could have saved them!"

Screams. Screams and weeping and fire. Screams and smoke and blackness.

Faron turned away from her and listened to the screams.

"I had to!" Vavelt pled with him, and he didn't know if he had been shouting or not. "I had to, Varek! To save others! Please, look at me!"

Synick was speaking, too, but Faron couldn't hear him. All he could hear were the voices of those who were dying all around him.

Heavy impacts shook through Anveil.

"To… save others," he replied more slowly. "For a life like mine—without choices—a slave's life, at the cost of others."

"Better," she said, "than no life at all."

She was wrong.

A corner of blackness swirled up with the threat of blindness—to spare him from what he was seeing—but it wasn't enough. He could *hear* them. He could hear the screaming that marked the passing of countless lives. He could feel, with hands that braced him against the parapet, each explosion that punctuated the snuffing out of more and more souls.

More weight to carry.

Synick was at his back, lending his one hand to keep Faron on his feet, and dangerously quiet.

The cannons fired again, but this time, the noise didn't die with an impact. The earth began to shake. Anveil began to tremble. Even here, atop the mountain, Faron felt a great rumbling that brought with it a sickening fear from his earliest days. Dead faces fled as a spike of alarm and adrenaline returned his vision to sharp clarity.

The screaming, the cannons, even the explosions of the firebombs were all washed out as one great section of Anveil's western wall shook, groaned, and crumbled under its own weight, grinding under the vast avalanche of a hundred feet of stone bricks stacked twenty feet wide.

Eyes wild and heart nearly bursting, Faron experienced the strangest sense of vertigo as, far below him, a curtain of stone bent like fabric in the wind, then toppled inward. Slowly at first, it began to fall, a wide sheet of rock above a mass of people packed body to body, then faster and faster until it crushed three levels of the mountain and everyone on it.

More of the black wall followed, curling inward and splintering those it was meant to protect—like a chain reaction of betrayal and death—until the opening stopped growing, and the wall turned inward, slowed, stopped, and held.

Shockwaves lanced up the mountainside, knocking Faron back off his feet and nearly off the balcony altogether; but, Vavelt held him, and he stayed. The keep behind them, though, built into the single high peak of the mountain, shook, quivered, and began to crumble. With the screeching cough of stone on stone, half the keep buckled and crashed onto the steepness of the peak. The Alabaster Guard screamed from inside until the roof caved in and crushed them. Had Varan been in there? And Yarow?

More weight to carry.

Cracked rock and broken bodies tumbled down the harsh slope of the mountain, leaving in their wake an open gash in the stonework where Faron could see the mountainside below and the thousands of citizens packed tightly together in the shadow of the mountain. The balcony groaned under its weight and shifted violently in that direction. Faron fell to his knees and clung to the parapet but was quickly recovered. Synick wasn't. Having given his one good hand to Faron's safety, he had nothing to grab hold of and teetered backward toward the opening in the balcony.

"Synick!" Faron screamed, true terror showing him the teeth it had kept back until now.

Synick's arm pinwheeled, searching for something to save himself. He didn't cry out for help or scream, but Faron could see the fear in his eyes, his balance pitched backward toward the new opening at the roof of the world.

Faron threw himself from the parapet, but he wasn't fast enough.

Vavelt was faster. Lunging across the tower, even as it tried to throw her down, she reached out with a bloodied arm and caught him by his belt of knives a mere instant before the void claimed him.

"Synick!" Faron choked. His heart raced to suffocate him.

"Dead gods," Synick cursed, collapsing on Vavelt and the safety of the stone below them. "Blackened body of Olsu."

"Not you!" Vavelt screamed as the earth stopped trembling. She crushed a cry of pain from him as his wrist was torqued between them. "Not you, too!"

Faron shakily rose to his feet, unable to process the nearness of it. "Synick…"

Wolves howled from the darkness.

Faron's hackles rose, gooseflesh running the length of his arms and legs, and he gasped as he finally understood the depth of his father's utilitarian brutality.

The flair machine drowned Anveil in light, but the remains of the keep and the highest peak of the mountain were behind them, cutting an ever-extending triangle of shadow in the perfect radial of white luminescence. Faron saw, in that dark shadow, the orange flash of light that was Sadagon's cannons, still firing through the gaping hole they'd created in the snow wall. They were placed in the one position where there would be no light, the one place where the wolves would all go, the one place safe from the catapults, where tens of thousands had fled to hide in the dark.

The cannons fired, the wall fell, and snow wolves flooded Anveil.

Even before the cannon fire faded away completely, the screams of prey were drowned by the howls of hunters. Anveil died in a maelstrom of white fur and yellow flame, caught between the hammer of fire and the anvil of teeth. Paralyzed, his worst fears made manifest, Faron watched as half the city was consumed by fire and half was consumed by monsters.

Screams.

"Dead gods," Vavelt gasped. "How have I come to this?" Her harrow was cutting and keen—bitter, like the scream that found him always. It, too, would haunt him, and he knew it.

More weight to carry. *Always* more weight to carry.

How much more could he bear? A city? A mountain? A *world*?

Screams. Horrible, heart-rending, whimpering screams.

Howls from the dark.

Dead faces.

SCREAMS.

Even with his back to the flare machine, the light was excruciating. It rebounded off the snow wall with enough force to burn his vision away, but for Faron, it was growing steadily dimmer. For him alone, the light faded, consumed by a black tendril that gifted him with blindness, and as it did, the screaming grew louder and louder and louder, climbing to a careening crescendo of suffering and fear that drowned out all else. It became so loud that had it been coming from anywhere but his own mind, his eardrums would have burst.

So overwhelming was the sound that it drove the whiteness to black, and there, the faces found him.

A nameless woman, who he had poisoned with a dust of red ivy in red wine. A tanner, whose life and family he'd destroyed with a fire in a warehouse. An assassin, who was his first real step toward the taint of violence, his bones crushed to splinters under heel. A slave trader, who couldn't see the harm he caused or didn't care, with a bolt in his head. Haka'een, with a dull knife splitting his eye, blood leaking into his open mouth in a way that seared to remember. Jaru'tal, who was a lacerated mess, his face full of glass and stomach full of poison—Jaru'tal, who was Hadria's *friend* and potential one-day husband. The man who was a guard for the Dunestrider, the two soldiers Faron had killed in his escape from Aru'barrahk, Jesika, Ulric, Galvin, Clarath, Jakab'een, Badune'ahl, Galena, Radast, Yarow, Varan, Sadagon.

How many lives had he ended in the pursuit of a greater good that he no longer believed in?

Faron turned into the light.

How many more could he carry?

How many more were dying *right now*?

He knelt before the furnace of phosphorous and gazed down at his deeply scarred and marred and burned hands.

More and more every second was the only answer he knew and the only one that mattered. Seventy thousand was not a number his mind could sufficiently visualize, but flame-scarred and haunted, it tried, showing him the countless dead who screamed from the grave or from a few moments before—it didn't matter. They were dead. Whether the fire or wolves had claimed them yet didn't matter. They were dead, and he had killed them.

Faron couldn't have better carried that weight than he could lift a mountain.

This was his weight to carry, and he couldn't lift it any longer.

Not for one second more.

Unfeeling of the hands at his back, Faron reached out

and picked up the phosphorous. He was aware of Synick shouting from someplace before the grave but couldn't truly hear him. Faron saw only the dead and heard only the dying.

He stood.

Vavelt was right that in the blood calculus of life and death, there was no real way to measure the worth of one life against another or nine against ten. The only moral way to trade lives was with the weight and authority of numbers, saving as many as could possibly be achieved.

She was wrong, though, about one thing.

Having the means to make that choice didn't grant the right. Having the power to play at god and balance the weight of lives didn't grant the responsibility. There was only one life Faron had the right to take to save others, and it was his own.

And now, in the blinding light of his father's broken machine, he could save seventy thousand or sixty or thirty or ten or whoever was left.

The world snapped back into focus, and Faron briefly saw Synick staring into him, Vavelt's hand twisted into his long hair, filling her fist with every inch of it she could. Her mournful eyes were only for the victims of her father's morality.

He flinched as he pictured them, dying for a cause that was not their own—a cause that was not *his* own.

Faron couldn't carry them.

But... he could carry this.

And maybe then he could put this weight down.

He lifted the blazing stone toward the one quiet blackness in the world, the one place where the faces wouldn't find him, the one deep darkness where he could fall forever in a quiet void and forget, and as he walked, his hands *burned*. It burned like a brand on his chest. It burned like a forest fire. It burned like lungfuls of smoke. It burned like… like… like a blazing beam that pinned a small boy in place, melting his skin and nerves as he was forced to watch a blackening skull on a bed of flame.

Screams.

Screams.

SCREAMS.

Not. one. moment. longer.

Faron stepped off the cliff.

Synick seized him from behind, the force of his body once again throwing them both to the edge of the remaining tower parapets. The force of it would have thrown the phosphorous from his grip, but it was already fused to the bones in his hand.

"No!" Faron screamed, so desperate to put his weight down. He twisted and pulled himself away, his lower body sliding further down the crumbled stone.

"Don't!" Synick screamed at him, face buried in Faron's neck, arm wrapped around his chest. "No! No, no, no, no, no, no, no, no, Faron, no, please, no, don't. Don't do this to me, please. Please, no. Don't go, Faron. Don't go."

"Let me go!" Faron pled. "Let me save them."

He pulled his hand and the phosphorous off the edge of the tower to fall below the lip. The light, like a drape of white fire, rose above the besieged city, shifting to drown the gaping hole in Anveil's wall in saving radiance. Faron screamed as the skin of his arm caught fire and began to burn his side.

"Let me go!" he screamed. "Please!"

"No!" Synick cried. "No, I won't! I can't! Don't do this."

Vavelt was there now, almost falling over the edge for her hurried grip. She stopped Faron's slow slide as she grabbed on to his flailing wrist.

"Faron, no!" she screamed. "Stop!"

"You can't help me!" he screamed at them. "Let me go! Please!" He gasped from the pain of the fire. "I. can't. carry. them."

"It was me," Vavelt told him. "It was my choice, Faron. Please, don't do this."

"I made a choice!" he accused. "One I could live with."

"No," she said with a weakness. "I couldn't... I had to save them... no matter the cost."

"What about this cost?" Synick forced through his teeth. "Can you? Damn you, Faron, grab the ledge!"

"Please," Faron begged them in agony and anguish. "Let me fall." The skin on the back of his hand burst alight, and he gasped an awful breath.

"I'm sorry!" Vavelt cried out. "How could I live with myself if I didn't do everything to save them all? As many as I can?"

"Can you?" Synick spat, sliding an inch as Faron struggled to free himself. "Can you live with this, Vavelt? Or are those your father's words? Look at him! Look around you!"

She choked with a gape as the city burned beneath them, paralyzed for her own weakness, and then her strength failed her. "No," she sobbed. "I'm not... strong enough," she betrayed, breathless for the depth of her failure. "I..." Vavelt wept. "I... I was wrong," she burst with a windless exhalation. "I cannot live with this."

The sleeve of Faron's shirt crumbled to ash, and the skin underneath caught fire. He screamed a terrible, deepthroated scream, and Synick jolted with a small cry.

"Let me go!" Faron begged again. "I'm burning you!"

"I," Synick seethed as his side blackened, "won't."

"I'm burning you!"

"Then I… will burn."

"Please!" Vavelt cried. "I was wrong! I can't live with this! I'm not strong enough, Faron, please. Please, Faron, help me. Grab the ledge." Long locks of her golden hair spilled into the open air as she nodded for him, and as they came close to the inferno of phosphorous, they withered and singed away from the heat of it. "Please."

"It's too late!" Faron said, the faces forcing him downward. "I can't carry them anymore!"

"Then don't," Synick said. "Put them down, Faron. Take the ledge!"

The fire climbed higher, white tongues of flame licking at his shoulder and swarming over Synick's own hand. Holding ever tighter, Synick committed his broken wrist to the fight, breaking it even further to keep Faron alive.

"Let me go!"

"He loves you!" Vavelt screamed as the fire bathed them both. "He loves you, Faron. Synick *loves* you."

How was it possible that here, now, burning once again and hanging from a cliff as Anveil died, that Faron could feel such new and visceral fear about something he had always secretly known? "I…" he choked. "I can't, Synick."

"Don't tell me," Synick breathed through clenched teeth, "that there isn't a part of you that doesn't want to live to carry this weight."

Faron trembled as his shoulder caught fire, his clothes shredding to dust in the inferno that consumed him.

"Don't tell me!" Synick screamed as he shared in Faron's flames. "That some part of you doesn't want to live!"

Faron shook his head as the phosphorous burned.

"Then, you'll have to kill me, too," Synick vowed. "Because I'm not letting go, you bastard."

"No, Synick!" Faron screamed with a fear stronger than death. "No!"

"Then take... the damn... ledge."

He cried out as the fire climbed higher up his shoulder and onto Synick's back, then found a breath long enough to say, "The light... it will kill them."

"But you," Synick gasped, "will live."

"How can I live with that?" he asked, writhing as hell consumed him. "How can I live with what we've done?"

Synick cried in pain.

"I'm sorry!" Vavelt lamented. "I thought I could wield the power of a god. I'm not strong enough, and I'm sorry. I'm no god. Maybe all I am—all I ever was," she cried, tears evaporating in the heat, "is a monster." The shaking of her head draped his face in her golden hair for a brief moment, sweeping at the salt stain of tears on his face. "Maybe..." she went on. "Maybe it's me the world needs to be saved from and not the Veil."

Faron gasped as her words struck him, and he saw, in its fullness, what he had become. In a desperate fear to put down the savagery of men when faced with the Veil, they became more savage and cruel than all the rest. To put down war, they razed a city. To protect the power of the strong and the name of unity, they sacrificed the weak.

Burning alive and dangling from the tower by the two people who loved him most, Faron saw that it wasn't the Veil he needed to save the world from but the people who would be consumed with the fear of it—people like Sadagon, and Varek.

Faron's eyes grew to great circles of understanding as he found a third path.

And he took it.

Faron grabbed the ledge.

With a heave and a heavy exhalation, Synick and Vavelt together hauled him back over the stone edge, plunging the burning side of Anveil back into the deathly light. Everything else became a blur as the catapults resumed, the wolves regrouped, and Synick and Vavelt sprang into motion.

Synick stepped on Faron's skeletal arm, boot igniting but ignored. Vavelt forced her hands down without a moment's hesitation and took the flaming stone in both hands, skin boiling but never stopping.

In a single motion, Synick drew his notched dagger with his burned left hand and sliced it deep between the phosphorous and the bones it had fused to, wedging it in far and yanking hard with his precious length of bluing steel. It came away with a crack, and Vavelt tore it off of him.

With hands that would forever look like her brother's, she threw the phosphorous over the edge.

The light fell behind the far side of the peak, lifting like a white curtain above the burning city and firmly illuminating the gap in the snow wall with radiance to blind the sun.

The catapults, now returned to the mundane darkness of morning, stopped firing, and the wolves that had been singularly spared from the harshness of the light were caught now in the fullness of it, bright and blinding and white and purifying. As the fireballs ceased on half the city, the wolves fled from the other, running like dogs from the dying star that shattered and burned all down the face of Anveil.

Synick dragged Faron to a sitting position and lay him up against a half-crumbled rampart, then tore off his shirt and shredded it to bandages. Faron gasped to see him, half his chin burned away and his shoulder and neck, too.

"I... burned you," Faron wept.

"And I didn't let you go." Synick shook his head and his flame-touched face as he knelt near to Faron. "I didn't let you go. I didn't, and I won't. I won't. I won't ever." Synick shuddered and trembled with a fervency and nakedness Faron had never before seen from him. "I won't *ever* let you go—fire take me, or Iron Halls claim me—*never.*"

Trembling alongside Synick, Faron reached out his remaining right hand and took Synick's functioning left, even if he didn't know why—even if he didn't know how.

Vavelt tamped at Faron's smoldering clothes with bloody hands and made what use she could of Synick's makeshift bandages to tend to the burns that were abundant and bloody. While she administered to them, Faron listened to the keening wails of the survivors of Anveil and let it fuel what he had to do.

His third path.

Braced against a weight he was finally ready to carry, Faron breathed long and deep in the peaceful quiet of his mind on a pyre of men and mountain.

No Matter the Cost

Flames cooled to embers, and embers chilled to char before the day turned much further. The brilliant light that had once signaled the catapults and cannons had been turned to flush the wolves from the city, except the few who were trapped in boxes of shadow and secret places. When Varan was found in the courtyard, mourning Yarow and Sadagon both, he was sent by his gods to organize the soldiers and all the phosphorous they had in their possession, to sweep the streets and purge the snowbeasts from within.

When the work was done, row upon row of soldiers filled the gap in the wall, blockading the way of any more dire wolves. The encampment would be moved there as a temporary measure while the wall was rebuilt, but for now, they held the line against the Veil and her teeth.

Faron lost his arm before it was done, amputated by a surgeon who had survived the collapse of the keep. The base of his shoulder was tied off in a tourniquet now, wrapped in a golden swatch of silk. It was laughably excessive, but Synick couldn't find the strength to acknowledge it. His mask was gone, shattered to a thousand pieces by the death of a city and the death wish of a companion.

The tears came and went, wracking through their frames as each of them came to see the closeness of their mortality and the cost of the lives they'd taken. Vavelt was the image of weakness and fatigue, regret personified, and Faron—well, he was Faron—dour, tired, and clinging to life by a thread, but at the same time, he was vibrant with a strength and a sureness Synick had thought lost.

He could only watch as they wept over their father and heard the mourning keens of Anveil around them. If there were words to mend such pain, Synick didn't know them, so instead, he said nothing at all and offered his good hand wherever it was most needed.

Eventually, Varan returned and the sun with him. Brilliant rays evaporated thin layers of clouds, breaking through in great crepuscular sweeps to fall on frozen char and pools of bloody ice. Only once he began to warm did Synick realize just how cold he had been.

When the High Archon approached, Synick read the dreadful lines of loss and awful realization on his face. His metal gauntlets were smeared in blood, but his finely engraved silver chest plate had been removed at some point; and, the white linen underneath was drenched with it. Synick could read from his eyes that he'd earned that sodden red stain, not by adding to the dead but by dealing with those who were dead already. Varan, it seemed, could not so easily grapple with his conscience when the corpses were more than numbers on a scale.

Slowly, he came before Faron, who was fortified and kept on his feet by a mixture of tarnic root and red ivy, and Vavelt, who was knelt in reverence by their father's pyre, low on one knee. They ignored him for a long minute. Synick resisted an urge to flick his fingers in quiet anxiety, laying his hand on Vavelt's shoulder, who seemed to need the support most for now.

She flinched away from him, and his breath caught. Head turned to deliver him a long glare, she eventually softened, nodded, and turned back to her grieving. Slowly, as if he were approaching a wolf, Synick rested his hand on her shoulder again, and she allowed it.

Eventually, when the quiet words were whispered and the silent tears were shed, Synick saw Faron's jaw clench as he turned to face his servant.

"Your report?" he asked, placing his one hand on his sister's other shoulder.

"It is done," Varan said, eyes drifting away from the body of his lord. "The city is as free of beasts as can be reasonably sure. Your army is assembled."

"Good."

He looked determined now, Synick thought, like he had rarely seen. He didn't know what Faron had planned, but Vavelt hadn't asked; so, neither would he.

"Take me to them."

"You're in no condition to ride, my lord god."

"I am no god, Varan. Not anymore." He shrugged. "And I don't care. I won't take a carriage through a carrion field. I'm walking."

Varan looked for a moment like he might object but then stopped himself and nodded instead. Faron lowered his hand into his sister's field of vision, where she took it and stood. When she turned to face Synick, he swallowed hard but didn't look away. Slowly, she extended her other burned and bandaged hand, and he took it in his left, his right still cradled in a sling. Linked together, they walked the sanguine streets of Anveil.

Broken crowds gathered on street corners and intersections, hollow-eyed and pained beside the piles of scattered and torn corpses. Apart from the withering glares, they left the guarded envoy alone, flinching away from the soldiers and from the rays of bright sunlight that fell upon them.

Seeing the mounded hillocks of bodies, Synick understood why Varan's shirt was so stained and his eyes so vacant. Wolves feasted here. If anything, Synick was shocked it wasn't bloodier. They passed, in their slow procession, an uncountable number of crumbled and crushed houses, mourning families and neighbors circling them all. Every broken building, sloughed-off home, or tavern on a corner made him think of Jesika, and somehow, he couldn't feel the hurt that he had hours before. He only felt numb. Even thoughts of Artur in that desperate explosion brought him nothing but weariness.

He suspected it wouldn't remain that way for long.

It was with a great relief that they arrived at the bottom of the mountain, eclipsed by the massive gape in Anveil's snow wall. For hundreds of feet across, it was empty, the great stones fallen to crush an indeterminate number of bodies below and curved threateningly above, looming loosely over the surviving citizens in morbid suggestion.

Varan led them up a staircase behind a tall building that had narrowly avoided being crushed by the fallen wall. Synick recognized it as a tavern somehow, but it was empty now, the hosts and inhabitants probably dead, among the very first eaten by the wolves. He tried not to think about it.

At the base, soldiers were crammed together between the

stones or atop them, making room for each other as tightly as possible. Synick could see from his vantage that Varan's wasn't the only bloodied armor. He could read plainly the look of horror on their faces at what these men and women had seen and done.

Vavelt quivered between them, holding their respective functioning hands in hers and more frightened than Synick had ever seen her. He gave her palm a small squeeze, and she squeezed back, even though it must have hurt. He looked away when she didn't return his gaze and looked over the crowd of soldiers.

They were silent, each and every one of them. It was then that Synick noticed the long lines of civilians behind them, watching soundlessly like beaten dogs.

"Do you trust me?" Faron turned to ask his sister.

"More," she answered, with evident effort, "than I trust myself right now."

He didn't argue the point and didn't validate it, only turning to issue a command. "Help me, Varan," he said, and Varan obeyed, stooping low to offer his support. Dangerously close to the edge of a twenty-foot drop, Faron climbed atop a wooden table and drew all eyes.

Synick inched closer.

Faron stood there, framed in the open white of the fallen wall for a long few seconds, saying nothing. The wind picked up for a moment, and gusts of ash and snow swirled in eddies around him.

When he spoke, it was loud, carrying, and clipped.

"You are, all of you, my slaves." His voice was brutal and staccato, drawing unsettled surprise from the faces below. "Every single one of you was taken from your old homes or born to become my property. You are people but also tools." He gestured with his arm, and Synick followed the movement to the freezing stacks of corpses and fragments of corpses.

"Look around you, tools of gods, and see the work you've been made to do."

They did, and not one of them seemed far from losing their enforced calm.

"Is this what you, as my tools, wanted?"

Sickly quiet wormed its way through the ranks, a suppressive blanket of nausea that smothered them all. Synick could practically feel the loathing from the crowds behind.

"You are living beings, men and women who breathe and think, and yet, as my tools—my slaves—you were made to feed the defenseless into the mouths of wolves and the maw of flame." He paused, shaking. "Is that what you wanted?"

Synick saw the flesh of Faron's knuckles turn white as he dug nails into his palm, and he swore he could have heard a pin drop, so silent were the soldiers. They looked around at their good work, truly seeing the half-consumed bodies they'd been tasked to create, then tasked to form pyres from, and there was a pervasive air of illness about them.

"As men and women without choices, are you proud of the choices that were made for you? Is this the salvation that you, as free people, would have given?"

Synick shuffled uncomfortably behind him and not alone. Where was Faron going with this? Was he trying to incite a riot?

Faron took a huge breath, then went on, "You have been made to slaughter the defenseless in droves—men, women, children. Their bodies litter these streets by the thousands, because of you—because of me. You, who were once weak and defenseless, have been made to prey on the weak and defenseless."

An almost palpable sense of guilt and furious indignation emanated from the harrowed slaves, galled by the heat of his accusation.

"Is this what you would have done as free people? Would these corpses be yours, were you free and not slaves?" His question rolled over the waves of soldiers, and all stirring ceased. Not a sound came from the haunted-looking army. He let the quiet extend for a long pause as prepared scribes scratched down his message and extended it to those beyond audible reach.

"Varek," Vavelt whispered. "What are you doing?"

"Don't," Synick said. "Watch." He could feel where this was going. This address, after all, was for the slaves, and that meant Synick, too.

When Faron spoke again, it was with more volume and conviction. "You have been used—without a voice or a choice—to dominate and destroy out of a fear that others might dominate and destroy. To prevent the wars of survival, you have been used to create wars here and now. As my weapons, you would be used to supplant future tyrants with greater ones and prevent future violence with displays of *greater* violence. You," Faron went on, breathing hard and angry, "have been wielded out of the fear of what others might do, and in that name, done something terrible."

Cold gusts of wind from the open maw of the snow wall spun about Faron while he shouted, "So again, I ask you, as my tools and my slaves, is that what you wanted?"

Calls of "No!" rose up through the ranks but not everywhere and not loud. Many still appeared hesitant. Faron kept going.

"You have killed and slaughtered in my name and my father's name. Look around you, slaves and tools, and see the work that we have done." Almost nobody did. More heads than one were hung low, disgusted and horrified by the violence they'd committed.

Synick squeezed Vavelt's hand again, and this time she looked at him.

"You are my slaves, and I am your master; but, answer me, soldiers of Aranath. Is there even a single one of you who does not feel the weight of this night on your back?"

The silence was his answer.

"Can any of you, who only followed commands, say that you feel no burden after what you have been made to do?" Faron raged on, "Can any of you, in good conscience, continue to kill for me? To make slaves for me?"

"No!" The cry was louder now, filled with frustration and the impassioned fuel of desperation. Faron stood taller on his orator's box, and Synick inched closer, just in case.

"What is he doing?" Vavelt asked.

Synick had to bite down on his emotion before he could say, under the roars of declination, "He's taking them."

Faron bellowed over the angry cries, "I am Faron Wolfheart, son of Vam Pyre, son of Atha and Olsu. I am the man you call a god, and I say, to each and every one of you, that you are free! I reject my ownership of you! I reject you as my slaves! I reject the idea that any man can own another. From this day, no one will call themselves your master. You will never again be forced to put those you might have loved to the sword or the tooth. From this day on, you are free!"

393

Faron's shouting was returned tenfold, excited yells breaking out among the previously disciplined and organized army, elated at the sudden direction of his heated oration.

Faron silenced them with his one palm. "And with this freedom, all of you are welcome to return to the homes you once knew or make new ones wherever you may go, but that is not you all. To those of you who, like me, feel the weight of what was done here upon your backs, to those of you who, like me, still feel the sting of enslavement, and those of you who, *like me,* need redemption for what was done here, I offer a bargain."

The world fell still as the jubilant militants fell to a silent whisper and leaned in to hear him.

"Come with me, as free people, and form together a new crusade, to destroy the men and monsters who claim to own their fellow man. Come with me, and end *all* slavery, not just here but for everyone, everywhere, in any form it might take—first, in Vam Aranath, where we will prepare for a great exodus, and then every city on this earth, one after the other until the tumor of subjugation is torn away!

"Form with me a single banner to root out the injustice of slavery wherever we might find it. March with me, and liberate the weak wherever they are hidden! March with me, and cast down the slavers one at a time until not a *single one* is left alive! March with me! Not to make slaves, but to free them!" He punctuated the speech with his fist in the air, trembling and weak, and for a moment, all was silent.

Earth-shattering roars exploded from the men and women as they chanted for their new captain. Spears slammed against shields in wild approval of the one who would lead them—the one called Wolfheart.

Slowly at first, then more and more, they took up the call, deep and tremoring.

"WOLFHEART, WOLFHEART, WOLFHEART!"

The stones under their feet vibrated with the strength of their cry, the very air seeming to quake from the intensity of the singular heart and mind of the men and women who, for the first time in their lives—and quite unexpectedly—found a chance to do what was right.

Varan spoke behind Synick, and he almost jumped in surprise, having forgotten he was there. "If you hoped," he began, "to lead them as a man, you will be disappointed. They will never believe you are anything but a god now, my lord, Wolfheart."

Faron didn't turn around, still receiving the shouts of the men who newly followed him.

"Faron," Vavelt said with wide eyes. Synick raised a half-burned brow to hear her use his preferred name. "Tell them about the Veil, about Aranath."

He gave a curt nod, then opened his fist to a palm, and the chanting stopped.

Defying the consensus of the crowd, Faron began, "There will be those of you who wish only to lead quiet lives, and to you, I will part with a gift of silver and gems as payment for your service and to help you find your way." Faron cast his eyes over the crowd, waiting for those who would accept his offer, but none did.

He harried on, "But to those of you who will join with me, I can promise only one thing: a weight to carry." He grimaced for a small moment, hand clenched tight, then said, "The *right* weight. To you who will join this war with me, I promise burden and toil. To you who will follow me, I promise pain and suffering. To you"—he trembled—"who will join me, I promise the chance to do what is right, no matter the consequences and no matter how heavy the weight."

Their cheers were unbearable.

"The Veil is coming," he went on, and Vavelt looked to Synick with anxiety in her expression. "And with it comes the violent fear of survival. With you who will march with me against the slavers, the work does not end there—not by half. To you who seek a weight to carry, we will open the way to Vam Aranath and evacuate Anveil. To you who seek redemption for the evil I have forced upon you, I promise a chance to save all who will come with us, to ferry them across the Veil, to be their guards and their protectors as we take them to safety, but that is just the beginning."

Several hundred voices called out in a cheer but just as quickly died with an eagerness to know what more they could do.

"Come with me to all the great cities and all the small villages, where we will extend the offer of asylum in Vam Aranath. For every single person who wants it, we will give our protection and our methods of survival, but that is just the beginning."

Somehow, Faron's fervor grew. "Come with me to all the great cities, one by one, where we will crush the blight of slavery with bloody authority, and for those who choose to stay behind, we will destroy the criminal lords, the warlords, the corsair kings, and the robber barons."

Faron's army cheered.

"With fields of mana beyond the walls and snow cloaks to all who need them, we will protect those who choose to remain from those who would steal up resources and seek to take advantage. With an order of those who are willing to carry a heavy burden, we will find those who would use tools of survival as weapons of war and *snuff them out* in defense of the innocent.

"My father," he cried, "sought to save the world by enslaving it, by taking the freedom from all men and forcing them to peace when they might not have fought—a solution where the strong command the weak, and the power of unity is maintained by subterfuge and blood."

He paused for a moment to look his sister in the eye, and terrified, she nodded. He turned back and yelled, "*Mine* is the opposite solution, not to save the greatest number of lives possible, but to give every man and woman a choice and to save the *right* lives—first, our duty to those who ask to be saved, second, our duty to those who will remain behind, and third, our duty to cast down the cruel and morally corrupt who would seek to kill their neighbors to secure power, when peace is still possible."

Synick saw Faron tremble.

"Join with me, and we will right the wrongs of my father and grandfather. Join with me in defense of the weak and the innocent, and we will free them from the oppressors and the cruel.

"Follow me," Faron promised, "and you will become a beacon for all slaves to rally behind, a banner for the downtrodden to gather together and join their strength to ours and this single purpose—to protect the weak from the strong, the slaves from the slavers, and the exploited from the exploiter, to overthrow the oppressors, no matter who, no matter where... no matter how.

"Follow me!" Faron cried. "And be sworn to no gods!

Follow me, and no rulers will have authority above you. March with me, as crusaders of the weak, and you will have the freedom to root out evil in whatever form it takes. Nations will surrender their tyrants to you; kings will bow before you! None can deny our authority, for we respect no authority but our own. No laws will bind you, for we will observe no laws but our own."

The clamor of metal crashing on metal rose up again with the chant for their captain, but Faron silenced it with his hand.

"You will be wolves, to hunt and tear the heart from evil, but that is not all. The work is great and plentiful. Follow me, and you will wield not just the sword but the plow and the trowel. Follow me, and we will plant fields of mana to fortify nations against the coming winter. Follow me, and we will sew clothes of white fur to protect the cities whose walls will fail them in the coming frost. Follow me, and we will ferry those who will come to Vam Aranath. Follow me, and we will teach those who stay to survive. *Follow me!*" he shouted. "And we will protect those who are weak from those who are cruel! We will feed those who are hungry! We will shelter those who are cold, and we will do it as men who are *free*!

"So, I ask you, as free men and free women, is *this* what you want?!"

The call was unanimous and screamed to sunder the earth. "YES!"

"Then I name you," he cried, "Crusaders of the Veil! Slave Bane! And Defenders of the Weak!"

They beat their shields harder. They cried out louder. They gloried in his names.

"You will be Knights of the White, Ferriers of Souls, and Destroyers of the Cruel. You will live to serve and protect the weak. You will be a force to throw down injustice, no matter how it appears or how it must be done. There will be no authority on this earth greater than yours." Faron waited for their echoes of support and furor to die down and raised a shaking palm when it didn't.

"Help me to begin," Faron plead, "by righting the wrongs I have committed here. Join me now, and deliver service to the people of this city, even though there is no hope of forgiveness. I will sow crops for them. I will bury their dead. I will rebuild their wall, and I will vow to never again shed blood that is innocent, no matter the cost.

"Who will come with me?"

The Last Chapter

Faron stood with his one arm raised, basking in the pure joy of the men and women who called his name, desperate, almost as much as he, to seek redemption, even if it took the rest of their lives. Ever since the night of the fire so long ago, Faron had known nothing but the cruelty of subjugation, and for the first time, with the exception of Synick, he wasn't alone. Here were thousands who understood his pain. Here were thousands who had been stolen from their homes and lives, thousands who had been made to do terrible things, and together, they were united.

"I will come with you," Synick said from behind, echoing the sentiment of the army. He gave a small bow, fist to heart.

Vavelt rushed at him and wrapped him recklessly in her arms. "I will come with you," she breathed. "Always."

Faron returned her needful embrace, heedless of the pain it caused him, then extricated himself to put a hand on Synick's exhausted shoulder.

"No," he said, with surprising intensity and a honed edge. "You don't bow. You *never* bow."

Synick looked up at him, those blue eyes cutting and deep and more exposed than Faron had ever known.

Faron, with fear that he shouldn't be capable of after all

this, approached that swelling in his breast and looked him in the eye.

"I don't know what you need from me, Synick, and I don't know what love means to you." Synick flinched like prey that wanted to flee. "But I do know what *you* mean to me." Faron peered back into his razor eyes. "And I will never let you go either." He looked to Vavelt and back. "Both of you." He breathed through his unfamiliar distress, fortified by Vavelt's touch on his arm. "I don't know if it's enough," he started to say, then Synick was on his feet, a rush of wind that embraced him tight and long, firm and unyielding.

"It," Synick said, "is enough."

Synick held Faron, and Vavelt held them both, immune, for a moment, to the chanting of 'Wolfheart' and calls for leadership. Eventually, Vavelt took them each by their hand, standing between them, and turned back to their liberating army.

"I will need you," he told them both.

"And we will be there when you do," Vavelt said.

"Always," Synick added.

"It will be hard," from Vavelt. "More bloodshed," she said. "Wars to put down. More weight to carry."

"The *right* weight," Faron answered. "Because it was never about strength or weakness, Vavelt. It was never about right or wrong. It was about finding the weight we can carry and we can believe in." He shuddered as a small exhalation stole away from him.

Vavelt set her jaw against the tears that were welling in her eyes, and then she nodded.

Faron breathed deep, reveling in the unity of their common goal, but it wasn't perfect. There were others like him, many far worse, who still bore the marks of slavery, who would join with them given the chance.

He remembered the many in Aru'barrahk, trafficked by Jaru'tal, who he had promised to return to and save; the small in Fayevew, looked after and sold by Aerik and Garad, who he had promised to return to and save; the familiar in Blackwood, gripped tight by Dageran and his unquenchable thirst for coin; and the rumored in Empyrion and elsewhere, who were surely exploited and indentured. There was an uncounted number of slaves to which Faron had sworn himself to save on his long and dreadful journey, and now, at the head of a free and zealous army, Faron found himself surrounded by others who craved the chance to bring freedom and mercy to the world.

Faron would give them that chance.

The thought brought eagerness to begin and eagerness to be finished, if ever that were possible, but it also brought joy. With an army of free men and women at his back, he would bring justice in his wake. The quiet it brought was vindicating, powerful, and long-awaited.

Because even if it was the wrong choice…

it was the one he could live with.

Epilogue

SEVERAL MONTHS LATER

I: The Cruel and Corrupt

Dageran stepped over the corpse of one of his toughs, rushing down the dark tunnel with a bag on his back. The body cried out for help, clutching a wound in his side, so he wasn't quite a corpse *yet*—but close enough. He ignored the slave and hurried down the rough stone corridor. There were far more important affairs to be about than saving the lives of his things—like saving his own life, for example, and his gold.

Another of those earth-quaking blasts shook the caves, and dust trickled from invisible cracks in the cavern ceiling. Somewhere behind them, a literal mountain of rock caved in, sectioning off one of his ancient tunnels. Good. Maybe that would slow them down.

Whoever was behind this attack was executing it flawlessly, pouring in from every entrance at the same time, even the secret ones—well, the *more* secret ones. It was clearly one of his own slaves who was responsible, in cooperation with that damn army that showed up out of nowhere, which was why he made sure to kill each one he came across, just in case. Even if he didn't get the one who ratted him out to those snowing invaders, it still felt good to call due a few of the lives he'd let run too long.

It was a shame he hadn't been able to find Clarath, though. He'd had about enough of her attempted escapes anyway and would have relished the chance to add her to his collection, but she wasn't in his chambers; and, time was pressing.

Another concussive blast shook the sanctuary, and he heard men yelling from behind. He'd ordered his most loyal to stay and fight the intruders, giving himself enough time to grab a few items and flee toward the Banshee Cliffs. The cowards had simply run and hidden, which wasted far too much time, as he'd had to run them down and slit their throats before making his own escape. Whoever was yelling behind him wasn't one of his thugs.

Now, he ran with Karus at his back, a newer lackey who'd been about to lose a hand for thieving before Dageran slipped a heavy bag into the right purse. The short girl ran with a bag filled with as much gold as she could carry, which wasn't a lot, unfortunately. She was quite small, even for her young age. She huffed as she ran but didn't complain or ask to stop.

Miles away, at the far end of the tunnel, stretched the Pale Sea, a murky and calm ocean that met the massive yellow-gray cliffs with surprisingly little energy at this part of the coast. An ancient rowboat leaned against the cavern wall, long unused. When Dageran finally arrived, ahead of the strange explosions that destroyed his great caverns, he pulled the boat onto its belly and heaved his bag of supplies inside.

"It's so small," Karus said, with her quiet, mouse-like way of speaking. "Even for me—and old. I don't think it can carry both us and the packs—not with all this." She hefted the pack of gold, clinking coins.

"I won't say it again, dear Karus. Gold and silver are replaceable, but so are you; and, gold doesn't talk." He pointed at the boat. "Now load it in."

She did, though with obvious reluctance. Dageran rolled

his eyes. He *hated* reluctance.

"What if it sinks?"

Dageran gave her a suffering look. "Then we'll shed some useless weight." He reached into Karus's pack, ignoring her small recoiling reflex, and withdrew a loose handful of gold coins, each one a fortune by itself, then threw it through the cavemouth and into the murky-teal water. It plopped and rang delightfully.

"You're throwing it?" she asked, frustration prompting at least a little bravery, or maybe it was greed. She shivered away as Dageran threw another handful of gold fortunes into the water with delighted laughter.

Karus shook her head. "Shouldn't we at least *test* the boat and see what it will hold?"

"Oh, no, you're quite right, my dear," Dageran answered. "It simply won't carry all this."

Karus stammered. "Then why... why make me carry it all?"

"Because," Dageran said in genuine confusion. "I could never have hauled all that gold by myself." Her huge brown eyes didn't even have time to light up before Dageran gutted her. Pity. She screamed as she fell to the ground, but there really wasn't enough time to stop and enjoy it.

Dageran reached out to take the knife back but stopped, grinned, and left it in Karus's stomach, turning around to push the boat. She'd live a few hours more that way and might even be dull enough to hope that someone might come to help her. That put a grin on his face. Losing his tunnels and slaves had put him in a foul mood.

Ignoring the slave's cries, he shoved on the small wooden craft, scraping it along the soft limestone until he entered the powerful spring daylight. How long had it been since the sun touched his skin? Months, at least, and he still hated it.

"Hello, Dageran," a familiar voice said from above.

He spun around, flipping a knife into his hand from a sleeve, and saw a ghost. Suddenly, it all made sense.

Synick grinned at him from an outcrop of stone above the cavemouth, smiling the way he used to when he'd been a good pet—before Dageran had been forced to kill him. Half his chin and jaw were marred by an angry red scar that looked like a brand. Dageran made a note of that. If he could get at that burn, it might still hurt.

"You? It was you who betrayed me, Synick? Impressive, especially for a dead man. I didn't think you had the spine."

He grinned. "I've been too busy to die—crumbling empires, felling deities, exacting revenge—you know how it is."

"Same as normal, then," Dageran said with a grin that could be friendly. "That's new, though." He motioned toward his own face in indication of Synick's fire scar.

"You like it?" he asked. "It was a parting gift from a dead god. I earned it, I swear. I'll be honest, though. It's made me less reserved to jump into the fighting. I was always so worried about my face, but now I see scars only make me prettier."

"You *hardly* have to do much fighting," Dageran said, drawing out the exchange, "with a mind like yours. Ambushing me inside my own sanctuary? Very clever and well-coordinated, too. I almost didn't manage to slip away."

Synick grinned again, hopping the twelve feet to the ground over the cave entrance. "I thought you'd like that," he said with a grunt. "Took a few well-placed bribes to ladder sentries, a few well-earned knifings here and there, but I managed it. Even got your whores out before. I'll point out, though, that you *didn't* manage to slip away."

Dageran nodded emphatically. "From a professional standpoint, I can certainly appreciate it. You've even managed to rummage together an army! I can't imagine what that must have cost you, and all for me?"

"Just borrowing it, I'm afraid. It's not actually mine. Glad you like it, though."

Dageran raised an eyebrow. "Borrowing? An army?"

"From Faron. He's got loads of them now. His sister, too. Turns out he's a god now or a captain or something. He's got men tripping over themselves to kill baddies for him. In fact," Synick confided. "They appointed me their spymaster, so *borrowing* might be a bit of a stretch, but not in the usual way since they actually gave it to me."

"Sounds like a difficult job."

"Eh, not really." Synick shrugged. "It's pretty satisfying, actually, and turns out, I'm *really* good at it. I have you to thank for that—a lot of breaking and entering, infiltrating, digging up paper trails, and learning secrets powerful people don't want me to know. It's almost like I was trained for it by a snowing madman, except now it's kind of a game to find out who the problem people are so I can kill them."

"Really?" Dageran intoned with an inquisitive eagerness. "All this from *Faron*?"

"And his sister. And me. It's kind of a group effort, actually, though I get the fun part, and they usually just clean up after me."

Dageran faked a long sigh. "I suppose I was wrong not to collect him then. I always knew it was my mercy that would be the end of me, and is that what this is, Synick? You've come to kill me?"

Synick laughed through his nose. "I thought that was obvious?"

"Yes, well, there seems to be an awful lot of talking and a pointed lack of killing."

Synick lifted two fingers and a thumb into the air. "You know, I've been waiting for a good moment for this, but I really couldn't have said it better."

Twenty men stood from the crags and crevices of the limestone cliff, all bearing heavy crossbows trained directly on Dageran. The weapons had springs in the limbs and small triggers in the stock instead of large levers underneath.

His eyes widened under an arched eyebrow. "My goodness, Synick, you've certainly outdone yourself. You've planned this all marvelously."

"Glad you can appreciate my handiwork in the face of certain death, old friend."

Dageran rolled his wrist slightly, shifting the weighted blade to his fingers. "Won't you at least do it yourself? Come, Synick, after all we've been through? It would mean an awful lot to me. I loved you, after all. You were meant to succeed me."

He couldn't move too quickly, couldn't let Synick's eye catch what he was doing.

A slight shuffling with his hands behind his back, and then the knife tip slipped into his fingers, ready to throw. All he needed was an opening—and to get the last word.

Only, Synick didn't respond. His raised fingers twitched downward, and the knife fell from Dageran's fingers as a chorus of bowstrings impaled him from twenty different directions. Dageran didn't even feel the arrows enter before being pummeled to the ground under the tremendous force.

"No," Synick said when the bows stopped singing. "And for what it's worth, I've always hated you."

Dageran's vision blurred away as he hit the ground, and it didn't come back. Where was his satchel? The gold? He felt it in his hands but couldn't see it. He fumbled with failing fingers to get at the kingpence but couldn't undo the buckle.

Desperate, he tore at it, lifeblood leaking away. He had to get the gold! He had to... to take it... with him...

Everything became black then, and Dageran saw something new. His collection—the heads he'd stolen over the years—was here, waiting for him in the darkness, only they were smiling now with bared teeth, and he wasn't.

Dageran screamed in the void, and the faces fell on him.

* * *

Synick closed the gap between himself and the feathered corpse that was his master—*previous* master. He drew all his phlegm and spat on the twitching body, then kicked it in the side. Dageran coughed blood, but it was only reflexive.

Slowly, with an anxiety he rarely felt and rarely showed, Synick reached his healed right hand to his hip and withdrew his precious knife from its sheath. It was beautiful—long, thin, and sharp on both edges, except for the blade catchers on the back.

Given to him on his first night inside the guild when Dageran had made him use it, this knife had been with Synick through everything. It had even stabbed him in the abdomen once, then stemmed the flow of blood long enough for him to find help.

Synick ground his teeth. It was bluish-black now, mottled by smoke and heat from the phosphorous he'd cut away from Faron's hand, the temper thoroughly destroyed. It didn't matter. There was only one thing he'd truly saved it for, and it would serve well enough.

Kneeling down with a gentle reverence, Synick settled beside Dageran and slit his throat.

The cut was jagged and gushing, spilling a well of sanguine water onto the already soaked floor of limestone dust.

Withdrawing it with a jerk, Synick set his jaw and sank it down into Dageran's eye, his collarbone, his neck. It was hard to find somewhere to get at underneath all the quarrels in his chest, but Synick managed, sinking the knife in and out and in and out until it snapped in his rib cage, the weakened blade shattering with a high-ringing fracture.

Synick didn't stop. He couldn't. He didn't want to. With shaking hands and the dull edge of his broken dagger, he stabbed and stabbed and stabbed at the man who had once called him a slave.

II: The Path through Apocalypse

Vavelt rode through a lifting Veil with an army at her back to find Blackwood in disarray. The gates were closed, of course, with the fear of the soldiers who followed her. It was a small portion of the main forces, only six thousand men and women, but that was more than she'd had when she'd ridden on Murcosta. The bulk of their army had swelled to over twenty thousand, according to her intelligence network, and was growing by the day. Faron's method of turning the weak against their oppressors had proven frightfully efficient, and people flocked to join the new crusade.

Supporting that large a company was a logistical nightmare and entirely untenable, so they were organized apart in a way that Vavelt could keep the supply trains going while still affording the manpower necessary to prepare fields, reinforce walls, police new systems of governance, and generally brace the world against the coming snow. The hardest part had been setting up and maintaining checkpoints for the escorting caravans that facilitated the exodus to Vam Aranath. It was an incredible drain on their supplies of food, fuel, wood, and coal, but she managed to keep it all running, if only barely.

Under Vavelt's careful hand, thousands of people were filing into her city by the day, where they would be safe from the storm. Now, she stood before Blackwood, the progenitor

415

city of her childhood village, and prepared to add them to the exodus. It was with a wash of mixed emotions that she approached the snow wall. This had been the culmination of her dreams as a child—to leave her small village behind as a bard and travel to a city such as this.

How small she had been.

The thought of Faron, as he'd chosen to be called, suffering here for long years without her filled her chest with sorrow and a strange melancholy. If anything, it only made her more eager to save this city—to wash away what it had done to her brother and to, perhaps, earn some sliver of redemption for what she'd done. It had been long months since that night on the mountain where she'd lost her father, her keeper, and herself. Most of that time had been spent between anguish for the morality she had failed and a servile ferocity with which she dedicated herself to redemption.

Faron was her guiding star, her example to keep going, no matter her regret or the depth of her guilt—to continually choose to be better and move on. For all the violent fervor with which he cast down the slavers and waged war against the exploiters who would ruin the world in the face of the Veil, he was nothing but gentle with her. Vavelt was not sure she deserved such kindness.

No, that wasn't true. Vavelt *was* sure she didn't deserve it. Still... maybe one day she might, if she could save enough lives, so she kept going. Faron made excuses for her, and Synick, too, perhaps with even greater vehemence, but she knew better than to accept them. It didn't matter that her father had groomed her to be unfeeling or had intentionally burned his vision of the world and his fear of the Veil into her. She had made a choice—at the behest of her father, yes—but she had accepted his logic and had learned that she could not live with it.

She would take that burden to her grave.

The thought of a grave was an entirely different topic she was still grappling with and still avoiding. She was, after all, no longer a goddess.

An internal debate for another time.

Surrounded by her guard and the morning mist, they came to the gate, dominated by a regal man in draping furs and too much brocade. His hair was long and black with greasy product, and Vavelt knew exactly who she was dealing with. He was the type to send her an entire cart of roses in another circumstance, thinking it would be enough to woo her and not a vapid display of thoughtlessness. She could practically smell his drenching perfumes from here.

Vavelt came to a stop on her great white horse, not so hot-blooded as the dire wolves, and the army behind her slowed.

"So it's true," the greasy man declared. "There truly is a new crusade led by a golden beauty."

Vavelt doubted that her brown divided skirts and black riding trousers were enough to confirm rumors like that, especially with the metal pauldrons on her shoulders and her hair braided and hidden behind her back. Hollow words, then, from a hollow man.

"I don't claim to be the arbiter of what is or is not beauty," Vavelt said. "Only the path through apocalypse. Open your gates, Ilrili Ariethi, that I might brace your city against the coming storm."

The wormy man flashed a grin. "Alas, my lovely lady, I am remiss to bear tragedy to you, truly, but I am not

417

Ilrili, but Alvani Ariethi. My father was brutalized, not three nights past, in a string of gruesome and most terrible assassinations." For the morbidity of his words, his smile was wide and fortuitous. "And so it is that I, his only remaining son, have been forced to resume his mayorship. You can understand, then," he went on, and Vavelt resisted the urge to roll her eyes. "Why I—a servant to a cause such as yours, truly—would be so cautious in such tumultuous and disturbing times as to disallow an untethered army inside my gates."

"And I," Vavelt countered, "as the head of such an army, find myself lethally curious as to the circumstances of your recent rise to power and what convoluted events brought you to it."

"An admirable question, and reflective of your noble quest, but evocative, in truth, of questions of my own."

Vavelt groaned internally.

"One hears such rumors, my lady, of a certain mountain city laid to waste, rumors of an army, such as this, leaving a dreadful trail of blood and instability wherever it goes. Such awful rumors—though unfounded, I'm sure—leave a man in my position to be more inclined to leave my gates shut to foreign armies. In truth, I'm terribly sorry for it because such a beauty as you has no place beyond the walls of my city—or my manor, for that matter."

Vavelt sighed. The glimmer in his eye was the same as every man who thought he'd said something clever to a woman.

She'd tried.

"Synick?" she called.

Alvani barely had time to raise a long and preened brow before he expelled a shocked breath of air. A long and unfamiliar dagger sprouted from his chest. Synick appeared from behind him, and Vavelt could just make out his words.

"Hey, Alvy. Remember me?"

He looked up to see who had impaled him, and the word that appeared to form on his lips was "Rogue," but there was no air behind it.

"Mhhmm, yeah, that's *Lord* Rogue, now. I got promoted…" There was an awkward pause as Synick caught the man as he lost his feet, thought better of it, and shoved him off the wall. "Bye, and thanks for all the contracts, git." Alvani impacted beside the gate with an unmoving thud.

"New knife?" Vavelt inquired.

"Dageran's, actually, or it was. Alvy can keep it." They stared at each other for a long pause, the usual grin on Synick's face giving way to a real smile as he lost his focus on her. She smiled back.

"Synick?"

"Yeah?"

"The gate?" Choruses of laughter from the free soldiers behind her roused Synick from a state of daze, and his grin returned.

"Right!" He turned around to see all the men who were supposed to be defending their self-declared mayor. "Consider yourselves liberated," he said. "Now open the snowing gates."

To Vavelt's pleasure, the gates swung open without much hesitation. This was going much more smoothly than in Murcosta.

Inside the wall, she was immediately assaulted by a city that had grown as much as possible within its stone constraints, both outward and upward. Tall, familiar buildings of blackwood and stone shingles were stacked neatly on top of each other as high as they would go, and she could immediately see where Synick's fondness for rooftops had begun.

In the street, crowded shoulder to shoulder, were men-at-arms, guards, shop owners, commonfolk, and ragged beggars, all wondering how to move forward with the suddenly shifting presence of seemingly new rulers.

She smiled and briefly wondered just how foreign the idea of democracy would be to them.

Synick was beside her then, descended from the wall with a quick jump, and his grin was broad.

"I missed you," he said.

"And I you. The month felt longer than I thought possible."

"More like five," he agreed. "Or fifty."

She gave him a small, slanted smirk, then turned her mind to task, breaking away from her guards to draw the attention of the crowd.

"Your false and corrupted officials are dead and their accomplices with them. Your crime lords are buried, and those who would oppress you are gone. I am Vam Vavelt," she said, beginning her lengthy address, "Lady of the White Crusade, and I will teach you to survive the growing Veil."

III: The Life Spile

With an Aranath lantern casting back the shadows, Faron ventured deep into the heart of his temple. Behind the gilded thrones and the golden false wall, a tunnel, long and deep, led him down an endless stair. The steps were wide enough for a single man, rough-hewn but semi-polished from treading feet, so Varan followed at his back. The dark passage was the only thing in the entire temple not plated in some form of precious material, and there was no light but his own.

Gradually, that began to change. The softness of an orange and hellish glow began to warm the walls of the narrow passage. It was difficult to see at first, but eventually, the orange matched the white for strength; and, Faron came to a rectangular door in the belly of the earth.

They stepped through the doorway into an enormous gash of a cavern, and Faron discovered the source of the light.

A river of molten rock languorously flowed in the distance, gushing like a viscous spring from the far right of the chasm and pouring hundreds of feet off a subterranean cliff to a burning lake far below. The light that lifted from the magma undercut the shadows and stretched them inside out, forcing an inverted dark toward the ceiling.

The stairs let out onto the steep side of a cavern wall where a wide balcony had been constructed, overlooking the molten river and lake. Stone railings with low arching designs rimmed the platform, and a black, octagonal hole in the floor punctured through its very center. Black iron spikes hemmed in the opening on all sides but one, through which thick chains hung from some dark place far above and continued down through the octagonal depression.

Varan placed a hand on a lever arm in the floor and slowly began to pull. For the briefest moment, Faron was on another balcony with another lever, and he began to cry out. He stopped himself but not before he had earned the full examining gaze of his keeper.

"This," Varan said, "is a lift, my lord, Wolfheart. Nothing more."

He took a calming breath and reassured himself. This was not the same balcony. This was not the same lever. That place was at the top of the world, and now he was under it.

He gave the nod to proceed, and Varan pulled the lever. The chains began to move, clicking together as the two lines passed each other, nearly drowning out the sound of spinning gears far overhead.

What Faron could only describe as a gigantic birdcage descended from the blackness above and into the light. It was formed of a thousand metal threads, intricately intertwined and connected at the base to form a solid metal floor. Once, it might have been reflective but had long since accumulated a black layer of soot.

"I've never seen anything like it," Faron said. "It's on a pulley? Who's on the other end?"

"Nobody, Lord Wolfheart," Varan answered. "Like many technologies lost to Atha's inquisitors, it is powered and controlled through careful manipulations of steam." He gestured to the lava. "Of which there is plenty." Varan stepped inside and gestured for Faron to follow.

The tall keeper manipulated a smaller set of controls inside the cage, and it began to move with shuddering slowness.

"We're going down," Faron said, though it was a question.

Varan only nodded.

"The lift came from above."

"There is another entrance, my lord, from the offices of the priesthood, where the ordained would enter the chamber—to preserve the secrecy of the throne room entrance."

"And below?"

"The Spile."

They descended—suspended by a cage—in the deepest of silences.

The clicking slowed as the lift came to a stop on what appeared for all the world to be an underground mountain. The magma swirled and bubbled still below, churning with white-hot flows that swallowed black spots on the surface. It was hard to look away.

Following Varan from the cage, they stepped into a small stone circle, carved into the steepness of a cliffside. Ancient steepled arches ringed the circle, towering above the most dangerous tool ever created.

In the middle of the platform stood two mirror-metal cylinders, with a brass arch on one side and what looked to be an iron maiden on the other. Cables hung from the arch, dangling over an unpadded, manacled, metal chair. It was warm to the touch.

Faron circled the contraption with contemptuous disgust and morbid curiosity. It was nothing like he had imagined. He opened the door to the coffin-like container and grimaced. Hundreds of fine metal spikes filled the walls and inside of the door, all pointing inward and all with barely perceivable openings. With the door closed, the spikes would overlap.

Faron shivered to imagine it and to know that it was more than just an imagined possibility. It was real, and it was more terrible than he had thought. It was a battle of its own to keep away his rising bile.

For each quiver of Faron's frame, Varan quaked.

At the back of the machine rested hundreds of tiny gears, smaller than Faron had ever seen, all perfectly smooth and forged from the same unfamiliar metal as the canisters. Its use was obvious now. A blood sacrifice would be forced into the sarcophagus on the right, impaled a thousand times over in a single moment, and the blood would be transfused through the cylinders and cables to the archon on the left.

Faron balled his hand into a fist. "Destroy it." Varan was slow to answer, and Faron caught him in a fiery stare.

"You display confidence in me I cannot meet, Lord Wolf-heart. I cannot destroy this machine."

"You will."

"I… lack the capacity."

"Then why lead me here?"

"I had hoped to appeal to you, my lord."

Faron put his hand at his belt, but there was no dagger there anymore. He only pinned Varan with his eyes.

"Can you, in good conscience, destroy this machine?" Varan asked. "There is none other like it in the world. Think of the advancement we might gain by studying it. Think of the stability that would come from using it. If you destroy it now, it will be lost to time like all the other technologies Atha and Olsu shut away. Can you do the same? Can you purposefully remove this knowledge from the world?"

A moment passed between them as they locked gazes. Faron was surprised to see a tear roll down his servant's cheek.

"You're afraid to die," Faron realized.

Slowly, he nodded. "I am terrified, my lord."

Faron stepped closer. "All men die, Varan. It is the only certain thing about life."

"Yes, but few are asked to consign themselves to it in the end."

Faron opened his mouth for a cutting condemnation, then snapped it shut. There was nothing to be gained from that now, and it was certainly what Varan expected.

With effort, Faron asked himself what Vavelt would do, were she here with him, then, "Why are you afraid, Varan? Does the idea of nonexistence really seem so bad?"

"The opposite, my lord," Varan said.

Faron remembered a conversation they'd had once before, standing above an army on its way to Anveil. There would be no taking back the words he'd said there.

Varan stared at the Spile with a hunger and a fear, the way a mouse eyes a hole in a cage. "Oblivion is the best I can hope for. If I am wrong, though, and there is another life after death?" He shuddered.

"Then you will be cast down to the Iron Halls," Faron finished the thought for him.

"I am a usurper," Varan begrudged. "I have dedicated my life to stealing the power of a god and done horrible sins in the name of it." The glint in his eye dimmed to regret. "Horrible sins. Yes, my lord. I am afraid to die. I fear eternity."

Faron pushed past his discomfort and put his hand on

425

the taller man's arm. "It doesn't matter what you've done, Varan. It matters what you'll do. I've killed men with cleaner consciences than yours, and I live with those choices; but, that's not your fate. You still have a mark to leave on this world.

"I'll never ask how many children died so you might live—because it doesn't matter. Nothing can bring them back. What matters now is that you use every minute of life you have left to outweigh the bad you've done with good. If, in the end, you save more lives than you took, perhaps whatever gods there might be will understand."

"How," Varan asked, daunted and dismayed, "could I ever hope to accomplish a feat such as that?"

"We all have weight to carry, Varan, and we do it the only way we know how—by choosing to, one step at a time. Synick killed for coin, compelled or otherwise, and he lives with that by killing the corrupt and the cruel in service to a greater cause. Vavelt thought only of the greatest number of lives and numbed her heart to the lives of thousands, and now lives in service to the individual. And I…" Faron choked on the words and almost didn't continue. "And I keep going, carrying this weight, so no one else will have to, ever again."

Varan trembled with the intensity of the damned.

"You move forward, Varan," Faron said, with words that were both heavy and familiar, ringing from the past in a high and silver voice, "by helping more than you hurt, by saving more than you sacrificed, by knowing that you do what no one else can, so others can live free of your pain."

The archon's shoulders shook as silent tears escaped him.

"I'm not a god," Faron continued. "And forgiveness isn't mine to give, but what else is there but to try?"

Quick breaths heaving through the High Archon's chest, he looked upon the Life Spile with a new vigor and pulled the greatsword from its sheath. Wordlessly, he drew it back into a wide arc and swung at the strange metal.

The blade chipped, but he didn't stop. He swung as if with a mallet, and large chunks of the glassy alloy broke apart, clacking as fragments broke away then flew upward instead of down, attaching themselves like lodestones to the canisters of the machine.

The silver cylinders hissed as they were rent apart, super-heated steam spouting in great streams, but he didn't stop. The brittle metal shattered under Varan's manic fervor as he struck the god machine again and again until his sword was nothing but mangled steel. Finally, the empty canisters fell next to the bloody cage, shattered metal chips spinning and smashing together with ferric affinity.

With a dreadful kick, the Spile toppled off the mountain-side, crashing and flipping and crushing and falling until it splashed with a magnificent eruption of molten rock and was swallowed by the earth.

Varan's tears stopped.

"It... is done, my lord."

"It's a start."

THE END OF BOOK THREE
of
THE GROWING VEIL SERIES
by T.S. Howard

Thank you, dear readers, for coming with me on this journey through the Growing Veil. It is my deepest and most sincere hope that you found some joy or lasting impact from the words I've put to page and the characters that brought themselves to life with my help. Thank you, all of you, for your support, your time, and your love.

Please consider leaving a review at one of the sites below to support my craft as an independently published author:
   amazon.com/author/ts.howard
   goodreads.com/tshoward
   bookbub.com/profile/t-s-howard

To stay updated on any future releases, join my mailing list, or order signed copies, visit:
   tshoward.co/

Thank you,
   T.S. Howard

About the Author

I'm T.S. Howard, and I am, above all else, a storyteller. I see stories with my two children, who I love unreasonably, with my wife, who is a grand adventure by herself, and in my daily duties. I see stories in the world around me and feel them burn inside until I can put them to page. I see stories in the faces of those I pass who I don't know and in the lives of those I do. Stories are my life, and it is my undying goal to make them a part of yours.

Ever since the second grade, I knew what I wanted to be: a bestselling author, and I dedicate most of my time to that pursuit. It isn't a vanity or desire to be a household name that drives me, but that same desire for my characters, their names, and their stories.

Still, we aren't only defined by our largest goals. When I'm not writing, I'm tending to my family, obsessing over the quality of coffee and various cheeses (I am, after all, a millennial), and playing as a hobbyist geologist. I am untenably obsessed with garnets and other gemstones and almost always carry one with me. Similarly, if you see me without my headphones, you can safely understand that I'm having an off-day. Finally, when I'm not writing, reading, cooking, cleaning, looking for something shiny, or listening to music, I'm probably getting my ass kicked in an FPS game online.